VIOLET FENN

THE HIGH GATE

Contents

Fish Are Friends, Not Food — 1

London Calling — 6

We Are Scientists — 20

Just Trying Not To Get Killed. Again. — 28

Martha's Harbour — 37

Midnight On Derby Square — 50

Everything's Fine, Thanks For Asking — 64

What Is Life, Anyway? — 75

Can't Beat A Bit Of Badalamenti — 89

England's Dreaming — 102

Secrets And Lies — 116

Fight The Power — 130

Never Trust A Man Who Doesn't Wear Socks — 141

Heart As Big As Liverpool — 153

The Ethics Of Death — 166

I'd Like To Escape Now, Please — 177

Family Ties — 188

Well, Someone Has To Take Charge — 199

Super Furry Vampire — 209

Smile At Your Enemies—It Makes Them Nervous — 224

A Tiny Knife — 236

It's A Gas — 242

You'll Never Walk Alone — 255

LARK RISING — 259

Author's Note — 265

"It is very certain that the desire of life prolongs it."

Lord Byron

Fish Are Friends, Not Food

My phone rang just as I was balancing precariously on a ladder that had been wedged into place by a table that was slowly sliding across the floor. I was also being berated by my best friend Izzy for having no vision when it came to interior design. She had unilaterally decided that Flora's, the Harrington Street coffee shop that I owned and lived above, needed to be 'brighter and more welcoming', and I hadn't had the heart to stop her. "Red and pink absolutely works together, so you can wipe that look off your face," had been the sum total of our discussions, before she'd put a 'closed for refurbishment' sign in the window and spent two days dressed in a boiler suit, painting anything that stayed still long enough. I actually thought it was great, but kept a begrudging expression on my face because Izzy loves it when she thinks she's got one over on me. So now I was hanging gigantic Roy Lichtenstein prints on the headache-inducing walls, while Izzy shouted instructions. I'd have ignored the call, but my phone was playing *The Final Countdown* by Europe, which signified it was either Eadric or Nikolaus. Both were perfectly capable of using modern technology but avoided it as much as possible on account of how one of them was two hundred years old and the other—well, let's just say that Eadric wrote some of the side notes in the original Domesday Book and leave it at that. Dropping the box of picture nails to the floor, I did my best to ignore Izzy's indignant squeaking as I fished the phone out of my pocket. I nearly fell off the ladder as I hit 'accept' on the screen, and ended up clambering down the freshly painted wall like a cockroach, hoping no one was walking past the windows to see it.

1

"If you don't come and do something with this repulsive pet of yours, I swear to the gods, I will fillet and shred her and make a nice kedgeree."

I sighed. "Morning Nik," I said, heading behind the counter. Flora's was due to open in an hour and the bakery order hadn't yet been put into the display units. I started pulling warm pastries out of boxes and arranging them on the counter. The almond croissants smelled like heaven, and I cursed the fact I could no longer eat human food. Izzy banged her way through to the staff room as I flipped the coffee machine on. At least espresso was still an option. "Daisy's a wild creature," I pointed out, "not a pet. I can't be responsible for her behaviour and you know that."

"Lilith," he said, "she climbed in through the bloody window. Then she dumped a pike on Eadric's desk. It was still *flapping*." I could hear noises behind him that suggested the piscine incident was still ongoing.

"Was he sitting at the desk at the time?" Eadric Silverton wasn't known for either his humour or his tolerance for wayward river creatures. Daisy lived in the Mersey and was free to come and go as she pleased—unfortunately for Nik and Eadric, her comings and goings were often via the top floor windows of their rooms in the Liver Building. And the fact she climbed up the outside walls in order to gain access did complicate matters slightly. Luckily, she generally only appeared when it was quiet and had somehow avoided being spotted by the public so far—or if she had, they'd presumably marked her down as a stunt actor for one of the film crews that regularly popped up in town.

"Yes," replied Nik. "And he isn't happy about it." Yowling noises from behind him confirmed this.

"I'll come talk to her," I soothed, reaching for the jacket hanging on the back of the kitchen door. "She just likes company sometimes." There was a crashing noise at the other end, some muffled cursing, and then Nik came back on the line. He sounded tense.

"Fish pie," he said through clearly gritted teeth. "Get down here now, or I'm making fish pie." The phone went dead. It wasn't my fault I had a river creature as an accidental pet. I'd first met Daisy a few months earlier, when she was being held captive in a sandstone cave dug out underneath the city

2

streets. No one had really wanted to keep her prisoner and she'd only been there a couple of days, but she stank to high heaven and had a spitting temper alongside several rows of the tiniest sharpest teeth you could ever hope to not see in a human lifetime. So it was no wonder that Joe and the boys had locked her up while they decided what to do. And then I'd turned up and been nice to her and she'd attached herself to me like a lamb that's been bottle-fed and doesn't want to go back to the flock. I'd only been dead a couple of days and didn't have a clue what the fuck was going on anyway, so I'd carried on being kind and got her back to her river and now we were all being stalked by an asrai with momma issues. The regular piscine gifts might have been more welcome if more of us could actually eat. In the end, Izzy installed a bigger freezer and bought a fish-themed cookbook. "I won't be long," I said to a grumpy-looking Iz, pulling on my jacket. I didn't feel the cold, but was becoming adept at fitting in with human behaviour. It might only be August, but there was a distinctly autumnal nip in the air. People would be wearing an extra layer this morning, so I did too.

***

It took some coaxing, but I eventually got the scouse mermaid out of Eadric's office by tempting her with a tin of mackerel that I keep in his drinks cabinet for just this sort of emergency. After seeing her off into the water with a promise to visit the next day, I headed back to Flora's. I'm pretty good at walking at a human pace now, even if I do say so myself. I've got the amount of times I scare random members of the public down to once or twice a week, max. The thing with becoming a revenant is that I no longer have any limitations on my physical abilities. I don't get cramp, I never get tired and I can run or climb or fight to the absolute limits of my human body's capabilities. And you'd be *amazed* by what you can be capable of when those human limits are removed. Only last week I climbed the Radio City tower, just to see if I could. Getting up past the overhang of the viewing platform was tricky, but I managed to swing up and over, before spending a happy hour or so peering at the view from my perch high above the city. Izzy had yelled a bit when I got back to Flora's and told her where I'd been. Apparently, I'm *an undead idiot with a perverse need to get found out*. I pointed out that if anyone actually spotted a woman with flaming red hair climbing up the outside of a four-hundred-and-fifty foot concrete tower, they'd probably assume they were hallucinating. We agreed to disagree on that one.

The sun was shining, passersby were smiling and I had a hopeful spring in my step as I turned the corner onto Harrington Street. Sean, my very favourite customer, often came into Flora's early. He liked to spend hours at his favourite table writing notes for the insanely popular thriller novels that had made his fortune. We chatted a lot, and I was pretty sure he was going to ask me out again any day now. I say 'again', because Sean and I actually went on a date a few months ago. It ended with Daisy frightening the life out of him and me having to wipe his memory. Only I messed up the memory-wiping thing badly enough that my friend Mapp had to redo it—and when Mapp wipes memories, he wipes them *properly*. So Sean had no idea that we'd actually already had our first kiss, let alone just how arse-wrigglingly *hot* it had all been. But he was definitely showing interest, and I was determined not to miss out again. As I bounced happily down the street towards the cafe, I saw that someone was leaning against the fire escape that leads up to my flat. Tall and slender, they were dressed all in white, from their fitted t-shirt and jeans, right down to their lace-up sneakers. Even their cropped, spiky hair was as white as snow. I slowed slightly as I realised they were waiting for me, pasting on a confident smile that I didn't quite feel. I'd had one too many nasty surprises at the beginning of my so-called afterlife, and I'd been enjoying the relative normality of the last few months (if being undead and having a pet mermaid could ever be classed as normal). As I approached, the person pushed themselves upright and stepped forward to greet me. I could see now that it was a girl in perhaps her mid-twenties and, other than being painfully thin, she looked to be human. Probably a student from the art school, looking for a part-time job. I sighed with relief. Flora's seemed to attract outsiders, and I was always happy to help people out where I could. After all, I knew only too well what it was like to be different. As I got closer, I opened my mouth to speak, ready to give her the standard 'leave your details and we'll get back to you' speech.

She beat me to it. "Lilith O'Reilly," she said in a soft, breathy voice. I thought I detected the faintest Irish lilt, but couldn't be sure.

I stopped and looked at her warily. It hadn't been a question. She knew who I was—and I didn't think she was looking for work. "And you are?" I asked.

The girl tilted her head slightly and smiled. "My name is Mab," she said, and if my heart was still beating, it would have stopped right then and there. Right at that moment, my phone started playing *The Final Countdown*, and I didn't think it was a coincidence. Mab took a step forward, and I had to force myself not to back away. "You killed my mother."

"I can explain," I said. But how was I going to explain? I had indeed killed Mab's mother. I'd chopped off her head with a meat cleaver in the living room of my flat, three storeys above where we were standing now. It had been my only option at the time, but I was pretty sure Mab wasn't going to accept excuses. Holding her gaze, I carefully slid the phone out of my pocket and pressed the speakerphone option. "It's not a good ti—"

"No, it absolutely isn't," interrupted Eadric Silverton. "I need you to visit the Queen," I dropped my gaze from Mab and stared at the phone in horror, "and I need you to go now."

"Something's happened here," I replied, more calmly than I felt. "There's someone you need to meet." I looked up at Mab as I said it—but the street was empty.

London Calling

"But I don't *want* to go to bloody London!" I scowled at Eadric across the vast mahogany expanse of his desk. "Anyway," I went on, scuffing the toe of my trainers on the expensively long pile of the carpet, "you're not the boss of me."

"I am well aware of that," sighed Eadric. "But this is important."

"So is running my business," I retorted. "Izzy's been looking after Flora's almost single-handedly since I was forced into this stupid bloody lifestyle," Eadric raised a neat eyebrow, but was wise enough to pick his battles, "and, well…" I trailed off, then rallied. "I miss it, Eadric. I miss running the cafe and chatting to normal people and just being bloody *human*." I glared down at the floor, trying not to cry. Okay, so I can't actually cry even when I want to, but the feeling was there and it's much the same thing.

"I'm sorry," said Eadric. I looked up at him suspiciously. Eadric Silverton had never given me the impression that he was sorry for anything at all, let alone the minor wailings of a thirty-something cafe owner. "I'm sorry," he said again, and I thought he might actually mean it. "I am well aware that you were dropped into this…." he groped for the right word, "*lifestyle*…without warning, and I'm sure it must be very difficult at times." *You can say that again*, I thought to myself. One day I was human with human problems, like did I have enough cat food in and would I ever meet anyone I'd want to have sex with again or was I doomed to a life of cat-lady spinsterdom. The next—*literally* the next—day I woke up dead and discovered that the city I'd called home for over a decade was actually jammed full of undead creatures of all denominations. And I had been expected to just crack on

6

without having even the teensiest of breakdowns about it.

"Anyway," I said, "I can't. Not until tomorrow night, at least. It's Izzy's day off tomorrow," I explained, "and I'm looking after Flora's."

"What about that boy you've taken on?" asked Eadric. "Can't he manage without you for a day or so?"

"Todd?" I snorted. "Todd is lovely," I said, "and very hardworking, but he doesn't know how any of the machinery works. There's the coffee machine to clean and fill, and the dishwasher gets a mind of its own at times and—"

"I think you're making excuses," interrupted Eadric. "Even I could refill a coffee machine, Lilith. The fact I choose not to doesn't mean I don't know how." *You'd get the staff to do it*, I thought to myself. Which was possibly a bit uncharitable, because other than a part-time admin assistant and a weekly cleaning lady—both of whom were absolutely human and apparently oblivious to the Silvertons' occasional oddness—Eadric didn't actually have any staff. "The fact you feel so—" he groped for words, "—*unenthusiastic* about joining the, uhhh, family firm," I sniffed loudly at that, "is unfortunate. For all of us." He leaned back in his chair and peered at me over steepled fingers. "But now you are here and we are all simply going to have to get used to that fact. Nikolaus and I are the only original members of the family that remain," *yeah because I had to kill the other one on account of how she was a conniving, manipulative, murderous witch*, is what I didn't say, "and we simply cannot manage everything alone. And right now," he went on, "we have something of an emergency brewing."

"You mean apart from Maria's long lost daughter turning up on Harrington Street and threatening me?" I snapped. "Cos that's enough of an emergency to be going on with, as far as I'm concerned."

Eadric frowned slightly. "Yes," he agreed. "Mab's appearance isn't the best timing." *You don't bloody say.* "Perhaps it would be better if you moved out of that cafe of yours, just for a while."

"Absolutely not," I eyeballed him sharply. "Flora's is my *home*, Eadric. And anyway, where would I go?"

"One of our properties is currently empty," Eadric replied. "A penthouse, up in the Colonnades. A very smart penthouse, for what it's worth. You are welcome to use it for as long as required."

I gaped at him. I knew the Colonnades apartments, alright. They're the converted upper floors of the Albert Dock—super fancy and with price tags to match. "Seriously?"

Eadric's face twitched slightly, as if he was trying not to smile. "Yes," he said, "seriously. I'm always serious, Lilith. Surely you know that by now."

"Oh, I know," I said. "No funtimes for Eadric."

"I have been known to enjoy myself on occasion," he said. "It does happen." I raised a sceptical eyebrow, but he ignored me. Eadric's got very good at ignoring me over the last few months, but I suspect it was a steep learning curve. "So you'll move, then?"

"No, I bloody well will not," I said. "I'm not being forced out of my home and business, just because some…*teenager* has got it in for me."

"Whilst I usually find your flippancy interesting," said Eadric, "if not actually attractive," he ignored my scowl, "it might be worth remembering we don't actually know what Mab's powers are. Or even if she has any. But what is certain," he went on, "is that she is undoubtedly much older than she looks."

"Around one hundred and fifty, by my calculations," I said. "But she definitely stopped ageing around eighteen or twenty, max."

"And that's strange in itself, no?" asked Eadric. "As far as we know, Mab had no idea of her mother's…abilities," his jaw clenched slightly, "yet she's clearly been around a very long time. I wonder how that happened? And, perhaps more importantly, who's been helping her over the years?"

"What do you think she is?" I asked him. "Quarter witch? She was a toddler by the time Maria died, so her father was presumably a human. But which bits of her mother's genetics has she inherited?" With a flash of guilt, I remembered Maria telling me the story of how her child had been taken from her when she was in the Brownlow Hill workhouse. Then she jumped into the Mersey in a fit of despair and walked back out some time later, undead and with a long-term plan for revenge. But whatever I thought of Maria's own criminal deceitfulness, she was still a mother who'd lost a child. And I'd killed her before they could finally be reunited.

"There's no way of knowing until she does something," said Eadric. "And we don't know what it is she might be planning to do. Which is why it would be better for you to get out of town for a day or so, while we figure out what's going on. And Elizabeth would very much like to meet you."

"Doesn't the queen have access to Zoom?" I asked. "Or is she another one who likes to pretend they're still in the Dark Ages?"

Eadric didn't bite. "Elizabeth is younger than that," he said, "as you well know." All I actually knew was that Middlesex—which is what Mapp and Eadric still insist on calling it, despite me pointing out that it's all pretty much all just London these days—had a queen ruling over it. An absolute, honest to god, Queen of the Dead. Eat your heart out, Anne Rice—the old country's not done and dusted just yet. Mapp had once told me that Lizzie (*"she doesn't like being called Elizabeth"*) was around my age and that he thought I'd like her. Of course, Lizzie had been my age for a lot longer than I had. "But no," Eadric admitted, breaking into my rambling train of thought, "she doesn't like using modern methods of communications. She doesn't trust them. And," he went on, "I can't say I blame her. Did you know Mapp has an account on the internet where he shows photos of the things in his shop to complete strangers? Why would anyone want to look at pictures of dusty books?"

"It's his online store," I said patiently. "It's where he sells things."

Eadric frowned. "Isn't that what the actual shop's for?" he asked, looking genuinely confused. "Never mind," he rallied, "I need to make sure Elizabeth is on our side right now. And she wants to meet you, so we have to make it happen. All you have to do is pay her a visit and try to make friends." He looked up at me with a bright smile and I swear it was as though the sun had come out inside the room. I gave myself a mental shake. Eadric Silverton was absolutely off limits, if only because he was my landlord. Okay, so he stopped charging me rent after the whole 'wife tried to kill me' thing, but still.

"On our side with what?" I asked.

He frowned slightly. "We both know," he said, "that Laithlind isn't going to just conveniently disappear." Ivo Laithlind headed up the north-eastern

9

chapter of Undead Anonymous. The entire country—along with pretty much every other country in the world—is secretly divided into territories that have nothing to do with human politics and everything to do with whichever supernatural entity is most powerful in that particular locale. And as far as anyone knows—anyone I've ever spoken to, anyway—the most powerful entity is almost always a revenant. Most humans would expect vampires to be top of the social heap, but they forget vampires have weaknesses. Vampires have to feed. And they have to skulk in the shadows, because real vampires do not look anything like their portrayals in films and books. It was a vampire who'd pushed me to my immortal doom back in the spring. All I'd seen before I'd taken an involuntary leap off a very high building was a tall, skinny human-shaped creature with a long thin face and rat-like teeth. I'd met Benjamin again after I woke up dead, and he hadn't seemed apologetic enough for my liking. And then he ended up permanently dead himself, so it was kind of irrelevant. But it certainly hadn't left me with any fondness for vampires. Nikolaus had once told me about strange creatures he'd met in Greece; similar in appearance to Benjamin but female, and with the ability to seduce their potential victims into giving themselves up willingly. I'd ask Nik how he'd managed to avoid having the life literally sucked out of him and he'd explained he was in love with a waiter at his guesthouse at the time and wasn't about to fall for the trickery of a mere woman. I'd have scolded him for being sexist, but by then he was gazing happily out of the window, deep in nostalgic reverie for his lost Greek love. Anyway, vampires have weaknesses where revenants do not. We don't need to feed, for one thing. Our bodies go into a form of stasis after death, creating a closed system that doesn't require sustenance and doesn't decay. And we look exactly the same as we did when we were alive—no flaky zombie skin for us. So humans are far less likely to be suspicious. What surprised me the most, at least to start with, is that we don't need to sleep. You'd think even an undead creature of the night would need to recharge their batteries occasionally, but nope. The last time I'd slept was the day after I'd been pushed to my death. I'd woken up in the car park next to my building the next morning with a sore head and a lurking worry that a fall like that really shouldn't have been survivable. After I got back into the flat and cleaned myself up, I'd slept for a good twenty-four hours. Then I woke up, threw up what felt like everything I'd ever eaten (don't ask what was going on down the other end; it's not a happy story) and slowly began the process of realising I was no longer entirely human. And I've never slept again. Which leaves an awful lot of hours in the day, especially as my best friend, Izzy, is still very much human and refuses to give up her beauty sleep in order to keep me entertained. Anyway, I've taken up knitting and everyone will be getting a terrible, lumpy scarf for Christmas. Including Eadric.

"Are you expecting him to try to take your territory?" I asked. Eadric's... *kingdom*, for want of a better description, includes the top half of Wales, a good chunk of the West Midlands and most of the north-west, with Manchester just squeaking inside the eastern boundary. The division line then runs up on a diagonal to the west coast, with Lancaster being the most northern of the major settlements under Eadric's control. Ivo Laithlind had been Eadric's oldest and most trustworthy friend, until he walked out on us all just as the shit was hitting the proverbial fan. We also discovered he was getting it on with Maria—but as she was trying to kill us all at the time, illicit affairs were the least of our worries. What wasn't up for question was Ivo's determination to hold on to power. Maria had helped him in that by spending a century and a half playing the role of Eadric's supportive and beautiful wife, all the time feeding information back to Ivo so that he could formulate a plan of attack. To give Maria the tiniest amount of credit, I don't think she'd originally planned for Eadric to be overthrown by Ivo. My theory was that she'd hoped Eadric would join forces with Laithlind's territory, creating a solid band of supernatural power across the entire mid-section of the country. With her as queen over it all, no doubt. Unfortunately for Maria and Ivo, Eadric Silverton had seen enough violence during his human lifetime to last him an eternity and he planned to spend that eternity being as reasonable as possible, thank you very much. He'd managed to rule for almost a millennium by sheer force of personality, instilling enough fearful respect in people during his lifetime that no one was prepared to risk upsetting him after death. Eadric had enough undead support that he could probably raise a zombie army, should such a thing ever be required. And when you have that amount of power, people rarely ask you to prove it.

"Ivo doesn't want the territory," replied Eadric, "but he needs the support. Which he knows I'm unlikely to give him, after his...*mistakes*." There was a thread of cold steel running through Eadric's voice that I'd never heard before. We'd discussed Maria's betrayal once, not long after I'd solved the immediate problem by chopping her head off. Think of it as clearing the air. Back then, Eadric was still mourning the loss of both his wife and his personal beliefs about her, so his attitude had been one of quiet sadness. Now, he just sounded flatly determined.

"Why does he need support?" I asked. "What he really ought to be doing is scuttling off back to Yorkshire and keeping his bloody head down for a century or two."

"You'd think," said Eadric, with a thin smile. "But something's rattling Laithlind's cage, and I want to know what it is. Not having the full details of whatever is currently brewing is dangerous, Lilith." He sat back in his chair and let out a sigh. "People think I don't do anything other than stay up here and hide away from the world." I opened my mouth to speak, but he held up a hand. "No," he said, "let me finish." I shut my mouth and shifted impatiently from one foot to another. "I stay here, Lilith," Eadric said slowly, "because the human world disappoints me. Centuries after my own death, humanity is still making the same mistakes that it was making back then—it's just that, these days, those mistakes are on a massive scale. We used to fight battles hand-to-hand, like real soldiers. These days," he gave a tiny, elegant snort, "someone in an office presses a button and *whoomph*, half a city is gone. People, animals, trees, *everything*—gone, just like that. Where's the sense in that?" I shrugged to indicate that no, I couldn't see any sense in it either. "And things aren't any better in the netherworld," he went on. "Everyone just plods along and pretends it's perfectly normal to be living a human life when they're actually anything but."

"I'm still human," I protested, "and so are you. And Mapp and Heggie. Although—" I trailed off. "Yeah, anyway, Heggie might not be the best example. But you know what I mean, Eadric. We might be dead, but we're still *human.*"

He looked unconvinced. "Then what are we doing," he said, "wasting eternity with businesses and coffee shops and pets?"

"Ohhh," I said, "don't you *dare* bring Grimm into this!" Eadric had only met my cat once and that was the day I killed Maria, so it hadn't exactly been a peaceful introduction. Maria had crumbled into dust after I'd cut her head off and, well, Grimm has always liked pouncing on the dustpan and brush. It's a game for him. Unfortunately, he stepped in the remains of Eadric's dead wife and proceeded to tread her into my sofa cushions. Eadric had clearly considered this disrespectful, even if the ashes were those of a two-faced, murderous cow. "You were on *his* territory then, whether you like it or not. Anyway," I went on, "he's my *friend.* Sometimes I need something other than whiny immortals or gossipy ghosts for company. I can't rely on Izzy for all my social interaction."

"Who's whiny?" said Nikolaus. He came in through the tower door, bringing with him a draught of warm air from the roof. The morning chill had worn off quickly and it was getting hot. Local radio was even predicting a heatwave, but as anyone who's ever lived near the coast will know, heatwaves only ever happen inland. Liverpool would have a few days of office workers getting sunburned in their lunch breaks up on Chavasse Park, and that would be it. "Apart from Bertie, obviously. That bird is honestly the most determinedly miserable creature this side of Manchester. I swear I'm going to refuse to visit him again unless he bucks his ideas up."

"He's just misunderstood," I said. "You don't appreciate him enough."

Nik looked sceptical, but wisely chose not to follow the path of avian argument. "So anyway," he said, "apart from cats and birds, who are we gossiping about today?"

"Apparently," I said, "I have to go visit the queen of bloody London." Nik raised an elegant eyebrow. "How come London gets a queen, anyway?" I asked, turning back to Eadric. "Does every area have a monarch? Are you secretly King Eadric?"

He looked uncomfortable. "I choose not to use honorifics," he said. "But in theory, yes. You forget, Lilith," he went on, "that many of us are from

13

times when absolute monarchy was an accepted thing. Kings and queens were chosen by gods, not men." Which sounded sexist to me, even making allowances for it being practically pre-history. "People—*our* people, whether technically human or not—still expect a framework of rulership. Without it, things would become very messy, very quickly."

"So if you're the king," I said, "shouldn't it be you going to London, rather than me? I'm just a low-level prole in the scheme of things."

"No denying that," said Nik as he sank into a chair by the window and casually draped his long legs over the arm. I narrowed my eyes at him and he grinned. "Can't have it both ways," he said.

"Will you two stop bickering?" asked Eadric. "This is *important*, Lilith. I need you to be my, uhhh," he struggled for a moment, "ambassador, if you will," he said finally. "Even the undead need diplomacy on occasion."

"Why can't you go?"

Eadric sighed. "I can't leave the city," he said, "because I think there is a very good chance that Laithlind is plotting something."

"So soon?" I asked, tensing. It had only been a few short months since Maria's death. We all knew Ivo would reappear at some point, but I'd assumed it would be a long way into the future. After all, time's different when you're immortal.

"He can't afford to wait," said Eadric. "He needs to establish his dominance in order to ensure his own safety."

"Safety from what?" I asked. "Ivo doesn't strike me as the type of person who gets threatened very often." Even older than Eadric, Ivo Laithlind had come to Britain with the Northmen in the ninth century and—other than getting himself killed a decade or so later and having to wait until the eleventh century to be reborn—had, as far as I knew, ruled his territory pretty much unchallenged ever since. It had been Eadric who had saved him from desecration and brought him into the undead fold, so I could see why the recent betrayal had stung a bit.

"There's always a bigger fish, Lilith," said Eadric. "We will forever be at risk, whether from suspicious humans or others of our kind." He leaned back in the chair and sighed deeply. "The trick is in making everything run normally, when things are anything but normal." I knew that feeling, at least. It really is surprisingly difficult to hide supernatural abilities behind the public image of a mild-mannered cafe owner, even when you're not climbing tall buildings for the fun of it. Even now, months into my afterlife, Izzy had to remind me on a regular basis that yes, humans were going to look surprised if I leaped onto tables like a gazelle in order to scoop up a sparrow that had flown in through the cafe windows, before jumping at the open window and throwing it back out. She did give me top marks for style, though. And I'd accidentally caused the river rescue team to launch their boat one night, when Daisy had persuaded me into taking a late-night dip in the Mersey. She'd wanted to show me a cute starfish she'd found on the wreck of the Sarsia, over at Birkenhead dock. We were arguing via some very basic sign language as to why she shouldn't eat it, when someone on the shore spotted me and called the coastguard. After giving Daisy a final hissed lecture about protecting local wildlife, I'd had to swim back to the Liverpool side entirely underwater, so the search team wouldn't spot me. I'd banged my head on the harbour wall because I hadn't been looking where I was going and felt guilty about the unnecessary 'rescue' for weeks.

"Who's bigger than Ivo?" I asked. "If you want me to be involved with undead politics, Eadric, I need to know exactly what the fuck is going on."

"It's about time she knew," said Nik from the corner. We both turned to look at him and he shrugged. "She might be the cause of it, for all we know."

"The cause of what?" I asked indignantly. "I've been dragged into enough bullshit already," I went on. "So you can bloody well leave me out of it this time."

"He's right, Lilith," sighed Eadric. "Things were...steady. Until you arrived. There'd been no real disturbances in our daily lives for a century or more. Then you appeared and, well." He gave me the closest he was ever going to get to an apologetic look.

"Well *what?*" I was pissed off now. I hadn't even been dead six months, and I'd spent most of that time defending myself from undead bullshit. "I didn't *ask* to be thrown off a bloody fire escape, Eadric! I was perfectly happy as a boringly normal human, living my boringly normal life." Okay, 'happy' might have been overstating it. I had definitely been very bored. And almost terminally single, which hadn't helped. But then suddenly terminal was the operative word, and I woke up to life that I hadn't asked for and which came with an awful lot of unwanted aggro.

"It cannot be denied," Eadric said, choosing his words carefully, "that things changed after you joined us." I glared at him. "And they changed quickly. But," he sighed, "I confess to having no idea whether you caused the change, or the change caused you."

"Stop talking in riddles, old man," I said sharply. "We both know the ratboys were only in my flat because your *wife* was trying to disturb the peace without you finding out. She'd made damn sure they knew there was access to Harrington Street from that tunnel. And in case you'd forgotten the most important thing, it was Maria who'd trapped the mother bird in the underground cavern." Everyone knows the legend of how, if the Liver birds ever disappear, the city will fall. Fewer realise there's a third Liver bird tucked away on a nearby building, who some consider to be the mother of the more famous Bella and Bertie. Maria's—admittedly very clever—plan was to kill off the mother bird under cover of the building works going on around Mathew Street, in the hope that the bird's bigger offspring would, well. I wasn't really sure what she thought might happen. Perhaps she'd been hoping Bella and Bertie would be so heartbroken that they'd smash the place up. Or maybe she thought they'd just leave the country. Which just shows how little she actually knew them, because Bella in particular is more bloody-minded than a toddler who's been told they can't have any more sweets. I reckon she'd have more likely stayed put and just bided her time until she could stomp Maria into pieces with her gigantic metal feet. Anyway, she tried to kill the mother bird, with me as convenient collateral damage. Luckily for me, Daisy had been close by in the river when it happened. I'd been credited with saving the bird, but in reality, it had made its own escape by following as Daisy dragged me out into the river to safety. "It was Maria causing the upheaval, and you know it. She wanted you to lose power so that Ivo could take over."

"That's as maybe," said Eadric, who absolutely does not like being reminded of his blind ignorance when it comes to his traitorous late wife, "but you're the first of our kind to be created in more than a century. Why you?"

"Gee, thanks for the vote of confidence," I muttered.

Eadric gave me a thin smile. "For what it's worth," he said, "you are a most worthy addition to the family. But," he went on before I could say anything, "there's no denying that you shouldn't have happened." I scowled, but he ignored me. "People die all the time, Lilith," he said. "They get sick, or injured, or they fall to their death from tall buildings after disturbing burglars. They *die*. But not you." He tilted his head slightly, as if inspecting me. "You woke up the next day as one of us, without even knowing we existed. You went back to work, for heaven's sake!" Actually, I'd taken a day off work until the vomiting finally stopped, but still. I'd take that gold star. "And you have that wretched tone of voice at times." Ah, the voice. Or *The Voice*, as Izzy liked to call it, usually in a doom-laden horror movie tone. The Voice is impressive by any standards, but I don't really have any control over it. I just have a limit to how much bollocks I can put up with, and once my patience snaps, out comes The Voice. It has no discernible accent—there's certainly no connection to my more usual Shropshire twang—and it sounds creepy as fuck, even to me. If I tell someone to shut up whilst using The Voice, they shut up. And they *stay* shut up.

"I can't help what I sound like," I said.

"I know," replied Eadric, "and that's what's so interesting. It's as if there's something else inside you. Something hidden, that only came to the fore after your death. Fascinating, really."

"Why not stick me in a specimen jar and be done with it?" I snapped back. "And if you're so suspicious of me," I continued, "why would you send me down to London on my own? How do you know you can trust me?"

"Oh, I'm not sending you alone," said Eadric. "What a ridiculous idea. No," he went on, "I'll make sure you'll have company. Anyway," a small smile, "it will do Nikolaus good to visit friends."

"Absolutely *not*," Nik spluttered, getting up out of his chair. "I haven't left this city for decades and I'm not about to start now. And you know it's dangerous for me!" He strode across the room and stood next to me in front of the desk. "What if I'm recognised?" I still didn't know who Nik had been when he was alive and I'd decided some time ago not to ask. I strongly suspected he liked the drama of his implied celebrity status and I wasn't going to give him the satisfaction of being curious.

Eadric rolled his eyes. "Nikolaus," he said, "you have been dead almost two centuries. There are no photographs from when you were alive and no one really knows what you look like. I'm truly sorry to break it to you, but unless you walk up to people with one of your old portraits held up to the side of your face, I strongly suspect no one will ever guess." I gazed off into the distance and attempted to look bored. "Anyway," Eadric went on, "Elizabeth has specifically requested your presence. She says," he tried and failed to hide a smile, "that it's been too long."

"That woman just likes baiting me," huffed Nik. "She's not actually interested in how I'm doing."

"That's as may be," said Eadric, "but someone needs to go with Lilith. And Elizabeth would like it to be you."

"Can't Mapp chaperone me instead?" I interrupted. If an enforced road trip wasn't bad enough, having to do it with Nikolaus Silverton for company was the miserable cherry on top of the rotten cake. I'd always found Nik slightly standoffish, in a weirdly fragile way. It was as if there was an invisible shell between him and the outside world. For all he liked to tease me with comments about his supposed fame, Nik struck me as someone who had been seriously damaged by his human life. I knew he'd died in Greece and made his way back to Britain on the same ship that was carrying his coffin, which was weird enough. And Mapp had once told me that there was a commemorative plaque in Nik's original name on the site of his old house. So he'd clearly been considered important at some point. But I didn't know him well enough to want to spend any length of time with him.

"Mapp stays here," Eadric replied firmly.

"Well, I'm not going until after Flora's closes tomorrow," I said. "Izzy gets her day off. And if I've got to go on a stupid bloody train trip with Captain Boring here," Nik made a choking noise, "then I think it's reasonable to expect it to be in First Class." At least that way we'd get snacks and legroom and a socket for my phone. I'd take earphones and just listen to audiobooks for the duration.

"I'm not putting you on a train when you can't even remember not to climb buildings in public," said Eadric. "It will be better if you drive."

"I appreciate the work you've had done to Basil," I snorted, "but it would take me about a week to get to London. *And* I'd get a numb arse." Basil is my beloved Beetle, who (yes, I anthropomorphize cars, what of it) was dropped halfway into a tunnel by Maria bloody Silverton during her final dramatics. He'd since been restored to almost showroom condition by a local specialist—thanks in equal parts to both Eadric's guilt and his platinum credit card—but there was no getting away from the fact that he has a top speed of about sixty miles an hour. And even then, he takes his own good time to work up to it.

"You're not visiting the queen of London in a bloody Volkswagen," said Eadric. "You can take my car."

"You've got a car?" This was the first I'd heard of it. "Can you even drive?"

Eadric shook his head. "I'm not as archaic as you think, Lilith," he said. "I've been driving since before anyone even had to take a test."

"Do you have a licence?" I was fascinated. I absolutely could not imagine Eadric Silverton behind the wheel of a car.

"Of course I do," he replied. "I forged it myself."

We Are Scientists

As I walked back up James St towards Flora's, it occurred to me I hadn't asked exactly *what* car Eadric drove. Christ, it was probably something from the forties. Actually no, that would be too noticeable. Eadric didn't do ostentatious—partly because when you're actually dead, it makes sense to not draw attention to yourself, but also because it just wasn't in his nature. Eadric was quiet, understated and quite possibly very, very dangerous. Something like a Ford Focus, I decided. Unobtrusive, but with plenty of room for the bodies of his enemies. The last thing I wanted was to spend hours driving down motorways with Nik for company, but I clearly didn't have any choice in the matter. Nor did I have the option of sharing the driving. I'd suggested to Nik that we could take turns, and he'd looked absolutely horrified at the prospect. "Oh no," he'd said, "no, no, no. I've never trusted those ridiculous machines. I don't mind travelling in them—and I can't deny that some are very sexy indeed—but I will absolutely not take control of one." It transpired that Nik hadn't *ever* tried learning to drive, not even when Eadric had encouraged him during the 1960s. "I thought it would be useful," Eadric had said when I asked, "but he pretended to have a nervous fit and collapsed in the road." I'd shaken my head at Nik in mock despair, but he'd just looked smug.

Flora's was open by the time I got back, and the outside tables were all occupied by customers eager to drink coffee in the sun while pretending they were leading a cosmopolitan lifestyle. Izzy must have called Todd after I'd left, because he was serving people from behind the counter. "Crikey," Izzy said when I walked in, "you're back! It usually takes forever when you get caught up with that lot," she went on, "so I rang Todd and asked him to come in." She passed a latte and an almond croissant to a man waiting at the counter. "Thanks love, sugar's on the side," before turning back to me. "Hope that's okay?"

"Course it's okay," I said, pouring myself an espresso. I'd realised early on that if I drank the same amount of coffee and tea I'd regularly got through when I was alive, it started coming back up after about the fifth cup. We need fluids in order to stop our eyeballs and the like drying out—and yes, that's as uncomfortable as it sounds—but can only absorb small amounts. So I stick to espresso and spread it out over the day. That way, I at least still have some connection to normality. "Could you feed Grimm for me tomorrow?" I asked, sipping the coffee with a happy sigh.

"You off running errands for the undead army again?" asked Izzy.

So much for normality. "Yup," I sighed. "Off to London, of all places. You and Todd are working tomorrow anyway, and I should be back by Thursday. I just need you to feed the cat."

"It's a shame Kitty can't work a tin opener," said Izzy. Kitty's my great-aunt. She and Grimm are buddies and they spend a lot of time hanging out together in my flat. It keeps them both out of mischief.

"We're working on it," I said. "Shall I just leave you to it?"

"Might as well," said Izzy, "as I've got Todd here now. I'll call you if we need anything." I grabbed my bag and headed out through the cafe. In theory, there's a staircase up to my flat inside the building, but I gave up on it a long time ago and just use the external fire escape. I was nearly at the door when I was stopped by the man Izzy had been serving.

"Lilith?" he asked. He had a friendly face and I thought I recognised him, but wasn't sure where from. His dark hair was combed into a neat quiff and his soft brown eyes crinkled quizzically at me.

"Who's asking?" I asked, warily.

The man smiled and held out his hand. "David Mansoor," he said. "We met earlier in the year."

I squinted at him as I shook his hand. "We did?"

"Yes, yes," he said with enthusiasm. "You came in for a health check and I

21

couldn't get my machines to work."

The penny finally dropped. "You're from the pharmacy?" I'd gone into the chemist on Castle Street to have my vitals checked, the day after I was pushed off the fire escape. David had become increasingly flustered by his inability to get a reading. And I got increasingly confused, until I decided that as I felt absolutely fine, it probably wasn't worth worrying about.

"I am indeed," said David. "And you stuck in my head for quite some time, let me tell you." I just bet I did. No detectable pulse or heartbeat, yet sitting there in his consulting cubicle like nothing untoward was happening. And now he was looking at me with what appeared to be rather unnerving excitement.

"Ah well," I said lightly, "I turned out fine, as you can see."

"I can indeed," said David-the-pharmacist, in an overly chirpy tone that was already becoming very annoying. "Which is why I would like to run the tests again." He tilted his head to one side and beamed at me with what I assumed he thought was a winning smile. He was wrong.

"Honestly," I said, "I'm fine. And I wouldn't want to waste any more of your valuable time. Now," I stepped past him and put my hand on the door, "if you don't mind, I've got places to be."

David leaned across and put his own hand on the door just above mine in order to stop me opening it. I stared at him and watched as his smile tightened slightly. "I really would like to check some things," he said, his tone less friendly now. "I might be able to help you."

A middle-aged couple heading into Flora's were forced to stop for a moment as David and I stared at each other in the entrance, neither of us willing to be the first to give way. "If you'll *excuse* me," I said eventually, giving the door enough of a yank to pull it out of David's hand, "I have business to see to." I stood back to let the couple in. They gave each of us a curious look, presumably wondering if we were having an embarrassingly public domestic. I nipped sharply out behind them as they walked past, before David could think of any more delaying tactics.

As I stepped out onto the pavement, I heard his voice behind me. "We'll be seeing you again, Lilith," he said. "Maybe sooner than you think." I forced myself to walk out of his sight slowly, as if I hadn't heard him. But as soon as I was safely around the corner, I raced up the fire escape so fast that a warm breeze blew across the sprawling wild buddleia that grew across the back of the car park.

"Oh," came a surprised voice from my living room, "you're home already!"

Dumping my jacket onto the small kitchen table, I walked through to where my great-aunt was sitting with Grimm in her lap. "Hey Kitty," I said, determinedly shutting creepy David out of my mind, "this is early for you." Kitty rarely turned up before mid-evening. I'm not entirely sure what she does all day, but I know she likes to call in for a regular gossip at Mapp's shop up on Renshaw Street. She then stops for a chat with Billy, the ghost in the empty shop doorway opposite Flora's. "Well done," I said, nodding to the armchair she was sitting on. "You've almost got it." Most people wouldn't have noticed, but from where I was standing I could see that, despite her best efforts, Kitty was hovering fractionally above the cushions. Other than that, there wasn't much that would give her away as a ghost these days. Having appeared just after I'd died—giving us both the shock of our afterlives, because neither had expected it—Kitty had originally needed to be around me at all times. It was as if she had to be almost literally tied to me in order to stay remotely corporeal. I think we were both a bit concerned we'd have to accompany each other everywhere until the end of time. Kitty hadn't seemed too perturbed by the idea, but I was still a functioning human, albeit a dead one. I didn't care for the implication that if there was to be any romance in my life in the future, it would be with my dead aunt in tow. Calling her 'great-aunt' makes Kitty sound ancient and creaky, but she was only three years older than me when she died. Her face is unlined and her blonde hair drapes over her shoulders like a heavy silk curtain. And the more I settled into the undead lifestyle, the more...*solid* Kitty became. Not always in a physical sense—her current position in the chair was proof of that—but she was definitely becoming more independent. Soon after she'd popped into existence, I'd discovered that she and Gaultier Mapp had known each other when Kitty was still alive. And yes, that's 'known' in the biblical sense. Despite there clearly being something going on between Mapp and

Heggie, Kitty had taken to disappearing off with Mapp on a regular basis, reappearing with a secret smile on her face hours later. No one else seemed to think there was anything odd about this, so I'd decided early on to just accept everyone and everything and try not to worry too much about the tangled webs they all appeared to be weaving.

"Are you not working downstairs today?" she asked. Grimm made a dramatic show of flopping over onto his back and wriggling in her lap. He squinted up at me through amber eyes as if to make sure I was witnessing his treachery. Grimm had been utterly in love with Kitty since the day she showed up, and I suspected he would choose her over me if it ever came to a custody battle.

"I'm just getting in Izzy's way," I said, collapsing onto the sofa. I kicked off my shoes and put my feet on the coffee table, ignoring Kitty's wincing expression. "I'm working tomorrow, though. And I need to go away tomorrow night. Just for a day or so."

"Without me?" She pulled a pouty face.

"Believe me," I said, "I'd prefer to be going with you. As it is," I pulled my feet off the table and tucked them underneath me on the sofa, "I'm going to London. With Nikolaus Silverton." Kitty pulled a suitably horrified face. "Exactly," I said. "And get this—" her faded blue eyes fixed on me in anticipation of some decent gossip, "—I'm visiting the queen."

Kitty's jaw literally dropped. "At the Palace?" she asked. "What on earth for? Oh my god," she went on, "at the crypt? Has the Queen come back as a revenant?"

"Not *that* queen," I said. Kitty subsided, a distinctly disappointed look on her face. "This one's apparently the queen of all undead London though," I went on, "which sounds pretty interesting."

Kitty perked up again. "Why on earth are you going to see her?" she asked. "I do hope it isn't anything dangerous."

"Kitty," I said, "I've killed two people already this year. I suspect an awful lot of people consider *me* to be the danger."

"But both of those were in self-defence," she said, loyally. "If it wasn't for you, poor Billy would be long gone." That was true, at least. Maria had tried to exorcise Billy as part of her last-ditch attempt at a scorched earth policy. Luckily for him, I'd lopped off her head before she could complete her weird incantation. Izzy and I spent a good bit of time afterwards wondering how the fuck no one had realised that Maria Silverton was actually a witch, eventually deciding it was probably because she was also an evil cow who'd put a lot of effort into covering her tracks. As Izzy had pointed out with a sigh, had she been a friendly, *modern* witch, she'd have been more likely to smudge some sage around the place while politely encouraging Billy to move on.

Billy had been murdered a couple hundred years earlier, by a woman who'd been ripping off Tom, an old friend of his. Tom had confronted the woman and, seeing the danger coming, Billy got between the two of them. Which is how he ended up dead in a Liverpool gutter. He's been here ever since, but doesn't know why. And he can't remember much about the first few decades after he died. Eadric later discovered that, just after I'd dropped head first into undead society, Billy's memory had started coming back. So yeah, something's definitely stirring in the undead state of Liverpool. As for Billy, the current theory is that it was Maria who killed him—probably when she was still human—and she needed him gone before his memory came back fully, in case he recognised her for who she really was. We're still waiting on Billy deciding to actually talk about it.

"How is he?" I asked. "I don't see him around so much these days."

"He's doing better than he was," she said, but I didn't think she looked entirely convinced. "His memory's definitely coming back—he tells me some of it. Honestly, Lil, it's enough to make your hair curl. The things that boy's seen over the years!" She shuddered. "Absolutely beggars belief."

"Do you think ghosts can get PTSD?" I asked, and stared at her bemused expression for several seconds before realising she'd never heard of the term. "Mental trauma," I explained. "From stress. Like shell shock."

"Well, why didn't you say so?" said Kitty. "Honestly, I'm sure no one even speaks the English language properly these days." She shook her head at the complications of the modern world. "Yes, I'd think so," she said. "He can't have been through all that and it not have an effect on him. And that...*woman* trying to get rid of him permanently—that's got to be difficult to cope with."

"Well, she's gone now," I said. "So that's one thing he doesn't have to worry about anymore."

"Perhaps it would have been better for him," said Kitty. "To be exorcised, I mean."

I was shocked. "You can't mean that?"

She shrugged. "I think I do," she said. "It's cruel that he's still here all this time later, don't you think?" My expression presumably made it clear that no, I did not think. "Think about it, Lili," she went on. "Billy's been out on that street for a century or more. Just...*existing*. And he knew he was a ghost from early on." This was true. Billy had told me himself that he realised within a day or two what must have happened, prompted by none of his friends being able to see him standing there right in front of their faces. "So even if he really can't remember the ins and outs of it, he'd have been aware he was trapped in a strange sort of limbo. He's watched people he cared for grow old and die, Lil. Some of them on the streets around him, right under his nose. And he couldn't do a thing about it." Kitty shook her head. "I can't even begin to imagine how lonely that must be."

"He's tied here," I said. "But don't take my word for it. I haven't had much experience with ghosts. Although there doesn't seem to be a shortage of you around these days, I have to say."

Kitty snorted. "That's enough about me and Billy," she said. "We'll both be fine. Tell me about this queen you're going to see." She suddenly looked worried. "Who's going to feed Grimm?"

"Izzy's going to pop in," I reassured her. "It's a shame you can't open a tin, mind," I went on. "A phantom cat sitter would be cool."

"Give me time," said Kitty. "Look!" She reached a hand over to the little table underneath the front window, where a small cactus sat rather forlornly in a plastic pot. She pushed the edge of the pot with her fingers and, to my surprise, it wobbled slightly.

"You're getting more solid," I said, unable to keep the astonishment out of my voice. "How?"

"Makes sense when you think about it," said Kitty. "I can hug you, and

I can…hug…Mapp," I raised my eyebrows, which she studiously ignored. "And Billy's as solid as you like, don't forget." She nodded her head towards the window, in the general direction of Billy's usual spot. "So if he can do it," she went on, "I reckon I can."

"I was wondering about that," I said. "About Billy, I mean." I walked over to the window and peered out onto Harrington Street. A bundle of blankets and old sleeping bags covered the shapeless lump that indicated Billy was at home. "How is he so human?"

"Well," said Kitty, "he *is* human. Just dead."

"But so are you," I pointed out, "and I can see through your head."

"No need to get personal," said Kitty. "Who's to say we all have to be the same? Everyone's different in life, so why not in death?"

"But living humans differ in things like hair colour and whether or not they like sprouts," I pointed out. "They don't generally vary in transparency and ability to pick up a tin of cat food."

"Things are different when you're dead," shrugged Kitty, and went back to stroking Grimm. I sighed and went into the kitchen to put the coffee machine on. There was a movement outside the kitchen door and I panicked for a second. If there was anything I'd learned since I died, it was that nothing good ever came from people turning up on my doorstep unexpectedly. I sidled into the kitchen in order to see out onto the fire escape. Outside my door—and staring straight at me—was Missy.

Just Trying Not To Get Killed. Again.

There was absolutely no good reason I could think of for Missy to be on my doorstep. One of Mapp's Renshaw Street mob, Missy had made it clear the first time we met that her tolerance of me was on sufferance, and nothing had happened since to make me think she might have changed her mind. I didn't think she actually resented me—there'd be no reason for it anyway, because Missy had been around a lot longer than I had—it was more a simmering air of distrust. Plenty of Liverpool's undead community had distrusted me in the beginning. And they had good reason, from their perspective at least. I'd appeared out of nowhere, killed someone within my first forty-eight hours as a revenant, and then made friends with all the cool kids in town. And I was the only one who had The Voice. Mapp once informed me in a jolly tone that there'd been some betting on how long it would be before they discovered I was possessed by something. He'd been very specific about it being 'something' rather than 'someone', which was not a comforting thought. Surely I'd know if someone—some*thing*—was inside my head? I'd once spent an entire day alone in the flat, consciously trying to use the voice. All that happened was that Kitty appeared and begged me to stop shouting, then Grimm stalked out of the flat in a temper and didn't return for nearly two days. I strongly suspect Grimm hides out under Billy's blankets when he's ignoring me, but neither of them is telling. Anyway, I'd never had cause to fall out with Missy—and I'd certainly never used the voice on her—so I didn't have a clue what her problem was.

I opened the door warily. She was standing as far back as possible on the small platform at the top of the fire escape, her feet carefully placed

JUST TRYING NOT TO GET KILLED. AGAIN.

between the collection of plant pots I keep out there. She had her arms wrapped tightly around herself, but as Missy isn't human, I assumed it was defensiveness rather than cold. "Hi," I said, eventually.

"Hi." Her voice was more subdued than usual, but still defiant. "I know this is weird," she said. "Believe me, I'd rather not be here." Charming. "But I need to talk to you." She sighed. "Can I come in?" I stood back and silently gestured for her to enter. She stepped through the door as though it was an invisible boundary and she was expecting an alarm to go off.

I closed the door behind us and turned to look at her. "To what do I owe this unexpected pleasure?" I asked brightly.

Missy scowled. "There's no need to be sarcastic," she said.

I shook my head. "Missy," I said, "I wasn't being sarcastic. Well," I went on, "not entirely, anyway. I don't know what your problem is with me," she narrowed her eyes, "but I promise you it's a one-way street. I have no issue with you at all, never have had."

She appeared to give this some real thought for a moment before speaking. "Can we sit down?" she asked, nodding through to the other room. "I promise I wouldn't be here without good reason."

"So you said." I peeked through the door to pre-warn Kitty, but she'd already made herself scarce. "Come through," I said to Missy, heading into the living room. As I passed my bedroom door, I saw Grimm rolling around on the bed as if playing with something, but he appeared to be alone. Only a faint flash of hologram-style light above the bed indicated Kitty's presence. And that was something else I'd yet to figure out—how Kitty appeared and disappeared, seemingly of her own free will. Parking that in the ever-lengthening 'weird stuff to think about later' section of my mind, I closed the bedroom door firmly and gestured Missy towards the sofa. "Have a seat," I said. She hesitated for a fraction of a second before visibly making a decision and sitting down on the squashed old cushions. I sat opposite her, in the chair I thought of as Kitty's. I pushed myself right back into it, hoping to project an air of confidence. What actually happened was that I sat down too fast and with too much force, sending the chair flying backwards into the bookcase that stands behind it. Cursing, I picked it up and sat back down, more slowly this time. "What can I do for you?"

Missy's face twisted up, as if she was still unsure whether to trust me. "I'm worried about Mapp," she said, finally. "Something's not right."

I frowned. "In what way?"

"He's keeping secrets," she said, looking uncomfortable.

"Well," I pointed out, "if something's secret, then he doesn't want you to know about it. Even Mapp's entitled to a private life."

"Not this kind of secret," she said. "This isn't the kind of secret that's fun and exciting, Lilith. It's something he really doesn't want anyone to know. He's sneaking around. Mapp's never been the sneaky type, not in all the centuries I've known him." I looked at the pretty, dark-haired woman sitting across from me and wondered just how old she was. I'd asked Mapp about the backgrounds of his Renshaw Street friends, not long after I'd first met them. Heggie I knew, of course. Not only had we been through the fight with Maria together, he spent most of his time with Mapp anyway, and I'd come to see them as a pretty much inseparable pair. When I saw Mapp alone, it was usually because Heggie had other plans, rather than the other way round. Which was funny because Heggie was a short, dumpy man who said very little and made even less sense. If anyone looked like the life and soul of the party, it was the tall and glamorous Mapp, but he did little without Heggie at his side. I'd occasionally wondered where Heggie went when Kitty 'visited' with Mapp, but finally decided that it was a mystery best left unsolved. I might not sleep anymore, but I prefer my daydreams not to turn into nightmares. Owain, the fourth member of the gang, had been a fisherman, I knew that much. He enjoyed lace-making, saying it reminded him of mending nets on his boat. Mapp had alluded to a dramatic near-drowning, during which Owain had been rescued by 'creatures of the sea' and returned to dry land. Quite what the creatures had done with Owain in the meantime, I hadn't asked. But it must have been impressive, because that was back in the eighteenth century, and Owain was still creating his delicate lace to this day.

Mapp had been vague about Missy's background. I knew she'd come over from the continent. And Mapp had once let slip that she'd been acquainted with King Charles I, so by my reckoning she'd been in this country for the best part of four hundred years. I also knew she'd started out in London, eventually coming up to Liverpool in order to be near Mapp, who she'd apparently been friends with for a very long time. When I asked him how they'd met, he'd laughed. 'It was a small world back then, Lili,' he'd said. 'Those of us who were different quickly learned to stick together.' But there was something in Missy's confrontational gaze that made me suspect there was more to her backstory than just wanting to hang out with her undead friend.

"What do you want me to do?" I asked. "Because I can promise you now, I don't have any control over Gaultier Mapp." A tiny voice in my head was wondering whether Missy was having me on, just to cause trouble. If that was her aim, though, I thought she'd probably do it from a distance, rather than having to deal with me at close quarters. And this really was the closest we'd ever been to each other, at least for any length of time. I noticed again that Missy didn't have the silver ring around her iris that would give her away as being a revenant. The silver ring was the first and only noticeable change in my own appearance after my death (aesthetically, I mean—if we're talking about all of it, then my newfound ability to run as fast as a cheetah was also a bit of a giveaway). I took a breath, just to check Missy wasn't secretly human. Well, you never know. And it's always useful to check—ghosts sometimes give off an energy I can 'taste' as well (and yes, it's as fucking weird as it sounds). But no, there was nothing. Missy was as dead as me.

"I thought he might have confided in you," she said, in a small voice. I squinted at her, definitely suspicious now. But when she looked up, she held my gaze with the confidence of someone telling the absolute truth. "The others clearly trust you," she went on, "because you're wearing that." She nodded towards my throat and I automatically put a hand up to touch the small but heavy silver key that hangs round my neck. It gives me access to the tower level of the Liver Building, and to the birds themselves. "Mapp doesn't always tell me everything," she explained, "because he doesn't like to burden me with what he calls 'heavy stuff'." She snorted. "As if I haven't carried my fair share of heavy, over the centuries." There was a sudden knock at the kitchen door. Christ on a sodding jet ski. Having any visitors at all was a rare occasion for me, and now there were two in one afternoon.

Missy looked nervously around her. "Would you come to my house?" she asked, already getting up from the sofa. "Tonight?" I stared at her. "I can talk properly there," she went on, "without worrying about who's around." She wrinkled her pert little nose as if considering something. "I probably," she said finally, "owe you some explanations."

"How do I know you're not planning to ambush me?" I blurted out.

Missy looked at me with utter astonishment on her face. "What the *fuck* are you talking about?" She was fishing in her pockets and finally came up trumps with a pen. "If I wanted to hurt you, I'd have done it by now." Well, that was a comforting thought. "Got a piece of paper?" I looked around and spotted a flyer for a vintage market that had been pushed through the door of Flora's while we were closed. I'd kept it with the vague idea of hunting out some new clothes that might be more interesting than my usual outfits. And then, as always, I'd completely forgotten about it and just carried on wearing variations of sneakers/leggings/skirt/t-shirt every single day, the same as I'd been doing for the past decade or more. Missy took the piece of paper and held it against the wall in order to write an address on it. She handed it back to me and I looked at what she'd written.

"But that's—" I started.

"Yes," she said, "it is. Come over after dark and I'll explain." Whoever was at the door knocked again, more urgently this time.

"I'll be off," said Missy, and I thought she was almost hiding behind me as we walked to the door.

I recognised the outline of the shadow. "It's just Izzy," I said, opening it to find Iz standing on the fire escape looking suspicious.

"You don't normally lock the—oh!" she jumped as Missy shot past her and headed down the fire escape so fast, she was nothing more than a blur. Izzy turned to look at me. "Who the fuck was that?" she asked.

"It's a long story," I said. "She's a friend of Mapp's. I only know her vaguely." I didn't explain the rest of it to Izzy. Best friends or not, some undead business stays undead business. Anyway, people only ask complicated questions. *'Are you supposed to be climbing that building on the outside?' 'Is that a mermaid you're talking to in the water?' 'Why does that...man...have such sharp-looking teeth?'* That sort of thing.

"You lot are weird," said Izzy, unnecessarily. She handed me a piece of paper. "This was dropped off on the counter for you," she said. "Don't ask who by, cos I don't know. I was serving a customer, and when I turned around, it was there." I took the envelope warily. Izzy had brought a mystery note to my doorstep only once before, and that had turned out to be an eviction notice from the Silvertons on the first day of the rest of my (after)life. This envelope was a standard white rectangle of exactly the kind of anonymous brand used in most modern offices. 'LILITH O'REILLY' was written in black Sharpie on the front, in block capitals. I tore the flap open and pulled out a single piece of paper. It was heavyweight, cream notepaper and bore the name of the hotel at the end of the street. The message written on it was also in Sharpie, and in the same anonymous block capitals. ***THE DANGER IS AT THE HIGH GATE.*** I turned it over, but there was nothing else. I stared blankly at the piece of paper until Izzy lost patience and took it from me. "What danger?" she asked. "And where's the high bloody gate when it's at home?"

"I have no idea," I said. "But I've already had enough of my life turning into an Agatha Christie novel." I slumped back against the door frame. "You really don't know who left it?"

Izzy raised an eyebrow. "You think I've got time to check out every customer?" she asked. "You know what it's like, Lil—it gets busy and you just turn into a smiling, coffee-making robot. Jason Momoa could walk in that place on a busy lunchtime and I'd barely register his presence." I doubted that very much. A movement by my feet made me look down. Grimm came stalking out of the kitchen and wrapped himself imperiously around my ankles a couple of times, before heading back inside. "I think his royal highness wants feeding," said Izzy. "Anyway, I have to get back downstairs. And listen, dead girl—I need you to promise not to get yourself into any more ridiculous situations. Okay?" She squinted at me, a look of concern on her face.

"I don't think it's something I can opt out of anymore," I said.

To my surprise, Izzy leaned forward and gave me a quick, tight hug. "I'm glad you're not dead," she said. "Well, no, obviously you're dead. I'm glad you're still here, is what I mean." She let me go. "But knowing that all the creatures from horror stories are real and living right here in Liverpool isn't the easiest thing to get used to, you know?"

"I know." Izzy had amazed me with how well she'd coped since my un-death in the spring. Once the initial shock had subsided, she'd just cracked on as if I'd done nothing more than change the opening hours at Flora's or dyed my hair a different colour. And she fitted in, somehow. Mapp adored her—I'd often walk in to find the pair of them giggling and gossiping as if they'd been friends all their lives. And I was pretty sure Nik had a crush on her, although she always brushed it off and accused me of having an overactive imagination. But it must have been a challenging time for her, all the same.

"What are you staring at?" asked Izzy. She patted her shiny black hair. "Have I got weird sticky-out bits again?"

"Nothing," I grinned. "Just wondering what I did to deserve such a brilliant friend."

She screwed her face up. "Don't be getting soppy on me now," she said, turning for the stairs. "Just try not to get yourself killed." She skipped down the first flight of steps, and stopped on the landing platform to look up at me. "Once is enough for anyone." And with that, she disappeared down the steps and back into Flora's.

***

"It's all going on today, and no mistake." I leaped sideways and turned to glare at my not-so-great-aunt, who had appeared next to the kitchen sink.

"Fucking hell, Kitty," I hissed, "how come I can be a supernatural being with unholy powers, but the ghost of a long-dead relative can still frighten me half to death?"

Kitty grinned. "Past halfway to death already, I reckon," she said. "Anyway," she turned to the kitchen worktop, "watch this." I'd left a couple of foil trays of cat food out on the side—the really pretentious sort, with photos of Persian cats on the lid and recipes that included words like 'terrine' and 'seafood broth'. They'd been out of stock of Grimm's usual brand in Tesco Express last time I went in, so I'd been forced to spend out on the fancy stuff. With a look of deep concentration on her face, Kitty put her hand on top of the nearest tray and caught hold of the pull-tag on the edge of the lid. I held my breath (well I don't actually breathe, but you know what I mean) as she visibly tugged the foil cover until it started coming away from the base. An interested mewing noise came from behind me and then Grimm shot past, leaping up onto the worktop with practised ease. Kitty grinned to herself as the cat nosed at the tray. "Good kitty," she whispered, "help me out." To my absolute astonishment, Grimm put a heavy paw on the foil tray and held it down on the worktop while Kitty concentrated on the lid. She managed to pull it a third of the way back before finally giving up. "Phew!" she said, turning to grin at me. "I don't know my own strength sometimes." Grimm was already helping himself to the smoked salmon pate inside the tub, so I reached over to pull it fully open and left him to it.

"You're determined to take over as the resident cat-sitter, aren't you?" I said to Kitty, who was watching Grimm eat with the sort of joyous expression on her face that's more usually seen on nannas committed to feeding up the grandkids.

She turned to look at me. "I can touch things!" she beamed. "Normal things, I mean. It kind of made sense that I could touch people like you and Mapp, because in effect, you're as dead as I am. But the living world! That's something I never thought I'd manage again."

"Well, I'll get Izzy to come in as planned this time," I said, "but just to help if you need it."

I swear to god, Kitty clapped her hands in excitement like a little kid. "We'll need some more of the fancy stuff," she said, nodding to where Grimm was licking bits of very smelly salmon off the worktop. "Tin cans are a bit beyond me just yet."

"Marvellous," I muttered, heading into the living room. "I'm going to be bankrupted by a cat-sitting ghost."

Martha's Harbour

The weather had turned sunny by late afternoon and it was well past ten o'clock before night properly fell. Not that a city centre is ever really dark, but at least I could take a few short cuts that were isolated enough for me to get away with running at full speed. It would have been easier to drive, but I needed advance notice to be able to use Basil. I keep him parked on the wasteland next to Flora's, because that way I can keep an eye on him. After he was nearly squashed during Maria's session of tunnel demolitions, Eadric had offered to buy me a replacement. Any make, any cost. I know he was trying to be kind, but he really needn't have looked so surprised when I turned him down and insisted that Basil be repaired instead. And now I've got him back, I like to keep him close to me at all times. The problem with this is that bollards block off the end of Harrington Street, and they're only lowered for a brief period each morning to let delivery vans through. I used to leave Basil parked up on the open car park at Hackins Hey if I thought I might need him, but these days I'm too precious about him for anything like that. As I ran across a dusky Everton Park, I wondered whether it might be worth persuading Eadric into allocating me one of the hallowed few parking spaces I knew were tucked away under the Liver Building. It would mean the Silvertons knowing my movements all the time, but I strongly suspected that Eadric kept tabs on everyone anyway, me included. I got to Priory Road less than fifteen minutes after leaving Harrington Street, speedy commuting times being one of the major upsides to undead athleticism. Slowing to something nearer a standard human walking speed, I followed the stone wall up past the main entrance and on to the address Missy had given me. Following the instructions she'd scribbled down, I walked straight past the house I was looking for and turned in a hundred yards further along, at the pair of small gates set into the wall. As I'd expected, they were locked. But they were also only about three feet tall, so, after checking that no potential witnesses were lurking on the road, I vaulted them.

So anyway, cemeteries at night are as creepy as you might think. I wasn't worried about paranormal activity; it was more that the very infrastructure of the place felt as though it was set up to be as unsettling as possible. The narrow road I was standing on was overhung with old, heavy trees that loomed in the darkness better than anything from a Hammer movie. I told myself to stop being ridiculous—after all, I was the lurking creature of the night these days, not the residents of this place. And actually, one of the strangest things I've discovered since my death is that the places you think are spooky when you're alive usually aren't, not once you're on the spooky side of life yourself. It's the 'normal' places—the pubs and shops and warehouse conversions—that give me the creeps these days. I once saw a vampire walk out of the Shankly on Victoria Street in broad daylight and say hello to a busker outside, without anyone marking him as being out of the ordinary. I can only assume he hadn't opened his mouth very far. My dad used to say, *'It's not the dead who'll hurt you, love—it's the buggers who are still living you have to watch out for,'* and he was only half wrong. It's the buggers who *look* like they're still living, who are the real danger. And now I was one of them. I headed through the trees and turned right. There was a break in the fence about halfway along. It looked as though the panels had just separated a bit, but when I pushed next to the gap, a section of the fence swung silently inwards, as if on well-oiled hinges. I stepped through and carefully pushed the fence closed again behind me. "Hey," said a friendly male voice in the darkness. I managed not to jump in fright, but it was a close call. There, standing by the open back door of the big Victorian house, was a man dressed in a suit straight out of those early Beatles photoshoots. He was neat as a pin, his narrow tie tucked into his jacket and his blond hair combed back into a quiff. I blinked a couple of times, just to make sure I wasn't imagining it. The man's angular face split into a broad, friendly grin. "Come to visit Missy?" His accent was local, but I'd never seen him before. And I was pretty sure I'd have noticed, had I ever walked past him in the centre of town. I nodded, and he gestured inside the house. "Into the parlour then, girl." I took a breath as I stepped past him into the house, and it nearly stopped me in my tracks. He tasted of grief and love and loss, and something my brain was telling me was adoration. Other people's adoration of him, rather than the other way round. He definitely wasn't a living human, I knew that much. And he was solid enough to be a revenant, but I didn't think he was one of us, either. Maybe another Billy—a ghost who was so attached to the place that he'd become absolutely solid. Shaking my head slightly, I walked through into what had clearly been built as a scullery. A heavy wooden worktop ran along the length of one wall, with a Belfast sink set into the middle of it. A table holding several dirty mugs and a sprawled copy of the Guardian sat in the middle of the room, with two mis-matched chairs tucked underneath. There was a door in the opposite corner of the room, through which I could see a dark hallway. Past that was what I assumed to be a sitting room, judging by the velvet three-piece-suite and open fire, which were the only things I could see from this angle. The fire was lit and several large split logs burned in the grate, despite it being a mild summer's evening.

"Thanks, Al," said Missy, walking in from the dim hallway. "We'll be okay now."

"Sure?" The man in the suit seemed to be protective of Missy. "I can stay down here if you like?"

Missy smiled at him. "That's very kind of you," she said, "but there's no need. And," she added, "neither is there any gossip. You'll only get bored and annoying."

Al pulled a face. "You always think the worst of me," he said.

"I can't imagine why," she said, "you being an absolute angel and all." He screwed his face up at her, but it was with an air of affection. "Honestly, Al," she went on, "I'm fine. Lilith and I are going out for a walk, anyway."

Al shook his head. "Girls sure are different these days," he said with a sigh. "It's like you don't even need us anymore."

"We never did," said Missy flatly. "So think yourself lucky some of us like having you around." She turned to me. "Anyway, Lilith," she said, "there's someone I'd like you to meet."

Anfield Cemetery is more properly known as the City of Liverpool Cemetery. Only a fraction over one hundred and fifty years old, it's a testament to the Victorian ideal of the 'garden cemetery', with its carefully laid out paths and wide-open spaces. It has gate houses and clock towers and a pair of the creepiest catacombs you ever did see. And that's before you even start looking at the graves themselves. If impressive tombstones and breathtaking monuments are your thing, then Anfield's where it's at. I'd visited it a couple of times before, back when I still had a regular pulse. Once was out of curiosity, not long after I'd started at university and was doing the tourist trail. The second was for the funeral of someone I barely knew—a colleague from back when I was still a desk monkey in a boring office. I'd taken endless photos of interesting graves on both occasions, but I'd never really noticed just how beautiful the cemetery itself was. Even at night, the place felt warm and welcoming. It was a very different feeling to the one I'd had when I'd first jumped the gates, which made me wonder whether it was because I was with Missy. As we walked through the gloom towards who knew where, she pointed out the occasional interesting resident, as well as an information sign that held the stories of local women of note. "They're a bit more forward-thinking up here," she said, pointing out a board that listed the names of women who'd served in the world wars, "which is lucky for them." I thought Missy's influence was probably stronger than I'd realised on our few previous interactions. I'd assumed she was just suspicious of me as a newcomer, but I was beginning to realise that Missy was just very single-minded. It was difficult to get my bearings in the dark and with little background knowledge, but I thought we were heading towards the very centre of the cemetery grounds, to the higher section where the catacombs stood in all their ruined glory. Sure enough, the thought had barely entered my head when the toppling arches of the nearest catacomb came into view. "Not this one," Missy said, as we walked past. "We're going next door." The second catacomb was as dilapidated as the first, and tightly protected with a ring of industrial metal fencing. "This way," said Missy, heading round the back of the crumbling stones to where a black iron gate was set into what remained of the old walls. She held her hand against the metal briefly, as if petting a favourite horse. Then she pushed, and the gate rolled inwards with a suspicious lack of creaking, considering it had appeared to be wedged into place by fallen masonry. "Come on," she said, turning back to me, "I can't keep it open for long." I stepped through, and could have sworn I felt—*felt*, not heard—the building let out a sigh. It would be just my luck to discover that the world of undead Liverpool included a revenant-eating crypt. And the maddest thing was that it wouldn't even be the weirdest thing to have happened since I fell off that bloody fire escape.

But once I was inside the skeleton of the building, my nerves eased. There was something...*kind* about the place, I realised with a jolt of surprise. This building, with its walls collapsed and insides open to the world, felt protective somehow. It was as if I'd climbed inside a cocoon. "Why here?" I asked Missy, who was standing silently in the dark while I took it all in. "Is it the gang hideout? Is Timmy the dog hiding in here, ready to bounce out and help us solve mysteries? Do we get scooby snacks?"

"You might turn out to be more irritating than Al," she said, without any apparent malice. "Which is impressive. No," she turned slowly on her heels, gazing round at what was left of the building's frame, "it's the place where I feel safest." I could understand that, at least. "Or anyway, it was." Oh.

"You said you wanted me to meet someone," I said, "not wander round ruined graveyards in the dead of night."

"We *are* meeting someone," Missy said. "Down there." I looked to where she was pointing, but couldn't see anything other than a stacked pile of broken masonry at the far end of the catacomb. The stones were cut into regular shapes and some were carved into columns—presumably pieces that had fallen off the building over the years and been stored safely out of the way of the accident-prone public. "Come on." She headed off towards them and, for want of anything better to do, I followed. When we were standing on either side of the stones, she bent down and put her hands, palm down, on the top stone. "Give me a hand, then," she said impatiently.

"A hand with what?" I asked.

Missy huffed slightly. "With this," she said, nodding down at the masonry as if it was obvious. "I need you to help move it." *Oh well,* I thought, *here goes nothing.* I followed Missy's lead and placed my hands down on the stone. The surface was unexpectedly warm, and I pulled my hands away without thinking. Missy looked up at me and her silent gaze explained clearly just what an idiot she currently considered me to be. *Of course the stone's warm,* I told myself. *It's the middle of summer, and it's a hot day.* But I wasn't convinced that was the real reason. I put my hands back down as instructed anyway, deciding I'd rather face whatever monstrous creature that might be in the crypt than have to deal with the wrath of Missy. The stones were solid, but not as heavy as I'd expected. As soon as we both had our hands on them, there was an audible creak and they moved fractionally across the old, cracked flagstones in a smooth way that definitely went against the laws of physics.

"What do you do if you don't have anyone to help?" I asked her.

"I push harder, obviously," she said. "But there's no point in me struggling alone when I've got you here." She shifted her feet slightly round to the front of the stones, so her weight was pushing them backwards. "Not that you're being much help at the minute." I debated walking off and just leaving her there to move the stones on her own, if they were that bloody important. But I couldn't shake the feeling that it was a big step for Missy to decide to trust me. Copying her movements, I stepped round to the front of the pile and pushed. "Mind out," hissed Missy. The stones suddenly slid backwards as if on rails and I nearly fell straight into the chasm that opened up beneath them. I only managed to stay on the surface by throwing my weight forward onto the stones and clinging on until they came to a halt against the back wall.

I slowly wriggled my way off the stones and onto safe ground before turning to confront her. "You could have bloody warned me!" I said sharply.

"What would you have done if I'd fallen in?"

"I expect she'd have told you to put the kettle on," said a croaky voice from below me. I jumped backwards before leaning forward and peering, slowly and carefully, over the edge. About twenty feet below me was a pale flagstone floor, the centre of which was illuminated by a candle lamp. A candle lamp that was being held up towards us by the oldest woman I had ever seen in my life.

"Hop in, then," said Missy, "before anyone sees us."

I glanced briefly around at the darkness. "Who's likely to see us?" I asked, trying not to sound as nervous as I felt. Being an undead creature of the night does not make you any less suspicious of things that lurk in the dark.

"Suit yourself," said Missy. Without another word, she stepped forward and dropped through the hatch. Landing lightly on her feet, she stood next to the old woman and looked up at me. "You staying out there all night, then?" she asked. Wondering what I'd ever done to deserve the amount of sheer insanity that coursed through my life these days, I gave myself a shake and jumped in after her.

We were in a large, rectangular basement that was entirely empty and undecorated apart from a pair of shepherd's crooks that hung from iron hooks high on the wall. There was also a cardboard box filled with what looked incongruously like plastic recycling, sitting in one corner. I stared at it. Endless milk cartons were squashed up and piled in on top of each other, some toppling out onto the stone floor. "Gotta recycle, girly," said the old woman. She couldn't have been more than four and a half feet tall, but was so hunched that I suspected she might scrape five feet if she was ever put on a rack and straightened out. Her clothing was made up of so many layered skirts and cardigans that she was almost round, but her wrinkled, birdlike face was thin and sharp. Bright little eyes gleamed at me in the candlelight and curly, iron-grey hair framed her skull like a tarnished halo. "Shut the door then, girls," she said. "You weren't born in a barn." Turning away, she headed towards a dark, square doorway in the far wall that I hadn't noticed. There was a creak of wood and a door closed on both the woman and her light. Undead eyesight isn't as super as the supernatural stories would have you believe, but it's definitely better than the human version. There wasn't much light coming in from the roof opening, but it was enough to see around me.

"Give me a hand, would you?" said Missy. She unhooked one of the crooks from the wall and indicated that I should get the other. "You need to catch it at the side," she said, raising her own hook up to where the edge of the stone pile was just visible in the roof opening. "There's a hook." I waved my hook helplessly through the hole for a moment, while Missy gazed pityingly at me. Then the end hit the stone and I scraped it around until I felt it catch. The crook slid into something that felt like a metal loop, and Missy gave a quiet grunt of satisfaction. "Finally," she said. "Now, pull." She leaned backwards, and I did the same. There was another creak, similar to the one when we'd first moved the stones, then they caught and slid. As their weight dropped into place, we were plunged into darkness. "For christ's sake, Martha," Missy said into the darkness, "bring that bloody lamp back out here."

"No need for that sort of language, young lady," said the old woman, opening the wooden door. "You only had to ask."

"Lilith," Missy said, "this is Martha. She enjoys being awkward," she went on. "Makes her feel useful."

"You learn to make your own fun at my age," Martha said, with a gurgling laugh. "Are you two coming in or not?" I followed Missy through the doorway into what was, to all intents and purposes, an underground living room. Another stone-walled room, it was maybe ten feet wide on each side and almost entirely covered in multicoloured, knitted throws. Stacks of books lined one wall and cushions were piled up under the blankets in a couple of places. A large oak door stood slightly ajar in the middle of the far wall, the darkness behind it broken up fractionally by light peeking through what appeared from this distance to be roof vents. "Tea first," Martha said, pulling a modern-looking plastic box out from a small set of shelves in a corner behind the biggest pile of cushions. "I hope you don't take sugar, because I'm all out." She placed the box onto an upturned crate and opened it to reveal a portable camping stove, which she held up to her ear and shook.

Apparently satisfied, she put it back down and lit the gas with a match. She then filled a tin kettle with bottled water and set it to boil while she rooted out a set of unexpectedly dainty teacups and saucers. The milk came from a chiller bag and I was relieved to see it bore a Tesco label. The way things were going, I'd half expected her to milk an actual cow. When she'd finally made what seemed to be the world's slowest cups of tea, Martha gestured for me to sit on the other pile of cushions and passed one over. I took a tentative sip, and then another when I was reasonably sure it wasn't going to poison me.

"Assam," said Martha, nodding at my cup. "Only decent tea there is." She looked from me to Missy and back again. "I assume there's a reason you've brought Lilith to meet me?" she asked Missy.

"How did you know my—"

The woman laughed again. It was friendly enough, but there was something about her tone that made me think I shouldn't take the nice old lady act for granted. "Oh," she said, "we all know who you are, Lilith O'Reilly." She clattered a spoon around in her tea as she fixed me with her beady eyes. "You're the bright new hope, aren't you? That's what they're saying."

"Who's saying?" I asked. "I'm not the bright anything, as far as I know."

"Can't disagree with that," muttered Missy, but it wasn't malicious. "Martha," Missy said, turning to the woman, "Lilith hasn't decided what she is just yet. Let her get used to us all for a while, before you start putting the weight of expectations on her bony young shoulders." There isn't a single part of me that even the most generous person would describe as 'bony', but I let it slide. "I just thought you two should meet, that's all."

"Ha," said Martha. "Ha! You do nothing without good reason, Miss Leschi." I hadn't heard Missy's surname before, and wondered how it was spelled. I'd assumed she was Spanish, but Leschi sounded more eastern European. "Talking of which," she went on, "when are you going to do something about Alan?"

Missy looked up. "Why would I do anything about Alan?" she asked. "He belongs here as much as you or I. In many ways he's more a part of this place than either of us, and you know it."

Martha snorted. "He needs to be wearing some normal clothes, then," she said, "instead of those fancy get-ups he wanders around in. People are going to talk."

"I can't control what Alan wears," said Missy. "I don't think even *he* can control what he wears, half the time."

"He's a ghost, then?" The words were out of my mouth before I could stop myself. Both women turned to look at me. I suddenly felt nine years old again, standing at the front of the class on 'show and tell' day, wondering why the model caterpillar I'd made especially and carried proudly in that morning was making the entire class snigger. It was another ten years before Izzy finally explained that my work of art had looked more like a curl of dog poo than the caterpillar of the giant hawk moth. "It's a reasonable question," I insisted, hearing the truculent tone in my voice.

"Yes," said Missy, in the sort of slow, polite voice people keep for very small children, "Alan is a ghost. He's a very solid ghost," she went on, "I'll give you that. But he's a ghost, nonetheless."

"Who is he?" I asked, having never found a hole I couldn't manage to dig that tiny bit deeper. Martha drank her tea silently, watching us with a mischievous gleam in her eye.

Missy decided to ignore me entirely. "How have you been, Martha?" she asked. The old woman pondered the question for a while, drinking her tea silently and looking perfectly comfortable with making us wait.

"Oh you know," she said eventually, putting her cup and saucer down on the floor with a clatter of china, "too old and too tired, same as always." I thought she was avoiding Missy's gaze, but couldn't be sure in the gloom. "The council have been poking around again," she went on. "I'll be needing you to remind your chap in the office that he's to leave me be."

"They won't come in here," Missy said. "They know better than that."

"How many people on the—" I scrabbled for the right word, "outside… know about us?" I asked.

"Too bloody many," grumbled Martha.

Missy pulled a face. "Yes," she said, "probably too many. But it's easy to underestimate just how much paperwork is involved in keeping people hidden in plain sight for centuries at a time. It's easy for you, Lilith," she tilted her head at me, "for now, at least. You're an average woman of an average age and average appearance—"

"Gee, thanks."

Missy raised an eyebrow. "But it's true," she said. "I'm sorry to have to break it to you, but you are—at least, as far as the general public are concerned—a thoroughly standard human being."

"That's not what Silverton thinks," Martha muttered, "Or so I'm told." We both turned to look at her, but she'd clearly finished speaking.

Missy turned back to me. "It's an *advantage*, Lilith," she said. "You can carry on without anything needing to change for a good few decades, yet. Worst that can happen is you might have to start wearing easy-fit clothes in maybe twenty years' time, in order to look older. Then just go away for a while when you get to retirement age, in order to reappear as your own niece or granddaughter a few months later. It's the reappearing as someone else that starts triggering paperwork—and that's why we can't do without Eadric. Or why those in the north-east are reliant on Ivo Laithlind. The people in charge might appear to be having all the benefits with none of the work, but in reality, they're mostly trying not to disappear under a tsunami of fake birth certificates and passports." I stared at her wordlessly. Perhaps naively, it hadn't occurred to me just how much was involved in running an undead community. I mean, obviously I knew Eadric was capable of 'fixing' things with people in high places, but I hadn't given any real thought to how it actually happened. "It needs a good level of political skill," Missy said, "not to mention diplomacy. So," she eyeballed me, "I've no idea why he's decided to send you, of all people, down to London."

"I don't actually *want* to go, if that helps," I scowled. "Neither do I fancy playing politics. So I can assure you Eadric's reasons for sending me are as much a mystery to me as they clearly are to you."

"Children, children," interrupted Martha. "If you don't mind, we were having a conversation about me?"

"We were," agreed Missy. "What sort of trouble have you been causing recently, Martha?" The old woman cackled at that. It rapidly turned into a breathless wheeze and it took us a good few seconds to realise that she was actually choking. "Bloody hell," muttered Missy, "not again." She got up and leaned over to slap Martha hard on the back. The force sent the older woman sprawling, and I was about to step forward to help her up when I realised she was laughing.

"Heee," she chortled, "heee heee, you nearly had me there, you wretch!" Slowly and painfully, Martha clambered upright and pushed herself back onto the cushions. "And it wasn't even that funny!" She snorted and readjusted her position. "Maybe I'm finally going senile."

"We'd never notice the difference," Missy said drily.

"You'll miss me when I'm gone," said Martha, "and don't you deny it."

"I'll be bored, for sure," agreed Missy. Something about this conversation was prickling my brain, and it took a good few minutes for me to figure out what it was.

"How can you choke," I asked Martha, who was looking around for her cup and saucer, "if you don't even breathe?"

She rescued the china from beneath the blankets. Miraculously, it hadn't broken. "Who said I don't breathe?" she asked. "You spilled tea on my blankets," she said accusingly, turning to Missy. "Put the kettle on again, for heaven's sake."

"I—well," I belatedly realised that I'd just assumed Martha was a revenant, purely because she looked too old to still be alive. "You're not dead?" I managed feebly.

"I'm human," said Martha, "living and breathing, like all the rest of them. Only difference is," she broke off to cough again, "I just keep getting older. Pretty sure I'll start desiccating soon." Another choking laugh.

"What the—" I started, but Missy gave me a sharp look.

"Martha isn't under any obligation to explain herself," she said. "We're not zoo exhibits, just sitting around waiting for you to come stare at us and take notes." I was going to point out that I'd be an exhibit myself and surely it was normal to be curious about it all, but decided against it. Life's too short for picking fights with people like Missy, even when you're immortal.

I was pretty sure she'd be able to bear a good grudge well into the next millennium, and things were complicated enough already. "And you're not going to bloody well desiccate, Martha," she said, getting up to fill the kettle. "You'd have crumbled years ago, if that was the case."

I looked at the wrinkled, hunched woman sitting opposite. "Can I at least ask how long you've been here?"

Martha turned her sharp gaze on me, and I almost regretted the question. She had bright blue eyes with an unusual lilac tinge, and they were boring into me as if she could see right down into my soul. "A long time," she said, finally. "You know the saying, 'be careful what you wish for'?" I nodded. "Well," she went on, "I made the ultimate mistake, didn't I? The one all the stories warn you about." That choking laugh again, but there was no humour in it this time. "I wished for eternal life, Lilith," she said, a small, sad smile breaking through her leathery face. "But I forgot to specify eternal youth."

Midnight On Derby Square

"And I've been here ever since," Martha gestured around the stone room, "hiding underground and wishing for nothing more than death's merciful release."

"You're so bloody dramatic," said Missy, sitting down between us and breaking the spell. "Here," she passed us both fresh mugs of tea.

"Let me have my fun, you miserable little wretch," said Martha, inspecting her tea. "Bit weak, this."

"You'll have what you're given," retorted Missy. "It's true though," she went on, turning towards me. "Our Martha here was offered eternal life, but she forgot to check the terms and conditions. Didn't you, you daft bat?" The old woman made a snorting noise and slurped her tea. "Yes," this was to me again, "she's human. And it was fine, for a good while. But then people started noticing that the old lady in the yarn shop was getting older and older but entirely failing to die, and I was worried we might be found out. Eadric helped me move her out before North West Tonight decided to use her as the token cheerful story at the end of their evening news bulletin."

"Who's 'we'?" I asked. Missy looked confused. "You said you were worried that 'we' might be found out. Did one of you do this to Martha?"

The outraged expression on Missy's face suggested that no, she probably hadn't been involved. Just as I was wondering whether it was time to make a hasty exit, her expression relaxed and she sat back in her chair. "I am going to give you the benefit of the doubt," she said, "because you are still relatively new. And clearly green as grass—which makes me wonder again why Eadric Silverton is so determined to push you to the front of things. No," she went on, "it was that bitch wife of Silverton's."

"Maria?" I was confused. "Not that I don't think she's capable," I said, "because I'm pretty sure she was the sort of person who'd drown kittens for fun. But," I frowned, "how is that even possible? No one knew Maria was a—" it sounded bizarre saying it out loud, but I forced myself, "*witch*. She was careful not to show it until the very end."

"That's what you think," said Missy. "Some of us started having suspicions a long time ago. And whatever he might say now, I think Eadric knew. He wasn't trying to be deceitful, I don't think," she continued. "He just got caught up in the romance of rescuing a poor waif from the streets and turning her into his glossy, immortal wife. And she played the part of an adoring spouse perfectly." She pulled a face. "Had us all fooled, when it came to her relationship with poor Eadric." It was the first time I'd heard the word 'poor' used in association with Eadric Silverton, and it didn't suit him. I'd only known him a few short months, but even though I'd felt sorry for him over Maria's betrayal, I didn't think he'd appreciate being described as 'poor' anything. "But I always thought there was something not quite right," Missy went on. "The rest of us get dropped into this life and start off making mistakes and not knowing how things work, as you well know." I frowned, but didn't say anything. "But Maria? She was different. Had it down pat right from the start. It was almost as though she'd been coached by someone already in the community. And obviously," her voice sharpened, "I was right. That duplicitous bastard Laithlind must have been *so* pleased with himself and his little puppet. Of course, none of us worked out that bit of the story until it was too late. But I wasn't the only one who was suspicious that Maria Silverton might not have been quite human to start with. Mapp didn't trust her, either."

"Why didn't Mapp like her?" I asked.

"I'd imagine it was because Heggie said she was a witch," said Martha, abruptly. "'*Martha*', Heggie told me, '*stay away from the witch*'. Of course," she went on, "I heard the word 'witch' and oh my gosh," she laughed hoarsely, "I'd tracked her down by teatime that very same day."

"How did you know Mapp and Heggie," I asked, "if you were human?"

Martha looked at me with bright, quizzical eyes. "How do people know you, Lilith O'Reilly?"

"Well, erm," I stumbled, "because I run Flora's and lots of customers come in and they get to know me that way."

"Well, there you go," said Martha, satisfied. "Heggie used to come into my yarn shop." I'd walked in on a meeting of the Renshaw Street Knitting Club the first time I'd met Mapp. These days, they're actually based in Flora's. On the second Wednesday of every month, we stay open late to accommodate a rapidly expanding group of people who knit, crochet and rag-rug their way through life, Mapp's interpretation of 'knitting' being a very loose one indeed. They even have button badges. Small black enamel circles with R/S/K/C laid out around crossed knitting needles, members wear them with pride, whether on silk kimonos (Mapp) or bouclé jackets (the elderly lesbian couple from up on Gambier Terrace, who've never missed a meeting). I'd assumed Mapp would change the club's name when they moved down onto Harrington Street, but he'd informed me loftily that it was part of the club's identity. "Good with a pair of needles, is Heggie," said Martha.

"He's been trying to teach me," I confessed, "but I don't think I'm a very good student."

Martha looked at me for a long second, her head tilted to one side. "Then you must be acceptable, I think," she said. "Because our Heggie is an excellent judge of character."

"Had any visitors recently?" Missy asked suddenly.

Martha looked taken aback. "Like who?" she asked, her eyes narrowing. "Your Alan came round last week," she went on, "but he just wanted to talk about a girl he likes. She comes to visit her dad's grave, over in the newer patch. Can't imagine she'd appreciate the scouse Elvis trying to chat her up while she's laying flowers, mind. Tells me he practises his stage moves round the tombstones, of all things."

"I'll have a word with him," said Missy. "God help us if he asks someone out on a date and they say yes." A frown. "Although I guess if he went into town and anyone recognised him, they'd probably just assume they'd had too much to drink." She shrugged. "Maybe we'll find out. Anyway," she got up, "it's time we left you in peace, Martha."

I followed Missy's lead and stood up. "It was lovely to meet you, Martha," I said, bending down to shake the old woman's hand. It was soft and squidgy, the skin like buttery leather.

"Ditto, I'm sure," said Martha. She gave me a strange little smile. "This might be interesting, after all."

"She's lying," said Missy, when we were walking down the main path back to the house, well out of earshot of the catacombs. "I've seen Mapp heading up to her place in the early hours on three occasions in the last fortnight alone."

"Why would either of them want to keep it secret?" I asked. "Surely they know you wouldn't mind them being friends?"

"They already *are* friends," she said, "so there's no need for the secrecy. It's not like I expect to be involved in everything, but it would be less weird if Mapp said hi on his way past, rather than skulking round the far end of the cemetery walls in order to avoid me."

"How do you know he's skulking," I asked, "if you're not watching him?"

Missy stopped in her tracks. "I realise we might have got off on the wrong foot when we first met, Lilith," she said, "and I am well aware that it was probably my fault. But I am not as cynical and cold as I perhaps come across. Mapp is my friend, and I care about him very much." A sigh. "Al saw him. Literally bumped into him the first time, which just shows how distracted Mapp was. He can pad around like a cat when he feels like it and no one would notice him, but apparently he was in a world of his own. Al went up to say hello and says Mapp nearly fell over a grave in surprise. He didn't bother telling me about it until it happened a second time—spotted him walking up to Martha's place a couple of nights later, clearly having got in over the back. Which, as you'll know," she said, "isn't the direction any of you lot would usually come from." She was right. Anyone heading into Anfield from the town centre would enter from Priory Road. But I still couldn't see what was so odd about Mapp visiting a friend late at night. If he was anything like me, he was probably just looking for something to do.

"What do you think Martha meant," I asked, changing the subject, "by 'this might be interesting'?"

Missy started walking again and I fell into step alongside her. "I don't know," she said, "but I don't like it. Mapp isn't the only person who's been in here when they shouldn't have been," she went on. "There was a strange blonde girl here, a week or so back." I almost tripped, but managed to stay upright. "Tall and thin, she was, with really short hair. I'd seen her earlier on in the daytime," Missy continued, "just wandering around like any normal visitor. But she was still here when I was going up to see Martha. And that was past midnight."

"What do you think she was doing?" I asked, somehow keeping my voice level.

"I don't know," said Missy, "but like I said, something isn't right." We reached the house and Missy pushed the fence panel open. "Will you come in and talk to Al?" she asked. "He enjoys having new people around."

"I really need to get back," I lied. "I promised my aunt I'd play cards with her."

"Aah," said Missy, "the pet ghost. I've heard about her. Maybe she'd like to come play whist one night?" She saw my expression. "It passes the time," she said with a shrug.

"That would be lovely," I said. Shit. Now I was going to have to learn to play cards. "I'd really better go." I was already walking backwards, just waiting to make a run for the gates and the safety of the main road. If Mab was lurking in Anfield, then I wanted to be as far away as possible, at least until daylight.

"If you hear anything," Missy said, "will you tell me?" She looked forlorn in the dim light coming from the house. "I'm worried about Mapp, Lilith," she said. "I'm worried about my friend."

"I promise I'll tell you," I said, already half turning away. "Let's catch up as soon as I get back from London."

"Oh," said Missy, "I'd forgotten about your London trip." So had I until I said it. Suddenly, I had more pressing things on my mind.

"I'm only going overnight," I said. "I'll be back on Friday. And Mapp will be fine." I was still backing away and had to speak more loudly. My voice seemed to echo through the trees.

"Okay," said Missy, but she looked doubtful. I gave her a wave and turned for the gates, leaping over them and out onto the road before she'd even got through the fence. I heard the panel click as I raced down the centre of Priory Road, which was thankfully empty of traffic. The more space I put between myself and Anfield Cemetery, the better.

The flat was silent when I got back in. The only light came from a small desk lamp on the side table that was trained on my latest disastrous craft project. I glared malevolently at the tangle of wool that lay on the arm of the sofa, looking more like a graveyard for fat spiderwebs than the cushion cover it was intended to be. Probably sick of the sight of the endless square throws I'd been knitting to keep myself busy, Mapp had convinced me to give Fair Isle patterns a go. It had looked simple enough when he'd demonstrated it to me, nimbly dropping the contrast wool in and out of the row as he'd click-clacked his way along. I had my extra wool wrapped round a peg to stop it unwinding and a print-out of the pattern wedged onto the sofa arm next to me, but all I'd produced so far was a knotted mess. Life in general was a knotted mess right now. I had no idea what Gaultier Mapp was up to, but I really hoped it didn't have anything to do with Mab. A faint rumbling noise coming through the wall behind me suggested Grimm was asleep on my bed, probably with Aunt Kitty lying next to him. She didn't sleep any more than I did, but was pretty good at giving me space. And Grimm liked the company. It was a long time since I'd been in a bed, and even longer since I'd had company in one. Sean hadn't been into Flora's for a while and even though I knew it was probably for the best, I couldn't help but feel a pang of loss over what might have been, had life—and death—not got in the way.

My phone suddenly pinged loudly, making me jump. I looked across at the clock on the bookshelf and saw that it was three in the morning. Panicking that something had happened at home—although surely that would warrant a phone call, rather than a text—I scrabbled around, finally locating the phone underneath the sofa. Sitting back on my knees on the hard wooden floor, I stared at the brightly lit screen.

Hey Red, the message read, *we need to talk. Meet me at the QV monument in ten mins?*

I glared at it for a few long seconds before tapping out a response. *Do you think I've got a fucking death wish?*

The reply came before I'd had chance to even put the phone down. *You're not in danger. You've never been in danger from me.*

I dropped the phone onto the floor. The noise disturbed Kitty, who appeared in the bedroom doorway dressed rather incongruously in a yellow kaftan. She had ghostly sunflowers perched in a crown around her head. "Is everything okay?" she asked.

I squinted at her in the semi-darkness. "Why are you dressed for Woodstock?"

Kitty looked down at herself and let out a pleased little laugh. "Oh!" she said, and twirled on the spot. "I must have dreamed it up!" Her hand went up to the flower crown and she beamed at me. "Isn't this lovely?"

"It's a very pretty look," I said, getting to my feet. "And also absolutely insane." Although being able to imagine clothes onto myself each morning would make life a lot easier, it had to be said. If people could just think up their daily outfit and have it appear on them from nowhere, that would be the 'fast fashion' problem sorted in no time. I was pretty sure it only worked for ghosts, though, thinking of Al wandering around Anfield in his smart suit. "I'm going out," I said, hunting my sneakers out from where I'd kicked them under the armchair. "Won't be long."

"At this time of night?"

I looked up at my great-aunt's concerned face. "I'm a creature of the eternal night, Kitty," I said drily, "I think I'll be safe."

"Do you want company?" She moved forward into the room. "I could come for a walk with you, if it's a change of scenery you're after?"

"NO." It was out before I could stop myself, the panic causing me to overreact. "Sorry," I said to her ashen face, "I really didn't mean to do that." Kitty stepped quietly backward in a way that made me feel like an absolute shit-heel. "It just...well, it has a mind of itself, sometimes. But no," I went on, "I'd like to go out alone. If that's okay."

"I'm sure you can do whatever you please, Lilith," said Kitty. Shit, I'd really upset her. "You're an independent adult with a life of your own to lead, after all. Far be it from me to attempt to involve myself."

"Kitty," I said, "that's not what I—" She disappeared even as I looked at her. Getting up, I walked over to the bedroom door. Grimm was just visible in the light coming in from the street, splayed out across the middle of the bed like the king of all he surveyed. I was pretty sure he was alone. Sighing, I put on my shoes and headed out.

He was sitting on the monument steps, a solitary shadow in the darkness ahead of me as I walked down Lord Street. As I got closer, he lifted his head and smiled. His eyes crinkled at the corners and my stomach did a traitorous backflip. "Evening, Ivo," I said, sitting down next to him. "How's tricks?"

He smiled into the darkness ahead of him. "Tricks have been...interesting," he said, "as I suspect you well know." He turned to look at me and I forced myself to hold his gaze. "How've you been, Red?" His voice was soft and I thought I saw his hand move as if to reach out to me, before he realised what he was doing. He folded his arms tightly and went back to staring determinedly ahead.

Twisting round to face him, I wedged my back against the stone wall alongside the steps. Having something solid behind me at least gave some sense of protection. "Well," I said, "Maria's long-lost daughter turned up." I hunched myself up. "And I'm pretty sure she's after revenge for her mother's death." I wriggled more firmly back against the wall. "So there's that." Ivo leaned forward with his arms on his knees. He was dressed informally by his usual standards, the dark roll neck sweater and trousers set off by suede Chelsea boots and a heavy grey pea coat. It looked like the sort of thing sailors used to wear, but this one had probably come via Harrods. Even in the shadows, Ivo Laithlind exuded a quiet, expensive confidence. "Why are you here?" I asked. "You must know it's dangerous."

"I do," he agreed, gazing into the distance. "And you must know it's dangerous for you to meet me." He turned his head to look at me. "Silverton isn't going to like it."

"Eadric isn't my boss," I said, "and he doesn't get to tell me what to do."

Ivo smiled in the gloom. "I'm not sure Eadric knows what to make of you at all," he said. "Neither do I, come to that."

"Then why did you ask me to meet you?" A young couple were walking towards us from the direction of Castle Street. They giggled and put their arms round each other as they studiously ignored us and turned down Red Cross Street, presumably heading for the Travelodge.

"It's so easy when you're human, isn't it?" said Ivo, turning to watch as the couple disappeared behind us. "Get a job, fall in love, go out and have fun until you decide to settle down and have kids. Then just sort of…moulder, until you finally die."

"You make it sound so romantic." I said.

He gave a quiet little laugh. "It kind of is, though," he said, "when you think about it. Everything's on a smaller scale when you're human. Just wandering ignorantly through life. Not that I ever got to experience a boringly modern human lifestyle, of course." He glanced sideways at me. "I guess it's all still recent memories to you, though," he said. "Do you miss it?"

I gave this some thought. "Yes," I said slowly, "I do." I remembered the conversation I'd had with Eadric earlier in the day. It was actually yesterday, I realised. That was the problem with revenant life—you could go weeks with nothing more than bakery orders and knitting patterns for entertainment, only to suddenly be confronted with a year's worth of action in the space of twenty-four hours. I was pretty sure I preferred the boring days. "I feel…" I struggled for the right word, "…bereaved." Ivo looked at me curiously. "Bereaved of all the possibilities."

"Did you want children?" he asked. "Marriage?"

"God no," I laughed, "nothing like that. It's more the fragility of humanity that I miss, I think. That feeling of not knowing where you'll go, or who you might meet along the way. Endless small adventures. Romance and lust and sheer, terrifying excitement." I looked at him. "I suppose that must sound very provincial, to someone who's been around as long as you have."

"It sounds…fun," he said. I looked at him sceptically. "Genuinely." He smiled. For all he was a duplicitous toad, there was something almost childlike and sweet about Ivo at times. I reminded myself sharply that he was also a scheming creep. Queen Victoria loomed above us in the dark, gazing out across her domain with the sort of confidence that only comes from absolute power. "She wasn't born to it, you know," said Ivo, seeing me looking up at the oversized monarch. "Should have spent her life in wealthy security with nothing better to do with her time than arrange flowers and find a suitably boring landowner to get married off to."

"I did a history degree," I reminded him. "I'm well aware of the background of the British royal family. Including," I continued, "just how much their hold on power depended on sheer luck."

"How do you mean?" Ivo asked. I squinted at him, waiting for the patronising mansplaining to start, but the question appeared to be genuine.

"It all relies on tiny little accidents," I said, waving dismissively up at one of the longest-serving monarchs in history. "She should have been nothing more than a spoiled little rich girl, but by an accident of birth—and the inability of her uncles to get their shit together—she ended up a spoiled little queen instead. Led a long and indulgent life being venerated by people who were nothing more than chattels in her financial inventory, while her private life was taken up with obsessing over her dead husband and being vile to her kids."

"You don't think very highly of her," Ivo observed.

"Nah," I said, "I don't. But it isn't personal." I looked back up at the statue. "She was just doing what she had to, in order to get through. I'd like to think others might have done it better, mind. But she certainly wasn't the worst this country's had."

"I quite liked her," Ivo said, unexpectedly. "On a personal level, at least."

I boggled at him in the darkness. "Oh god," I said, "you're going to tell me you knew her, aren't you?"

He laughed. "I did know her," he said, "yes." He looked across at me. "You'd be surprised who knows about us, Red," he said. "Some never find out for sure, of course," he shrugged. "But plenty do. There's fewer these days," he went on. "I wouldn't trust the current lot to boil a kettle, never mind with the secret of our existence."

"The royals?" I asked. "Or are we talking politics now?"

"Both," he grinned. "You can say what you like about Vicky," he nodded his head backwards towards the monument, "but she knew how to keep a secret. I can't promise to control her, Red," he went on, and for a moment I was left wondering whether I was going to be hunted down by a dead queen. "Mab, I mean. I'd like to be able to reassure you that you're safe," he gazed off into the distance, "I really would. But I'm not sure anyone's safe from Mab."

"But you're working with her," I said, "aren't you?" I'd expected Ivo to at least attempt to deny it, but he gave a small nod. "You're happy to have her on your side," I went on, "regardless of the danger she poses to the rest of us. Such loyalty to your friends."

Ivo winced. "I deserved that," he said. "For what it's worth, I would have preferred to stay loyal to Eadric."

"Ivo," I snorted, "you were fucking his wife!" It came out louder than I'd intended. We sat in silence as my words echoed around Derby Square. "How is that any kind of loyalty?" I hissed, keeping the volume down this time.

"I hadn't had a..." he struggled for the words, "...*physical* relationship with Maria for a long time," he said eventually. "But yes," he went on, "we had a connection. Maria and I understood each other, Red." He looked me in the eye. "We were similar creatures. At least, we were back then. We both understood the need for control. The need for power."

"How long ago?" Ivo looked confused. "You said 'back then,'" I pointed out. "How long ago was 'back then'?"

He sighed. "Before she met Eadric," he said. "But I rather think you know that already."

I glared at him, my arms folded tightly around myself. "Yeah," I said, "we figured that one out pretty quickly." I sighed. "Eadric was your oldest friend, Ivo. He *saved* you." His eyes twitched slightly at that. "And you repaid him by setting him up with a conniving, vicious cow, purely to bolster your own power. Nice move, big boy."

"Maria wasn't conniving or vicious," he said quietly. "Not back then."

"Don't you dare try to tell me it was some ridiculous love story," I hissed at him. "All that *I didn't mean for it to happen, we just couldn't help ourselves*, and *It must be fate*, bullshit. That sort of crap is only ever an excuse for idiots who aren't intelligent enough to self-reflect about their own inadequacies, and you know it."

He smiled despite himself. "Ever considered being a relationship counsellor, Red?"

"Funnily enough," I retorted, "no. And don't try to deflect me, Ivo Laithlind. You need to come up with some better excuses than 'oh she was nicer back then', you hypocritical little shit."

"No one's ever spoken to me like that before," said Ivo, quietly. "No one's ever dared."

My internal animal brain made a tiny squeak of fear, but I trod it down hard. "No one's ever been as much of a dickhead as you, to be fair." I said. We sat there for a while without speaking, each digesting the last five minutes' conversation. "Is she going to try to kill me?" I asked eventually. Anything was better than the icy silence.

"I think so," Ivo said. "Wouldn't you?"

I gave it some thought. "Yes," I said flatly. "If someone did to my mother what I did to Maria," my cold, dead heart clenched at the mere thought of it, "I'm pretty sure I'd want to kill them." Something else occurred to me. "Mab's only just turned up," I said, "yet Maria's been wandering round Liverpool for the past hundred and fifty years. Where was her daughter all that time? And," I went on, "how come Mab's even *been* around all this time? I'm pretty sure she's not a revenant," Ivo tilted his head, "but she must be *something*. Because she looks like a twenty-something hipster when she's actually got to be a good century and a half old. You're not telling me she conveniently grew to adulthood and then just stuck like that for the hell of it?"

"I would assume she didn't know about her mother until recently," said Ivo. "News of Maria's death spread rapidly through the entire community, as you can imagine." I could indeed imagine. "Across continents," he went on, "as well as the British territories." I shuddered. Hopefully Maria Silverton hadn't had too many undead European allies, because otherwise I was going to be watching my back for a very long time. "As for Mab's presumably unusual genetics," he shrugged, "I can't help you there. She was born before Maria even went into the workhouse up on Brownlow Hill. So she's technically half human, at least."

"Maria didn't seem very human to me," I said, remembering all too clearly the vengeful look on her face when she stood in the middle of my living room and tried to destroy Billy. "Where was Mab?" I asked. "Before she came to Liverpool, I mean."

Ivo shrugged. "Who knows?" he said. "It's been a long time, Red. Mab had disappeared from official records before Maria had even died. The story she told you was true, by the way," he went on. "About trying to drink herself to death and then throwing herself into the Mersey. It's just that it was me who found her. Originally. It made sense to use the same story again when I…arranged…for Eadric to rescue her. That way, she was more likely to keep her story straight."

I shook my head. "You are a really awful person," I said. "And believe me, I don't mean that in a 'funny ha-ha' kind of way."

"I don't believe you," said Ivo. He slid closer to me, along the stone steps. "You don't think I'm awful," he said. "Not deep down."

I looked him in the eye as he gazed earnestly at me. "I think you underestimate my self-control, Ivo," I said. "I've had years of—"

"Red!" The voice carried across the square and broke whatever spell it was that Ivo thought he was casting over me. I stood up to see someone striding towards me from the direction of Castle Street. *Shit.* I had no idea how I was going to explain why I was sitting in the middle of town with Liverpool's number one enemy.

"Billy?" I obviously knew he left Harrington Street occasionally; the occasionally unoccupied stash of blankets in his doorway was proof of that. But I'd somehow been under the impression that he only went as far as Rainford Square or Mathew Street. I'd certainly never seen him down this way before. I looked down at Ivo in the hope he could come up with something believable, but the steps were empty.

Everything's Fine, Thanks For Asking

"You okay, Red?" Billy's expression was one of concern as I walked forward to meet him.

"Absolutely fine," I said, feigning what I hoped was a casual manner. "Why wouldn't it be?"

"I could have sworn there was someone else here," said Billy, looking around. "Weren't you talking to someone?"

"Checking up on me now?" I raised an eyebrow. "You're getting as bad as Kitty."

He looked sheepish. "Well now," he said, "it might have been Kitty who was worried about you. Don't you go being cross with her," he added hurriedly, "she cares, is all."

"Cares enough to send someone out to check up on me, you mean." I scowled. "Anyway," I said, "I'm heading home. Coming?" I set off up Lord Street without waiting for a response. I'd got as far as the jewellers on the corner with North John Street before he reappeared next to me, making me jump. "How do you do that?" I asked as we crossed the road.

"Do what?" he asked. It was getting light now, and I turned to look at him as we reached the turning for Harrington Street. He seemed taller, somehow, and less weatherbeaten than when I'd first got to know him. I thought back to the day after I'd died, when I'd spoken to him properly for the first time. We'd exchanged the odd greeting before that, of course. But on that strange day when I was beginning to realise that something really big had happened, I'd sat down next to Billy on the pavement outside Flora's and spoken to him as an equal for the first time. Which says a lot about human privilege and the treatment of homeless people. I'd have counted myself as someone who genuinely cared and tried to make a difference—I took coffee in a takeout cup out to Billy regularly, and we always gave him the leftover pastries at the end of the day—but until I was an outsider myself, it had never occurred to me to have a genuine conversation with him. Of course, I now knew he'd never been able to make use of the cakes and coffee anyway, on account of being a dead man walking. Turns out he'd been passing it on to other rough sleepers, so these days we try to mix it up with some fresh fruit and veg and the occasional pack of new socks. Anyway, that first time we'd spoken, Billy had resembled the absolute archetype of someone who lived on the streets—crumpled up leathery face, scruffy hair, the lot. But now... Now something was different.

"You're looking well," I said eventually, coming to a halt just underneath the arched Harrington Street sign. "Outdoor life suiting you, suddenly?"

He grinned. "Turns out," he said, "it depends on who you hang around with." He nodded towards the fire escape that led up to my flat. "Been talking to your Kitty about it, so I have. Obviously I knew she was like me from the minute she appeared," which was interesting in itself, because at the time Kitty first appeared I'd yet to figure out that Billy was anything other than your average human man, "so it was nice to feel less alone, anyway. Then I realised she was changing her clothes." I thought of the flower child outfit Kitty had been wearing when I'd left the house in the early hours and hoped she was feeling happy enough to still be wearing it. I really needed to learn how to control that bloody voice. "And I got to thinking," Billy carried on, "about whether I could do the same. Turns out," he shrugged, "I could. Guess it just hadn't occurred to me before then. And once I'd got used to having nicer clothes on, I thought maybe I could do the same for my physical appearance." This certainly explained why Billy's usual camouflage ensembles had looked a lot neater recently. "What do you think?" To my absolute astonishment, he did a twirl, right there in the middle of the street. He was actually quite handsome, I realised, albeit in a blokeish sort of way. Brown hair flopped in crooked bangs, and his kind eyes almost twinkled in the early morning light.

"Very impressive," I said, smiling back at him. "What's next, then?" I asked. "Going to find yourself a good woman and settle down?"

I'd meant it as a compliment, but Billy's face fell slightly. "Can't see that happening, Red," he said, "not with me being dead, an' all that."

"Oh, come on," I said, trying to gee him up a bit. "If we started letting a little thing like dying get in the way of our fun, where would that leave us?"

"I think it's different for your sort," Billy replied. "You're never anything other than absolutely, one hundred per cent human, and you never have been. Whereas those like me and Kitty," he went on, "we're a bit more..." He paused. "Ephemeral, you might say."

"Don't let that stop you," I said, rolling my eyes. "It certainly doesn't stop Kitty getting up to god knows what."

"Jealous, Red?" Billy said, his eyes crinkling with laughter. "There's nothing to stop you dating, you know." He nodded towards Flora's. "What happened to that chap you liked?" he asked. "The one the mermaid frightened off?"

I sighed. "That's the thing, Billy," I said, "isn't it? Human women don't have bloody asrai popping up in their living rooms without warning, do they? Normal, human women don't have to worry about whether their long-dead great-aunt might appear in the doorway at an unfortunate moment in proceedings." I sighed. "If I'm honest," I said, "I'm not sure the success rate for human/revenant relationships is likely to be very high."

"Ah, get on with you," he said kindly, rocking back on his heels and looking me up and down. "You're still a bit of a catch, aye." I could feel myself turning pink under his gaze. "Someone'll snap you up sooner rather than later, Red," he went on, "you mark my words."

"I've got to survive first," I said with a sigh. "And there seems to be a lot of people who'd like me out of the picture right now."

"There is that," agreed Billy. I raised my eyebrows at him. "Sorry Red," he went on, with a little apologetic shrug, "but it's true. You're a threat to many. And that's without the vengeful daughter hanging around."

I froze where I stood. "You've seen her as well?"

Billy looked down at me, his face concerned. He was definitely taller than he used to be. It suited him, but I suddenly had more important things on my mind. "She's been around a couple of weeks now," he said. "At least, that's what people tell me. She stands out in a crowd, let's face it. And," he went on, "I don't think she's trying to hide, anyway."

"What do you think she's doing?"

He considered this for a minute. "I think she's making sure everyone knows she's here," he said eventually. "Trying to unsettle things, maybe."

"Oh, she's definitely trying to unsettle things," I said. "She made it very clear that she's intending to make me feel uncomfortable, at the very least. I'd assumed she'd only just got into town, but," I thought of my earlier conversation with Missy, "I think she's been sussing the place out for a while. Do you know where she is now?" I asked. "Have you seen her around here?" I was pretty sure Izzy would have noticed someone as striking as Mab, had she come into Flora's at any point. But then I remembered Izzy didn't know about the current 'bereaved daughter intent on revenge' situation. And Mab wouldn't look all that different to any number of the university students who'd started using Flora's as their base. Business had picked up over the last few months, probably down to a combination of Izzy's friendly management and Mapp's rather niche craft groups. What with meetings of the local beekeepers' society (I'd been very surprised to find several hives on top of the Liver Building when I first went up there, but had soon discovered they weren't the only locals with their own honey-making setup) and the endless art students who liked the fact we didn't mind them making one latte last two hours, Flora's was quite the social hub.

So no, unless she'd known what to look out for, Izzy wouldn't have given a second thought to Mab coming into the cafe. And I wasn't about to tell her, either. I hated keeping secrets from my oldest friend, but the less Izzy knew about undead dramas, the safer she'd be. At least she had Damon around these days. Well over six feet and built like the proverbial brick outhouse, Damon worked as security-for-hire for anyone in need of some well-muscled backup. Izzy had met him when he was doing a side job for his cousin, the owner of a local construction firm. Damon had been put in charge of ensuring no one disappeared down the bloody great hole in the ground next door to Flora's—the one that had almost swallowed Basil whole. Iz had started taking him the occasional coffee, Damon had been thrilled by her apparent interest in how industrial diggers work (Izzy is nothing if not devious) and within about a week, they were a bona fide couple. I'd found it hilarious at the beginning, because what *isn't* funny about a tiny Welsh-Japanese girl dating a walking, talking man-mountain? Izzy looks like a starlet from the fifties even on her off days, while Damon gives the distinct impression he eats concrete for breakfast. Turns out he actually has a Masters in Biology, was bluffing about the digger knowledge and the security work is just a side gig while he studies for a PhD in some obscure field of plant biosynthesis. At least I think that's what he's researching—I've learned to zone out when he gets onto the differences between various secondary metabolites. Iz, on the other hand, appears to find it genuinely fascinating. Which would infuriate our high school biology teacher, who regularly put us both into detention for giggling at the human anatomy modules. Anyway, she's certainly got protection, should she ever need it. I couldn't help feeling it was me who needed protection right now, though, not my best friend. "Only time I've seen her at all was yesterday," said Billy, "when she was waiting for you." He gazed at me thoughtfully. "Shouldn't Silverton be helping you out?" he said. "After all, it's his wife who caused all this trouble in the first place." *And Ivo*, I thought. Ivo, who was presumably hiding out in his hotel suite up on Hope Street right now, as if being a manipulative, thousand-year-old revenant taking a city break was normal behaviour.

"He's asked me to go to London," I said, "tomorrow night. It's a business trip," not *exactly* a lie, "but I suspect he's also thinking it might be a good way of getting me out of town for a day or so."

"But you can't just stay away," said Billy. "Not for long. He needs to do something about it."

"Billy," I said, "this entire situation is an unholy mess." I shrugged. "I just have to try to survive it, I guess." And as I said it, I realised it was true. A good bit of my human nervousness had disappeared on the night I was pushed off the fire escape. There isn't much else can frighten you when you've already died once. All I had to do these days was survive.

Billy looked unconvinced. "I dunno, Red," he said. "I'll feel better when I know you're safe."

I smiled at his concern. "I'm not sure I'll ever be safe, Billy," I said. "Not any more."

***

The next day I did the only thing I could, under the circumstances—I opened up Flora's and pretended everything was normal. Todd came in and impressed me with his eagerness to please, as well as his overwhelming air of general niceness. I couldn't remember the exact details of Todd's connection to Izzy's family, but thought he might be the son of one of her cousins. Presumably on the Welsh side, if the occasional twang to his accent was anything to go by. Like so many of us, Todd had moved to Liverpool for university and then couldn't bring himself to leave, working his way through endless bar jobs in order to pay the rent. At least at Flora's, he was earning a proper wage. Since Eadric had stopped charging me rent, the cafe's overheads were ridiculously low. And of course, as a dead woman with no need for sustenance, my own expenses were minimal. Izzy had made a half-hearted attempt to persuade me into spending some of my extra income on clothes and makeup, but rapidly gave up in the face of my determination to cling to what remained of my human life. Maybe one day I'd develop a taste for the fancier things in life, but it didn't look to be happening just yet.

It was a busy morning, helped along by the sun being out and the street filling up with tourists. Harrington Street is usually quiet compared to the rest of the area, but the repair works needed on Mathew Street after the whole 'collapsing tunnels' incident had pushed the swell of visitors outwards and all the surrounding streets had benefitted. I could hear Ifan playing an acoustic version of an old grunge song from his pitch up towards the turn for Rainford Square. Ifan's a well-known musician in his own right, but he pulls a hat down over his face so that people don't recognise him and just plays for the sheer joy of it. Makes a lot of money, as well. Izzy once told me he donates it all to a local detox centre. There was a lull after lunch and I sent Todd out for a break. I was cleaning down the outside tables when I heard someone calling my name. Billy was back in his spot opposite Flora's and we both looked up to where Sean was approaching from North John Street. "Hey Lil," he said as he got closer, "lovely day for it." I straightened up and tried to remember how to act normal. Sean isn't anything out of the ordinary to look at—six feet tall with scruffy brown hair and the sort of dress sense that makes him look like he works in a book shop. Which is kind of in the right ball park—he's actually one of the biggest crime writers you've never heard of. If you have, it's probably because you picked up one of his bestsellers in a two-for-one deal in Waterstones before going on holiday. He's sold millions of paperbacks, been on every bestseller list there is, and I fancy the absolute arse off him.

"Hi," I squeaked. I swear I could hear Billy's eyes rolling at my hopelessness, but I determinedly didn't turn to check. "How's it going?"

Sean grinned as he came up to the table I'd just finished wiping down and dumped his bag on one of the chairs. "Better for seeing you," he said. I wished I was standing closer to Billy so that I could kick him hard—it might have stopped the audible groaning noise he was making. "Can I have my usual?" Sean always drinks Americano—black, no sugar. I was just about to reply when something behind me caught his eye. "Hey Soph!" he called out. I turned to see a blonde woman walking towards us, her hand already up in greeting. She was maybe a few years older than me, beautifully dressed in the sort of floral tea-dress Izzy kept for special occasions and with a figure that would make an hourglass weep with envy. Huge sunglasses covered her eyes, but she took them off as she reached us. Big blue eyes blinked at me in a friendly manner, long eyelashes framing the kind of perfectly winged liner I'd never be able to manage even if I spent the rest of my afterlife practicing.

"Hello," she said, and to my abject horror, leaned in to kiss Sean full on the lips. "I've never been here before," she went on, nodding at Flora's. "It looks lovely."

"Told you it was great," said Sean, winking at me. I realised I was literally gaping at the pair of them and somehow remembered how to shut my mouth. "Espresso?" he asked.

Sophie nodded. "Of course," she smiled. "You should know that by now."

"Just checking," said Sean. "Wouldn't want to take you for granted." I thought I might be sick. Then I remembered I can't actually be sick, and took a deep breath instead, just for the hell of it. To my utter disgust, 'Soph' smelled absolutely bloody lovely. Flowers and kindness and generosity, as well as the oddly sour tang I've learned comes from an intellect sharp enough to cut through iron railings. I'd taken enough sneaky little huffs of Sean over the months—yeah it's a bad habit, so sue me—that I knew his mixture of shampoo and cleverness by heart, but now it was overlaid with something else. With a sinking heart, I realised that Sean absolutely adored this woman. They were perfect for each other and I hated them for it. "Be right back," I said through gritted teeth. They were already chatting so animatedly that they didn't even notice me leave. By the time I'd got behind the counter and could look back out through the window to where they sat in the afternoon sun, Sophie was leaning into Sean's lap as he showed her something on his phone. She was laughing, and he had his arm wrapped protectively across her back. A movement behind them broke my gaze. I looked up and saw Billy making shrugging 'whatcha gonna do?' gestures at me through the window. I shook my head at him. I should have known things were going too well.

***

I still take a lunch break from Flora's, mostly because if I don't, a surprising amount of people ask questions. It's easier to just bugger off for half an hour than it is to explain that no, I'm not on a diet. So when Todd came back after his own lunch, I nipped upstairs to pack for London. I had an overnight bag open on the bed and Grimm was staring into it, as if trying to decide whether he'd like to come with me, when Kitty appeared in the doorway. Grimm immediately shot over to greet her, like the traitorous little scrote he truly is. It was the first time she'd shown herself since I'd accidentally yelled at her the day before. The sunflowers had disappeared from her hair, but I was pleased to see she was still wearing the yellow flowered dress.

"Hey," I said. "I'm sorry about yelling at you. Truly I am. Thank you for caring."

"Of course I care," she shrugged. "You're my family, Lili. I didn't have anyone for so long, and then I found myself here." She gestured around herself. "You're important to me."

"You're important to me as well, you know," I said. "And I promise I didn't mean to shout at you like that."

Kitty came into the room and perched on the edge of the bed. I could have sworn I saw the duvet flatten slightly underneath her. "I know you didn't," she said. "I need to learn not to be so touchy. Anyway," she went on, nodding to the open bag, "you're heading off on your travels, then?"

"Yep," I said, throwing a spare t-shirt into the bag, "whether I like it or not." I added spare socks and knickers and decided it would have to do. The plan was that we'd only be away overnight, and I'd made Eadric promise faithfully that I wouldn't have to do any formal socialising apart from meeting and talking to Lizzie. We were staying at her house in north London. I'd asked Eadric for the address for the satnav, but he said he'd never written it down. He'd also asked me what a satnav was, so I'd updated Google Maps on my phone, just in case. He'd reassured me that, so long as I got us as far as Finchley, Nik would know the way from there. I wasn't convinced, but there didn't seem to be much option other than just hoping for the best. "You sure you're going to be okay?" I asked Kitty. "I'll feed Grimm before I leave, and Izzy will pop in before she opens Flora's in the morning."

"Did you get the little trays?" asked Kitty excitedly, getting up off the bed.

"Yup," I said, walking round the bed to the door. "They're on the worktop, so you don't have to do anything other than open them," I said. "Come and have a look." I headed into the kitchen just as something moved on the other side of the window. "Fuck*sake*," I hissed, moving to the door with lightning speed, "can't I just have some bloody *peace*?" I wrenched the door open onto the fire escape and stepped outside. Which was probably foolish, because who knew how many hit-lists I was currently on, or what manner of horrors might be lying in wait. But there was nothing to see other than a couple of plants waving in a breeze, and that could have been from me throwing myself out of the door. I thought I heard the faintest of footsteps running away in the distance, heading toward Button Street. I did a slow turn on the top platform of the fire escape, checking the car park below as well as the stretch of Harrington Street that was visible from where I stood. Nothing. Sighing, I turned to head back inside—and found Kitty staring at the back door. A piece of paper was stuck to it with what appeared to be masking tape, and its message was written in the same large letters as before. ***BEWARE THE HIGH GATE.***

"What's going on, Lil?" Kitty asked, concern evident in her voice.

I pulled the paper off the door. It was the sort of paper you buy in bulk to refill home printers—completely anonymous and untraceable. "I have absolutely no idea," I said honestly. "But someone's definitely trying to tell me something." I walked back into the kitchen and closed the door firmly. Leaning back against the cupboards, I held the piece of paper up to Kitty. "And it would be a clear message," I said, "if only I knew which bloody gate they were talking about."

"Has that girl been around again?" Kitty asked. "Maybe it's something to do with her?"

"If it was Mab," I said, "she'd be ambushing me, not warning me."

"Maybe it's time to take Eadric up on his offer," said Kitty. I stared silently at the piece of paper. "Go live somewhere a bit more secure," Kitty went on, "just for a while."

"I'm not moving," I said, still staring at the paper. "This is my home."

"And it always will be," said Kitty. "But only if you don't get your head knocked off by the vengeful daughter."

"I think she's being manipulated," I said. "Like a puppet. She's been around since the eighteen-hundreds, Kitty. It's a relatively small country, and news travels fast. Especially when you're dead. If I'd been taken from my mother as a child and then discovered she was hiding out in Liverpool, don't you think I'd have been up here searching the city within a couple of decades?" Kitty tilted her head slightly in agreement. "Nope," I gave up hunting for clues on the almost-blank paper and put it down on the worktop, "someone told her what had happened to her mother *after* I'd killed her. But why leave it until Maria was dead? Had she known earlier, Mab might have headed up here and helped her mum in her takeover bid." I looked at Kitty. She was shimmering slightly, something she always does when she's nervous and trying to hide it. "I mean," I went on, "obviously I'm glad they didn't. But why tell her now?"

"To unsettle the area even more," said Kitty. "Eadric's been betrayed, lost his wife and now the stepdaughter he didn't even know he had is hiding out in town somewhere. Probably plotting his demise. That would unsettle things, if it were me." She folded her arms and looked straight at me. "You do realise Ivo Laithlind is the only real suspect?"

"Yes," I sighed, "I do. But," I turned and slid the note into the cutlery drawer, weighting it down with the teaspoons, "I don't think it's him. Ivo doesn't want Eadric dead. Not really. And if he wanted *me* dead," I shrugged, "he'd just do it himself." God knows, I thought, he's had the opportunity.

"And you're just going to stay here in this flat," Kitty said, "so everyone knows where to find you?"

I nodded. "Better than skulking in the shadows," I said. "I'd rather stay out in the open, so *everyone* knows where I am. That way," I said with a confidence I didn't entirely feel, "it should be easier to spot any potential attacks before they happen." Kitty didn't look convinced. "Anyway," I went on, "I need to get back downstairs. Don't let any murderers in while I'm out."

What Is Life, Anyway?

Well, this is an unexpected delight," said Gaultier Mapp, when he found me standing on his doorstep. I'd had to wait for the last customers to leave Flora's and he'd closed the shop for the day by the time I'd got up to Renshaw Street. I waited for what felt a very long time while he clattered his way through the endless locks and bolts on the other side. "Business or pleasure?"

"Both," I said, as he bent to unlock the wrought iron security door that was the bookshop's last line of defence against the outside world. "Why do you have so much security?" I asked as he straightened up. "It's hardly as though a dusty shop filled with ancient knickknacks is likely to be near the top of any self-respecting burglar's hit-list."

"Ooh," he squeaked, "such hurtful words! You *cut* me, Lilith O'Reilly," I rolled my eyes and stalked past him into the shop. "Cut me to the veritable *bone*."

"Whatever," I said, hopping up to sit on the countertop next to the cash register. "Why, though?"

Mapp was locking the door behind us again, but he limited himself to the iron gate and one set of bolts on the inner door. "Habit, I guess," he said, turning to face me. "I've lived through eras where you really did have to lock yourselves and your belongings away from the world at all times, or risk losing them." He was wearing what appeared to be gold harem pants over matching ballet slippers, topped off rather incongruously by a night-shirt with a large Sylvester and Tweety Bird cartoon across the front. Tweety was gazing out at the viewer with a cutesy look on his face, while Sylvester snuck up behind him with a baseball bat. Despite being dressed for bed, Mapp still wore his usual collection of necklaces. They wrapped like a metallic serpent around his neck, draping down past his sternum.

I spotted something on the shelf to my right and suddenly realised what Mapp's jewellery reminded me of. "What's that?" I asked, pointing to the velvet-covered display board.

Mapp looked at where I was pointing. "Aah," he said, walking over and picking up the large square card. "This, my darling, is a chatelaine." He lifted the ornate oval disc out of the notches that secured it to the card and held it up to show me. "It means 'keeper of the castle'." Several chains hung from the bottom edge, attached to the filigree design with beaded loops. They dropped in groups of three or four, each set coming together on a smaller version of the main disc. Below the smaller circles hung even more chains, each with a different item fixed to its bottom loop. "This one's a really beautiful example," said Mapp, draping the chains across the back of his other hand so I could see them more clearly. "Belonged to the lady of the house, at one of the big places just out of town. When it still *was* out of town." He grinned at me. "They've all been sucked up into the deep, dark city since then, of course. Probably been converted into luxury flats by now. Anyway," he held the chains closer to me, "she must have had a husband who wasn't shy of spending cold hard cash on her, because this one's got pretty much everything." I reached out a hand and lifted what looked to be a small metal box at the end of one of the chains. "That's a notepad," said Mapp. "Still got the paper in it. The one next to it," I picked up the piece he was nodding towards, "is a vinaigrette. A scent holder," he explained, "like the old pomander balls, but these were more fashionable by the eighteenth century. She'd have dipped a piece of linen into vinegar and lavender, and the scent would have wafted around as she walked. There's also a mirror, a sewing kit and a pair of scissors." I couldn't find the scissors for a moment, then realised that they were made to a clever folding design that disguised their true purpose. "Priorities were different back then," he continued. "She'd have spent her days sewing and writing letters and checking she looked and smelled perfect. Of course," he arched a well-manicured brow, "the pay-off was that she had no control over her own life. Just had to sit around looking useful and pretty. And now here *you* are, Lilith O'Reilly," he stepped backwards and turned to put the chatelaine back onto its stand, "being both useful and pretty and doing it for no one except yourself." He turned to look at me. "I'd say that was progress, wouldn't you?"

I shrugged. "Seems I'm having to do a lot of things for other people right now," I said. "You know I'm going to London tonight?"

Mapp pulled a chair out from behind a bookshelf and sat down, crossing one leg and holding his ankle, as though he was going to start pulling yoga poses. "I do indeed," he said. "I gather you are to enjoy the company of the younger Mr Silverton?"

I nodded forlornly. "What did I do to deserve *that?*" I wailed.

"Ah," said Mapp, "our Nikolaus can be good company when he wants to be. I think you might actually enjoy it." I made an unconvinced huffing noise and Mapp laughed. "Give him a chance, Lili," he said. "Nik's been around for a good couple of centuries now, yet I think he's only just getting to know himself, let alone anyone else."

"Why have you been lurking up at Anfield?" I blurted out.

Mapp looked genuinely shocked for a second, but recovered himself rapidly. "I see the grapevine still hangs heavy with gossip," he said eventually. "Why does it matter to you what I do when you're not around?"

"It doesn't," I said, honestly. "But it's clearly worrying Missy."

"And since when have you and the delightful Ms Leschi been friends?"

"We're not," I said. "I don't think." I remembered Missy asking me in for tea, with an almost wistful look on her face. "Not yet, anyway. But I was up at her house last night," Mapp gave me a curious look, which I chose to ignore, "and she mentioned that Al had seen you up by the catacombs."

"You've met Alan then," he said. "Delightful chap, don't you think? Little bit naïve, maybe."

"I got the impression that Al was quite interesting as a human," I said.

Mapp grinned. "I think Alan is still rather interesting now, don't you?" he asked. "He certainly has a certain style about him." I thought of Al's sharp suit and raised an eyebrow. "Better than just wandering around the afterlife in jeans and a t-shirt," said Mapp. He winked. "Ah, Lili," he went on, "there are some things I don't really want others to know about. Is that so surprising?"

"Of course not," I said, thinking of how mortified I'd be if people knew about my disappointment in the face of Sean's budding romance. Obviously Billy knew because he'd been unfortunate enough to witness the entire embarrassing scene, but somehow I didn't think Billy was one to gossip over tea and knitting. "I guess she's perhaps more concerned than she'd normally be. Because of everything else that's going on."

"And what else might be going on?"

"Oh, come on, Mapp," I said, "you know it's all kicking off. In a metaphorical sense, maybe," he raised an eyebrow, "but things are weird, regardless." I thought about it for a second. Mapp stayed silent. "It's all so...*untethered*," I said, finally. "As if the foundations of...everything...are shifting, and no one knows where or when it's going to settle." I frowned at my own feet, swinging above the old wooden floorboards. "Does that make any sense?"

"It does," said Mapp. "It does indeed. And for what it's worth," he unfolded himself up out of the chair and leaned against the wall instead, sliding his hands into the pockets of his enormous trousers, "I agree with you. Things are changing. But we knew this from the day you arrived. And for what it's worth," he went on, before I could say anything, "I don't think it's because of you. I think," he appeared to choose his words carefully, "there was something bigger already stirring, and you just got caught up in it. Who knows," he shrugged, "maybe if you'd been pushed off that building six months earlier, you'd have just fallen to your death. Your literal, human death. Our beloved Izzy would have been heartbroken, but eventually she'd have had to get on with her own life. Maybe she'd have taken on Flora's for herself and still be there now. She'd have a framed photograph of you tucked away somewhere discreet behind the counter. Your parents would have had to face the death of a child for a second time," I flinched at that, "but by now they'd have settled back into some kind of quiet sadness. And I'd be sitting here now without the benefit of your delightful company. But," he

WHAT IS LIFE, ANYWAY?

pushed himself suddenly upright and spoke loudly and brightly, giving me a jolt, "that didn't happen. You fell and died, but you didn't. You're still here and we're all very grateful for that. Swings, as they say," he said, spinning around on the spot with a loud clanking of jewellery, "and roundabouts." He stopped twirling and grinned at me. "Don't you think?"

"You still haven't told me why you were lurking in Anfield cemetery," I said doggedly, trying to get the image of my grieving parents out of my head.

"Why should I?" Mapp asked mildly. "It's not as if I can't have any secrets," he went on, "so long as they're not hurting anyone else." He saw my expression. "And I promise, Lili," he said, "I'm not hurting anyone." He sighed. "Anyway," he shrugged, "it really isn't that much of a secret. I've been visiting a friend, is all. Someone who isn't going to hurt anyone, so don't be worrying about that."

"Martha?"

Mapp looked genuinely surprised. "Yes," he said slowly, "as it happens. You've met her, then?"

"That's why I was at Missy's," I told him. "She wanted to introduce me to Martha."

"Now, why would she want to do that?" Mapp mused. "The meddling little minx."

"Maybe she didn't realise Martha already had a social life going on," I said, narrowing my eyes at him. "Surely you must have known Missy would worry if she didn't know what you were doing?" I asked. "And it *does* look suspicious," I went on, "because Martha didn't mention you, either. Which is strange behaviour, if there's nothing sneaky going on."

"If you must know," said Mapp, with a sigh, "Martha found out about my, uh, talents. And she wanted to talk to me about them." I boggled at him for a second, wondering which of Mapp's no doubt endless 'talents' someone as old and frail as Martha might be interested in.

Then a lightbulb pinged on in my head. "The life force?" I whispered. Mapp was able to literally breathe life into people, a talent considered all but impossible by other immortals. I'd been under the impression that me and Eadric were the only people who knew about it. And the only reason *I* knew

79

was because it was how Mapp had fixed the mess I'd made when I'd done a terrible job of wiping Sean's memory after our ill-fated date earlier in the year. In my defence, it had been an emergency. I'd invited Sean in for coffee after what had been a very pleasant date, only to find Daisy in my living room looking particularly, well, 'feral' is probably the only word that would cover it. I'd panicked and attempted to wipe Sean's memory by sucking some of his memory. But because I was new to the afterlife and didn't know how to control things very well, Sean turned into a forgetful shell of a man. In desperation, I'd asked Mapp for help. He'd helpfully replaced some of the life force I'd taken and suddenly Sean was back to normal. The main downside was that he couldn't remember ever having had the faintest of romantic interest in me, but at least he wasn't walking round in a daze. So yeah, I'd been an eyewitness to Gaultier Mapp's more esoteric talents. And Eadric knew all about it, because apparently Mapp had saved *him* at some point in the past. Quite how far into the past I wasn't sure, but I knew the two of them went back a long way. "Does she think you might be able to make her younger?" I asked.

Mapp pulled a face. "That's what she wanted to know, of course," he said.

"How does it work?" I asked.

He gave me a thoughtful look. "Haven't you ever wondered where your energy comes from?" he asked.

I had to think about that for a minute. "I guess I just assumed it was the whole 'closed system, don't need anything extra' thing," I replied. "Y'know, no human restrictions, living our best lives, all that stuff."

"What about the physics?" asked Mapp. "Movement burns energy, no?"

"If we burned energy," I said, "we'd run out pretty quickly, I reckon. Like batteries."

"Exactly," said Mapp. "But the movement has to come from *somewhere*." I must have been looking particularly blank, because he took pity on me. "Okay so," he said, "humans eat food and their bodies turn it into energy, yes?" I nodded. "Revenants don't need to eat, but they can get extra power from breathing in the life force of living humans."

"With you so far."

"When you die as a human, it sends an enormous store of potential energy into your undead, revenant body," Mapp went on, "and that's what's powering you now."

"I can promise you," I said, "that after I woke up dead, my digestive system got rid of every last bit of food that might have been lurking in its depths."

Mapp pulled a face. "Thank you for that delightful image, Lilith," he said, lifting a hand to his mouth in a delicately repulsed gesture. "But this isn't just energy from food. It's all the *potential* energy your human body contained, both physical and mental. In fact," he went on, "that's part of my theory. About why some people become revenants, but most don't."

"One biology lesson at a time, Darwin," I snarked. "You're telling me that everything I can do now—the things I couldn't do as a human, like climbing buildings and beating Ferraris in a sprint—are powered by the energy I already contained?" Mapp nodded. "So what happens when it runs out? You lot have been around for *centuries*. How much did you eat when you were alive, for fuck's sake?"

"Well now," he smiled, "there's the really clever bit, innit? Humans are everywhere—wandering blindly through their lives, throwing out energy all over the city. No ordinary city, either."

"Tell me something I don't already know," I said. "This place is *weird*. I mean," I shrugged, "I love it more than anywhere else in the world and I wouldn't ever want to leave it. That's a given. But there's no ignoring the fact that Liverpool is really fucking bizarre at times."

"Exactly," said Mapp, with evident satisfaction. "That's because this city has power of its own. As you well know." I remembered being trapped underground with the spirit of the city losing its unholy shit in an uncomfortably enclosed space, and shuddered at the claustrophobic memories. Yeah. Liverpool certainly had power. "And it encourages the humans within it to be more free with their own emotions, whether for good or bad. People are more...*themselves*, here. Don't you think?" I thought. About how I'd chosen the university here purely because it wasn't Birmingham or Aberystwyth (the obvious choices for most students from Shrewsbury) and nor was it London or Edinburgh (too far away and way too intimidatingly cool—or at least, that's how they'd seemed at the time). And mine *definitely* hadn't been the sort of senior school that considered Oxbridge an option. So Liverpool it was. Close enough to see my parents if necessary, but also far enough—and different enough—to make me feel I was starting a new life in a far more exciting place. Izzy had moved up a year or so after me, citing terminal boredom back in Shropshire, and that was it. We'd never left, and I doubted we ever would.

"Are you saying you think the city itself pulls people here?" I asked.

Mapp grinned. "Oh, she's a flirtatious beast and no mistake," he said. "Started out tempting the fishermen, then it was the sailors. And of course, the money always follows—even if most of it has stayed in the pockets of the undeserving few, over the centuries. This city is *alive*, Lili. It's vibrant and humming with excitement and heartbreak and love and tragedy, every hour of every day. And because of that," he went on, "the people within her streets are generous with their emotions—they can't help it. So you and I and the rest of the undead and unholy gang find ourselves living in an atmosphere that's so heavy with energy that we can't help but absorb some of it, even if we never go near a living human being."

"And that's what keeps our energy levels up?" I asked.

"Well," Mapp said, "some of us do it better than others. You and the Silvertons can absorb as much as you'd ever need, and that's why you have such physical capabilities. Others—Joe Williamson, say, or even my Heggie—aren't so good at keeping their levels up. I guess it's a form of metabolism," he shrugged. "Some are more efficient than others."

"How does yours work, then?" I asked. "Why can't I breathe life back into people?"

"Got the most efficient metabolism of anyone, innit," he grinned. "Turns out I can just hoover up all that good ol' energy stuff by just hanging out in the city and being my usual approachable self. Or maybe I just don't use very much energy myself, on account of my laid-back personality." He shrugged. "Who knows? Either way, it just builds up inside me, like interest on a savings account at the bank."

"What would happen if you didn't push it back out occasionally?" I asked.

"Would you burst? Would a flame pop out the top of your head, like the gas burners at the refineries over the river?"

"I'd bloody hope not," he said. "I'm very fond of my hair." He patted his close-cropped scalp protectively. "I don't know, is the honest answer. It's never been a problem in all my many centuries on this godforsaken earth, so I choose not to think about it. Don't be taking a gift horse to the dentist, is what I'm saying."

"And Martha wants you to—what?" I asked. "Give her back her youth?"

"Yes," Mapp replied, "but I can't help her, and she knows that now. It would take everything I have, and more. But she's discovered my secret, so now I have to be sure that she won't betray me to anyone who might seek to use it—or me—to cause actual harm."

"How did Martha find out in the first place?"

"Well now," he said, "that's what I don't know. It won't have been Eadric—apart from the fact he rarely leaves the bird house," he nodded in the vague direction of where the Liver Building sat four-square in front of the Strand, solidly protecting the waterfront, "it's not his style. And it can't have been you," Mapp smiled, "because you and Martha have only just met."

"I might be lying," I pointed out.

"You might," he agreed, "but Martha wouldn't have been able to keep it to herself. Believe me," he winked, "Martha likes a good bit of gossip."

"Are you sure Missy didn't tell her? I know," I put a hand up to stop him interrupting, "she's your friend. I'm just going through the options, is all."

"Missy doesn't know," Mapp said. "I've never had cause to tell her about my abilities, not in all these past four hundred years. But," he went on, "I helped her boyfriend out once. And he doesn't strike me as the sort who could keep anything to himself for very long."

"Boyfriend?" I asked. "You can't mean Alan?" I thought back to my visit to their creepy old house. They were clearly close, but I didn't think they were *that* close.

"You don't think?" Mapp looked genuinely curious.

"No," I said firmly, "I absolutely don't think. Al is very sweet—if a bit ostentatious—but I think Missy sees him more as a younger brother who needs supervising."

Mapp appeared to consider this. "Maybe I just made assumptions," he said, "based on it being the two of them being in that house. I mean," there was a twinkle back in his eye, now, "what else would they be doing all the time, shut away in that big old place that far out of town?"

"Bloody hell, Mapp," I said, "have you ever considered not judging other people by your own moral standards? Not everyone is getting into everyone else's pants, you know," I informed him, "just because they spend time together. I see plenty of people and no one is getting in *my* pants. Which is unfortunate for me."

"I'm sure I could put a good word in for you with some of the more interesting members of the community?" Mapp offered. "See it as an undead matchmaking service. Actually," he brightened noticeably, "that might be fun! Why don't you tell me what you're looking for and I'll consult the undead hordes? Just the single ones, of course."

"Don't you bloody dare," I said. "The last thing I need is you meddling in my love life. It's disastrous enough as it is, I don't need help to make it worse. And for what it's worth," I went on, "Anfield isn't all that far out of town."

"It is when you're having to sneak in at the far end in order to avoid being questioned by your mate at the front gate," he said.

"Then just tell Missy what's going on," I suggested. "Although if Al knows your secret, then I'd be very surprised if he hasn't told her already."

"I'm not sure he really understands the details of it all," said Mapp. "It happened soon after he died. Most people are a bit fuzzy-headed for a long while, when they first wake up in...Netherweird." He grinned. "I like that name, by the way," he said. "And not just because it drives Eadric mad."

"I wasn't fuzzy-headed when I woke up," I pointed out. "I mean, I felt like shit and I definitely had a headache, but I just got on with stuff." I paused. "Is that really so unusual?"

Mapp gazed at me thoughtfully. "Yup," he said, "it's as rare as rocking horse shit. I've heard talk of one or two others who've woken up bright as a button over the last couple thousand years, but you're the first I've met myself." He tilted his head slightly. "The only one. Usually we have to hide them away somewhere until they can pass as reasonably human."

"What if they can't?" I asked. "What happens then?"

"We sent the last one to Telford," said Mapp. "He seemed to fit in okay. Luckily, it's not a problem we have very often. We're rare beasts, us revenants."

It seemed as good a time as any to ask the question that had been bothering me since the day I woke up without a pulse. "Why do some people turn into revenants, and others don't?"

"Well, that's the million-dollar question," Mapp replied, "innit? My theory is that it's down to sheer force of personality. Most people accept that they're human, their bodies get the message and when either accident or old age gets them, that's that." He looked thoughtful. "Maybe that's why so many revenants are those who were over-achievers in their human lifetimes. The sort who have enough personal *oomph*," he flicked his hand elegantly in the air for emphasis, "to keep going, purely to spite the grim reaper. Your famous poets and Viking warriors and all that jazz."

"I could hardly have been described as an overachiever," I pointed out. "I'm just...normal."

"Are you sure about that, Lil?" Mapp asked. "Cos from where I'm standing, there must be *something* about you that's kept you here."

"Billy and Kitty are normal people as well," I said, warming to my subject. "Or at least, they were. When they were still alive."

"They're ghosts, Lil," Mapp said, "not actual, real people. They're just echoes of what used to be."

"I dare you to say that to Kitty's face," I said, "next time she pops in for some quality time."

"So I'm not bigoted," he replied blithely. "I judge people by whether I like them, not by whether they technically exist. Regardless, they're not human. At least, not in the way you and I are. We're still flesh and blood, yes?" I nodded. "And however powerful or fast we are, we still have to live by the physical rules. We might be able to jump a ten-foot wall," he shrugged, "but we wouldn't be able to walk *through* it."

"So why am I here?" I asked, struggling to tread down the faint wailing tone creeping into my voice.

"Ah, the eternal question," said Mapp. "Look," he said, in a softer tone, "I don't know why you're here, any more than you do. None of us know. And believe me," he gave me the tiniest of winks, "we've put the hours into trying to figure it out."

"Oh brilliant," I grumbled, "weirdo Lil's the hot topic of undead gossip. Again. Like I didn't have enough to be paranoid about already."

"What do you have to be paranoid about?" asked Mapp. "Other than me and Eadric trying to figure out who or what you actually are, of course. At least our ideas were polite. Our money's on secret family connections to the netherworld, that sort of thing. Nik's original theory was that you were some kind of shape-shifter," he grinned. "He reckoned we'd be best to just chop your head off and be done with."

"What the fuck? I thought Nik *liked* me!"

"He does," Mapp reassured me. "Nowadays. Took him a while to be convinced, though. He had this mad idea that maybe you were looking to usurp Maria. Had set her up in order to take her place, something like that."

"Take her place?" I boggled at him. "Where? In Eadric's bed?"

"Would that have been such a terrible place to end up?" asked Mapp. To my horror, he appeared to be serious. "You'd have taken over as joint head of the family and been the public face of Silverton Corps. Money and power, Lil," he went on. "Two of the most tempting things on the planet. And many would be happy to keep Eadric Silverton company in the undead boudoir, I'd wager."

"You're a grubby old man, Gaultier Mapp," I said tartly.

"I like to make the most of my artistic freedom these days," he replied. "That sort of talk didn't go down well in the church."

I gaped at him, trying to get my head around what he'd just said. "You were a *priest?*"

He grinned. "Oh," he said, "it was a long time ago. And I was merely an assistant to those higher up in the church. But yes, Lilith, I was a man of god. Is that such an unlikely thing?"

"Yes, it bloody well is!" I spluttered. "You're...well, you're—"

"A delight?"

"Yes, well, obviously," I floundered, "but you're *Mapp*. Mapp the bookseller, who wafts around town in silks and satins and enough jewellery to open a small stall down the Red Brick market. Everyone knows you!"

"They do indeed," he said, an air of smugness in his tone. "And they always have. I travelled, you know. When I was still human. Studied at the Sorbonne, no less. Wrote a fair bit—sometimes my humour went down well, other times less so. I had a good life, Lil. Of course, I had to lie low for a good while after I...died. Mostly to get over the shock," he continued, "if I'm honest. I know my bible stories, of course, but even I hadn't expected to rise from the tomb like that."

"Where did you hide?" I was struggling to imagine Mapp staying undetected anywhere for very long.

"Herefordshire, mostly," he said. "Some people knew who I was, of course. But I was a local boy and they protect their own."

"I thought you were from Dingle?"

"I am," he said. "Nowadays. But I was born on the borders. Child of Offa, if you like."

"You don't sound very Welsh," I pointed out.

"Hereford isn't Wales," Mapp replied, "and I've been in Liverpool a long time. Anyway, Lilith O'Reilly, do you not have a trip to be packing for?"

"Don' wanna," I mumbled.

Mapp laughed. "You'll like Lizzie," he said. "I promise. And while you're away, Eadric and I will investigate the spooky goings on in the old town of Liverpool."

"We *are* the spooky goings on," I pointed out.

"Same difference," Mapp shrugged. "You go do the schmoozing, we'll be the muscle. It'll be like the old days, when women knew their place." He ducked as I picked up a notepad from next to the till and threw it at his head.

"Where's the high gate?" I asked suddenly.

Mapp looked confused. "How do you mean?" he asked. "High geographically, or high as in high falutin'?"

"Doesn't matter," I said, hopping down off the counter. "Forget I asked. I need to go pack."

Can't Beat A Bit Of Badalamenti

I could still hear Mapp turning keys in his endless locks as I headed down Renshaw Street. It was a warm, sunny evening and the streets were busy, with locals and tourists alike making the most of the weather. I love summer in the city. So many people complain about it—the noise and the outside drinking and the busy pavements—but because most of the students have gone home for the holidays, Liverpool's often quieter in August than it is in September, when freshers start arriving. The older students arrive a week or so later and then we have a month of insanity, while they all compete in drinking games and who can burn through their student loans the fastest. I occasionally hear customers in Flora's moaning to each other about how students are taking over the place and sending rents sky-high, but I just smile and nod politely and ignore them. After all, I was a newbie student here myself, once upon a time. I've thrown up in pretty much all the bars at some point over the years and I definitely spent my student loans on anything other than education. Although a night out at Popworld was often an education in itself. I was smiling to myself at the memories as I swung a left onto Heathfield Street. If I cut through to Bold Street, I'd at least have a more scenic walk home. Maybe I'd nip into Matta's food store and spend ten minutes staring longingly at all the different things I couldn't eat. Izzy said I was a masochist who would be better off avoiding anything edible, and I thought she was a heartless beast who should probably consider the deprivations of the undead lifestyle. Mind you, I did have my nose in her newly opened box of baklava at the time.

I was a few yards into the narrow little passageway that squeezes past the Central Village car park, when the faintest of noises behind me made me swing round. Catching the vampire by its straggly hair, I wrenched it round and up against the brick wall. Grabbing its arms with my other hand, I pinned it so it couldn't move. Vampires might be strong, but revenants are stronger. I twisted the vamp's hair up and back, and wedged my knee up into its groin—a move which might have had more effect had my undead stalker been male. She was screwing her face up against the afternoon sun, but I knew from experience it wasn't hurting her. Vampires hide from the daylight because it shows them for what they are, not because it's dangerous to them. "What the fuck do you think you're doing?" I hissed, my face briefly close up against hers before I thought better of it and pulled away. Not because I was scared—she just stank to the point it was wafting up through my nostrils, even though I was determinedly not breathing.

She twisted her head round in a snarl. "Tryin-to-help," she said. She did the usual vampire thing of running all her words together as if speaking was a massive effort, but was more understandable than most I'd come across so far. Not that I'd met many. They're a rare thing these days, mostly because they're so obviously paranormal that they get hunted more than any other supernatural creature. Often, the hunting is being done by revenants. It's not that the two species are at war or anything like that. We just don't enjoy being associated with stinking, murderous creatures that look more like rats than humans. This one wasn't any different. Her face was long and thin, with jagged yellow teeth just visible behind narrow lips. She had pale blue eyes, which was unusual. Most vampires have dark brown irises, but no one really knows why. Nik's theory is that it's from the used-up blood they consume. I don't like to shatter centuries-old myths, but most humans have nothing to fear from vampires. They feed mainly on rodents, and aren't averse to picking up roadkill if it's sitting around uneaten. I once saw a vampire being attacked by a pair of angry magpies because it had tried to steal their food. It was such a ridiculous sight that I ended up ripping the poor dead fox into pieces myself and sharing it out between the various would-be hunter-gatherers. I've read a lot of urban fantasy books in my time, but none of them warned me I'd find myself refereeing spats between

90

angry corvids and vampires that looked like they'd just climbed out of a bin.

"How is sneaking up behind me being helpful?" I asked. I loosened my grip enough to let her head drop slightly, but was careful to make sure she couldn't make a run for it. Vampires can wriggle like you wouldn't believe, and holding onto one that doesn't want to be held is like trying to cage an octopus with a string bag.

"Helpyou," she wailed. "Warnyou!"

"Warn me about what?"

"High-gate," she said. "Dangerdanger."

"Where's the gate?" I asked, but she just shook her head in response. "Why are your eyes blue?" She looked confused by the change of topic, but I could feel her body tensing in my grip. "Oh no you don't," I said, pulling her away from the wall and swinging her round so she had her back to me. I twisted her arms up behind her back and pressed my other hand up into her throat as I pulled her behind a large industrial bin. "Now tell me the truth," I hissed in her ear, giving her arms an extra twist for emphasis.

She made a pained squeaking noise, and I loosened my grip on her throat slightly. "Neverdrinkblood," she managed to get out.

"Never?" This was a new one on me. Vegetarian vampires? I peered at her carefully and was extremely relieved to see that she definitely didn't sparkle. She shook her head, sending her straggly hair into my mouth. I spat it out and tried not to retch. Vampires don't have any life force in them—they're like a walking black hole into which humanity disappears without trace—but their smell is all-pervasive. I was going to have to have another shower before heading down to the Liver Building. Deciding I'd had enough bullshit for one day, I let her go. She backed away quickly as she spoke.

"Not-all-bad," she said, before spinning round and racing off back towards Renshaw Street.

***

I'd promised Eadric I'd be at the Liver Building by eight o'clock, so Nik and

I wouldn't be leaving it too late for the four-hour drive down to London. I'd said surely it didn't matter *what* time we got there, because presumably ol' Queen Liz didn't sleep, anyway. Eadric had pointed out in an annoyingly reasonable tone that we were less likely to be noticed if we travelled when the human world would still be reasonably active. "I'm not risking you being picked up for speeding just because you're the only car on the road at three in the morning," he'd said.

"How do you know I'm the speeding type?" I'd retorted. "Anyway, that depends entirely on how shit your car is." Nik had snorted, but Eadric just rolled his eyes and asked me to 'at least wear something presentable'. Which was why I was currently pulling on leggings, a tartan mini skirt and a scruffy t-shirt that had 'WORKING CLASS HERO' written across the front in huge black letters. I'm not in the habit of being patronised by someone who isn't even one of my parents, no matter how many centuries they've been around. My clothes were clean—I'm not a complete skank—and I'd had a shower and pulled a wide-toothed comb through my hair, but that was about as far as my preparations were going to go. I sighed as I picked up my bags and walked into the living room, where Kitty and Grimm were curled up together on the sofa, watching old episodes of QI. "I'm off, then," I said. "Try not to miss me too much."

Kitty paused the TV and turned to look at me. "I think we'll manage," she grinned. Grimm turned to blink slowly at me and made a noise that sounded something like a grunt, before turning back to stare at the frozen television screen.

"Is that cat learning to communicate?" I asked, suspiciously. "Are you infecting him with your paranormal weirdness?"

"Paranormal weirdness?" asked Kitty. "You can talk." She snorted. "Grimm isn't doing anything he couldn't always do." She scratched him under the ear and he purred loudly, "He just chose not to. Maybe he feels more comfortable in himself these days."

"Huh," I said. "Well it's on you if he starts walking round on two legs and frightening the neighbours."

"We're in Liverpool," said Kitty. "A humanoid cat would not be the strangest thing that's happened round here."

I couldn't argue with that. "Anyway," I said, "I need to go. Might pop in on Mum and Dad on the way home. You're welcome to come with us, you know," I added, trying not to sound too pleading.

"No thank you," said Kitty firmly. "I'll be fine here with Mister Grimm. Won't I, baby?" she cooed at the cat, who looked up at me with a definitely smug air.

"Okay," I sighed, turning to leave. "I'm off. Wish me luck." But she'd already switched the TV back on.

***

"Just promise you'll try not to damage it." There was a distinctly worried tone to Eadric's voice as he frowned at me across the bonnet of the car. My guess that Eadric Silverton would drive something solid and boring had been so far off the mark it was practically on a different continent. His car sat between us like a child waiting patiently for its estranged parents to decide who was keeping it for the weekend. It was certainly solid, but that was the only thing I'd guessed correctly. Huge and sleek, with a smoke-grey finish that was so glossy you could use the bodywork to do your eyebrows, it was less a car and more a wild beast that just happened to get around on wheels.

"Give me the keys, granddad," I said, struggling to keep the grin off my face. My unexpected trip was beginning to look more fun. Nik was leaning against the boot, studiously ignoring us and reading one of his endless supply of tattered old paperbacks. Izzy had found a stash of trashy romance novels in the charity shop up in St Johns a few weeks earlier. In a fit of philanthropy, she'd bought the lot, dumped them up in Eadric's office and Nik had been happy as a pig in muck ever since. Eadric held the keys out across the bonnet, clearly not wanting to risk my catching abilities. "How many gears?" I asked as I pressed the button to open the doors.

"None," he said. "It's automatic. You *have* driven automatics before?"

"Course," I lied. "Easy peasy, lemon squeezy." I slid into the driver's seat and gazed around at something that resembled the cockpit of a fighter plane. The Alfa Romeo logo on the steering wheel gleamed expensively. "Fuck *me*," I blurted. "You've had this thing hidden away all along?"

Eadric walked round to the driver's side and peered down at me through the open door. I thought I detected a faint air of nervousness. "It's valuable," he said, "as I'm sure you can imagine."

"Would you rather just hire me something instead?" I asked, really hoping he wouldn't. "Because I'm not sure you're really one hundred per cent committed to me borrowing this car, if you want my honest opinion."

"I have standards," he replied. "*We* have standards. If you turn up in a hire car, the assumption would be that I don't entirely trust you. Which I don't," I narrowed my eyes at that, "but we will make a good pretence of it."

"Cheers," I said. "Your confidence in me is appreciated. As always." There was a click behind me as Nik opened the boot and dumped our bags inside. From what I'd seen before I got into the car, his packing had consisted of nothing more than a leather messenger bag that looked as old as he was. He opened the passenger door and slid in beside me, leaning over to speak to Eadric.

"You owe me one," he said.

"The break will do you good," said Eadric, stepping backwards away from the car. He then stepped forwards again when he realised I was struggling to find the car's ignition. Leaning in, he took the key fob from me and dropped it into the central console. "It just needs to be in the car," he said. "Put your foot on the brake pedal." I did so, and Eadric leaned in to press a button on the dashboard. The car roared into life and I squeaked with astonished excitement. "Sometimes," said Eadric with a smile, "I really enjoy the modern world."

We'd crawled our way carefully out of the Liver Building, while I got used to how the car worked. Telling myself it was pretty much just an overpriced dodgem car, I pulled it out onto the Strand with a squeal of brakes that no doubt made Eadric clench his ancient teeth up in his tower. We were soon heading out of town on the M62, the big car making mincemeat of the roads. To my astonishment, I'd discovered the onboard stereo was already connected to Spotify. "He's not as archaic as you might think," Nik had said, when I expressed my surprise.

"So why does he hide away from the world?" I'd asked.

"I think he just doesn't like humans very much," Nik had said, which was fair enough. After a brief argument about what we were going to listen to, we settled on a compilation from David Lynch movies. "Can't beat a bit of Badalamenti," said Nik, before closing his eyes and ignoring me. It didn't bother me. I've always liked driving, and the Alfa was a leather-lined joy. We skirted north Warrington and I grinned to myself as I headed down the M6 slip road, pushing the accelerator slightly in order to shoot past an Audi that was cruising at boringly normal speeds in the left-hand lane. "Can you *not?*" hissed Nik from beside me.

Glancing across, I saw he was holding on tightly to the handle above the passenger door. "Can I not what?" I asked. "I'm only doing—ah." I took my foot off the pedal a fraction and checked the display again. "I'm only doing eighty," I informed him, "which is practically within acceptable limits. Anyway," I pressed my foot back down just enough to make the car leap forward and then eased off again as Nik made a choking sound, "you must have been in fast cars before now. Man of your glamorous background, and all that."

Nik snorted. "I do not step foot into these ridiculous machines if I can possibly help it," he said. "I'm only here now because Eadric asked me. And he wouldn't have asked if he didn't think it was important."

"You've been summoned by this Queen Elizabeth," I pointed out. "It doesn't sound like it was Eadric's decision."

"Lizzie," he sighed, "is an absolute minx. She enjoys tormenting me."

"Why?" I asked. It began to rain, but before I could attempt to figure out which button controlled the windscreen wipers, they sprang into action of their own accord. "Ooh!" I squeaked. "How clever is that? Look," I poked Nik in the thigh to ensure I had his full attention, "they know when to come on!"

"There's a sensor in the windscreen," he said in a weary voice. "Lots of cars do it."

"Basil doesn't," I retorted. "This thing is five-star luxury when you're used to driving a Beetle."

"Ah yes," said Nik, "the people's car. The Nazi dream machine."

I scowled as I drove. "It's not the car's fault it was thought up by a psychopath," I said. "Anyway, how do you know so much about cars if you hate them so much?"

"I don't hate them," said Nik. "I just think that if the gods had intended us to travel this fast, they'd have cut their losses and given us wings."

"You didn't answer my question," I said. "Why does Elizabeth enjoy winding you up?"

Nik stared out of the window at the green fields flashing past. "We've known each other a long time," he said, finally. "When you've been in each other's company as long as we have, I guess there's a tendency to fall into something like a sibling relationship."

"Dead or alive?" I asked, swinging out to pass an articulated lorry.

Nik winced. "I wish you'd drive more carefully, Lilith," he said. "Not that I don't think this car couldn't get us out of most scrapes, but," he turned to look behind us as if to push his point home, "I'd really rather not get pulled over by the police."

"We've had this discussion," I said. "Or rather, I've had this discussion with Izzy and Kitty." I pulled back across in front of the truck, giving its driver a friendly wave that didn't seem to be appreciated. "Rude," I said. "Anyway, yeah. I've already thought about this. I'm still only thirty-two, Nik," I glanced across to where he was gripping the door handle for dear life, "and I've got a full, clean driving licence. No one's going to give a shit for a while, yet. So," I went on, "dead or alive?"

"What on earth are you talking about?" Nik looked thoroughly bemused, but it might have just been stress.

"You and ol' Liz," I replied. "Were you already dead when you first met, or still breathing?"

"Oh," he said, "I was long gone before Lizzie made it into society. Shame, really," I glanced sideways and saw he was gazing out of the window with a quiet smile on his face, "I think she'd have been huge fun to have around. As it was," he shrugged, "we were both well and truly deceased by the time we got to know each other properly. I know I sound negative about her," he glanced at me, but I kept my eyes on the road, "but that's only because she knows me better than most. Better even than Eadric does, maybe." A small laugh. "So she finds it very easy to irritate me. It amuses her."

"How come she ended up in charge? I know about the failed coup," Mapp had told me the story of how Elizabeth had been the 'close companion' of the previous ruler of Middlesex, and had taken her revenge when he'd been murdered, "but how come everyone just let her take over? She couldn't have been very old at the time, and she hadn't been dead for long. If I tried that," I frowned, "I reckon I'd find myself dumped in the Mersey pretty quickly. Probably in many different pieces."

"You could try it," Nik offered, "and see what happens?"

"Ha," I snorted, "as if I'd even *want* to take over from Eadric." I couldn't think of anything worse than being put in charge of several counties-worth of bickering dead people. "But that's my point," I went on. "If I tried to overthrow you lot," I waved a hand vaguely in Nik's direction, "people would complain. It'd be all *'Oh she doesn't have enough experience* and *actually we'd rather someone with a few more entries in the Encyclopaedia Britannica'.* They wouldn't just leave me to crack on with it." I saw a sign for motorway services a couple of miles further along and pulled into the left-hand lane in preparation.

"What are you doing?" asked Nik, as I flicked the indicator on.

I nodded to the display on the car's dashboard. "We need diesel," I said. "Somehow Eadric's happy to throw wads of cash on buying one of the most top-of-the-range cars in existence, but has apparently forgotten it requires fuel." The discreetly flashing symbol reassured me I had quite some distance left before it would dry up completely, but I wasn't going to risk it in a car like this. If nothing else, being towed would be bloody humiliating. "So why," I said, "did a city as big as London let an inexperienced young woman pretty much just walk in and take over?"

"Lizzie didn't just walk in," Nik said, as I swung off the motorway and pulled the car round the tight access road that led to the services. "People knew her already." I bypassed the petrol pumps and pulled up in the service station's car park. "What are you doing?" he asked, as I opened my door and got out, leaning backwards to stretch my spine with a satisfying cracking noise.

"I need coffee," I informed him. "I still haven't really got the hang of not eating and drinking, and driving without a coffee on the go just feels bloody weird." I put a hand on the driver's door and peered in at him. "Want anything?"

"No, thank you," Nik said primly, pulling his book out of the inside pocket of his jacket, "I'll just wait here."

"Suit yourself," I said. "Won't be long." I headed inside and, disappointed by the lack of a Costa, headed for the automatic machines inside WHSmiths instead. I added an extra shot to my espresso and took the ticket to the counter to pay. As I held my phone up against the contactless payment machine, I wondered idly what my bank balance was looking like. I'd always been able to get by financially, even though it had been a close squeak at times. I'd done my time living on instant noodles when I was at uni, and spent way too long living in shared houses that were so cold I'd have to get dressed under the duvet in winter. Then I'd moved to Flora's and, after a few tight months to start with, things had levelled out and I'd been, well, if not comfortable, then at least not entirely destitute. These days I had hardly any bills to pay and very few living costs. For all I'd moaned about Grimm's newly developed taste for expensive cat food, it was actually my only regular expense. As I wandered slowly back to the car, sipping my coffee, I checked my balance online. And then I walked back to WHSmith's and bought another coffee, to replace the one I'd dropped in my shock.

**

"What the fuck?" I said, the minute Eadric picked up the phone. I was sitting on a low wall outside the service station. The Alfa was parked a couple of rows away and I could see Nik watching me curiously.

"Good evening, Lilith," he said politely. "What can I do for you?"

"You can tell me what the hell's going on with my bank account, is what you can do," I spluttered.

"I'm not sure what the problem is?" Eadric sounded genuinely confused. "I was concerned that you might need petty cash for your trip, so I sent some money over. Did I do the wrong thing?"

"No," I said hurriedly, "I really appreciate it. I'm just wondering what sort of expenses you thought I might have, to be sending that amount?" I stared bug-eyed at the five-figure balance that was showing on my banking app. There was also a pop-up ad from the bank, suggesting I might like to talk to someone about investments. *I bet that gave the algorithms a shock*, I thought.

"I'm a bit out of touch on the cost of things," Eadric admitted, "so I overestimated, to be on the safe side. See it as a thank you for helping out."

"All I'm doing is going to say hi to your friend," I said to him. "Unless there's something you haven't told me?"

"No," said Eadric, "there are no secrets. You just have to pay Elizabeth a visit and the rest of us just have to hope that she likes you."

"I think I'm an acquired taste, to be honest." I said. "The Marmite of Netherweird."

"I wish you wouldn't call it that," sighed Eadric. "It makes us sound like something out of a fantasy novel. And what's Marmite?"

"Never mind," I said. "I'll explain when I get back. Have you and Mapp started planning yet?" It occurred to me I was discussing things with Eadric as though we were working together as equals. It felt surprisingly natural.

"There have been more sightings of Mab," said Eadric, and I tensed. "Once at Anfield again, and a couple of times in the area around the Anglican Cathedral. Mapp's theory is that she doesn't know exactly what happened to Maria and is going round the cemeteries in the hope of finding her grave."

"But there isn't any grave for her to find," I said.

"Exactly," said Eadric. "So whoever told her about her mother wasn't there at the end, or she'd know that already. Which at least gets you and your friends off the hook."

"Excuse me?" I spluttered, "since when was I *on* any hook? It's me that Mab's threatening, don't forget."

"And it's the rest of us who are at risk from her," Eadric said. "We don't know who she's working with, so we can't take any risks."

"Ivo," I said flatly. "She's working with Ivo. I spoke to him a couple of nights ago."

There was a long silence. "I appreciate you sharing this information," said Eadric eventually. "Do you think Ivo himself is a threat?"

"No," I said, "I don't. He's trying to protect himself and his territory, not attempting to take over yours. Ours. Oh, whatever." I drained the espresso. "But Mab's attached herself to him somehow," I went on, "and I'm not entirely convinced he can control her. They've got different priorities."

"It depends if they're prepared to band together in the face of danger," said Eadric. "And that depends on precisely what that danger is."

"Do you think there's danger?" I asked. "Other than from Ivo, I mean."

"There's always danger, Lilith," said Eadric. "The trick is in figuring out where it's coming from. And where it's headed."

Nik gave me a curious look when I finally got back into the car, but I didn't offer any information and he didn't ask. I switched the music back on and we drove down the motorway in silence. I'd filled the car with as much diesel as I could get in the tank, on the principle that it would save us from having to stop on the way home. People always talk of the dramatically romantic possibilities of immortality—never ageing, having superhuman powers, all that jazz—but in reality, the most useful aspect is not having to stop for a wee when driving long distances. Nik had read his book for a while, before reclining the seat and closing his eyes, looking for all the world as if he was having a nap. Maybe some revenants *could* sleep? It occurred to me I'd never actually compared notes with any of them. We might all have different habits, for all I knew. I gave Nik a nudge as we hit the outskirts of London and the traffic began slowing down. "Hhhnnngh?" he said, opening his eyes blearily. Perhaps he really had been asleep.

"We're getting close to London," I said. "I'm going to need directions."

Nik peered out into the darkness and squinted at the signs flashing past on the side of the road. "We're not coming off until junction two," he said, settling back down. "Let me know when we get to Edgeware." And with that, he went back to what I was beginning to think really was sleep. When the signs for junction two began to appear, I prodded him again, and he pushed the button to bring his seat upright. "Off at two," he said brightly, "and head for Finchley. It's the A1 that we're after. Get onto Archway Road and then we pull off to the right almost immediately." My vague knowledge of London geography was beginning to set off the quietest of alarm bells. Nothing major just yet, but my subconscious was definitely beginning to prickle. As the Alfa cut smoothly through the north London traffic and I started recognising more place names on the road signs, the prickling got stronger.

"Nik," I asked quietly, "where exactly are we going?"

"Didn't Eadric tell you?" he asked, as he gazed out of the window. "We're going to Highgate."

England's Dreaming

Highgate started popping up in local records in the early fourteenth century, when the Bishop of London began allowing people access to a track that went across his deer park, in return for paying a toll. Two hundred years later, deer hunting had stopped and the incumbent bishop began leasing out parcels of land. Highgate itself developed slowly, around the new roads that had been built in order to give travellers convenient access to the north. And where there are travellers, there is business to be had, so it wasn't long before a tavern was established at the site of the gatehouse. Set five miles out from central London and on top of a hill that enabled its residents to look down on the rest of the city, Highgate was always going to be an area popular with London's wealthier inhabitants. By the time it had developed into a suburban town, its residents had become precious enough about their separation from the rest of the grubby city to begin calling their patch Highgate Village, despite most of it being within a hefty stone's throw of the northern arterial roads. The busiest of these roads is the one we were currently travelling on.

The traffic slowed to a crawl as the A1 turned into Archway Road. "Take a right here," said Nik, almost as soon as we'd got onto the hill. "Then left." I followed his instructions silently, my mind spinning. Highgate. The high gate. But we were in London, not Liverpool. How would a vampire know to warn me about problems over two hundred miles away? I didn't think it was anything to do with Joe Williamson and his little family of foster-vampires from Edge Hill. Joe had only been out of his beloved tunnels once in more than a century, and that had been just a few months earlier, when I'd helped

102

save him from Maria. Even then, he'd only stayed on the surface until the tunnels had been stabilised, disappearing back underground the second Eadric's very discreet—and presumably highly paid—structural engineers had declared it safe. The messages had been very clear about the danger being at the 'high gate', but they'd been short on useful detail. But perhaps Joe knew Elizabeth of old? He'd certainly been around long enough. And he'd been quite the society figure in his time, albeit one who wasn't overly bothered about fitting in. Maybe he'd travelled more than I'd assumed. But if he'd had thought I was in real danger, Joe would surely have warned Eadric as well. At least, I hoped so. Straight over," instructed Nik, as we came to one of those annoyingly tiny mini-roundabouts where no one really knows who's got right of way. On the principle that I was driving a big car that didn't belong to me, I pulled determinedly out straight across the middle and took the road Nik was indicating, past the Gatehouse Inn. I thought of all the people who'd walked this hill over the centuries. Some heading into the big city in the hope of a better life, while others were leaving it, perhaps with no idea whether they'd ever return. "Keep going," said Nik. "This bit goes on for a while."

"How much d'you reckon these houses cost?" I asked.

Nik gazed out of his window. "Obscene amounts," he said. "And you haven't even seen Lizzie's place yet." Which was true, but I was pretty sure I knew where we were headed. Sure enough, I found myself driving down Highgate West Hill, with its increasingly impressive houses that backed on to the Hampstead bathing pools. "Left at the roundabout at the bottom," said Nik, but I was already indicating for the turn.

"You cannot be telling me she lives where I think she lives," I said sourly, turning the car onto Swain's Lane. Despite the sky-high property prices, every last resident seemed to have parked their car on the road, and I had to slow to a crawl in order to weave my way up the hill.

"Well," said Nik, "that depends entirely on where you think she lives, doesn't it?" I didn't bother dignifying that with a response and just kept the car moving until we came to a huge stone gateway, where I pulled the car in and switched off the engine. Nik looked at me. "Why are you stopping?" he asked.

"I'm assuming we've arrived," I said flatly, scowling at the signs welcoming tourists to Highgate Cemetery. Despite it being the middle of the night, a small group of people were wandering down the road towards us. They stopped to take flash-lit selfies in front of the gates. For a mad second, I was tempted to get out and scale the enormous stone walls in a show of superhuman undead strength, just for the hell of it. Why should I live by the rules set down by others? I hadn't asked to be made immortal. Maybe it was time for me to start doing things my own way.

"We're not there yet," said Nik, breaking into my thoughts, "Lizzie's place is further up. On the left." Oh. Maybe I should stop jumping to conclusions after all. I started the car up again and pulled back out onto the road, feeling more than a little foolish. We drove in silence as the road narrowed to a single lane and the trees closed in above our heads. "Here," said Nik, indicating a high, flat wall on the left. "Wait in the car and I'll get them to open up for us." He hopped out and walked over to a nondescript door that was almost invisible in the black wall. I watched him lean in to speak into what I assumed was an intercom. Almost immediately, a section of wall to Nik's left started rolling upwards, and he gestured at me to pull the car in. Which was alright for him—he wasn't the one driving a car the size of a tank on one of the narrowest streets in London. Somehow, I squeaked the car in through the opening. I was quietly pleased with myself—despite my distinct lack of experience with cars less than fifteen years old, I got it inside with only one shouting session from the onboard sensors. I switched off the engine and sat in silence for a moment, while the shutter door rolled back down behind me. Not six months earlier, the furthest I generally drove was the sixty-odd miles back to Shrewsbury from Liverpool. Even that was a rare trip. And now here I was, driving the most expensive car I'd seen in my entire life into what for all I knew might be the underground lair of the real, twenty-four carat, Bad Guys ™. Nik appeared through a door to my right, and tilted his head at me questioningly. *Oh well*, I thought, *here goes nothing*. I got out of the car and waited for him to get our bags out of the boot, before locking it. I tucked the keys safely into the pocket of the leather jacket I'd decided at the last minute was perfectly suitable clothing to meet a real-life Queen of the Underworld. "Come say hi to Lizzie," said Nik. He sounded genuinely pleased to be here, which was reassuring.

I looked around at the garage, which was cleaner than the kitchen in my flat. "She doesn't have a car herself, I presume?"

Nik laughed. "Lizzie never goes anywhere," he said. "So she doesn't need a car. Anyway," he pushed open a small door that was tucked into the wall and gestured at me to enter, "people generally come to her." I stepped past him into an atrium that appeared to be constructed entirely of glass and angles. Open-tread staircases zigzagged upwards at the far end, and whatever was to our left was blocked from view by a glossy, piano-black partition. "We're going upstairs," said Nik, nodding to the stairs. "She's looking forward to meeting you." Feeling more nervous than I'd ever have admitted publicly, I followed him upwards. As the staircase turned back on itself and the next floor became visible, I stopped dead in my tracks. The far wall of the room at the top of the stairs was made entirely of glass. I barely registered the enormous sofa in the centre of the space, so distracted was I with the view.

"Bloody *hell*," I blurted out.

Nik was already at the top of the stairs. He turned to look back down at me, a wide grin on his face. "Beautiful, isn't it?" he said. I nodded silently and stepped up next to him. Spread out like a huge and glorious homage to the dead, its details slowly making themselves visible as my eyes focused, was the cemetery itself. I squinted my eyes out at the darkness and tried to get my bearings.

"This is the old side?" I asked. Nik nodded beside me. I took a few steps forward across the deep pile carpet and peered down through the glass. Just below me in the darkness were the tops of several ancient stone memorials. One—a delicate stone pillar—was higher than the others. It felt almost as though I could reach out and touch it.

"Do you like it?" asked a quiet voice behind me. I spun around and found myself face to face with the most beautiful woman I'd ever seen in my life. Maybe a couple of inches taller than me, she was wearing a green silk dress that draped down over her bare feet, its long, loose sleeves pulling into buttoned cuffs at the wrists. Her pale grey eyes were huge and doll-like, framed by long red hair that wrapped itself heavily around her shoulders before falling down her back in a cascade of fiery gold. I suddenly felt very self-conscious about the mop of twisted gingery curls that spewed from my own head. The woman smiled and held out her hand. I shook it, still struggling to think of something to say in the face of such aesthetic perfection. "I'm Elizabeth," she said. Not Lizzie to me, then. "You're Eadric's lark." It was a statement, not a question. I wasn't impressed by being described as Eadric's anything—and certainly not a bloody bird—but decided to keep it zipped for now.

"Hi Lizzie," said Nik from behind me.

"I'm going back to Elizabeth," she said with a smile, "now that I'm the only one again." She turned to me. "I've heard a lot about you, Lilith."

Yeah, I bet. "How long have you…lived here?" I asked.

"A long time," said Elizabeth. She nodded towards the sprawling cemetery. "For all it's a citadel to the departed," she said, "it's also a beautifully peaceful place to live. Of course, I've improved my living conditions over the years. This," she gestured around her at the house, "is perfect. I can put on a show of normality for the humans, while staying close to my roots."

"It's an amazing house," I said, truthfully. "Do you live here alone?"

"Gosh no," she said, "how boring would that be? Others pop in and out. And I have Jude, of course." Right on cue, someone walked in through a door at the back of the room. Even taller than Elizabeth, Jude was dressed in a loose cream shirt and matching trousers, with pale bare feet that had shell-pink polish on the toes. Their short, cropped brown hair stuck out in all directions. They walked up to Elizabeth and, to my surprise, sat down cross-legged at her feet. She put a hand down without looking and ruffled Jude's hair.

"Hi," I said to Jude, waving my hand slightly like an idiotic toddler. "Nice to meet you." Jude raised the fingers of one hand slightly in response, but said nothing. "So," I said, trying to sound lighthearted, "I'm here. Apparently I'm supposed to be, like, an envoy or something."

"Told you she was fun," said Nik, appearing beside me. "Although fun does sometimes turn into a chaotic mess." He shrugged.

"I'm here, aren't I?" I said to him. "I came because Eadric wanted me to. I'm not so much of a cow that I won't help out when needed. And *you'd* be more helpful if you knew how to drive a fucking car, so you can cut the sarcastic crap. Why," I turned to Elizabeth, "am I here?"

"I think," she said, clearly suppressing a smile, "we're supposed to be talking politics and discussing loyalties. That sort of thing." She shrugged. "Boring, I know."

"Could we not have met in the middle?" I asked. "Although that would be somewhere around Dudley, which is a bit much to ask of anyone. Maybe a bit closer to your side. Banbury would have been fine."

"Will you come for a walk with me, Lilith?" Elizabeth asked, putting a sensible halt to my pro-level rambling. "I think we'd be better off talking alone." Nik must have opened his mouth to say something, because she held a finger up to shush him. "We'll be just fine," she said to him, "you know I think better outside. Stay here with Jude. Play cards or something." I waited for Nik to argue, but to my surprise, he just walked over to the enormous sofa and sat down in the middle of it.

"Come on then, Jude," he said, "crack out the pack." Jude padded over to sit down next to him and reached under the table. They produced a packet of cards and began shuffling with the deftness of a professional croupier.

"Those two will be happy for hours," said Elizabeth in a low voice. "Let's make our escape." Beckoning me to follow her, she turned and headed out through the same door Jude had appeared from. Following her, I found myself in a large, open plan bedroom. The wall to my left was floor to ceiling glass, and a whitewashed four-poster bed sat in the centre of the room. The only other furniture was a long, low chaise longue, positioned in front of the glass wall in order to make the most of the view. The chaise was draped with woven throws in muted forest tones and looked as though it was used more often than the bed. Elizabeth stepped over to the glass wall and pushed it with one hand. To my surprise, the entire panel began to slowly move downwards until it disappeared entirely. "It slots into the cavity wall below," said Elizabeth, "which is clever. Sometimes I am very impressed with modern technology, despite my best efforts to ignore it all."

"Is that why I had to come to you?" I asked. "Because you don't like the modern world?"

"Do any of us?" asked Elizabeth. "I'm sure you've seen how... uncomfortable Eadric can be with the trappings of modern society."

"Well," I said, "I've seen how he'd rather hide out up in his tower instead of mingling on the streets with the rest of humanity. If that's what you mean."

"I wouldn't have called Eadric the hiding type," said Elizabeth. "He's more of a plotter." She grinned at me. "Sits around looking quiet and inoffensive, all the while planning his next move. Which is why," she went on, "I insisted on him sending you down here. Whatever people like to think, I am perfectly capable of leaving the cemetery. Although," she held a hand palm out towards the monuments just visible in the dark, "why anyone would want to is beyond me. But if I'd come to you—or even met you halfway, as you so politely suggested—I am immediately at a disadvantage. Eadric's territory stretches a long way down, and the second I set foot out of my own lands, I'm at risk."

"Surely I'm equally at risk, then," I said. "I've stepped right into *your* territory."

"You have, indeed," agreed Elizabeth. "I'm sure I could make life quite... difficult for you, should I choose. But," she held up a hand before I could say anything, "you're not at risk. Or at least, not in the way Eadric or I would be. We're the leaders of our territories, Lilith. Our power is as symbolic as it is physical. We have to be seen in our ivory towers, looking down over those we're dedicated to protect. At the risk of sounding disrespectful, you're a less important target."

"Correct," I said, "that *is* very disrespectful. I'm pretty sure my friends and family would consider me more important than either of you. And my cat," I added. Although I strongly suspected I was definitely less important to Grimm, now Kitty was becoming capable of looking after him. "Had Eadric told you about Maria's long-lost daughter reappearing?"

"Ah, the lovely Mab," said Elizabeth. "Quite the character, don't you think?"

"You know her, then."

"Not well," said Elizabeth. "I've met her once. She came here before going on to Liverpool, but we had little to say to each other. I don't appreciate people turning up without an invitation, and she didn't appreciate what she perceived to be my lack of support. We didn't even know she existed until recently, of course."

"Of course." I stared out into the darkness. "What am I supposed to do about her?"

"Let's walk," said Elizabeth. "I think better when I'm walking." With that, she stepped off the edge of the room and dropped into the darkness below. I stepped forward and peered over the ledge. "Come on," she said, nearer than I'd expected. Stepping out from underneath the house, she gestured at me to follow her. "I'll give you the tour." *Here goes nothing*, I thought, stepping out into darkness. I landed neatly on soft grass and wondered irritably how long it was going to take me to feel entirely confident in my undead abilities. "It gets easier," said Elizabeth. "I promise."

We walked together down the gravel path, Elizabeth occasionally trailing her fingers across the surface of the gravestones. "You've been here before?" she asked

"Once," I said, "years ago. Had a weekend in London with my parents and we spent an afternoon wandering around the newer side. Dad wanted to visit Marx's grave."

"Aah, Karl," said Elizabeth with a smile. "It's a shame he didn't stay to become one of us. I think he'd have been fun."

"What's your theory behind revenants?" I asked her. Well, she brought it up. "Mapp says it's to do with strength of character. But surely, if that was true, then people like Marx would be all over it."

"Gaultier Mapp has theories for every occasion," said Elizabeth, "and some are more likely than others."

"You've known each other a long time, I guess."

"Yes." She didn't elaborate.

"You made a point of introducing yourself as Elizabeth," I said. "But Mapp told me you preferred Lizzie." He'd been definite about it, as well. *Call her Lizzie if you value your head*, was what he'd said at the time.

"Mapp," said Elizabeth, "is from my old life. Quite literally. We knew each other when I was still alive, and I was definitely called Lizzie back then. However," she glanced at me as we walked, "that name was given to me by my husband, who was not always a good person. But the name stuck, and I convinced myself I liked it. Even after I died." She gave a small chuckle. "That was back when I still thought my identity depended on those around me. I've learned to value myself more since then. And of course, it's less confusing now that there's no longer a living queen with the same name."

"I guess it's lucky you're the only undead one," I said. "Anyway, you're the boss."

"I'm not, though," said Elizabeth, "and that's the problem. Here," she gestured around her, "I am absolutely in charge. And I always will be, if I have my way. But there are many other territories, as I'm sure you are aware."

"Eadric's tried giving me some history lessons," I said.

"And I'm sure you were a most diligent pupil," said Elizabeth. I looked to check whether she was mocking me, but she appeared perfectly serious. "Eadric is a wise man—wiser than most. It is definitely worth learning the background of our world, Lilith. I feel you will become an important part of it."

"You didn't answer my question," I said.

"As to why some become revenants and others don't?" I nodded. "There are questions without answers, Lilith, even in our world. If there was any real scientific theory behind our existence, then I'm sure mortals would know about it by now and would be manipulating it to their own ends. They can't stop poking and prodding at things. Usually to see if they will break."

"Do you think Mab is a revenant?" I asked.

"I'm not sure what Mab is," said Elizabeth, "and that's the truth. I don't think she's the same as you or I, no. She's at least a century old by my calculations, yet looks to be in her twenties at most. Her mother was at least partly human before she died. We don't know who—or what—her father was, of course. Let's sit down for a moment." We'd walked down far enough that I could see the outline of the stone entrance gates through the trees. Elizabeth sat cross-legged on the edge of a small space between gravestones, which was empty but for the ivy that scrambled across it. She patted the ground next to her and I reluctantly perched myself on the edge of the path, a few feet away. "Why are you so wary of me, Lilith?" Elizabeth asked. There was no inflection in her voice to suggest it was anything other than a straightforwardly curious question, so I decided to be honest.

"Because a vampire has been warning me to stay away from the 'high gate,'" I said. "So it doesn't take a genius to figure out why I'm feeling nervous right now."

"*The* high gate?" asked Elizabeth. I nodded. "Then I don't think the threat is here," she said. "Or if it is, it certainly isn't coming from me. The high gate in question round here isn't even in the cemetery grounds." Which, of course, I already knew.

"So, why were you so keen to meet me?" I asked. "Why did it have to be now? I've been part of this," I gestured my hands around vaguely, "since the spring and I don't recall there having been any urgency for me to meet anyone so far. Then Mab turns up completely out of the blue and makes it very clear that I'm top of her murderous shit-list and I'm dispatched to meet-and-greet with you a couple of days later. And between all this, a rogue vampire starts sending me warnings about a high bloody gate. Even by weird paranormal standards, that's all a bit spookily coincidental. Don't you think?"

"There was no rush to meet you on my part," said Elizabeth. "Eadric had informed me of your arrival, of course." Of course. I could just imagine how *that* conversation went down. *This woman should have died but she didn't and now she's poking her nose in oh and by the way she killed my wife but I'm not holding it against her.* "But I trust him to make the right decisions. He wouldn't have lasted as long as he has if he made mistakes."

"So why now?" I asked again. "Why just as Mab arrived?"

"I'd actually intended to contact Eadric in order to request your presence as soon as Mab left here," said Elizabeth. "Following her surprise visit. I thought I might be doing you a favour, in fact, by getting you out of the way before Mab got to Liverpool. I got sidetracked, unfortunately." She was stroking her hand across the ivy-strewn ground next to her. "Notice this small patch of land, Lilith," she said softly. "See how unassuming and unremarkable it is." She looked up at me, her hand flat against the ground as if feeling for a heartbeat. "And yet," she said, "ten women lie here. Ten. All of them fallen from grace and all of them on top of each other. Purposely laid down with little to protect them, in order that their bodies might break down more easily and make room for later additions. This, Lilith," she patted the ground again, "is what history thinks of women who don't follow the rules. And that is why I wanted to meet you—because it became clear very quickly that you weren't following the rules. This community—this undead, perhaps unholy community—needs people like you. Like us."

"You called us 'unholy'," I said. "Why should it matter whether or not we're considered holy? I've been an atheist since the day my brother died and I realised he wasn't coming back, not ever. One of the teachers at school said Cally was lucky because he'd gone to heaven to be with God and I was so angry I screamed in her face." Elizabeth tilted her head sympathetically but didn't say anything. "I told her only a selfish and horrible god would take children from their families and I thought it was all made up and stupid." I looked her in the eye. "And nothing I've seen since has changed my mind. So I don't actually care about being unholy, if it's all the same to you."

Elizabeth gazed at me in silence for a moment, then smiled. She really was unbelievably beautiful—more like a living, breathing china doll than any human woman I'd ever met. Perhaps I should ask Mapp just how attached she was to Jude. He had said he was all about the matchmaking, after all. "It was the taint of being seen as unholy that led to this grave," she said eventually, nodding down at the patch of ground. "So no, I have no objection to your beliefs. Not that it would matter if I had. All of us in this undead world have faced battles of our own—whether they happened when we were still alive, or after we were long dead. As a result, we tend not to judge each other. And we stand by each other in times of threat. Which is why I wanted to meet you, Lilith O'Reilly." She reached out a pale, delicate hand and took my fingers in hers. "I declare that I stand by you. Whatever the incoming threat, you will have the support of Middlesex."

"Thanks," I said, unable to think of anything more coherent, "I think. Although I suspect Eadric was hoping the show of support might be for him."

Elizabeth laughed and dropped my hand back into my lap. "Eadric knows better than most just how this world works," she said. "For whatever reason, you are the current focus of attention, both good and bad. Therefore, you are the priority and *you* have my support. Now," she sprang up, her bare feet digging into the ivy surface of the mass grave, "let us see who's winning at cards."

***

Jude had just won the hand when Elizabeth and I got back to the house. Nik was insisting on playing for best of three. Elizabeth and I sprawled on the floor, watching them. That woman could even sprawl elegantly. "You're playing for the honour of the North," I warned Nik, just as the still-silent Jude laid their hand down. Nik looked crestfallen. "Never mind," I reassured him, "it's kinder to let them win, really. Poor souls, having to live down here in the heartless southern wastelands."

Elizabeth prodded me with her foot. "Some would say we're more civilised," she said. "I hear you're currently dealing with a vampire outbreak." I looked up at Nik, who just shrugged.

"They're certainly...around," I said carefully. If she had to ask, then Elizabeth presumably didn't know that my very existence was down to the actions of an idiot vampire. "They don't really cause much trouble."

"Didn't you say it was one of the vampires who'd been trying to warn you about something?" she asked.

I nodded. "A *vegan* vampire, would you believe?" Elizabeth's expression suggested that no, she would not believe. "Normal blue eyes and everything," I said. "But definitely a vampire."

"How do you know?" she asked. "If this...*vampire* doesn't feed off living things and has normal human eyes, then how do you know they're a vampire?"

"She smelled like one," I said. "And looked like one. Just not the eyes. And she's clearly still got some kind of moral compass, to be trying to warn me."

"Warn you of what, though?" asked Elizabeth. "Obviously, I can see why you thought the high gate might be a reference to me, but I can assure you it isn't. I might be many things, Lilith," she looked at me with her clear grey eyes, "but I'm not sneaky. If I was going to attack you, you'd know about it. I don't ambush people. Some of us," I thought I detected a slight flick of her eyes towards Nikolaus, but couldn't be sure, "still play by the rules."

"Well, if we're going to be open and honest about everything," I said, "what are you planning to do about Ivo Laithlind?"

"Why would I be doing anything about Laithlind?" Elizabeth asked, her gaze steady. "He's already well aware that I've no intention of intervening in a battle for territory, and I haven't changed my mind about that. Nor will I support Eadric in such a move, should he decide to become involved."

"But you said—" I started, but Elizabeth put a hand up to stop me.

"I said that *you* had my support, Lilith," she said, "not the rest of your clan." I felt Nik's eyes twitch towards me, but he carried on playing cards. "You and I will perhaps become friends. I think I'm going to enjoy having another woman around, even if it's from a distance. Eadric and I are equals, but we're not friends. I'm sure Nikolaus here can confirm that."

Nik snorted. "Don't drag me into your games," he said. "You are a terrible woman, Elizabeth."

"And yet still you all fight for my attention," she said calmly. As she spoke, I felt a flash of power emanate from her. It was brief, and neither Jude nor Nik seemed to register it. Although it might just be that they were both used to it by now. "It's not even because of my feminine wiles, is it?" She glanced slyly across at Nik. "It's because you're all still little boys at heart. Little boys who are desperate for mama's attention and approval. It's sad, really," she turned to me, "they're all so *obvious.*"

"I can't say I've noticed," I said. "Personally, I'm more bothered about when and how Mab is going to attempt to get her revenge."

"Yes," said Elizabeth, "that's an interesting one. I'm not really sure what she thinks she can do. After all, you are already dead." She smiled at me. "I think she might try to capture you instead," she said, frighteningly calmly. "Perhaps as a bargaining chip."

"People have been trying to use me as collateral since the day I died," I said sharply, "and it's getting quite tedious now, thank you very bloody much."

"Then you'll have to make a stand, Lilith," said Elizabeth, as if it was obvious. "Show them what you're made of." Nik was openly watching us now. Jude put their last hand down and then scooped all the cards up and replaced them in their packet.

"Show who?" I asked.

Elizabeth smiled. "Everyone, Lilith," she said. "Show *everyone*."

Secrets And Lies

"We don't turn off here," said Nik, as I indicated left and pulled onto the slip road that led to the M54. We'd taken our leave of Elizabeth and Jude as soon as it was clear that Nik wasn't ever going to make back his metaphorical losses at cards. I'd insisted on stopping at the first services for coffee again, but after that we'd ploughed up the M40 without stopping.

"We're taking the scenic route," I replied. "I texted my mum before we left London. Figured I might as well say hi, as we're passing anyway."

"This was absolutely not part of the deal," said Nik. "I will not wander around Shrewsbury like a bloody tourist."

"You're free to do as you please," I said, picking up speed just to annoy him. "Wait in the car, if you'd rather. Like a toddler." There was a quiet huffing noise beside me. "But I am going to catch up with my mother." We drove in silence, taking in the Shropshire countryside as it flashed past. It was late afternoon now, and the sun was dipping towards the Welsh hills in the distance, bathing the landscape in golden light.

"Beautiful, isn't it?" said Nik. "I can see why Housman loved it so much."

"I never got on with Housman," I said, "despite my English teacher's attempt to drill it into us at school. Most of it was bollocks, anyway."

"In what way?" asked Nik.

"Well," I said, "he barely ever came here, for one thing." I pulled out to overtake a tractor. It was almost certainly not supposed to be on the motorway, but most Shropshire farmers claim to have missed that memo. "I looked him up once, can't remember why. Probably to annoy my teachers.

116

Anyway, yeah. He made a lot up. You know the 'blue remembered hills' bit?" Nik nodded. "Housman didn't even know which hills he was talking about, half the time. He got most of his information from an old walking guide. And the closest he got to most of the county was seeing the hills on the horizon, when he was growing up in Worcestershire. Bloody poets."

Nik snorted. "You remember a lot of the details, for someone who doesn't like the poems."

"I do," I agreed, "and that's the weirdest thing. I glanced across at him as I drove. "Because I'm pretty sure I wouldn't have remembered it when I was alive," I said. "Things are becoming clearer with distance, as if I'm looking back through the wrong end of a telescope. Housman's comments about Shrewsbury being an island were spot on, mind. Bloody place goes underwater every year, without fail."

"You'll remember everything, eventually," said Nik. I waited for the rest, but he stayed silent.

"Do you?" I asked. "Remember everything, I mean? From back when you were still alive?" We were swooping down into Shropshire proper now. The road changed from motorway to dual carriageway as we did so, as though such modern inventions weren't acceptable in the old county.

"Yes," said Nik eventually. "At least, it feels like it sometimes. As if my head's filled with everything I did and everyone I knew and everywhere I went. I'm not always sure whether the memories are from before or after I died, to be honest. It's been a long time." A quiet laugh. "My daughter would no doubt tell me I'm not being very scientific."

"You've got children?" I couldn't keep the astonishment out of my voice. "Seriously?" I glanced sideways at him. "I assumed—I mean..."

"You assumed," said Nik lightly, "that I wasn't interested in women."

"Yeah," I said. "Sorry. That was presumptuous of me."

"People aren't always what they seem, Lilith," he said. "I certainly wasn't. I was married, once. To a woman." He flashed me a grin. "She was a delightful girl, and I was an absolutely appalling husband. These days we'd have perhaps understood each other a little better. But back then, marriage was the thing, and it rarely occurred to anyone to check whether it was the right thing for the people involved. Parents decided for their children, even when those children were adults." He sighed. "But I couldn't change my nature then, any more than I could do so now. She ended up with a husband she didn't understand, and I ended up with a reputation that followed me everywhere."

"Is that why you went to Greece?"

"I loved Greece," he said. "It's warm and welcoming and people don't care so much about who you are or what you do."

"Have you ever thought about going back?" We were coming up to the turnoff for the Shrewsbury ring road. Ignoring the road signs, I headed straight towards the town centre.

"I thought your parents lived on the outskirts?" asked Nik, as the traffic slowed to a halt outside the abbey. "Bloody hell," he said, peering up at where the ruins of its old transepts were still visible, "I'd heard they were putting the road through here, but I hadn't realised they were going to plough straight through the church."

"Yeah," I said, trying not to smile, "that happened nearly two hundred years ago. I take it you don't know the area well?"

"I know it as well as anyone needs to," he said, as the traffic started moving and we drove into the town centre. "But it reminds me too much of Chester."

I found a space on High Street and pulled the car in. "What's wrong with Chester?" I asked, as I switched the engine off. Before Nik could respond, there was hammering on the glass next to him and we both jumped.

"Lilith O'Reilly!" A woman's face appeared in the window.

"Shit," I said, louder than I meant to.

"Is there a problem?" asked Nik, looking between me and the woman, who was leaning down to wave at me with unnerving enthusiasm.

"Claire Fenton," I said, undoing my seatbelt. "We went to school together." Somehow it hadn't occurred to me that by coming back to Shrewsbury, I risked bumping into people I knew. I'd only been back once since I'd died and that had been a flying visit to my parents' house. "I'm going to have to get out and make small-talk," I said to Nik, "without her realising I'm...well," I trailed off.

"A bit odd?" Nik finished. I nodded. To my surprise, he unfastened his own seatbelt and put his hand on the door to open it. "Come on," he said, "let's get it over with." I got out and walked round to the pavement. Nik stood in front of Claire, blessing her with his best high-wattage smile. It was clearly working—Claire seemed dazed and was just gazing silently up at him.

"Hi Claire," I said, with an enthusiasm I definitely didn't feel, "how lovely to see you." It took her a few seconds to even register I was there. Finally, she gave herself a visible shake and turned to me.

"Wow, Lilith," she said, shaking her head in amazement, "you *have* done well for yourself!"

"The man or the car?" I asked, confusion making me blunt. Claire gave a girlish little giggle that was at odds with her appearance. She was wearing a neat skirt suit that had probably come from M&S, and her short hair had that angular undercut that announces its owner as having recently broken up with someone. Dump the partner, then cut the hair—it always happens in that order.

"Both, I'd say," she giggled again. "You lucky thing!"

Before I could say anything, Nik put his arm around my waist and pulled me to him—a move so surprising that I was stunned into silence. "I think you'll find it's me who's the lucky one," he said to Claire, who was all but wetting her no doubt very sensible knickers. "Fished this beauty out of the Mersey," he went on. "It was a good catch that day." I tucked my head down slightly so that Claire couldn't see me struggling not to laugh and elbowed Nik sharply in the ribs. In return, he kissed the top of my head. "I'm a very lucky boy."

"Of course," stuttered Claire, "very lucky. My Darren used to enjoy fishing, but he was never the romantic type." Yup, that explained the haircut. Darren had spent one too many Sunday mornings out on the riverbank rather than at home in bed with his wife, and she'd had enough. I hoped Claire would find someone nice sooner rather than later. We'd never been what anyone would describe as friends, but I liked her. We'd sat together in Biology at school, but always went off with our own friends as soon as the lessons ended. "Anyway," she said, "I'd better crack on." She shook her car keys for emphasis. "Need to get back and do the boys' tea. They turn feral if I leave them alone too long. Say hi to your mum for me, Lilith."

"Will do," I said. We watched Claire walk off down the street, and I was impressed that she only turned around once to look back at us. Nik gave her a little wave and she waved back, before turning into the alleyway that lead down to the main car park. I pulled away from Nik. "What the fuck?" He was grinning at me. "Honestly Nik," I said, pressing the button that locked the car with an expensive-sounding *thunk*, "you'll have started enough gossip to keep anyone who knows me busy for *weeks*. I won't be able to visit again until it's long enough for me to pretend we've split up, for fuck's sake."

"Ah well," he said, looking absolutely unrepentant, "it won't hurt them to think you're doing marvellously well for yourself, will it? Up in the big city."

"Liverpool isn't *that* big," I said. "And since when was having a boyfriend and a fancy car enough to impress people?"

"I think you'll find people are still very easily impressed by that sort of thing," said Nik.

"Huh," I said. "Then they need to up their standards. Anyway, I'm going to meet Mum. Want to come?"

Nik put his hands in the pockets of his immaculate trousers and looked around him. "Actually," he said, "I think I'm going to have a wander round, after all. It'll be nice to have a change of scenery."

"Get you," I said approvingly, "being all sociable and stuff. Meet you back at the car in an hour?" He nodded. "If you get bored before then, I'll be at the Birds Nest cafe in the market hall."

"Ooh," said a voice right by my ear, "I haven't been inside the market for years!" Nik and I both leapt backwards in surprise. Standing in front of us—and grinning broadly—was Aunt Kitty. She was wearing a blue boiler suit and had her hair tied up in a scarf. It made her look surprisingly contemporary and as though she shopped in very expensive vintage stores, but I strongly suspected the outfit was all her own.

"What the *fuck*?" I hissed, looking round to see if anyone had noticed a full-sized adult woman materialising in the middle of the street. Thankfully it was a busy afternoon and my dead aunt's sudden appearance seemed to have gone unnoticed.

Kitty grinned at me. "Hey Lil," she said, "thought it'd be nice to see your mum again."

I gaped at her. "How?" I spluttered, eventually. "How did you get here?"

"I'm a ghost," she said slowly, as if that explained everything. Perhaps it did. "I can get around in ways you can't."

"Yes," I said, "but how the fuck did you get from the flat? I assume you were in the flat?" Kitty nodded. "How did you get from the flat to here? We've been driving for hours! There's no way you could have known when we were going to arrive."

"I'll leave you two to…discuss things," said Nik. "Don't go home without me. I'm not capable of teleporting like your delightful aunt here." He turned without waiting for an answer and headed off up Pride Hill. I watched him sauntering along as though he was just another tourist, rather than a two-hundred-year-old walking corpse. Standing there on the high street of the town I'd known for decades, I wondered—not for the first time—how the *fuck* my life had taken such a weird turn. Claire bloody Fenton was probably driving home right now with nothing planned for her evening other than feeding her kids and seeing what was on TV. I was standing here figuring out how to go for coffee with my mum without anyone discovering I had my dead aunt in tow. Never mind the sentient zombie I could still see in the distance, perusing the window display of the Hobbes shoe shop.

"You'd better behave yourself," I said, turning back to Kitty. "Come *here*," I hissed at her, as she turned to walk into the Joules clothes shop on the corner of the street. I caught hold of her arm and pulled her backwards.

"What?" she asked. "I haven't been shopping in years. It might be fun!"

"No fun for you today, lady," I muttered, stalking down Shoplatch and dragging Kitty along with me. It occurred to me I was holding her as though she was solid, but when I looked at her, her usual holographic shimmer was still visible. I wondered what it would look like to anyone watching us—would they see Kitty being dragged along like a child, while she ooh'd and aah'd at the shops we passed? Or would they just see me stomping down

121

the street with my hand held out at what would presumably look like a very awkward angle?

Kitty suddenly ground to a halt, so suddenly that I was forced to stop with her. "Bloody hell," she said, looking upwards. "It didn't look like that last time I saw it." I followed her gaze up to the market hall, which was looming above us in all its ugly retro glory. It was built in the mid-sixties and replaced the faux-gothic spires of the Victorian original. I've seen photos of the earlier version and can only assume the town planners had taken mind-altering drugs on the day they signed off on the new design. There is nothing about Shrewsbury market's brick-and-steel exterior that isn't utterly repulsive, yet it contains one of the best indoor markets in the country. Which tells you a lot about the tenacity of the people of Shropshire.

"Well," I said, tugging her across the road with me, "that's because you've been *dead* a long time."

"Honestly, Lil," said Kitty, "do you have to keep going on about it? You don't see me constantly blethering on at *you* about being dead, do you?"

"That's because I'm not prone to turning up in public spaces out of thin air," I said to her, as we made our way up the stairs to the first floor of the market. "I walk. Or drive. You know," we were up on the main floor of the market now, "like normal people. I arrive looking *human*, Kitty."

"Well, you say that," grumbled my aunt, "but most humans aren't dragging a ghost along like a piece of old baggage."

"Most ghosts don't just turn up without warning and ask to go shopping," I muttered. "Anyway, there's Mum," I nodded towards the cafe in the corner, where my mother was sitting with a coffee already in front of her. "I have no idea whether she'll be able to see you this time, so for god's sake, try to be subtle." Kitty had met my mother—her niece—a few months earlier, when I was freshly dead. She—Kitty, not Mum—had decided to be moral support on my first visit back home, whether I liked it or not. The intention had been to pretend nothing had changed and that I was absolutely one-hundred-per-cent live and kicking, but Mum had seen through it straight away. Mostly because she'd been able to see through Kitty, who she recognised from her childhood. Kitty had already been dead when a very young Mum had first met her, which led to an awkwardly hissed conversation when Dad was out of the room about how Mum could see things others couldn't and yes she'd realised I was dead but it's not really that big a problem is it, not if everything's carrying on as normal. And that is how I'd discovered my mother is a spooky little bastard who's just never bothered to mention it because apparently my dad 'doesn't hold with that sort of thing'. Families, huh—can't live with 'em, can't drop dead and hope they won't notice.

Mum stood up as we reached the table and stepped around it to hug me. "Hey Lil," she said, "good to see you. And you've still got your sidekick!" She let me go and hugged Kitty as well, who held her tightly while grinning at me over Mum's shoulder. Well, that answered *that* question.

"Can I get you ladies anything?" chirped a waitress as she approached our table. Dressed in black jeans and a black fitted t-shirt with a butcher's-style apron over the top, she looked exactly the same as every member of waiting staff in any cafe you might walk into in Liverpool (other than Flora's, because Izzy says uniforms are a crime against humanity). She smiled and held a pencil over her notebook.

"I'll have an espresso," I said, "thanks." Mum lifted her cup in greeting, to show she already had a drink.

"And anything for you?" To my astonishment, I realised the waitress was talking to Kitty.

"Oh!" said Kitty, clearly flustered, "ummm, an espresso for me too, I think." Mum and I made boggle eyes at each other. "Thanks so much," said my aunt. The waitress saluted with her pencil and walked off. The three of us just stared at each other for a moment. "She can see me," said Kitty, eventually.

"No shit, Sherlock," I said, pulling a heavy wooden bench out from under the table and sitting down opposite Mum. "You'd better sit down. And at least *attempt* to look normal?" Kitty sat herself next to me and looked between me and Mum, clearly trying to make sense of what just happened. "I don't know," I said, "so don't bother asking. And anyway," I narrowed my eyes at her, "if you're here with me, who's looking after Grimm?"

Kitty grinned. "Oh," she said, "we have had *such* fun! Izzy's been popping in, don't worry. But I haven't needed her once! He's such a clever cat, you know." She smiled happily to herself. "So helpful."

"I'm sure he is," I said sourly. "Has he been doing the dishes and folding the laundry?" Mum was drinking her coffee in silence, clearly enjoying the sight of her immortal daughter bickering with her ghostly aunt. I wondered again how I'd never noticed Mum's...*odd* side when I was still alive. I'd lived with the woman for the best part of two decades, for god's sake. How had I missed any of this? Although Kitty hadn't been around back then and I was still alive, so maybe there just hadn't been anything odd for her to deal with.

"Not quite," said Kitty, breaking into my thoughts, "but he's getting very good at helping me open his food trays."

"I bet he is," I said. "That cat's always had his priorities straight."

Kitty laughed. "He can open the cupboard door now," she said. "And just this morning, he pulled out the carton he wanted for breakfast. Honestly Lil," I could see the excitement on her face, "I'd swear he checked through them all first, picking out his favourite flavour."

"Which is?" I asked, drily.

"Lamb terrine," Kitty said with certainty. "I think he likes—oh! Thank you!" This was to the waitress, who was leaning over the table with our drinks. She slid an espresso each in front of Kitty and I, before wishing us a cheery *"Enjoy!"* and wandering off to clear tables. Kitty stared down at the tiny ceramic cup in front of her.

"I'm kind of morbidly curious to know what would happen if you drank that," said Mum.

"I don't think I should risk it," said Kitty, "not in public. Not until I've tried at home first, anyway." She grinned at us. "How exciting, though! I'm becoming more real by the day."

"Which doesn't answer my question," I said. "Who's looking after Grimm?"

"Oh," said Kitty, "I forgot. Hang on." And with that, she disappeared. Literally, honest-to-god disappeared, right in front of our eyes.

"Well," said Mum, "that's impressive."

Before I could say anything, Kitty popped back up beside me. "He's fine," she said. "Napping on your bed."

"Okay," I said slowly, "am I the only one here who thinks this is not remotely normal?" Mum and Kitty both looked blankly at me. "Come on," I said, "she just disappeared! Right in front of us! What if," I looked around at the busy market, "someone had seen?"

"What would you have done if someone disappeared in front of your eyes?" asked Mum. She dropped her voice. "When you were alive, I mean."

"I'd have, well…" I had to think about that one. "I'd have assumed I'd just missed them moving, I guess," I said, finally. "Or muttered to myself about getting new glasses."

"Exactly," said Mum. "People don't believe their own eyes, half the time. If something really weird happens in front of them—something that *shouldn't* happen—they don't think 'oh crikey, ghosts must be real after all'. They think, 'That's odd, anyway I wonder what's for tea'. Never doubt the capacity of the human brain for ignoring things it doesn't understand, Lil." She nodded at me for emphasis. "Let's be honest, love," she smiled, "*you* don't make sense. But you're here and I am very grateful for that. Shall I take care of that for you, Kitty?" With that, she quickly tipped most of Kitty's espresso into her own drink and put the cup back down on the table.

"Thanks, Helen," said Kitty.

"So," I said, "how does the disappearing act work?"

Kitty looked blank for a second. "Oh, me?" she asked.

"Well I don't see anyone else popping in and out of various realities," I said. "So what gives? Did you really go back to the flat for a minute just then?"

"Yes," said Kitty, with a grin. "You asked me how Grimm was, so I checked on him and he's fine."

"How, though?" I asked. "You're sitting here looking real enough for the waitress to bring you a drink, yet you can just zip up to Liverpool and reappear back here seconds later?"

"I was never one for science," Kitty shrugged unhelpfully. "It's not like actually travelling though, I don't think." She pushed her empty espresso cup with a fingertip and it moved slightly on the table. "I just disappear in one place and reappear in the other."

"Could you go anywhere you wanted?" asked Mum.

Kitty appeared to give it some thought. She stared down at the wooden surface of the table for a minute, then looked back up. "No," she said. "I thought about Southport then, because I know it from when I was alive." A small smile. "But I didn't go anywhere. I think it's still somehow connected to you, Lil."

"Well, that's comforting," I said drily. "Just mind that if I ever get any form of love life back, you don't turn up in the bedroom at an inopportune moment."

"Yeurgh," said Kitty, "as if." She went back to prodding her cup experimentally.

"How's Dad?" I asked Mum.

"Absolutely fine," said Mum. "Honestly. He started picking up again a few days after your last visit. You'd never know he'd been poorly, now. It's a bit strange, but I'm learning not to question these things. He doesn't know I'm seeing you today, mind." She smiled at me. "I wasn't sure how well you were managing the whole 'pretending to be human' thing," she did the little rabbit-ear finger moves for emphasis, "and thought it would be easier to come on my own, just this once. And I'd have had a job explaining Kitty to him."

"Good afternoon, ladies." We all looked up at once to see Nik standing at the end of the table. "Ah," he said, seeing Kitty, "I forgot about you." As he said it, Jonny—Shrewsbury's resident revenant and, more importantly, Kitty's ex-boyfriend—appeared from behind him.

"Oh," said Jonny. He stepped backwards slightly. His reticence was understandable, given that Kitty had thrown a very heavy statue at him the last time they'd met.

I looked across at my aunt, who was clearly fighting many different thoughts at once. "You could go back to the flat," I suggested.

Kitty was looking thoughtful. "No," she said slowly, not taking her gaze off Jonny. "Jonny and I have things we need to discuss." The look on Jonny's face suggested he'd rather not discuss anything, thank you very much, but Kitty was already getting up from the table. I put my hands over our empty coffee cups, just in case.

"Then I shall join these fair creatures," said Nik, sitting down next to Mum, "and wait for you here. Have fun, children." We all stared silently as Kitty took Jonny's arm and marched him down the nearest row of market stalls until they were out of sight. "I do hope they don't break anything," sighed Nik.

I looked across the table and saw Mum staring at Nik, her face a mask of concentration. "I know you," she said to him.

"I very much doubt that, my dear," he replied, smiling politely. "I've been dead these last two centuries. Nikolaus Silverton, at your service." He held out his hand and Mum shook it politely, a mask of confusion across her face.

"My parents had a painting of you in their hallway," she said, doggedly. "I'd recognise you anywhere."

Nik scowled at me. "I warned you, Lilith," he said. "This is why I don't go anywhere. I hope you will advise Eadric of his mistake."

"Mum isn't just anyone," I said. Out of the corner of my eye, I saw her preen slightly. "She sees things other people don't notice. Your secret's safe with her."

"I've got some of your books," Mum ploughed on. I stared at her. I still hadn't figured out who Nik had been in his human life, yet here was my mother telling him she was a big fan, got all his work. She'd be asking for his autograph next. "Maybe you could sign them for me one day." Bingo.

Nik laughed. "I don't think my signature would pass muster, these days," he said. "Any antique bookseller worth their salt would point out that the pen used would be too modern for the author himself to have ever used it."

Mum sighed. "I hadn't thought of that," she said. "Fancy, though," she went on, her face brightening up, "you being a friend of our Lil's!"

"Claire Fenton thinks he's my boyfriend," I told her. "We bumped into her before I came to meet you. So let's just hope she's not a fan of ancient literature, or whatever it is mister fancypants here was into."

"You mean you don't know?" asked Mum, incredulously. She looked from me to Nik and back again. "He's—"

"He's desperately wanting to get back home to Liverpool, is what he is," interrupted Nik. "It's been a joy," he took Mum's hand and actually *kissed* it, "but I am afraid we have urgent business to attend to. Don't we, Lilith?"

"I, erm, yes, I guess we do," I replied, struggling to drag my eyes away from my mother, who I swear was about to faint like some pre-teen Harry Styles super-fan. "We've got to find Jonny and Kitty first, though."

"I think Kitty will find you," said Nik, "wherever you are. She and Jonny clearly have plenty to talk about."

I just bet they bloody do, I thought. "Yeah," I said, "we'd better go. Sorry it was such a quick visit, Mum."

"It's absolutely fine, love," she said, still gaping at Nik. "Perhaps...*Nik?*" he nodded, "could come with you again, next time you visit."

"Or perhaps you would like to visit us, Helen," said Nik, as he got to his feet. "I could give you a tour of our offices. Lilith keeps pets on the roof, I'm sure she'd love to introduce you to them." I glared at him. As if I was going to take my mother to the top of the Liver Building and introduce her to the residents. *Oh hi mum, I'd like you to meet Bella! Yes, she is an enormous metal sculpture, you're right. But she doesn't let that stop her making the most of city life! Don't mind Bertie there, he's a grumpy sod.*

"It's a good job you're already dead, Nikolaus Silverton," I growled. He just grinned in response.

We walked out of the market hall together. There was still no sign of Kitty, but I was pretty sure Nik was right and she'd reappear when it suited her. Or when Grimm demanded his supper, whichever came first. Mum walked back with us to where I'd left the Alfa, saying she'd parked her own car further down the road. "Wow," she said, when she saw what I was driving. I rooted the keys out and unlocked it with a grin. "Bloody hell, Lil," Mum said, "don't let your dad see this. You'd never get it back. Now," she hugged me, "don't leave it so long next time." She turned to shake Nik's hand. "And it's been an absolute pleasure to meet you, George."

Nik's gaze flickered, but he shook her hand firmly. "Likewise, Helen," he said with a smile. "And I meant it about visiting. The invitation's always open." I folded my arms and watched in despair as my mother fluttered excitedly, before turning and walking off down the hill.

"Get in the car, *George*," I said. Nik winked and slid down into the passenger seat. I stalked around to the driver's side and got in silently. I wasn't going to

128

give him the satisfaction of asking. He could keep his stupid bloody secrets. See if I cared.

Fight The Power

The drive from Shrewsbury back up to Liverpool was uneventful, if you discount the screeching emitted by me and Nik when my dear departed aunt suddenly reappeared. We'd just got to the A55 junction between Wrexham and Chester, and I was carefully negotiating the confusing filter lanes when Kitty popped up in the rear view mirror without warning. *"Jesus FUCKING Christ will you stop doing that!"* I howled, gripping the Alfa's steering wheel in panic. Nik stared straight ahead in grim silence, but his jaw was clenched tight enough for me to see the muscles twitching in his neck.

"What a lovely evening," Kitty said, gazing out of the window at the sunset and happily ignoring me. I glanced in the mirror and saw that not only did she have a smile on her to rival the Cheshire Cat, the flowers were back in her hair.

"Someone had fun, then," I observed drily. "Made it up with Jonny, have you?"

"Might've," said Kitty. "Haven't decided yet. Ooh, we're near Chester! I haven't been there in years."

"And we're not going there now," said Nik. "Dreadful place." With that, he leaned back against the head rest and closed his eyes.

"So what's going on with loverboy, then?" I asked Kitty. "Spill the tea, you terrible old woman."

"Might I remind you I'm only three years older than you, Lilith O'Reilly," she said. "So less of the old woman, thank you very much."

"That's a bit mad when you think about it," I said. I glanced in the mirror in order to move lanes and saw she was fastening her seatbelt, which was a headfuck in and of itself. Presumably a ghost would just be able to teleport themselves out of any road accident, whatever the damage. That said, if Kitty really was becoming fully visible, then it was better if she did at least try to appear human. I wouldn't like to have to explain my magically disappearing passenger to any random road cop who decided to stop me. "You're my mum's aunt, but she's getting on for twice your age."

"If you think that's the strangest thing that's happened round here recently," said Kitty, "then you're not very observant. If you don't mind me saying." She went back to staring beatifically out of the window and I just concentrated on getting us back to Liverpool in one piece.

***

Officially called the Queensway Tunnel, the subterranean connection between Liverpool and Birkenhead was opened in 1934 by King George V and is still the longest road tunnel in the UK. I prefer it to the much newer Wallasey tunnel (aka the Kingsway), because it pops you back out right into town, opposite the row of excessively grandiose buildings that house the city library and museums. "I'll never get my head around the things modern engineering can do," said Nik, as we drove through the tunnel. It was the first time he'd spoken since Chester. He pulled himself upright in his seat and peered forward through the windscreen. "We're *literally* at the bottom of the riverbed," he said. "Imagine that."

"We're underneath the riverbed," I pointed out, "not at the bottom of it." I knew all about the construction of the tunnel. This was because I'd once said to Dad how clever it was that they could put a road in a tube, low enough down in the river for ships to avoid scraping along the top. In my defence, I was about eleven at the time. And even then I did actually know how tunnels are bored through bedrock underneath water, because we'd once watched a Discovery channel documentary about it. But half asleep in the back of my parents' car after a day out in Crosby, I'd imagined us driving through a long, snaking tube that was laid out through the sediment and river weed, from one side of the Mersey to the other. Dad had laughed so hard he shook, so it was lucky Mum was driving at the time. But I could see her head shaking with the effort of not snorting out loud. I'd rapidly woken up properly and realised what I'd said. But however much I insisted I did know how tunnels work, it had been a running joke from then on that the Mersey tunnels were basically giant underwater hoses, with cruise ships and ferries alike having to be careful not to knock against them in case the water leaked in.

There was barely any traffic on the roads as I drove up and out of the tunnel. The heatwave was still showing no sign of breaking, and the night air was hot and sweet as I turned left onto Dale Street. Kitty disappeared again as we dropped down into the Liver Building's subterranean entrance, so it was just me and Nik locking up the Alfa. "George, huh?" I said to him as we walked towards the exit that would take him up to the tower and me back out onto the street. "You don't look like a George to me."

"I never *was* a George," said Nik, "not really. It was my birth name, but it didn't suit me then and it doesn't suit me now. The version of me that was alive and creating endless drama all those years ago was just a front. I was scared of who I might really be, underneath the glossy surface." I stopped walking and stared at him. "What?" he said, coming to a halt a few paces ahead and turning to face me.

"I think that's the most personal information you've ever given me," I said.

Nik shifted uncomfortably on the spot. "Well," he said eventually, "you're a good listener. And you're clearly here to stay. So maybe it's time I gave in to the inevitable and just accepted you."

"You didn't accept me before?" I asked, in mock offence. "The very cheek."

Nik grinned. "There's still enough of George left in me," he said, "to occasionally resent someone else being the centre of attention. But I'm getting used to it. And I'm getting used to you, Lilith. I think I might actually like you. A tiny bit."

"I'm honoured," I said drily. "But for what it's worth, Nikolaus Silverton, I like you too. I think."

To my utter surprise, Nik held his fist out to me. After a moment's confusion, I bumped it with my own. "Friends?" said Nik.

I grinned. "Friends."

***

I got back to the flat to find Kitty already installed on the sofa and Grimm happily eating his supper from a bowl on the kitchen worktop. He was supposed to eat on the floor, but maybe Kitty hadn't quite worked out how to put the bowl down without dropping it. Although, given the way things had been going recently, I had to consider the possibility that Grimm might have learned to put it back up onto the counter himself. I decided not to think about that too much and left him to it. Heading into the living room, I flopped down into the armchair and glared across at Kitty. "Alright, Doctor fucking Who?"

"I can't imagine what you might possibly be talking about, Lilith," said Kitty.

"Don't give me that, you insane woman," I said. "You've taken to bloody *teleporting*, for chrissakes! Since when was *that* normal behaviour?"

"Since when did the supernatural have to conform to normality?" I belatedly noticed that Kitty had a copy of the *Echo* in her hands. "And since when could you pick up a newspaper?"

"You'd be amazed by what I can do these days," she said. She waggled her eyebrows alarmingly.

"You are a vile and horrible creature," I said. "I hope you realise that." With one last waggle, she raised the paper up in front of her face. I was just reaching for my phone to let Eadric know I still had the keys for the Alfa and maybe I'd be keeping them a while, thank you very much, when it started ringing.

"Hey Iz," I said, wedging the phone under my chin and heading into the bedroom. Revenants might not sweat, but we get coffee stains down ourselves like any normal person. Actually, most of them probably don't—I've certainly never seen Eadric Silverton looking anything other than perfectly presented, even in extremis—but some of us like to get down with the mortals and still appreciate a decent espresso. Okay, so maybe that's just me. Switching Izzy to speakerphone, I let her talk while I found myself some clean clothes.

"Hey dead girl," she said, "survived the big, bad city, then?"

"I already live in a city," I pointed out, "and I'm already dead."

"True, true," she agreed. I found a pair of pyjamas in the laundry pile—the clean pile rather than the dirty one, although sometimes it was admittedly hard to tell the difference. I gazed around at clothes draped over everything and my makeup and hairbrushes scattered across the dresser, and wondered—not for the first time—why I hadn't developed an innate elegance alongside immortality. "So anyway, it turns out Damon's parents are visiting him tomorrow and he'd like me to meet them." Taking my crumpled clothes off, I lobbed them half-heartedly at the laundry bin on the other side of the room. Most of it hit the target, but my t-shirt sailed out through the window.

"*Shit.*"

"What's the problem?" asked Izzy. "I've been seeing him for ages now, why wouldn't I meet his parents?" Pulling my pyjamas on quickly, I stepped over to the window and peered out to where Billy sat in his usual spot opposite Flora's. Spotting me, he reached an arm up and lazily waved my t-shirt in the air.

"Fuck*sake,*" I said, "what an *idiot.*"

"Excuse me?" Izzy sounded indignant, and I hurried to pick the phone up as I realised the confusion. "Just because you can't get yourself a boyfriend, Little Miss Undead Princess."

"I wasn't speaking to you," I said. "I just did something stupid."

"Oh," she said. "Anything I should know about?"

"No," I sighed, "nothing major." I stopped in my tracks as I belatedly realised what she'd said. "And what do you mean, I can't get myself a boyfriend?" I reached underneath the bed to pull out my slippers. I couldn't feel the cold anymore, but somehow it still felt weird walking around outside with nothing on my feet. Elizabeth had wandered happily barefoot around Highgate Cemetery without appearing to give it a second thought, but then Highgate was probably less likely to harbour lurking dog turds than

Harrington Street. Doggy-do between the toes is still grim AF, even when you're an undead creature of the eternal night. As I pulled the slippers on, I noticed my nail polish was wearing off my toenails where they'd been pressing against my sneakers. I couldn't remember exactly, but was pretty sure it had been Easter the last time I'd painted my nails. It was August now, yet they'd stayed determinedly short and neat. Maria Silverton had once told me how her hair had been shaved off during her time at Brownlow workhouse, but by the time I'd met her, she had heavy chestnut curls down past her shoulders. She'd said at the time that things like hair and nails still grew, just with glacial slowness. By my reckoning, it had taken her the best part of a hundred and fifty years to grow it back. Which kind of dwarfed the wailing I used to do as a human when the hairdresser occasionally cut my fringe too short.

"Of course you could," Izzy soothed, "if you really wanted to."

"How do you know I even want a boyfriend?" I peered at my reflection in the hazed mirror above my dressing table. I was by now several months into immortality, but the silver rings around my irises still gave me a start occasionally. Amazingly, no one had ever asked me about it. Izzy said people probably just assumed I was an ageing emo with a taste for naff contact lenses. Apparently she'd meant it comfortingly, but as I was currently being reminded, Izzy cared about as much for verbal filters as she did for people who supported blood sports. And Izzy considers a session with the local hunt saboteurs a fun day out.

"Girlfriend, then," she said. "Heard from Laura recently?"

I glared at the phone. "No, I have not," I said. "As you well know." Laura and I had drifted apart long before I'd died, in that slow, tedious way that laid no blame on anyone whilst also not really having any closure. We just gave up bothering. The only thing approaching so much as a sniff of romance since then had been my abortive date with Sean. And the less said about Sean right now, the better. "I need to go rescue my clothes," I said. "Was there actually a point to this conversation?"

"A'right, mardy," said Izzy, not sounding the slightest bit actually offended. "I just want to know if you can man the fort in the morning, while I go meet the in-laws. Woman the fort. Undead it. Whatever."

"I'm sure I can manage," I said. "See you at lunchtime?"

"Absolutely," she said. "Be with you by one. You're the best zombie pal a girl could have, you know that?"

"I am," I agreed. But she'd already gone.

***

"Nice shoes," said Billy, as I walked over.

I looked down at the ragged bunnies that adorned my feet. The slippers had been a cheap impulse buy more than a year earlier and were already at least six months past the point where they should have been consigned to the trash. Their ears now drooped sadly and their fluffiness was long-deflated, but I liked them. "Warm feet, warm heart, as they say."

"Does anyone actually say that?"

"No idea," I said, holding my hand out for the t-shirt. "But they probably should."

Billy twirled it on the end of his finger before sending it flying towards me with a flick of his wrist. "Didn't have you pegged as a fan of the big man," he said, as I caught the t-shirt and tucked it into my waistband. It took me a second to realise he was referring to the quote on the shirt.

"Well," I said, "a working class hero is always something to be. Don't you think?"

"I preferred his later stuff," said Billy.

"I'd have thought the skiffle period was more your scene," I teased. "Before they went mainstream."

"Nah," said Billy. A lopsided smile creased his face. "He was a pain in the backside back then. Fell over me after he'd had a skinful one night, up on Whitechapel. I gave him a kicking, but he never held it against me. Liked him much better later on. When he was doing the softer stuff." A pause. "Shame about what happened."

"Yup." I said. "And thanks. I forget my own strength sometimes."

"It's growing, isn't it?" Billy looked up at me, his head tilted quizzically.

"What's growing?"

"Your power." He smiled again. "It's interesting."

"I don't know what you're talking about," I said. "I'm no different from always. Well," I reconsidered, "no different from when I first died, anyway."

"That's what you think," said Billy. "The rest of us maybe see it more than you do. It's a good thing," he went on, "so don't be worrying about it."

"I wasn't worried at all until you brought it up," I said.

Billy leaned his head back against the wall and smiled up at me beatifically. If anyone was changing, it was him. Gone was the hollow-eyed, generically blank look of the rough sleeper. In its place was a friendly, open expression and a pair of the greenest eyes I'd ever seen. "Something's happening," he said. "Not just to you. To the city, as well. It's waking up."

"This city never went to sleep in the first place," I said. "It wouldn't know how to if it tried."

"Don't divert the conversation, Red," Billy said. "You must be able to feel it." I thought for a minute about everything that had happened over the last few months. About Mab and Elizabeth and Ivo, and how they all seemed to accept—for good or bad—that I was somehow connected to everything. And also about the power I'd felt washing over me down in the cavern underneath the Cavern, months earlier. Coming face to face with the spirit of the city itself had been terrifying and exhilarating, all at once.

"Yes," I said finally. "I can feel...something."

"Some say you're the catalyst," he said. "That it was your arrival that started things."

I'd heard this one before and it was getting boring now. "Yeah," I said, "so I keep being told. But as I keep reminding people, I'm just a cafe owner from Harrington Street. Average woman, average cafe, average street. Nothing exciting about any of it."

"You're *dead*, Red," said Billy, as if I didn't already know. "Average women don't keep on running cafes after they've died."

"Look," I said, "we all know that my death was an accident. An accident caused by a stupid bloody vampire with not enough spatial awareness to keep from knocking me off the fire escape. Sometimes, Billy," I raised an eyebrow at him, "shit just *happens*."

"And triggers an unexpected chain of events," he said stubbornly. "Come *on*, Red!" He gestured at the street around us. "I've been on this street for more than a century, but you're the first undead shopkeeper I've ever met. Okay," he'd clearly seen the look on my face, "the first undead cafe owner. Mapp's had the bookshop a while, I'll grant you that. But he stayed up on Renshaw Street for decades and we barely saw him or his friends. And the Silvertons rarely showed themselves. It's only recently they've all started coming out of the woodwork. And by recently," he shrugged at my frown, "I mean since you woke up dead."

"You knew," I said, "didn't you?" Billy looked up as I frowned down at him. "You knew I was dead—undead," I corrected, "from the minute I woke up in the car park. When you stopped to ask if I was okay."

"Well," he said, "I had an idea you might be. Couldn't be sure for a while, like. It's not something that happens very often. So I decided to just keep my head down and wait. Remember the next day, when you came back from killing that bloke down at the docks?" I nodded. Accidentally killing a would-be rapist might have been understandable under the circumstances, but the speed and force with which I'd done it had come as a shock, even to me. It had been my first inkling that things maybe weren't quite right. And I'd come back to Harrington Street and told Billy all about it. Which, given we'd barely spoken before that, had perhaps been another sign that something was different. "You just sat down here," he patted the folded sleeping bag that lay on the pavement next to him, "and told me all about it. Almost manic, so you were. And you had that glint in your eyes."

"Your own eyes have changed," I said, deciding it was high time I pushed back, "and you were already dead. So what's that all about?"

Billy shrugged, which seemed to be his current go-to response to just about everything. "Told you," he said, "things are changing. We're *all* changing, Red. You and me, the Silvertons, everyone. The power is growing, and it's affecting us all. It's been growing since the day you woke up dead. Ivo Laithlind certainly noticed it."

"He's not the Messiah," I said, "he's just a very naughty boy." Billy looked confused. "It's an old quote," I said, wondering where on earth it had popped up from. "Ivo's more likely to be the reincarnation of Beelezebub himself."

"There's no Messiah," said Billy, "and no Beelezebub. There's just us, Red. The ones who can't die."

"Not that I enjoy pointing out the obvious," I said, "but we *did* die. It's just that for whatever reason, our mortal forms still exist in some way."

"Why do you think that is?" he asked.

"Is this a trick question?"

"No," said Billy. He had a strange expression on his face that I could only describe as yearning. "It's a genuine one. Because I really don't know, and I'd like to."

"Well," I said, "when I find out, I'll be sure to let you know." I'd originally assumed Billy had been hanging around as a ghost because he'd been murdered in his early thirties, rather than dying peacefully in his sleep as an old man, like he should have. I was pretty sure I hadn't been the only person who'd assumed that once his killer had been identified, he'd waft off this earthly plain in a cloud of peaceful doves or whatever, never to be seen again. But then we'd discovered that the guilty party had almost certainly been a then-mortal Maria Silverton and, even though I'd lopped off her evil little head, Billy was still here. So it must be something else tying him to Harrington Street. I just had no idea what. Kitty was also still here, of course, but I strongly suspected dear old Jonny M might be the reason for her continued spectral existence. And as he was also dead as a doornail, Kitty would presumably be going nowhere. Which I was pleased about, because I'd kind of got used to having the company.

"You hanging round for a while now?" I thought Billy meant right that minute and opened my mouth to say no, I was going back inside, but he beat me to it. "Here, I mean," he nodded to the street. "You're not planning to move somewhere safer?"

"I'm not going anywhere," I said, only realising the absolute truth of it as the words came out of my mouth. "This is *my* city, Billy. I might not have been born here, but it's mine now and I belong here. Mab knows where I am if she wants me."

"Good," said Billy. "I'm pleased." He pulled the sleeping bag over himself and settled back against the wall, for all the world like someone who actually needed to sleep. "Night, Red," he said. "See you in the morning."

Never Trust A Man Who Doesn't Wear Socks

The next day dawned sunny, and it was already noticeably warm by the time Grimm started shouting to be fed. He'd already pulled today's breakfast of choice out of the cupboard and was sitting next to it with an expectant look on his face as I walked into the kitchen. I tipped it out into the bowl and put it back down on the floor. He glared up with what was definitely an attempt at an indignant expression. "Cats don't eat on the worktops," I told him. "Not even spooky ones." He made a huffing noise, but then decided breakfast was more important than arguing and settled down to eat. I stabbed at the coffee machine until it begrudgingly delivered me a cup of espresso and took it out onto the fire escape. Billy's sleeping bag marked his territory, but the man himself was nowhere to be seen. I was idly wondering if he could teleport himself in the same way as Kitty and if so, where he might go, when someone walked into view from the John Street end.

"Good morning," said David Mansoor, from below me. He was dressed in a dark, short-sleeved shirt over matching trousers that were short enough to show his bare ankles. *Never trust a man who doesn't wear socks*, my mum always said.

I frowned down at him. "Can I help you?"

"Perhaps we could talk?" said David politely. "I was perhaps a bit too forceful the last time we met. I would like to apologise." He was talking loudly in order to be heard from a distance, which meant he didn't know as much about me as he seemed to think. Revenants never need hearing aids, put it that way. Deciding it might be prudent to leave him misinformed wherever possible, I made a show of sighing, before getting up and sauntering slowly down the steps. Stopping halfway—no need to make him feel *too* confident—I leaned against the handrail and sipped my coffee.

"What would you like to talk about?" I asked.

David shifted uncomfortably. "Perhaps we could go somewhere more private?" he said.

I looked up and down the empty street before turning my gaze back to him. "This is private enough for me," I said. "Anything you've got to say to me, you can say here."

He didn't look convinced, but clearly realised he wasn't going to get anywhere and decided to plough on. "As I said a few days ago," he said, "I would like to re-run your health check. As an apology for my original failures."

"No need to apologise," I said. "I hadn't given it another thought." Which was true. The day David tried and failed to get a reading on his monitoring devices in the backroom of his Castle Street pharmacy had been, I later realised, the first day of the rest of my afterlife. No wonder he hadn't been able to find my pulse—it was already practically nonexistent. I'd actually put a fair amount of time into researching my own bodily functions in the intervening months—what can I say, even the undead need hobbies—and discovered that I *did* still have a pulse. It was just that it only actually popped up maybe once an hour or so. There had then followed a very geeky session with a calculator and a pen and paper, during which I figured out that, assuming a revenant had the same maximum amount of heartbeats as an average mortal, I could potentially expect to last nearly four hundred thousand years. At which point I'd needed a little lie down, because the thought of potentially outliving the entire planet had made my head hurt. Although at least people like David Mansoor wouldn't be around to annoy me by that point. The thought cheered me slightly.

"Anyway," he said, "perhaps you would like to come with me now and we can do it before you have to..." he paused, as if fact-checking, "open your cafe."

"No thanks," I said.

David clearly hadn't been expecting a flat refusal. "It will only take a few moments," he insisted. "Back in a jiffy, as they say."

I'd had enough. "Why are you so determined to check my pulse, David?" I asked, slowly walking down the steps towards him. He took an automatic step backwards before realising what he was doing and stopped.

"Just being neighbourly," he said, but the tension in his jawline betrayed his nerves. "Wouldn't want to lose my reputation amongst the great and good of Liverpool. Ha!"

"I'm neither great," I said as I got closer to him, "nor good." The part of David's brain that was forever a squeaky prey animal took over, and he stepped backwards. "I think it's time you left."

"You okay, Red?" I heard Billy behind me. He came to stand by my right shoulder. "Is this man annoying you?"

David looked genuinely nervous now, and he put his hands up to protest. "No, no," he said, "I was just leaving. I thought maybe I could assist Miss O'Reilly here. But she clearly has things under control."

"That's more than you have, mate," said Billy. "You look a bit sweaty, if you ask me." He wasn't wrong—dark patches were beginning to appear in the armpits of David's neatly pressed shirt and beads of sweat were visible on his upper lip. "You should probably go have a sit down for a while. It would be unfortunate if you developed heatstroke and started imagining things that weren't actually there, don't you think?"

"I was just trying to help Lilith," said David, but he was already backing away. "If I don't help her, then others will take matters into their own hands. You mark my words."

"Your words are duly marked," said Billy, and I wondered why he was speaking so carefully and politely. Right now, it was like standing next to Jeremy Paxman when he was particularly irked by a team faffing around on University Challenge. "Now we'd appreciate it if you buggered off." A sweary Paxman. David backed away a few more steps, before turning to walk off at a pace more usually seen in those weird walking races at the

Olympics.

Turning to face Billy, I narrowed my eyes. "What's going on?"

"How do you mean?"

"Your voice," I said. "You don't usually speak as though you're presenting the bloody news."

He looked sheepish. "Don't you like it?" I raised an eyebrow. "I've been having fun improving myself," he said, gesturing down at himself. He was still wearing the same sort of clothes he always had, they just looked a lot more expensive than they had the day before. I gazed down at his feet, which were clad in a pair of new-looking walking boots. Before I could stop myself or even think about what I was doing, I bent down and poked Billy's left foot. The shoe was absolutely real—leather and canvas stitched over the top of heavy ridged soles. But I was pretty confident Billy hadn't been shopping at that outdoor clothing store over on Church Street, however conveniently local it might be.

"How does it work?" I asked, straightening up to look at him.

Billy shuffled on the spot, his cheeks pinking slightly. "I don't know," he said. "And that's the truth. I just saw them in the shop window and got to thinking how they'd look better than the ones I had on." Billy had been wearing worn out boots for as long as I'd known him, complete with flapping sole on one foot. "Next thing you know, I look down and there they are. Right on my feet."

"But also still in the shop window?"

He nodded. "Like magic, so it was." I grinned at the return of his distinct Irish twang. "What?" he asked, blushing again.

"I really do prefer your normal voice, for what it's worth."

Billy appeared to consider this for a minute. "So do I," he finally said. "For what it's worth."

I shook my head. "I'm pretty sure I'll never get my head around all this weirdness," I said. "All my human life I thought I had a pretty decent handle on how the world worked, and it turns out everything I ever thought I knew was wrong."

"Nah," said Billy with a grin, "it wasn't wrong. You just didn't know the half of it."

"You're telling me," I said. "These days, most of my friends have walked straight out of a book of children's fairytales. And the local pharmacist thinks he's some kind of, I don't know. An investigator for *Most Haunted*, maybe."

Billy looked dubious. "I don't think he's that naïve," he said. "He knows something. Or suspects, at least."

"He's just a pharmacist," I said. "There's not much he can do if I refuse to play his silly games."

"True," said Billy. "Maybe he'll try telling someone about you and end up sectioned." He sounded hopeful.

"Never mind the local weirdos," I said. "What are your plans for the day?"

"Thought I'd change it up a bit," Billy grinned. "Y'know. Do a bit of sitting outside Flora's, mebbe wander round to Mathew Street to see whether Ifan's been outed yet."

"It's only a matter of time," I said, turning back towards the fire escape. "No one as famous as Ifan can sit on one of the busiest streets in the city for long without being recognised."

"I dunno, Red," said Billy, "he's managed a good few months now. Just goes to show," he sat on his pile of blankets, "people don't see what's right under their noses."

***

Billy stayed on his pitch for most of the morning, curled up facing the wall as I served customers and cleared tables. Flora's wasn't as busy as it had been the previous week, so I managed fine on my own and enjoyed the distraction of normality. The drop in customers was probably down to the weather, which was getting hotter by the day. It hadn't broken any records for Liverpool's highest-ever temperature yet, but the general consensus was that it was only a matter of time. I went out to have a chat with Billy during an early afternoon lull, but he wasn't there. *Probably gone to annoy Ifan again,* I thought, sitting myself down in his spot and looking back over at Flora's.

He could see pretty much everything from here, I realised. Although I was sitting down on the pavement, the cafe's front window was big enough to give a clear view right past the customer tables and through to the small staff room behind the serving counter. I wondered how often Billy watched me and Izzy at work. Not that I minded. We'd be just about the only activity on the street most of the time, so I couldn't blame him for taking an interest. Looking up, I spotted Grimm in the window of my flat, peering out over what he presumably thought of as his domain. Grimm's domain is actually quite small. He rules my scruffy car park with an iron paw, seeing off rival cats and taking great joy in killing any rodents stupid enough to scuttle onto his territory. Not that he ever eats them, of course. Freshly killed rat is far too downmarket a meal for Grimm, who definitely prefers the expensive trays of ridiculous feline recipes. But he takes enormous joy in torturing them to death, usually before gleefully dumping them beside my bed. If he's feeling particularly generous, he'll leave it on my pillow as a special treat. I rarely go to bed these days—when you don't need to sleep, beds become useful for pretty much one purpose only, and I hadn't had any of that purpose in a very long time—but that doesn't stop it being a shock whenever I spot a tiny bloodied corpse on the white sheets. Clearly sensing my eyes on him, Grimm looked down at me from the window. As I watched, he raised a front paw slowly, before lowering it again. If I was entirely insane, I might have suspected he was giving me a friendly wave. But I'm not, so I just got up and headed back into Flora's. I waved back first though, obviously. I've got *some* manners.

∗∗∗

"There you go," I said to the woman at the counter. "Sorry about the wait."

"It's fine, love," she said. "I'm just pleased to see this place so busy. Almost like the old days again."

"You remember it?" I asked. Flora's had been popular under its previous owner, an Italian man called Marco with the sort of creased and crumpled face that had probably made him look at least eighty since he was in short trousers. I only vaguely remembered Marco from the odd occasion I'd met Izzy at Flora's for a coffee, but anyone who'd ever been a regular seemed to remember him with genuine affection. No one had wanted to take on a cafe on an otherwise empty street after he'd died, so it had lain neglected and empty until I'd come along and opened it up again.

"Course I do," she said. "Older than I look, aren't I?" She grinned. "Had some good times in the place next door as well, I can tell you. Rough as a bear's arse, that place was. Brilliant fun!" She took her coffee and pastry and went to sit with a friend at the window table. I knew exactly where she meant. There'd once been a nightclub in the basement of a building that used to sit next to Flora's, pretty much on the spot where Basil was now parked in all his newly shiny glory. I also knew for sure that there wasn't much of it left, because I'd walked through it on my way to an underground date with a furious firebird and a murderous witch. It had been a busy few months. Which was why I was currently getting so much enjoyment out of making coffees and chatting with customers. I still technically worked in Flora's, but my stints behind the counter had become far fewer recently. Not out of choice—it was just that keeping on top of undead politics and general weirdness took up more of my time than I'd ever expected. Izzy didn't mind, thankfully, but that was probably as much to do with the pay rise I'd given her as anything else. It had been the least I could do, after she'd dealt so brilliantly with the discovery that her best friend was basically a zombie. And that was *before* she'd realised just how many of the city's other residents weren't entirely what they seemed, either. So yeah, she'd deserved a raise. I thought I'd probably have to hand over all the day to day running of Flora's to her at some point, but I was holding off as long as possible. I *liked* this tiny bit of normality.

I was filling the temperamental dishwasher that sat behind the counter when I felt someone step up to the counter. And it was definitely 'felt' rather than 'saw'. I had my back to the counter and my face in the dishwasher, but I knew he was there as clearly as if I was standing up and looking right into his face. I carried on stacking dishes, putting off the moment I'd have to deal with this fresh problem. Why couldn't I just have *one* day of peace and quiet, for heaven's sake?

"I know you know I'm here," he said. "So what's the point of playing games?"

I sighed as I stood up and slowly turned to face him. "Hello, Ivo," I said. "Coffee, is it? Piece of cake? We've got a very good carrot and walnut sponge in today, everyone says it's—"

"I don't have much time," said Ivo, "so it would be really helpful if you would cut the crap." I did as requested and glared at him instead. "Look," he said, "everything's an almighty mess. We both know that."

"Well there's the understatement of the century, right there," I snapped. "What the fuck are you even *doing* here, for chrissakes?" I stepped forward to the counter and leaned over, so I was less likely to be overheard by the few customers who were sitting at the inside tables. "We all know you're going to go up against Eadric. But why? Why are you doing this?" He stayed silent in the face of my quiet fury. "I was having a *nice day* and you've turned up in the middle of it and now people will start suspecting that I'm in on whatever ridiculous plan it is you've got going on."

"I don't have a plan," he said. "Not when it comes to you or Eadric, anyway."

"So, why are you here?"

"I can't find Mab."

"Tell me something I didn't already know," I sniped. "Did you ever really know what she was up to? Or were you just so quick to assume she'd be useful backup in your ridiculous power struggle that it didn't occur to you to check whether she'd actually be loyal?"

"She *was* loyal," said Ivo. "Right up until the point I told her I wasn't going to agree to anything that might put you at risk."

"Me?" I laughed hollowly. "Since when have you cared about what happens to me? You told me when I came to meet you on Derby Square that you thought Mab would try to attack me at some point."

"I can't control what Mab does," said Ivo, "but I can refuse to get involved with it myself. She asked me to help, and I refused. Called me pathetic and disappeared off into the night."

"When was that?"

"Last night," he said, "around midnight. She'd come to see me at my place on Hope Street. We ended up having a bit of a disagreement."

"I hope the disagreement wasn't expensive," I said drily. Ivo's 'place' is actually a suite of rooms that he keeps reserved at the Hope Street Hotel. The hotel is one of those places that's just expensive enough to feel like a treat, while at the same time being affordable enough for hen parties and illicit affairs.

He gave a wry smile. "I've promised to replace the furniture," he said. "And I'll pay the scaffolding costs. But regardless of my personal embarrassments, Mab is on the prowl somewhere in the city. And I currently have no idea where that might be."

"What is she?" I asked. "Has anyone figured her out yet?" Right at that moment, a group of students came in and headed for the counter. Ivo stood aside to give them room, tucking himself into the corner with his back to the window. Over the heads of the students, I could see Billy back in position outside. He was watching me and Ivo intently. I held up a hand to reassure him everything was under control, but he didn't drop his gaze. After making the students one pot of tea for the four of them and handing over a plate that held one piece of cake and four forks, I turned back to the revenant lurking in the corner. "Ivo Laithlind," I hissed, "I am sick and fucking tired of all this undead bullshit. If you don't tell me everything you know about your rabid little pet, I swear to god I will hunt her down myself and chop her bloody head off, same as I did to her mother."

To my surprise, Ivo appeared to be trying not to smile. "That's the spirit," he said.

"Hey hey!" said Izzy, bouncing in through the front door and propping it open behind her. "God it's hot in here, you need to let some air in! How's my favourite girl?"

"Anyway," said Ivo, stepping backwards to let Izzy through, "I'll be off."

"Oh no you don't," I said, but he was already at the door. "Ivo," I said pleadingly, "I need some answers! You can't keep popping up like this and then just disappearing again, for god's sake."

Izzy looked from me to Ivo and back again. "Something up, Lil?" she asked.

"Not at all," said Ivo smoothly. "I think Lilith is going to be just fine."

"Don't you dare leave," I said. "We have to talk."

"The time for talking is long gone, I fear," said Ivo, stepping out through the doorway. "You need to consider taking action." With that, he disappeared. I watched Billy's gaze follow Ivo as he presumably headed in the direction of the river, before turning back to me and raising his hands in a '*wtf?*' gesture. I did the same back at him, before turning to where Izzy was already finishing off the dishwasher. She shut the door on it with a thud and pressed the button to start the wash cycle.

"So what gives?" she asked. "That was the bloke you ran after that day, wasn't it? When you were first..." she paused. "Whatever. You know."

"Yeah," I said, "that's him." I'd first met Ivo when he helped me dispose of my would-be attacker, just after I'd died. He'd disappeared before I could question him, only to reappear outside Flora's a day or so later. I'd been so eager to find out what the hell was going on that I'd walked out of Flora's in the middle of a busy lunchtime and left Izzy with only a very confused Sean to help her with the rush. It had definitely been written on Izzy's list of 'things to remind Lil about when she gets annoying'. Probably in thick red marker pen.

"What did he want this time? Thank you," this was to the woman who'd mentioned the nightclub to me, who was putting her empty crockery on the counter. "Hope to see you again soon."

"Oh, I'm sure you will," said the woman. "It's nice to see some life back in the place."

"Isn't it just?" Izzy said with a bright smile. "We're all about making the most of life round here, aren't we, Lil?" I made vaguely agreeing noises and the woman just looked faintly confused. With a last smile and a nod, she and her friend left the cafe.

"Somebody clearly took their sarcasm pill," I said, rounding on Iz.

She grinned back at me. "Not at all," she said, "just doing my best to carpe the fuck out of every diem and all that. You should try it sometime." She took the dirty crockery off the counter and dropped it into the sink with a clatter of china.

"What's that supposed to mean?"

"Lilith," said Izzy as she straightened up to look at me, "you can't escape it. Not this," she gestured around the cafe, "but *this*." Her hands flew up to indicate the wider world. "Something, somewhere, clearly thinks you're in charge. Or that you should be. Thinks you're important, anyway. So," she held my gaze, "maybe it's time you just went with it."

"Went with what, though?" I asked. I'd been so looking forward to a day of normality, but so far I'd been threatened by a weaselly pharmacist and visited by someone who scared and excited me in equal measure. And now my best friend was lecturing me on undead politics, despite being resolutely human herself. I sat down hard on the high stool we keep behind the counter and winced as I felt the metal legs buckle under the force.

"With all of it," said Izzy. She leaned back against the counter with her arms folded and gazed at me thoughtfully. "Look, Lil," she said, "there's no getting away from the fact that you're dead. Dead sexy," she added, as a lone customer sitting near the counter looked up in interest. She lowered her voice. "But also very dead. Dead, but still here. With a whole heap of side characters who seem to think you're the second coming of Bela Lugosi, or something. And there's nothing you can do about it, because clearly none of them are going away. So maybe it's time to think about leaning into it."

"And how would I go about doing that?" I asked. "It's not like anyone wants me to take over, or anything. And I wouldn't want to, anyway. So what am I supposed to do?"

"This woman who's after you," said Izzy. "She's lurking and making you nervous. Don't pull that face, I've known you long enough to be well aware when you're on edge. It makes you twitchy."

I dropped the scowl and sighed. "You know me too bloody well, Isobel Jones," I said.

"Call me Isobel again," said Izzy, "and I'll take a machete to you myself."

"I'm relying on it," I said. "You're my safety net if things get too much."

Izzy frowned. "Well hopefully it won't ever come to that," she said. "But I do think you need to go after Mab. After all," she grinned, "attack is always the best form of defence."

Heart As Big As Liverpool

The rest of the day was, thankfully, absolutely normal. Not one supernatural creature stepped foot through the door to Flora's and both Izzy and I were kept busy with late afternoon customers making the most of Harrington Street being shaded from the sun more than many of the surrounding streets. We even stayed open later than usual, both of us loathe to turf out loitering customers on such a nice day. By the time I'd seen Izzy off and locked up the cafe, it was early evening. I walked round to the mini-supermarket on Lord Street to top up Grimm's food supplies and was surprised by how busy the streets still were. Tucking myself into a doorway, I took a minute to just watch the world go by. The steps of the Victoria monument where I'd met Ivo were barely visible for all the people sitting on them. I watched as a young woman sprawled across the lap of a man who looked more interested in his phone. "He'll lose her," said a voice next to me. I turned to look at Ifan, who was gazing at the couple with a smile on his face. "She'll find someone less easily distracted, you just watch."

"And that would be you, I suppose?" Ifan grinned in response and set off across the square. I didn't doubt that the girl would soon be finding him far more interesting than the current target of her affections. *Yeah,* I thought, *the kids are still alright.*

***

"It'd be nice if things stayed settled," said Kitty, when I finally got back up to the flat. "Just for a while. There's always something dramatic going on

153

around here. It's enough to make my nerves jangle." Grimm was wrapping himself round my ankles in a hopeful manner, so I emptied a tray of food into his dish and left him to it. "You're a ghost," I reminded her, as I walked into the living room. She was curled up on the sofa with her legs tucked up beneath her and her arms clasped tightly round her knees. "Ghosts aren't supposed to be nervous. Anyway," I flopped down into the armchair, "it's getting late. Everything's settled down for now. Let's leave the fretting til tomorrow." Which was, of course, the point at which the shit well and truly hit the fan.

Suddenly there was a frantic hammering on the back door. Grimm shot past me and leapt into the safety of Kitty's arms as I raced into the kitchen and ripped the door open. Heggie was hitting it in such a frenzy that he fell in on me. I caught him and we swung around the kitchen, looking for all the world like the strangest double act to ever appear on *Strictly Come Dancing*. Even in my panic, I registered that he was far heavier than I'd ever expected. It felt as though he was hewn from rock rather than being some form of human. I'd never really worked Heggie out, but right now, he was hyperventilating in the middle of the room—a pretty neat trick for someone I was pretty sure didn't actually need to breathe. "I can't find him," he was gabbling, "nowhere, he's nowhere, oh ohhh where is he doyouknowwhereheispleaseohplease—"

"ENOUGH," I said, the sudden shock enough to bring out The Voice. Heggie froze, his wailing cutting off sharply as if someone had pressed a hidden mute button.

"What's going on here, then?" said Kitty from the living room door. Grimm perched on her right shoulder like a witch's familiar, perfectly balanced and utterly unruffled.

"I have no idea," I said, "but I suspect I'm not going to like it." I put a hand on Heggie's shoulder and he jerked in fright. "I'm not going to hurt you," I said. "You came to me, remember?"

Heggie shook himself down like a small animal who'd been out in the rain. He looked up at me with pleading eyes. "I can't find Mapp," he said. "He's not anywhere and I need to find him I need to—"

"Okay," I interrupted, "so you've lost Mapp." Heggie nodded silently. "But

154

you go out without him all the time," I said, "so why is it such a panic now?"

"You don't understand," said Heggie, shaking his head. "He was coming back we were going to have an evening together and we had plans and I went to the shop and he wasn't there and I thought he might be here but he isn't and I don't know—"

"That's enough." I said sharply. Heggie's eyes widened, but he shut up and stared at me, his eyes wide. *"Where does he go?"*

"Who is that," asked Kitty, "and what have you done with Lilith?"

I turned to glare at her. *"You'll do well to remember who you're speaking to, woman,"* I said. We stared at each other in mutual horror.

Kitty broke first. "I'll remind you that I'm not any old woman," she said archly. "I am your aunt. And as your aunt, I am telling you now that I'm not sure what's going on in that head of yours, but this ain't you, Lilith O'Reilly."

How dare she question us? The voice said inside my head. *She thinks she knows better than us. Perhaps we should prove her wrong.* "NO!" I yelled. Heggie and Kitty both stepped backwards away from me. I looked up slowly to find them both staring at me. Grimm was on top of Kitty's head, his back arched and his claws digging into her scalp. For a long, insane second, I wondered why it wasn't hurting her. Then I remembered she was dead, which set me off laughing.

"What's going on, Lilith?" asked Kitty carefully.

I got myself under control and straightened up, but for some reason she didn't look remotely reassured. "I'm fine," I said firmly. Heggie was looking really scared now. I took a moment to pull my scattered thoughts back together before I spoke again. "Why are you so worried about Mapp?" I asked him. "He's probably out visiting one of his many other...friends."

Heggie visibly winced. "I'm the most important one, though," he said determinedly. "He always says so."

I tilted my head and looked at him, hunched and defensive. *Poor little creature*, said the voice in my head, *so weak and fragile, even for an immortal. Not the sort we want around us, not if we're going to take control. Emotionally vulnerable, wouldn't you say? It would be so easy to break him down and send him away forever. So easy*—"SHUT THE FUCK

UP," I said loudly, clutching the sides of my head. "I'll deal with you later," I said, more quietly this time. I wasn't speaking to anyone except myself, and by the expressions on their faces, both Heggie and Kitty had realised that. "I'm sorry," I said, and now I was talking to them. "I'm not sure what happened then."

"I'd wager you've got someone in that head of yours," said Kitty bluntly. "And not a very nice someone, either." *She has no idea what we've been through*, said the voice. *Or why we're here in your head. But you know, don't you Lilith? You should know why we're here.*

I absolutely did not know why a strange voice was suddenly inside my head, but I wasn't going to admit it. Ignoring the voice—which was just as difficult as it sounds—I turned to Heggie. Fixing my best sympathetic smile onto my face, I took his arm again, and this time was sure to do it kindly. "He's probably gone over to see Missy," I said. "Maybe he just lost track of time."

"Missy's looking for him as well," said Heggie miserably. "I saw her just now. Everything's wrong and Mapp's not here and your voice isn't right and—"

"Come on now," said Kitty, stepping past me towards Heggie, giving me as wide a berth as the narrow kitchen would allow. Putting her arm around the little man, she turned to me with a defiant expression on her face. Grimm was back down on her shoulder and was managing a very good attempt at glaring. "I have no idea what's going on in that head of yours, Lilith O'Reilly," she said sharply, "but I would suggest that you get it under control and go find Gaultier. Heggie's right," she gave his shoulders a squeeze, "it's not like him to disappear entirely. One of us always knows where he is."

Of course they do, said the voice. *They rely on him for everything. He's like their father, just with added*—"STOP IT RIGHT NOW," I yelled. Heggie and Kitty—and a very pissed off-looking Grimm—stared silently from the end of the kitchen. I was between them and the door, I realised, and they desperately wanted to get away from me. I hadn't a fucking clue what was going on in my head, but I clearly needed to sort it out before anyone else had to deal with it. There was a reasonable chance Izzy would fight back out of sheer terror if I did it to her, and she was worryingly handy with sharp implements. "Right," I said, "I'm going to be honest with you both, because I can't think of anything else to do right now. Something is talking inside my head," Heggie leaned even tighter into Kitty, "and I need to figure out what it is." *You already know us, Lilith.* "Because I don't have a fucking clue." *Take that, invisible head-psycho.* "I'm going to go outside and have a good talk to myself in the car park," okay that sounded absolutely insane even to my own ears, "and then I'm going to find Mapp. Heggie," I said, "I'm not going to hurt you." He didn't look convinced. "Stay here until I come back. Okay?" He nodded, but stayed absolutely silent. "Kitty," she looked at me and held my gaze without wavering, "I'm going to try my best to sort this mess out."

"It's all anyone can ask," she said calmly. "I'm sure you know what you're doing, Lil."

I only wished she was right. "Take Heggie into the living room," I said, stepping backwards away from them towards the kitchen door. It was still open, and I stepped out onto the fire escape to give them as much space as possible. "Smoke me a kipper," I said as I left. "I'll be back for breakfast."

Where the fuck did that come from? I wondered, as I vaulted down the fire escape. I knew the quote because Dad used to say it all the time, but I was pretty sure that was the first time it had ever come out of my own mouth. I was relieved to see Billy's spot opposite Flora's was empty. One less potential victim to terrify this evening. I stalked down to the far end of the scrappy wasteland car park and crouched in the darkest corner I could find. "I'm sorry to burst your bubble," I said out loud, "but I haven't a fucking clue who you are. So you'd better explain yourself before I get Izzy to sort the problem out permanently. With a machete."

She'd never do it, said the voice. *And you appear to have your fingers crossed. Fancy thinking you could lie to yourself.* I uncrossed my fingers with a sigh and leaned back against the wall. Looking up at the night sky, I wondered how many stars were above me, hidden from view by the city's light pollution. *There's no need to fear us, Lilith.* The voice was softer now. *Do you really not know who—what—we are?*

"I absolutely do not know what you are," I said, "and I'd tell you to fuck off only there is clearly yet another bloody crisis brewing and I need to look for Mapp pretty fucking quickly. If it's all the same to you."

We're on your side, Lilith. We've been with you since you woke up. I'd woken up on this very car park, wondering how on earth I'd managed to survive a fall from the top of the fire escape. It had taken a while to realise I hadn't. Life—and death—hadn't been the same since.

"Then you're going to have to start being nicer to my friends. And why are you in my head?"

There was a quiet, sad little laugh that sounded like it was coming from far away, but was definitely inside my head. *We're what's made Liverpool the city it is today. We're what gives it such power. We're everyone and everything that has ever been rejected because they didn't fit in. Centuries of love and loss, survival and triumph, neglect and resurgence. We're the city with more soul than any human could ever imagine and a heart big enough to take on the world.* I knew then that it was real.

I'd felt this kind of power only once before, when I'd come face to face with the firebird in the cavern underneath Mathew Street. Anyone who believes their own hometown has the biggest personality has clearly never visited Liverpool. There's an atmosphere in this relatively small city that can't be found anywhere else and it's why so many—including me—turn up for a supposedly temporary stay, then never leave.

"You're not answering my question," I said firmly. If an entire anthropomorphised city was going to take up residence inside my skull then it could bloody well explain why, before Eadric had me disposed of as a threat to the undead community.

He wouldn't dare. There hasn't been one like you until now. Silverton knows it. Everyone knows. Everyone who matters.

"Well Kitty and Heggie clearly don't know," I said, "and they matter to me. So you're going to have to explain yourself." I paused for effect. "Or it'll be Izzy and the machete for all of us."

You wouldn't.

"Try me." I got to my feet. "I'm sick and bloody tired of being a pawn in other people's games. Whoever you are, you're already getting on my nerves. If Izzy says no, then maybe Missy would have a go at exorcising me."

We're here to help you, said the voice hurriedly. **We're part of you, Lilith. And you're part of us.**

"So why has it taken so long for you to show yourself?" I said, walking out onto Harrington Street. It was a warm night and people were still wandering around in twos and threes, some more drunk than others. I thought I heard thunder rumbling in the distance, just on the cusp of hearing. I got to Button Street and stopped. "Izzy lives up there," I said, looking up at the dark windows of my best friend's flat. "I'm sure she'd help me if I asked her."

We *can help you*, said the voice.

"You have to promise not to make me say mean things to my friends."

A pause. Then, **You are not what we expected.**

"Well I wasn't expecting you at all, so I reckon you're still getting the better part of this deal, quite frankly. And you still need to promise."

We will try.

"And you're definitely not a figment of my imagination?"

No.

I sighed. Having myself committed to a psychiatric unit would have been a pleasantly simple alternative to dealing with whatever undead bullshit was clearly lurking in my immediate future. I was pretty sure Eadric could have arranged it. "Are you the voice I use sometimes?" I started walking again, with no actual idea where I was headed. "The one that pops up without warning and scares people?"

No. A brief pause. **That's all you.**

"I don't suppose you can tell me how to control it?"

Nothing for a moment. Then, **You have to accept it, Lilith. Accept that you are it and it is you.**

"I'm getting sick of riddles,"

You'll figure it out, said the voice, **eventually.**

I broke into a run. Suddenly, I knew where I had to go.

***

I made it to Priory Road in record time, even by undead standards. It had taken a while for me to get the hang of moving at speed, but I was finally beginning to manage it. At the beginning of my so-called afterlife I'd often trip over my own feet, purely because I thought too much about the actual process of moving around. You know that feeling of forgetting how to walk when you have to get from one side of a room to the other and people are watching? You've been happily walking around on your own two feet for decades, but suddenly you're consciously thinking about the action of putting one foot in front of the other and how weird it is that your brain usually does all this stuff automatically but now you're actually thinking about it and it's all incredibly complicated…and suddenly you're stumbling on a non-existent fold in the carpet and everyone assumes you've had too much to drink. Turns out that doesn't stop just because you're no longer breathing. About two months into my immortality, Izzy had decided I was finally, just possibly capable of accompanying her out for a drink without too much embarrassment. To be fair to Iz, she'd had to calm nervous customers on several occasions after I'd accidentally done things too quickly for the human eye to see, so I was happy to let her be the judge. She chose Ma Egerton's up by the Empire, on the basis that their clientele was usually either very drunk or just downright theatrical. Her logic was that they were therefore less likely to notice or care about someone acting a bit odd.

Halfway through the evening I went to the ladies' loo to check my makeup and an older lady who was clearly several bottles to the wind barged through the door in a hurry to throw up. Now, if you've ever been into Ma Egerton's, you'll know it has what seems like the tiniest loo entrance that was ever retro-fitted into an old building. I'd been trying very hard to act normal all evening, but spun around so quickly at the woman's unexpected appearance that I pretzel'd my own legs and had to take evasive action. So anyway, it turns out that even really drunk people are a bit shocked by the sight of a thirty-something woman bouncing up onto the top of a toilet door like Spiderman's nervous aunty.

Izzy had informed me I wasn't going to be allowed out in public again until I could prove I had things under control. So, in order to not become the most tragically lonesome undead spinster on the block, I'd spent a few nights down on Otterspool promenade, practicing undead parkour. It wasn't until the third night that I realised it really was the thinking that was getting in my way. I was racing up and down the prom as fast as I could manage, taking different routes each time, because after the first night I'd realised my feet were starting to leave tracks in the concrete pavement. Occasionally Daisy would pop her head up out of the Mersey and wave me on encouragingly. I sometimes thought there were others in the water with her, but they slipped from view before I could see them properly. Around three in the morning, I realised I was now so used to the Otterspool layout that I wasn't having to think about where I was going and instinct was doing the work for me. When an urban fox wandered out of a hedge, I automatically lengthened my stride and zipped over him fast enough to make the fur on his back flatten in the down-draught.

Confidence duly boosted, I'd taken the scenic route home, heading up Jericho Lane and doing a couple of laps around Sefton Park before heading back down to the riverfront via Lark Lane. Other than one surprised milkman who nearly got blown over in front of the Lodge pub, no one seemed to notice me. I'd only risked running in public at full speed once before then. That was on Bold Street, when Mapp and I had been saving people from Maria and urgency had taken over from discretion. But I was slowly realising that humans really didn't believe their own eyes half the time. And I can run *really* fast—fast enough that people assume they'd just felt a rogue gust of wind, rather than five and a half feet of red-haired undead woman pounding past them. So maybe the better option would be to just go at things full throttle, instead of giving anyone—including myself—time to think. I hurdled the cemetery gates and immediately skidded to a halt in the darkness as an awful thought hit me. I looked back towards the locked cemetery entrance.

You entered through the gates, agreed the city.

"I was warned about a gate," I said, definitely trying to convince myself as much as anyone else. "Singular. Those are plural."

Do you really want to waste valuable time querying vampire grammar?

161

"You think it's the vampires, then? They're the source of the threat?"

Danger rarely comes from one direction, said the city, most unhelpfully. *But right now, the vampires are certainly on the move. And if they're on the move, they're on the rise.*

"Vampires, though?" I asked. "Did it really have to be the naffest possible option?" I started walking slowly round towards Missy's house. "And why," I asked grumpily, "are vampires so bloody ugly? I'm sure I'd find their existence far less stressful if even just a few of them made the effort to look like Gary Oldman."

The netherworld isn't a glossy movie, Lilith. It's real and dangerous and it lurks in the shadows. Just waiting to show its teeth.

"That's what I'm worried about."

You worry because you still think like a human.

"That's because I *am* still human," I said. "I just happen to be dead."

It would be easier for you if you gave up being human.

"Ain't never gonna happen."

Then you will have to be braver than most, Lilith. It takes strength to be both a human and a monster.

"So now I'm a monster? Cheers, like."

We're all monsters. Monsters created from experience and memory and cruelty and kindness. Monsters bigger than humanity could ever imagine.

I thought back two days, to when I was standing on the edge of Elizabeth's bedroom in Highgate, still nervous about stepping off into the darkness. "Fuck it." I said. "We'll sort out what's going on right now, and worry about the rest of it later."

Finally, said the city. *We've been waiting for you to wake up.*

"If you're the spirit—*a* spirit—of this city," I said, "you're as tough as old boots. You might *want* my help, but I'm pretty sure you don't actually need it." All the lights in Missy's house appeared to be on and the back door was wide open. I was basically walking into the plot of every terrible horror movie with a lower than twenty per cent rating on Rotten Tomatoes.

You might be surprised.

"I'm spending most of my life being surprised right now," I said, "and honestly, it's getting tedious. Can't I get a break? Just for a while?"

Not until you're in control.

"In control of what?"

The city. And the territory it commands.

I stopped dead in my tracks. "Are you fucking *kidding* me?" I asked, fully aware that if anyone could see me from the house, they'd assume I'd finally lost the very last of my marbles. "Eadric's in control. He always has been."

He was never destined to hold power here. He merely saw a space and stepped in to fill it.

"So he's filling the space," I said. "He can keep it. I'm not interested in anything other than my cat and my cafe. And my friends."

You might not have a choice.

"There's always a choice," I said. "And right now, my choice is to help my friends."

"Who are you talking to?" Alan came out of the kitchen door. He'd replaced the sharp suit with a loose shirt and narrow-cut trousers over what looked distinctly like winkle-picker shoes. His quiff flopped to one side, as if it was too exhausted to stay upright. Humidity clearly affected ghostly hair as much as it did the human version.

"Myself," I said. "I find it's the best way to ensure interesting conversation. Is Missy home?"

Alan squinted at me in confusion. "I thought she'd be with you," he said. "She was fretting about something but deffo didn't want to chat to me like, so I told her to go find you instead. You know stuff, girl." Oh, just fucking *brilliant*. Everyone and their bloody dog had decided I was the font of local spooky knowledge, somehow without ever realising I was simply crashing through life—and death—with absolutely no idea what I was actually doing.

"Have you seen Mapp recently?" I asked. Alan shook his head and his quiff jiggled like half-set jelly. "Why have you got all the lights on?"

He looked up at the house behind him and seemed genuinely surprised to see all the windows glowing brightly. "Shit," he said, "I forgot to turn them off. I was dancing," he said, turning back towards me with a sheepish expression on his face, "and I like to make a grand entrance down the stairs.

I guess I should go switch off my stage lights." I shook my head in wonder. Everybody around me was, quite literally, *completely* mad.

"Yes," I said, "I think you probably should." Alan turned to go back inside, seemingly oblivious to the fact that half his friends had suddenly gone missing. "I'll go look for Mapp, then." Maybe he'd offer to come with me. A bit of moral support would be nice.

"Okay," he said, already back inside the house, "I'll tell Missy you called." And with that, he closed the door.

***

"We need to talk," I said as I headed up towards the catacombs. Although I'd lost both the ability and the need to sweat since the day I first woke up dead, the air was still uncomfortably thick and hot, despite the late hour. The occasional rumbles of thunder were definitely getting closer. I really hoped the weather would break soon, if only to give Alan's poor, wilting quiff a break. Sticking to the paths, I walked at a human pace, not wanting to disturb anyone whose eternal rest was maybe not quite as comfortable as it ought to be.

This is perhaps not the best time.

"There's never a good time to ask an invisible sentient being why it's lurking inside your head," I said.

You—

"I what?"

There is danger ahead.

"Well, that's just fucking peachy," I said. "I've been in danger pretty much constantly since the day I woke up dead and I've just about got to the end of my rope with it all, if you must know." I stopped walking and looked around me. The cemetery was in almost complete darkness, and the air felt heavy under the gathering storm.

You're learning, though. You're learning to control...everything.

"Well I'm clearly not learning how to control you, am I?" I said. I was in the middle of the cemetery now, and the catacombs were visible in the

164

gloom ahead. I thought I could see lights flickering in the one furthest away. Hopefully I'd find Martha having a nicely boring evening. Maybe I could stay for a cuppa with her and Mapp. "Not without threatening violence, anyway."

Violence against yourself, the voice pointed out.

"It'd be worth it," I said, "if it meant you shutting up."

You might yet find us helpful, said the voice. ***But not now. Someone's here.***

The Ethics Of Death

"Good evening, Lilith." David Mansoor stepped out from behind a nearby tombstone. "It's nice to see you again."

"Fuck*sake*," I spluttered. "You must be kidding me." Every time I thought the world couldn't get any more insane, it proved me wrong. Fat drops of rain were beginning to fall and the oppressive atmosphere wasn't helping my mood.

Don't trust him.

"As if I'd ever trust this idiot," I sighed. "He can't even talk to me without breaking into a nervous sweat."

"Who are you talking to?" asked David. "And what do you mean, nervous? Why would I be nervous of you?"

"Oh, come *on*, David," I said, "you're backing away even now!" He stopped shuffling backwards, but was careful to keep his distance. I took a step forward just to mess with him and he visibly flinched. "What *is* your problem?" I said, the last dregs of my patience draining out of my already-frazzled mind. "Why are you so interested in me?"

"I want to help you," he said.

"Help me what?"

"I know...people," he said. "People who are aware of your...situation. People who could help you."

"What if I don't want to be helped?" I asked. "What if I'm perfectly happy with my situation? I don't think you even know what my situation actually *is*, David, if you don't mind me saying."

"You're not normal," he blurted. "You shouldn't *exist*. You should be dead,

166

but you're not. And I keep trying to help you, but you won't let me."

"How is following me around like an annoying fanboy helping in any way?" I saw movement in the trees behind him. Hopefully Mapp had finished chatting with Martha and was heading down for a nosy at the next potential bit of gossip. He could help me give David the bloody pharmacist a dunk in the lake down at Everton Park. Maybe that would shock some sense into him.

"I know people," said David, stubbornly. "People who can *help*."

Lilith—

"Don't *you* start interrupting me," I hissed. "Like who, David?"

"He means us." A voice with the tone of a tenor bell came from the darkness. Before I could do or say anything, the tallest, scariest vampire I had ever seen in all of my undead life stepped out in front of me. He stood next to David, whose face immediately froze into a mask of pure, unadulterated fear. The vampire had to be the best part of seven feet tall and was dressed entirely in black. I was somehow aware that it was human-shaped, but its outline refused to stay fixed in my vision. However much I tried to focus, my gaze slid off it as though on an opposite magnetic pole. It had a human face, I thought, but its features were hidden in the shadows.

"So this is the threat," I said. "The big, scary vampires are trying to take over the city. Would someone like to explain to me why I appear to have been dropped into an episode of Buffy?"

You have to fight, said the voice of the city in my head. **They cannot be allowed to succeed.**

"No shit," I hissed. "Pardon my rudeness like, but you seem to have taken your eye off the ball quite a lot, just recently." Silence. "What the fuck were you thinking, letting this shower of maniacs in?" I'd have sworn I heard an embarrassed cough, somewhere in the depths of my mind.

We didn't realise they were back until it was too late.

"Too late for what?" I asked out loud.

"Who are you talking to, Lilith?" asked David again. "Do you have someone with you?" He looked around the dark cemetery with what looked distinctly like a hopeful expression on his face.

"She has no one with her," said the vampire. "We, however, do." Four more figures emerged from the shadows and ranged themselves behind David and the head vamp. I didn't have to turn around to know there were more behind me, because I could smell them. On the plus side, El Vampo clearly didn't know I had the spirit of the entire city rattling round inside my head. Unfortunately for me, the city in question currently appeared to be shuffling in silent embarrassment.

"You said you were going to help her," said David. "I told you about her because I thought you knew how to fix her. You said—"

"We said no such thing," said the vampire, sharply.

David flinched, but no one could accuse him of a lack of dogged determination. "You know I need her for my research," he said. I wasn't liking the sound of this. "She has to be saved, so I can gather the information—"

"Enough," said the head vampire. He made a zipping gesture with his hand and, to my astonishment, David's mouth snapped tight. By the panicked look on the face of my least-favourite pharmacist, it wasn't voluntary. That would definitely be a useful talent to have, if only to shut Kitty up when she got overexcited and started rambling on about Grimm's endless talents. The rain started in earnest as the vampire spoke, drumming onto the concrete paths and bouncing dust up into the air off the dry grass. "You asked if we could help her," said, "and I said yes. Because we could—if we chose to." He looked at me, then back at David. "We do not choose. This—" the vampire gestured towards me with an attitude of faint disgust, "—*creature* is the reason our kind are being hunted again. She is the reason the revenants know we're here. We were building our power, preparing to take over. And then *she* arrived."

"Excuse me," I interrupted, "but it was one of your lot who kicked off this absolute shitshow in the first place. If that scrawny little rat of yours hadn't pushed me off a building, I'd still be human. Human and happy and working in my cafe without having to worry about what a million and one undead asshats are doing every minute of every bloody day. And you," I turned on David, "need to start choosing your friends better. What the fuck were you *thinking?* Why on earth did you think this bunch of blood-sucking idiots might be any help?"

"I have an interest in the ethics of the afterlife," said David helplessly. "I'm working on a PhD," he actually gave a faintly self-satisfied smile, despite the somewhat tense circumstances, "investigating what constitutes actual human death."

"Well," I said, sourly, "I'd suggest that not breathing and having no pulse is a fairly good indicator. Wouldn't you?"

"No," said David, "and that's why I'm so interested in you. Did you know that even now, the only accurate indicator of human death is active decomposition?" His head bobbed enthusiastically as he warmed to his morbid topic. "We assume it's brain stem death, but who's to say that's correct? Some cultures believe the act of breathing is enough to indicate life, regardless of anything else. People are kept on life support machines for years after their mind is long gone, because their families believe that they're still alive as long as the machines are breathing for them."

"Well, that's all very interesting, David," I said. "But right now, I think we have a rather more pressing ethical dilemma." The other vampires were suddenly closer, yet I hadn't noticed them move. Just to increase the drama levels, there was a sudden loud clap of thunder overhead as I considered my options. There was no way I could take on all the vampires at once, even with my increasing strength.

You must try, said the city.

"That's easy for you to say," I muttered, "you're just a passenger." I was gritting my teeth and trying to decide which one to take out first, when something flew past my head and sent the head vampire flying. I launched myself forward and pulled David out of the way. With a start, I realised the newcomer was the vampire who'd tried to jump me on the way home from Mapp's a few nights earlier. Maybe it was because she was younger, or perhaps she'd just taken the older vampire by surprise, but she was giving as good as she got, despite the size difference. Thunder rolled and the rain spat down as they fought like a pair of gigantic black tomcats. The others didn't move to help—instead, they stayed at a distance, making panicked hissing noises. I wondered why, until I realised my would-be saviour had a bloody great crucifix swinging around her neck. "Well that proves one myth true, at least," I said, pulling David backwards with me until we were safely wedged up against the trunk of a nearby tree. "But I'd love to know how she's managing it."

"Maybe she's been feeding off atheists," croaked David.

"Give him to me, girl." To my absolute astonishment, Al materialised out of the darkness beside me. "I'll hang onto him." Deciding not to question potential help, however unlikely the source, I gave David a hefty shove. Unfortunately, Al was beaten to it by a smaller vampire I hadn't spotted before, who must have been lurking behind the tree. The tiny bloodsucker caught hold of David round his neck and began dragging him backwards at speed. His screaming choked off as they disappeared into the gloom. I turned to go after them, but a yell from the other direction spun me back round just in time to see the bigger vampire rip the crucifix from the girl's neck.

NOW.

Energy suddenly poured into me. It was as though I was possessed by a demon with the strength of twenty undead men and a fury to match.

"LEAVE HER." The two vampires in the centre didn't seem to hear me—or at least, it didn't stop them fighting—but the others backed away slightly. "YOU HAVE NO PLACE HERE." Stepping forward, I spoke again. "HEED ME", I said, my voice booming out across Anfield Cemetery. But there was a flatness to it, as if the sound waves weren't travelling anywhere other than inside my head. I still didn't know how the voice worked, but it did—the vampiric wingmen disappeared as though they were smoke blown away by the wind.

Save her.

I looked down to where the two remaining vampires were still sprawling on the ground. The one I'd met before had somehow managed to pin the giant bloodsucker face down on the path, with his arm wrenched up behind his back. She was struggling, though, and I didn't think she'd be able to hold him for long. He looked fractionally more human now. The edges of his silhouette still danced in my vision, but now I could see him for what he was. I moved forward and stepped on his back, pushing him down hard. Grabbing his repulsive straggly hair, I pulled his head up and backwards. The younger vampire fell backwards onto the ground, hissing quietly to herself in either fear or pain, I didn't yet know which. Gritting my teeth, I yanked the vampire's hair again, putting all my strength into it. There was a sharp, loud crack as his neck broke.

"Aaaaaahhhahaaahaa," he gasped through his twisted windpipe, "you think you're better than us. We're all just darkness come to life, Lilith." Another gasp. "And the old ones are more powerful than you can ever—" He trailed off and started making a revolting wheezing noise. I looked around for something to put him out of his misery.

"This might help," said Missy, emerging from the gloom. She stepped forward and handed me a carving knife. "It was the best I could do at short notice," she said apologetically. "Sorry." I rolled my eyes but took it anyway.

"Can you do it?" managed the vampire. I could see into his eyes now. They were entirely black, glinting up at me in the moonlight. "Do you really have what it takes, Lilith? Ahahaa I don't think—" his voice cut off as I sliced through his neck. His head lolled and a sickening crunch suggested it had broken away from his spine where I'd crushed the bones. I dropped him down onto the grass with a heavy thud and leaned over to pull the knife out of his throat. "*Aaaaaaaaaaahahahahahahhaaaaa,*" the vampire's eyes snapped open, "as if you could—"

That was quite enough amateur dramatics for one night. Ripping a branch from a nearby tree, I rammed it into his gaping mouth with enough force to send the splintering wood straight through his skull and into the grass beneath. Broken yellow rat-teeth scattered down his bony cheek as his eyes widened briefly in horror before he slumped lifelessly. "What?" I said to Missy, who was staring wordlessly at me in what appeared to be shocked amazement. I straightened up and wiped my hands on my jeans. "He had it coming, the absolute gobshite. You going to help me clean up?"

So anyway, it turns out cutting the head off a fully-grown vampire with a basic kitchen carving knife is quite the task. It took a lot of sawing to get through the tendons and I was pretty sure I wouldn't forget the sound for the rest of my undead life. In a grim re-run of what had happened to Maria when I'd put her out of her evil misery in the spring, the vampire had crumbled into a pile of grey, sticky dust as soon as his head had left his shoulders. As I'd watched the rain wash his pathetic remains away, I wondered queasily whether it was the same for all supernatural beings. I'd heard stories of revenants literally pulling themselves back together after being chopped into kitty kibble, but who knew if they were really true. What if we just collapsed into dust, the same way Maria and the vampire had? If I ever got ambushed outside Flora's, would Izzy be able to sweep me up and drop me neatly into a bin? It felt like a 'when, not if' scenario—I was certainly building up a hefty list of Creatures That Wanted Me Dead.

"What are we going to do about her?" Missy asked, pointing to where the female vampire was still sitting on the path, her arms wrapped around her legs and her head hunched down onto her knees. "She can't be allowed to live." The vampire flinched, but didn't move.

"She saved me," I said flatly. "And she isn't alive, anyway. So it's moot."

"Can't-go-back." The voice was quiet but defiant.

"Well, you can't stay here," said Missy firmly.

"Will-kill-me," said the vampire. "Betrayed-them-will-be-destroyed."

"She can come home with me," I said, surprising even myself. "Maybe," I thought fast, "I could make her, I don't know, a mock-up crypt or something." Missy was looking at me with the sort of expression kept for people who've gone entirely off the rails and started collecting those china figurines you see advertised on the back pages of trashy weekly magazines.

"You're going to *keep* her?" said Missy incredulously. "Like a *pet?*"

"No," I said, the solution coming to me literally as I spoke, "she can move in below me. At Flora's," I said in the face of Missy's rising astonishment. "There's two empty flats between me and the cafe. She can have one of those. Look, Missy," she looked, but didn't appear to be any more understanding, "she saved me. Even you can't deny that. I owe her one."

"You are completely and utterly insane," said Missy. "Like I told them you

172

were."

"Charmed, I'm sure. Anyway," I said, "have you found Mapp? He's the only reason I'm up here, so this is basically all his fault."

He's here.

"Where here?"

"Look," said Missy, "I know we're all having a stressful evening. But most of us are managing not to talk to ourselves."

Tell her.

"Tell her what?" I said. Missy narrowed her eyes at me.

Who you're talking to. She will understand.

I looked at Missy for a long moment, deciding whether to trust her with the news of my apparently incipient insanity. "It's the city," I said eventually, keeping my tone flat. "It's in my head."

She tilted her head slightly. "Actually in your head?" Well, at least she wasn't immediately accusing me of losing my undead marbles. It was a start.

"Yes," I said. "There's a voice in my head and it says it's the spirit of the city."

"The entire city?" asked Missy, who was clearly struggling to process this philosophical development.

Just the spirit of the city. Not the soul. That would be too much for anyone to carry, dead or not.

Great, I murmured. *You're telling me there's more than one of you?*

The soul of this city is older and more powerful than anyone could comprehend. We're merely the part of it that still takes note of human activity.

"Most of it," I said. "It appears to have some kind of job-share scheme going on."

"Oh bloody hell," said Missy. "Mapp was right, then. I didn't want to believe him."

"Believe what?" I asked.

"I didn't want to believe you might be important," she said. "I know that sounds rude. But the stone cold truth is that you'd have been better off if I'd been right and Mapp was wrong. Gaultier Mapp saw something in you

I didn't want to see." She shrugged. "I guess I liked things how they were. Settled."

"I can promise you I didn't plan to disrupt your peaceful life," I said. "However boring things were when I was still alive, I'd have definitely preferred it to stay that way."

"Nah," said Missy with a grin. "I reckon this new life will turn out to suit you just fine, Lilith O'Reilly."

"I'm glad someone thinks that," I said, "because right now I'm not convinced. Anyway," I looked down at the female vampire, who was still hunched up on the path, "can you take her back to the house? She won't eat you," Missy looked unconvinced. "I promise. I just want to nip up to Martha's."

"I've been up there myself," said Missy, "and no one's answering."

"Not even Martha?" I raised an eyebrow. "Don't you think that's weird in itself?"

Missy pulled a face. "I decided to leave well alone," she said. "If she's really been trying to get Mapp to reanimate her ancient ass, I want nothing to do with it."

"Okay," I said, "but I'm going to check, anyway."

"Your funeral, I guess." Missy bent down and dragged the female vampire up by her arm. "Come on then, ratty," she said.

"Stop it," I said sharply. "She's not like the others. You've seen that for yourself." Missy looked unconvinced. "What's your name?" I asked the vampire, who shrank back. "If I was going to kill you," I pointed out, "I'd have done it by now." *My*, said a tiny voice in my head that was definitely all my own, *how times have changed. Six months ago you'd have struggled to squish a spider, but now it's all 'AARGH MURDER KILL KILL' on the reg. Who'd have predicted that?* I trod down my lurking conscience. "You must have a name?"

"Rachel," said the vampire.

"Your pet has a name," said Missy.

"Pack it in," I said, without malice. "Take Rachel back to the house and I'll come fetch her as soon as I'm done giving Martha a telling off."

"If she stinks the house out," said Missy, "you're paying the cleaning bill."

"Get Al to babysit her," I suggested. "He likes an audience."

***

I thought about Missy's comments as I made my way—admittedly slowly and reluctantly—up towards the catacombs. 'Settled', she'd said. Everything had been settled—until I turned up.

Nothing is ever settled, said the city. *We're constantly moving. Shifting. Alert.*

"You weren't very alert when you let me walk into that vampire trap," I pointed out. "I must have had a face on me like an angry haddock." I paused. "Why did I just think of fish? Grandad used to say the haddock thing, but I never have."

Everything's coming back. All the memories you've ever had.

"Oh no they're fucking not," I said. "No one needs to remember that time I asked Dave Betsall to dance at the school disco but he said no and I burst into tears in front of everyone."

Yet clearly you remember it well.

Of course I remembered it—who could ever forget that level of humiliation? It was one of those memories that would be funny to tell people when you were, I don't know, maybe ninety or something. Many decades after it happened, anyway. In the meantime, it got locked away deep down in the mortification vaults. Along with that time I fell over at the front of the lecture hall during my first week at uni and was helped up by two girls who then giggled to each other as they walked away. And the day I thought an unusually cute traffic warden was writing down his number for me, only for him to slap a yellow penalty notice onto Basil's windscreen and walk away without a backwards glance. "Oh fuck."

Indeed.

"I can't have every single memory I've ever had popping back up in my head," I said. "There isn't room."

The mind is infinite.

"My patience bloody well isn't," I said.

We could be very useful, now you have accepted your fate.

Martha's catacomb was right in front of me. With an easy bounce, I vaulted the fence and stepped towards the iron gate. "So what *is* my fate?" I asked.

No one's future is ever truly predictable, said the voice. *But you appear to have arrived at your destination.*

I'd Like To Escape Now, Please

S hit. *Shit.* I froze, one hand already on the iron bars of the gate. *This was the High Gate.* All that worrying about driving into London, yet the supposed danger had been back home all the time.

Like many historically important port cities, Liverpool drops towards the river, its outskirts scrabbling up the surrounding geological ridges. The highest point of the area is technically down towards Woolton, but in the city itself, you can't get much higher than Anfield. Anfield, though? Really? The city centre, I could understand—it's loud and vibrant and definitely has potential for danger if you don't know your social geography. But I was standing in a garden cemetery in what optimistic estate agents liked to describe as an 'up and coming' neighbourhood. Anfield Cemetery is the sort of place people come to walk their dogs when they want some peace and quiet. Even since my death, Anfield wouldn't have been top of my list of places that might harbour a secret hotbed of malevolent paranormal activity. Mind you, I'd have said the same about the Cavern, and look what happened there. Peering in through the bars, I could see there was definitely someone at home down in Martha's crypt. A faint chink of light glowed from the edges of the stone that covered the entrance, and I thought I could detect voices at the very edge of my hearing. Hopefully it was Martha and Mapp, sitting around gossiping and drinking tea.

Mapp's in danger. We need to go to him.

Bollocks. So much for my musical theory. "In danger from what?" I asked.

Himself, mostly.

"Same old, same old," I said. There was no point sitting around waiting for backup. No one else knew I was in Anfield.

We're with you, said the city. *We'll always be with you.*

"Yeah," I said, "that's what I'm afraid of."

There are worse things than us to be afraid of, Lilith.

"Well, that's reassuring," I muttered. With a resigned sigh, I pushed the gate open as quietly as possible and stepped through. I knew that whoever was down in the crypt would be alerted to my presence the second I started shifting the stones above their heads, but couldn't see I had much choice.

There's another way in, said the city. *An entrance even Martha doesn't know about.*

"That's more like it," I said. "It's about time you made yourself useful."

You're not going to like it.

"I haven't liked anything very much since the day I woke up dead," I said, "so why change the habit of an eternal lifetime?"

***

And that is how I found myself sliding down through a small hatch around the back of the catacomb, into the darkest, tightest space ever thought up by a particularly grim nightmare. *Can you hear me?* I asked the city.

We can always hear you, Lilith. Marvellous. Now I not only had a ghostly aunt who liked to pop up in front of me at inopportune moments, I also had an entire city in my head and it was privy to my every thought. *It doesn't work like that*, said the city. *We're only here when you need us.*

Well, I'm going to need you to promise not to spy on me, I grumbled silently. *I might not have a love life to speak of right now, but it would still be nice to not have my every thought inspected while it's still inside my head.*

Believe us, it said, *we don't need to know what you're thinking. Although your suspicions about the cat are almost certainly correct.*

What's Grimm done now? I wriggled down and found myself having to lie flat inside what felt like a rectangular space. The walls were close up against me and felt like cold stone. *Oh, you are fucking kidding me*, I said, as I realised where I was. *I'm in one of the coffin niches, aren't I?*

Yes. There are many down here.

This one had better not be occupied, or you and I will be having words after this is over.

Why fear the dead? said the city. **It's the living who would try to hurt you.** I felt around the space in the darkness, wondering what would happen if I couldn't get out. Presumably I'd just have to stay here until Nik or Eadric realised I was missing and came to find me. They'd never let me forget it. *There's no one in here,* said the city, eventually. **And there's a hatch by your feet. Not yet**—I'd pulled my right foot up to kick out at the end of the niche, but stopped myself—**we'll tell you when.**

How do you know what's going on? I asked. *You're in here with me.*

We're everywhere, it said. **But our only true consciousness is here with you.**

Well, thanks for clearing that up. Not.

Not everything is explainable, Lilith.

Yeah, so I keep being told.

Empty your mind, said the city in my head. **Listen.** Emptying your mind is, as anyone who's tried mindfulness can tell you, difficult at the best of times. Now imagine trying to do it when you're wedged into an underground space the size of a coffin—on account of how it *is* a coffin—with an entire city jabbering on inside your head. After many failed attempts at meditation, I'd eventually learned that while I will never be able to actually empty my thoughts, I *can* fill my head with other stuff that pushes the conscious thinking out and allows my mind to wander. So I lay in that cold, dark stone coffin underneath Anfield Cemetery and thought of the river. Of swimming with Daisy, and floating peacefully while the Liver Birds spun their ephemeral dance in the sky above my head. The vast, open sky was dark in my imagination, but filled with promise. Promises of future peace and present troubles, all of them washing around me on the surface of the Mersey. My angst about vampires and vengeful witches slowly ebbed away, until all that was left was the here and now. Voices became audible, out beyond where my feet pressed lightly against the hatch.

"You know why I'm here," said someone in the darkness. *Mab.*

She doesn't know you're here, but she's expecting you. She needs backup and she sees Mapp as a potential source of help.

Then she really is insane. Mapp would never help Mab.

*It's **not** his **help she wants**,* said the voice in my head. *She thinks he can bring her mother back. She's planning to join forces with Maria.*

Over my undead body.

That's our girl. NOW. Before I could think about whether it was a wise move, I kicked the hatch. The impetus propelled me out of the niche at speed, and I only just managed to stay upright as I dropped onto the floor of the catacomb. I'd been higher up than I'd thought. Glancing back up at the wall, I could see the hatch hanging open a good few feet above my head.

"Evenin'," I said brightly, to my astonished audience. Martha was hunched over Mapp, who was, I was amazed to see, chained down to a stone slab in the middle of the crypt. Mab stood on the other side of them, glaring at me across the surreal diorama. The entire scenario looked like something out of a Hammer movie.

Mapp twisted his head to look at me, and his face broke into a relieved grin. "Iron," he said, nodding his head at the chains holding him down. "Part fae, innit." He attempted an apologetic shrug, but I didn't know whether he was embarrassed not to have told me, or just at having been caught out. "Managed to avoid the stuff for centuries, but now here we are." Martha glanced up at me. To my astonishment, she looked younger than she had the last time we'd met. And far less frail. "My...*friend* here," he indicated the no-longer-quite-so-old woman, "took matters into her own hands."

Martha stood up and glared at me. Gone were the hunched shoulders and grey frizz, replaced by flowing silver hair and posture straight enough to make her my height, at least. "I have been hidden away down here," she spat, "for longer than anyone could be expected to tolerate. Hiding out like an animal in the dark and damp, reliant on freaks like you to keep me fed and watered."

"Heggie likes you, Martha," said Mapp, from his prone position. "He's going to be so disappointed when he finds out what you've done."

"I'm not planning to kill you, Gaultier Mapp," said Martha, "so don't you be panicking. I'm just taking what I need."

"You're draining him," I said. Mapp's dark skin was definitely starting to take on a weirdly chalky tone, and his irises looked even more faded than usual. "You'll kill him permanently if you carry on." But before I could say anything else, Mab took things into her own hands. Launching herself across the room, she knocked Martha flying into the corner and wheeled round to look at me and Mapp. The all-white outfit from a few days earlier was grubby now, the knees of her jeans worn and dark with dirt and her t-shirt torn at the neck. Smudges ran up her neck and onto the side of her face like dark bruises, and her pale blonde hair stuck out in all directions.

"My turn," she said.

"As it happens, darling," Mapp's voice sounded weak. "I really think I'm done." His shoulders twitched in a faint shrug.

"You're going to help bring my mother back, whether or not it kills you," said Mab.

Mapp actually laughed. "I think the fuck not," he said. "Your mother was a nasty piece of work from day one. Nothing good would come from her being back in the city."

"I need my mother back," insisted Mab, "and you will bring her to me."

"You know this isn't going to work, Mab," said Martha, from the corner. "Mapp can work miracles, but even he has limits."

"You just want to keep his abilities for yourself," said Mab sharply. "You're a desperate old woman who got greedy. You didn't know what you were asking for and now you've got it, you're resentful. A nasty, resentful, bitter old—" I barrelled into her before she had a chance to see it coming. We flew across the room together and hit the wall on the far side, although I took great pleasure in using her as cushioning against the stone. We still ended up in a tangle of arms and legs and she managed to punch me in the side of the head, hard enough to make me fall backwards away from her. I bounced back onto my feet, but she was already standing over Mapp's impromptu altar. Even in my panic, I could see Mab was being careful not to get too close, and I wondered why. To my horror, she slid a small, folded pocket knife out from her jeans pocket. When she flicked it open, I saw that although the knife's case was silver, the blade itself was made of a dark, flat-coloured metal. As she twisted it in front of her face, there was a nasty glint from the blade's razor-sharp edge. Before I could do anything to stop her, she leaned forward and nicked Mapp's arm. He shrieked in shock and pain. She cut him again—just a tiny, slicing movement, but he writhed in agony. "Bring my mother back," she said, stepping sideways in order to press the knife up against his jawline, "or I will make the rest of your undead life very short. And *very* painful." Another small nick, this one high on his cheekbone. Mapp screamed in a way I'd never heard before and desperately hope to never hear again. It was the noise an animal makes when it's caught in a trap and knows there's no hope of escape.

What am I going to do? I asked the city in my head. *I can't attack her again. She's insane enough to kill Mapp out of sheer spite.*

Talk to her.

What the fuck about? I shook my head in frustration and Mab saw the movement. She was watching me closely, but the hand holding the knife was now pressed hard against Mapp's closed eyelid and I couldn't risk surprising her.

Anything, said the city. **Help is coming, but you need to buy time.**

"What are you trying to achieve, Mab?" I asked her. "Maria's gone. I'm sorry for your loss and all that, but there was no option."

"There is *always* an option," she hissed. A tiny spot of blood appeared under the knife's blade and Mapp made a quiet keening noise under his breath.

"I swear to god," I said, "if you hurt my friend any more, I will make your existence a living hell."

Hold your ground.

I plan to, I thought. *The only way out is through.*

Always.

"From what I can see," I indicated Mapp, "you've got a prisoner, but he's not actually of any use to you. Not even Mapp can bring someone back from absolutely nothing."

"Oh, but I think he can," said Mab. "And if he doesn't," she moved slightly and Mapp flinched, "I will destroy him. And then I will destroy you, Lilith O'Reilly."

"How do you plan to do that?"

"You have no idea who I really am," said Mab, "do you? No idea *what* I am." As she spoke, she raised her right arm into the air and the entire world went white. And I mean that in a literal sense. There was nothing metaphorical about the way the catacomb suddenly filled with the brightest, whitest light ever imaginable. I closed my eyes, but it made no difference. The whiteness forced its way into my head, blinding me from the inside out. I felt my way backwards until I was pressed up against the wall.

Open your eyes.

Are you shitting me? The light was painful even with my face scrunched up as tightly as I could manage. *That little bitch is trying to blind me!*

She's trying to distract you, said the city, **not blind you. Open your eyes.** Against all better judgement, I opened my eyes. I knew I was still in the catacomb because I could feel the stone wall beneath my fingers, but the structure had disappeared. In its place was—nothing. Pure white as the opposite of pure black, but with the same effect—complete absence of *anything*. As my eyes began to regain focus, I could make out the vaguest of shadowy shapes. The horizontal hint of darkness directly in front of me was, I was pretty certain, Gaultier Mapp. Presumably still chained to his slab like an upmarket Rocky Horror cosplay. And almost certainly enjoying the drama, even as his immortal life was being threatened. A small, scrabbling movement in the far right of my vision was probably Martha. And the vertical, darker shadow to my left was definitely Mab.

Are you still with me? I rubbed my fingers against the stone behind my back in an attempt to ground myself.

We'll always be with you. No one can separate us so long as you are not destroyed.

That isn't as reassuring as you seem to think it is.

Concentrate, Lilith. Think about who you are. The shadow version of Mab moved, getting bigger and darker as she moved closer to me. She was almost human-shaped now, but in a slippery way, like waking up from a dream that slides away from you faster and faster, the more you try to remember the details.

"How do you like the view?" said Mab. Without warning, she was right in front of me, just inches from my face. The shadows moved from left to right, as if inspecting me. "There's no escape from this, Lilith," she said. "No escape from yourself."

"Some of us aren't scared of ourselves," I said out loud, my voice echoing into the void. "Some of us, Mab," I didn't know whether she could actually see me, but scowled at her just in case, "aren't filled with resentment and bile and whatever else you're made up of. Because it definitely isn't sugar or spice. And absolutely not anything nice."

"I know what I am," she said, "and I came to terms with it a very long time ago. I've never been fully human, Lilith. Not ever. Not even when I was what you laughingly call alive." She spat the last word out, as though it disgusted her. "Do you have any idea," the shadow pushed up into my face and I pressed my head back hard against the stone wall, "what it was like growing up an orphan in the nineteenth century? Of course you don't," I felt a breath against my cheek, "because you're a modern, go-getting woman! Aren't you, Lilith? A single woman with a business and an apartment and a family. A *family*, Lilith. People around you. People who care about what happens to you." The shadow moved away slightly, but I was pretty sure that, in some reality at least, Mab was still standing right in front of me.

You're still in the catacomb, said the city. **Help is coming, but it's slow. The one person who can stop this isn't sure they should.**

Tell whoever it is that if they don't make their mind up very bloody soon, I will give them a bloody good shoeing when I get out of this.

"I don't know who you think you're having a conversation with," said Mab, "but it's all in your head. Imaginary friends can't help you, Lilith. Perhaps you'd feel better with some company? There's someone here who'd like to see you." The shadow faded away and for a second, I was staring into nothing. Then I saw someone walking towards me from what seemed a very long distance away. As they got closer, I realised it was a child—short and sturdy and grinning from ear to ear.

"Hey Lil," said my little brother, coming to a halt a few feet in front of me. "Whatcha doin'?" Cally was still dressed in the clothes he'd been wearing the day he died. The day I hadn't been able to save him from falling into the river and had been left standing helplessly on the banks of the Severn as he was washed away in front of my eyes. I stared at him in wonder, taking in the absolute realness and solidity of him. His t-shirt was red with blue and white stripes, and I could see the remains of the Pokemon sticker that he'd refused to take off, so it had gone through the wash several times. All that was left was an outline and the pale zigzag of Pikachu's tail. The spare pair of school PE shorts he'd worn that day, because his favourite jeans were in the wash. The shorts still looked crisp and new, just as they'd done when he'd pulled them on before asking me to go looking for squirrels with him. He was still wearing odd socks. I'd always remembered them as one black and one navy blue, but I could see now that the black one was actually dark grey. It had a small embroidered picture on the side, but I couldn't make out what it was because of the loose threads tangling over it. I realised he must have put the sock on inside out and the sudden thought made me want to cry. "Why you sad, Lil?" Cally asked. "Let's go adventcha!" He turned to walk away from me.

"Come back!" I shouted. "Cally, come back!"

The little figure kept walking, but turned to look back at me. "Nope," he said with a grin, "I'm gone, Lil. You can't look after me, can you?" his voice was getting harder now, and older. "You're rubbish, ain'tcha? Couldn't even look after one little boy, Lil. One little boy who just wanted to see the squirrels then go home to his mum and dad. I just wanted my mum, Lil." I clutched my ears in an attempt to drown the voice out, but it was insistent. "And now you've got her and I haven't. Do you know how much Mum's cried for me over the years? How much she's wondered about what actually happened? About whether you could have saved me, if only you'd tried just that little bit harder? I bet you don't, Lilith. You've shut it all out because you feel guilty and bad. You're a bad sister, Lilith. A bad, rubbish sister. Seeya!" Cally thumbed his nose at me, eight years old again, and turned to walk away.

185

"*Cally!*" I shrieked, but even as the words left my mouth, he disappeared. He faded to a shadow before his silhouette fragmented and shattered into a million pieces. The shards disappeared into nothing, right in front of my eyes.

It's not real, said the city. **He's not real. She's got into your memories.**

Well she can fuck right off out of them. How dare *she bring my brother into this?*

She's looking for a way in. She knows she can't beat you in a fair fight, which was kind of reassuring, because it was more than I knew myself at that precise moment, **so she's going to try to get into your head and throw you off that way.**

"Mab," I said, forcing my voice to sound calmer than I actually felt, "you didn't deserve what happened to you. You were a little kid. You had no choice."

"You know nothing about me," hissed Mab. Her voice came from right next to my ear, and I struggled not to pull away.

"I know you were a scared little child who deserved better," I said. "It wasn't your fault you ended up an orphan. And it isn't your fault your mother was how she was. But you don't have to be the same." Silence. "You could join us," I ploughed on. "Eadric cared about your mother, even after she betrayed him. He would support you."

"You think I don't have support?" Mab made a choking sound that I thought might have been a laugh. "You really think I'm doing all this on my own? I'm not that stupid, Lilith." Her voice was moving round me now, but all I could see was white nothing. "I've got allies you could never dream of."

"Like Ivo Laithlind?" I asked. "That two-faced little shit-heel?" I snorted. "As if he's ever going to do anything that isn't best for himself, whatever the risk to anyone else."

"Ivo has power," said Mab. "And he doesn't have a soft heart, like you and those pathetic Silvertons. Who do they even think they are, anyway?" Her voice moved away slightly now and I risked moving my head around slightly. There was definitely an edge to the whiteness around my peripheral vision, suggesting the enforced hallucination—or whatever it was—only existed within my field of vision. I remembered Izzy going through a phase of playing Minecraft and showing me how the scenery only built itself around your character's immediate environment, in order to save processing power. As you moved the character through its artificial world, things appeared in front of it and disappeared behind it, like a small island of blocky reality that was moving independently through space and time. "A tired old man who's sick of his very existence, and a poet who bored people to death even within his own lifetime. The Silvertons are a *joke*, Lilith." She was closer again now, and I thought I could feel her breath against the side of my head. "My mother was the best thing that ever happened to them and they couldn't see it. She had the will to use their power in order to take control of this entire immortal country, but they didn't want it. They *wasted* her, Lilith."

"You didn't know Maria," I said loudly. "Everything you think you know about your mother is based on rose-tinted daydreams, Mab." No response. "Any kid brought up in your situation would do the same. But you don't know the truth. You don't *know* what your mother was really like. How she betrayed the one person who really cared for her, because he wouldn't give her the power she wanted. Because he knew she'd abuse it. But still, he loved her. *That's* a waste, Mab. Your mother wasted the love she had."

"She loved Ivo," said Mab, quieter now. "He told me."

"She did," I agreed, "and he let her down. The same way he'll let you down, and anyone else who doesn't toe his exact line. You're useful to him now, Mab," the light was receding now and the catacomb was once again becoming visible around the edges, "but one day you won't be. And what will Ivo do with you then?"

"He'll stand by her," said Ivo Laithlind.

Family Ties

The brightness suddenly drained away, and I was back in the dark underground room. Martha was still in the corner, but standing upright again now and looking more like a well-preserved woman in her forties than the ancient crone she'd been. Mapp was lying silent and unmoving on the slab. For a brief panicked second I thought he was truly dead, but a slight wince reassured me he could clearly still feel the iron chains. Mab stood by his head, staring at the new arrival in the manner of a small furry animal caught in full-beam headlights. Ivo was standing underneath the open hatch entrance, presumably having dropped in while we'd been distracted by Mab's mind-reading abilities. He was, of course, dressed immaculately, from the tip of his neatly coiffed head to the toes of his stupid shiny boots. My stomach lurched at the sight of him and I couldn't decide whether it was outright lust, or nausea from knowing he made me feel that way. Probably a combination of both.

"Hello, Red," he said, giving me a small wave.

"Why?" I asked him, struggling to keep the anger out of my voice. I was in no position to lose my shit right now, but it was definitely going to happen in the very near future. I shifted away from the wall a fraction, trying not to make it obvious. "Why do you need her, Ivo? Planning to add her to your list of sad little conquests, in the hope she'll do anything you ask?" His jaw clenched and I half expected him to come at me. He didn't move. "Just like her mother before her, huh? I don't know what it is you're capable of in the sack, Ivo Laithlind," *although it would be interesting to find out—just for research purposes, you understand,* "but you've clearly got something that pulls

188

in the ladies. More fool the—" Mab careered bodily into me, cutting me off mid-sentence. We bowled across the floor and this time it was pure cat-fight, the sort more usually seen down Seel Street on a Friday night as the clubs are emptying. She grabbed a handful of my hair and pulled hard, making me screech as I discovered being immortal didn't make you immune from the pain of having your scalp yanked. In return, I remembered something from a self-defence class I'd taken at uni years previously and shoved my little finger hard into Mab's ear. The idea is that you disrupt your attacker's thought process and they're forced to concentrate on getting you out of their ear hole, rather than continuing their assault. But obviously I'm much stronger than I was back when I was a human student, and I felt a distinct *pop* as my finger ruptured Mab's eardrum. She shrieked and rolled away from me, clutching her head in her hands as I got back onto my feet. "Aren't you going to help her, Ivo?" I demanded, picking up Mab's knife as I did so. It felt like nothing more than a small, sharp knife to me, so I guessed that meant I was just a boringly normal human. I flicked it closed and slid it into my waistband. Ivo was still standing in the same spot, looking distinctly torn as to what to do next. "Why are you waiting?" I asked him. Mab was wailing quietly now, and I wondered if I'd done more damage than intended.

"She needs to learn to stand on her own two feet," said Ivo. "If she's to survive."

"Needs to learn how to be a power-hungry sociopath, you mean?"

Ivo frowned at me. "As much as I like you, Red," he said, "even I have my limits. I will not," he took a step forward and I had to force myself not back away, "risk losing my territory. The power of the netherworld is rising, and that brings new threats and new enemies. Eadric has always refused a direct fight for his own reasons, and until now I have respected his approach. But the risks are increasing. And with them comes a need to be proactive. I will not wait for the threat to come to me, Red." He moved towards me.

"GET OUT OF MY CITY, IVO LAITHLIND," The voice was coming more naturally now. "BEFORE I REMOVE YOU PERMANENTLY."

Ivo stopped in his tracks. "Who are you?" he asked, looking genuinely shocked. "Who are you *really*?"

I took a moment to tread down the anger that was bubbling inside me. "I'm still me," I said, speaking in my normal voice. I just hoped to hell I was right. "And I have had enough of your shit, Ivo. I don't know what threat you think is coming, but if it isn't coming from you, then I'm willing to bet we're going to have to work together at some point. Which is why I'm not going to kill you. Yet. Don't assume that means I like you," I warned. "Because in my opinion, you are a no-good, nasty little worm with zero conscience."

"Ooh," said Mapp from behind me, "I love it when you talk dirty."

"SHUT UP." Mapp shut up. "I'm not killing you, Ivo," I said, my eyes fixed on him, "because right now, the alternative is clearly your creepy new girlfriend there." I nodded to where Mab sat on the floor, clutching at her ear. "And if you really didn't care what happens to Liverpool, you'd have stayed away. But you're back. And that's interesting in itself, isn't it?" Ivo's face was a mask of bland impassiveness. "Eadric is still in charge round here and I'm not going to overstep his authority. Mostly because I still have no idea how these stupid bloody undead politics actually work."

"You're definitely still you," said Ivo, with a faint smile. "I recognise the confused tone."

"Like I said," I glared at him, "I am absolutely still me. But now I'm getting a grip on *what* I am. And I quite like it, Ivo. I quite like having some power and strength and the ability to make my own decisions again. So just be careful how far you push me. Because my patience is limited right now."

"For what it's worth," he said, nodding towards Mab, "we're definitely not romantically attached. I can assure you of that. So do let me know if you're ever free for a dinner date."

I scowled and was about to say something suitably rude, when a low noise from behind me reminded me that Mapp was still trapped. "Get him off that slab," I said, turning to look briefly at Martha. She didn't move. "GET HIM OFF THERE BEFORE I RIP YOU LIMB FROM FUCKING LIMB, YOU NASTY LITTLE COW," I instructed again, and this time she moved. I turned to look at Ivo again, but kept flicking my gaze backwards to make sure Martha was following my orders. Ivo stared at me wordlessly, still not moving. I heard clanking noises behind me and a groan. Turning my head slightly, I saw Mapp being helped off the slab and half-carried by Martha into the far corner of the catacomb. I'd worry about her later.

"What am I to you," asked Mab, "if not equal partners?" She was talking to Ivo, not me, I realised. Her pale face turned to look up at him from her hunched position on the floor. "Why have you been helping me all these years, if it wasn't me you wanted?"

"Years?" I said. "He's been helping you for *years*?"

Mab glared at me. "What of it?" she asked.

I ignored her and looked at Ivo. He held my gaze, but there was a faint flicker in his eyes. "You've known of Mab's existence for years," I said carefully, "but didn't think it was worth telling Maria?"

"I did what I had to do," he said flatly. "The two of them together would have been dangerous, Red. For all of us."

"What are you talking about?" asked Mab. She was still on the floor, looking from me to Ivo as she tried to figure out what was going on.

"Your would-be boyfriend here," I said to Mab, "was always in touch with Maria. With your *mother*, Mab. All those years alone. The decades you spent trying to track her down. And Ivo here knew where she was all that time." Mab's face was a mask of horror. I didn't feel great about what I was doing, but ploughed on regardless. "He knew you were alone and desperate for your mother, Mab. He *knew*. But he chose not to tell either of you. All that time you and Maria were losing your minds to grief and loss, and Ivo-fucking-Laithlind here could have fixed it for both of you." Mab was slowly getting to her feet. I suspected I was no longer her primary target and stepped carefully out of her path. "But he didn't. I wonder why?"

Mab moved slowly towards Ivo. "You *knew*?" she asked him. "You knew, and chose not to tell either of us? What sort of monster are you?"

"A pragmatic one," said Ivo. "I've been around long enough to know how this game plays out, Mab. There are bigger threats than any of us here in this room. Maria was unhinged enough to put us all in danger."

"You *bastard!*" screeched Mab, and flew at him. He stumbled backwards but kept his footing, twisting out of her way and using the impetus of Mab's own weight to swing her over his head and into the wall. She howled like a banshee and made another attempt, ripping at his clothes in her fury. Despite the evening having been a fun-packed festival of stressful activities already, I realised I felt stronger than ever. I needed to take out Mab, before she could do serious damage. Not that I was averse to someone getting Ivo back for his shitty behaviour these last few centuries. But he clearly knew more about potential incoming threats, and I needed to get the information out of him while he was still capable of speech. Grabbing Mab from behind, I hauled her off him and dragged her backwards, tripping and sprawling onto the rubble-strewn floor of the crypt with a painful thump. As we scrambled around on the floor, Mab grabbed a handful of my hair and I really wished I'd thought to tie it up before heading out. She wrenched my head backwards with painful suddenness and I found myself looking straight up at Ivo. "Fucking stop her," I yelled, "while you've got the chance!" Ivo just stared at us both, seemingly at a genuine loss as to what to do. "DO SOMETHING!" I bellowed. He flinched backwards but still didn't come to my aid. Mab was shaking with fury, and my voice clearly no longer had any effect on her. I jammed my elbow backwards into her stomach with all my strength and she gasped, but didn't let go. I was pretty sure she was going to attempt to literally rip my head off my shoulders if I didn't stop her. Kicking my feet against the floor, I caught a section of solid stone against my heels and used the leverage to twist myself sideways. Ducking my head down, I managed to get an arm up and grabbed Mab's wrist. "You are a fucking maniac," I hissed, and slammed her arm down into the floor. Her wrist broke with a horrible crunching noise and she screamed loud enough to make my ears ring.

"Get out of the way," said Martha from behind me, and I was surprised enough to do as I was told. As I flattened myself against the floor, something heavy flew above me and, going by the sudden increase in Mab's howling, presumably hit its target. I risked a glance upwards and saw her laid flat on the ground with the iron chain across her. So that was why the barrel of her knife was silver—Mapp wasn't the only one vulnerable to the effects of iron. Martha stood over her with a vicious gleam in her eye and another chain in her hand. She raised the chain and I only just got to her before she had a chance to slam it down into Mab's face. "She needs putting out of her misery," hissed Martha, as I pinned her hard against the wall. She'd clearly regained her strength along with her youth, but I was stronger.

"Let Mab go," said Ivo, quietly.

I turned to look at him, all the time keeping a firm hold on Martha. "What the fuck?" I gave him an incredulous look. "Why on earth would I do that? She's a fucking liability. For all of us." Ivo stood facing me, just a few short feet away. Mab lay on the floor between us, still pinned by the iron chain. Her face was a mask of pain and her bright pale eyes fixed on me grimly. "What's so special about your little pet, Laithlind? What is it about her that makes you willing to sacrifice everything? Because that's what you'll be doing if you carry on. You *need* us, Ivo. We could probably manage without you if we had to. We have a spirit that you're clearly lacking. But you won't survive without us."

"Don't push it," said Ivo in a low voice.

"Why?" I asked, taking a step forward. He didn't move backwards, but his eyes flinched slightly. *He's genuinely nervous*, I thought. *Why is Ivo Laithlind uncomfortable around me?*

He's hiding something.

"Come on," I said, taking another small step towards Ivo and Mab. "What is it I'm not supposed to push? If you're waiting for me to bow to your masculine superiority, Ivo, we're going to be here a long time. You're just one more egotistical man in a world full of egotistical men. I'm supposed to play nice because I'm a woman, right? I bet you think I'll back down if it comes to the crunch. But if that is what you think, then you don't know me as well as you hoped." Before he could think up a smart-arsed response, I lunged forward. Dragging Mab out from under the chains, I pulled her back against me and held her as a shield. Slipping the knife out of my pocket, I had the blade out against her face before Ivo even realised what I was doing. She made a panicked gargling noise.

Be careful not to make threats you can't carry through.

If you think I won't carry out any threats I make, then you don't actually know me very well.

Fair enough.

Holding Mab's arms behind her back with one hand and careful not to tug at the wrist I'd already broken, I used my other hand to press the blade tight up against her face. She'd fallen silent again and was now heaving steadily with her back against me. Sliding the knife across her face, I pulled it against her earlobe. It only cut her very slightly—just a couple of millimetres and definitely surface damage only—but the noise she made was dramatic. Recoiling from the knife, she thrashed and flailed in an attempt to get away. Unfortunately for her, I was getting stronger by the minute. I looked down briefly to where I was holding her arms and gave them an experimental twist. Mab yowled in response and I laughed hollowly. "I think we've safely established," I said, "that you are not entirely human yourself." She stayed silent. "I wonder where that unusual bloodline comes from. What exactly *was* your mother, Mab? I'm happy to take suggestions." She moved to shake her head in mute fury, but unfortunately for her, the knife was still against her face. I felt the blade pierce the skin and almost immediately hit bone. *Fuck.* Her yelling put even Mapp's in the shade. We'd be lucky if half the Merseyside police force didn't turn up at the cemetery gates, the way things were going. "It's just a flesh wound," I said, "for heaven's sake."

"Put her down, Red," said Ivo. "Before I take matters into my own hands."

"Oh, shut *up*," I said sharply. "I have spent this entire bloody evening trying to stop people fighting each other."

"Not me," same a weak voice from the corner. I turned to look and found Mapp grinning weakly at me. "I'm a lover, Lil," he said, "not a fighter."

"You are all as bloody ridiculous as each other," I said. "Regardless," I turned to Ivo, "you're not getting Mab back. This madwoman," I gave her a shake for emphasis, "stays here. She's a liability. Eadric can decide what to do with her."

"You're not keeping her," said Ivo flatly. "She belongs to me."

"I don't belong to *anyone*," spat Mab, suddenly fully focused. She made a move to wriggle out from my grasp, but I held onto her. My strength really was increasing now, as though someone had replaced my batteries with fresh ones.

Is the power coming from you? I asked the city.

No, it said. **That's all you. The power is building, and it's channelling into you.**

Not the others, though? I asked. *Not Ivo?*

No. Other...things are waking up. Well, that was something to look forward to. **But they're not here. Yet.**

"Why does she belong to you?" I asked Ivo. "Did you miss a chunk of the last century, Laithlind? You know—when women gained their independence? We," I shook Mab again, "don't need you. I would suggest that you fuck off back to Yorkshire and only come back here after you've given your head a good wobble. You keep rattling on about danger on the horizon, but I've already met that danger out in the bloody cemetery. You're late to the party, Ivo. But you're evidently not going to keep your head down and stay out of it, so we're better together. It's time you decided who your friends really are."

"You don't understand," he said. "I can't leave Mab in danger."

"Why not?" I asked. "She's been nothing but trouble since she appeared on the scene."

"It's my fault," he said. "I could—should—have kept her out of this."

"Yes," I agreed, pressing the iron blade against Mab's delicate, pale cheek, "you should. But you didn't. So what gives, Ivo? Why is she so important?"

I could almost hear the cogs turning in Ivo's head as he considered his response. Eventually, he appeared to come to a decision. "Because," he said with a simple shrug, "she's my daughter."

"What?" Mab and I asked the question at the same time. I pushed the blade against her cheek and felt mean about the hiss of pain she emitted, but at least it shut her up. I could feel her entire body shaking against me as I stared at Ivo Laithlind in absolute astonishment. "How the fuck can *this* be your daughter?" I asked him, my voice incredulous. "You're not even alive, for christ's sake! It wouldn't even—" for reasons known only to that part of my brain that has no filters whatever, I nodded at his crotch for emphasis, "—*work*. Surely?" I was genuinely lost for words. And, as Izzy would happily confirm, that doesn't happen very often.

Ivo looked straight at me. I forced myself to hold his gaze. "I can assure you, Red," he said, "I might be more than a thousand years old, but every part of my body functions as it should." I probably shouldn't think about that too much. I couldn't afford to get distracted right now. There was absolutely no comment from the city, which had presumably been stunned into silence. "Mab was..." he paused. "A mistake."

Mab threw me backwards off her with inhuman strength and was on Ivo before I even realised what she was doing, her anguished screams enough to quite literally wake the dead. Grabbing hold of his head, she cracked his skull down onto the floor so hard I thought she must have smashed it. "You bastard!" she shrieked, punching and kicking Ivo even as he lay slumped and unmoving on the floor. His eyes were open, but he made no attempt to fight back. "My *father*? And you knew all this time? You *knew* who my mother was and that she was still around, but you didn't tell me?"

"*Oh no you don't—*" I grabbed Martha before she could go at the pair of them with the chains again and pushed her backwards hard enough to send her sprawling onto Mapp, who was curled up in the corner. "Stay there and see to Mapp," I hissed. "You've done enough damage already." Hefting the chain in my hand, I turned and gauged my aim in the hope of dragging Mab off Ivo—just as an angel dropped through the roof.

***

The pale figure was thin and lightly built, but it landed on Mab and Ivo feet first, the force enough to knock them flying in opposite directions. Its white clothes were far cleaner than Mab's and they seemed to glow in the darkness of the crypt. A flash of light from above made me realise that the newcomer was actually being illuminated by moonlight, which was breaking in through the hole in the ceiling. The figure stood in-between Mab and Ivo's sprawled figures with its hands facing up and out, as if pushing them back with an invisible force. I could see now it was wearing heavy boots—and those combats definitely came from Gap, rather than heaven itself.

"Jude?" The angel looked up at me and grinned. Mab took advantage of the distraction and bounced to her feet. Before I could get to her, she somehow propelled herself up against the wall and out of the hole Jude had dropped through. Launching upwards, Jude grabbed at Mab's disappearing legs and managed to catch hold of one foot. They clung on tightly, despite Mab's frantic kicking. Ivo suddenly launched himself forward, throwing his entire bodyweight into it. Jude turned and kicked out at him, sending him flying into the stone wall with enough impetus to make a cloud of ancient mortar puff up around him. But his tactic had worked. With a final shriek of triumph, Mab disappeared up and out into the night. I grabbed Ivo and pulled him up off the floor. "You'd better have a bloody decent explanation for all of this," I hissed at him. "Because right now, I'm struggling to find a good reason to not finish you off."

"You can't kill me," gasped Ivo. Given that he didn't need to breathe, the gasping was probably more to do with me having my elbow wedged against his windpipe. "You need me."

"Wanna bet?" I dug my elbow in harder, and he grimaced. "I'm beginning to think we'd be better off without you," I said. "Eadric's already offered me that apartment down at Albert Dock, but it's starting to feel like a bit of a cheap pay-off, given all the drama I'm having to deal with. Maybe he'll help me take over York instead."

"Eadric knows the truth," Ivo managed. "He knows none of us can do this alone."

"Do *what*, Ivo? Deal with your demonic crotchspawn?"

"Who's crotchspawn?" Missy dropped through the hatch. "Al's looking after Rachel. They seem to like each other. Have you found Mapp ye—" She looked round at the assembled company. "What the hell is going on here?"

"You missed the excitement," I said drily. Jude stepped forward and helped me pull Ivo to his feet, each of us holding an arm so he couldn't make his escape. "Don't suppose you saw someone running off into the darkness on your way in? Wearing white, got a face like a wet weekend in Rhyl?"

Missy shook her head. She caught sight of Mapp, still slumped in the corner of the crypt, and ran over to him. "Are you okay?" she asked. "What on earth happened?"

197

He managed a weak smile. "You'd better ask Martha, here," he said. Missy looked at the woman sitting next to him. Her mouth opened and closed a couple of times, but no sound came out.

"Our Martha figured out the secret to eternal youth," I said. "I haven't decided what to do with her yet."

Missy got slowly to her feet and turned to face me. "I take it he," she nodded at Ivo, who was standing silently between me and Jude, clearly having given up the fight, "had something to do with all of this? And," she said, seemingly noticing Jude for the first time, "who the fuck is that?"

"This is Jude," I said. "They're Elizabeth's..." I looked at Jude for help, but got nothing, "...friend. I can only assume they realised something was happening and decided to come help."

"What an honour," said Missy, her tone making it sound like it was anything but. "I've never known Middlesex take sides before."

"Elizabeth has promised me her support," I said, glancing sideways to make sure Ivo was taking note of the conversation. His eyes flashed, but he stayed silent.

"Well now," said Missy, "isn't that fortuitous?" She nodded. "I'm very pleased to meet you, Jude."

For the briefest of seconds, Jude was distracted and their grip on Ivo loosened. "*Now!*" I said. He kicked out at Jude, bounced up onto my shoulder and disappeared out into the night.

Well, Someone Has To Take Charge

As soon as Ivo had made his escape, Jude turned on me, but I was expecting it. "Oh no you don't," I hissed, when they tried to grab me. "You're on *my* territory now." I stood my ground and for a few ridiculous seconds, we must have looked like a pair of comedy horror characters stuck in the middle of a dramatic standoff. Then Jude narrowed their eyes at me and, with one last shrug, bounced up and out of the crypt. I turned and looked across to where Missy had moved to sit back down next to Mapp. She put an arm round him, and he rested his head on her shoulder.

"Will he be okay?" I asked. Rain hammered down through the roof hatch, pushing fresh air into the dank room.

"I think so," said Missy. "He'll need to take it easy until he's built his strength back up."

"Can you let Heggie know?" Mapp's voice was croaky. "He'll be frantic by now."

"He's with Kitty," I said, "at my place. I'm sure she'll have kept him busy teaching Grimm new tricks that he shouldn't really be capable of."

Mapp raised his head slightly and managed a weak smile. "That cat," he said, "is capable of far more than you could ever imagine, Lili."

"Yeah," I said, grinning back at him, "that's what concerns me."

"What are we going to do with her?" said Missy, jerking her head towards Martha. The older woman was also sitting against the wall, but she was ramrod straight and gazing at me with clear and unrepentant eyes.

"Who's running the yarn shop now?" I asked.

"It's gone," said Missy. "We cancelled the lease after Martha was moved up here."

"I've still got all the stock," said Mapp unexpectedly. "It's in boxes, up on the top shelves in the bookshop."

"Do you want to stay here?" I asked Martha. "In Anfield, I mean."

"What is it to you what I want to do?" she said. "I'm a free woman, I can do whatever I—" I stepped forward, looming over her as she stared up and attempted to hide her panic.

"I asked if you wanted to stay in Anfield," I said, glaring down at her. "It's as much free choice as you're going to get, so make the most of it."

"How dare you," she started, but I'd grabbed her throat and had her pinned against the wall.

"Don't even think about giving me that shit," I hissed into her face. "You nearly killed my friend, Martha. You nearly killed Mapp." The man himself lifted a weak arm in agreement. "The only reason you're still sitting here now and not shoved into one of those storage niches in many small pieces is because you didn't succeed. So," I pressed even closer into her and a look of fear finally crept into her eyes, "you will do as you are fucking told. Do you understand?" She nodded. "So I suggest you make a choice."

"Yes," she mumbled. "Yes, I'd like to stay here. Not in the crypt, though," she added hurriedly.

"No one's staying in the crypt," I said. "It's about time this place was left for those who are properly dead. You can stay at Missy's until I sort something out."

"What the fuck?" began Missy, but I held up a hand to stop her.

"Whether or not any of us likes it," I said, "—and believe me, I don't—I'm clearly going to have to take charge of at least some of the organising around here. She won't be with you for long. Hopefully Eadric's property portfolio includes something in the Anfield area. And if not, I'll just have to find him an investment project. Martha will make an excellent long-term tenant. Plus," I turned to Martha, "you can run some classes down at Flora's. Give back to the community." She attempted a scowl, but I could see she was struggling not to look pleased. "No one will recognise you," I went on, "and if they do, you can pretend to be your own granddaughter or something. As for you," I turned to Gaultier Mapp, "you'll stay at Missy's until I get Heggie to come take you home. Then you will avoid any and all excitement until you get your strength back. Understood?"

Mapp raised a hand and gave me a wobbly salute. "Aye aye, Cap'n."

"Right," I sighed, "I'd better go face the music."

***

Leaving a bemused Missy to deal with Mapp and the youthful Martha, I clambered out of the crypt and let myself out through the gate back into the cemetery proper. It was still raining heavily, but the occasional distant clap of thunder suggested the storm was moving out to sea. I've got one of those shipping apps on my phone because I enjoy identifying the boats I spot on the Mersey, and I thought briefly of the little brave fishing boats that would be bobbing around in the creeping morning light, with the thunder pounding above them. I'd have liked to have checked who was out there this morning, but I'd left my phone in the flat when I'd left in a hurry the previous evening. The early morning traffic was building as I walked casually down into town, and the pavements were dotted with brightly coloured umbrellas as people walked into town to start another day in the endless shops and offices that take up most of Liverpool's real estate. I was in no hurry to make it back to the Liver Building. If Jude was here, then so was Elizabeth. I pictured her and Eadric standing in front of me with their hands on their hips, like irritated parents waiting to hear their child's excuses for the latest scrape they'd got into. *Well*, I thought, *they can just bloody wait.*

You have done nothing wrong.

Still here? I'd got as far as St John's Lane and remembered to stop at the edge of the road to check for traffic before crossing over to Whitechapel. It was too easy to slip into undead speed and simply zip through the city, but today I wanted to make the most of it. I risked a breath when I was sure no humans were around for me to accidentally drain of energy and the petrichor scent hit me like a brick wall to the face. I could smell warmth and chlorophyll and a sweet scent of something unidentifiable, but which

I was fairly sure was a flower of some kind. Turning towards the smell, I spotted an overgrown honeysuckle clambering heavily over a crumbling wall, its flowers already pushing their faces up to the morning light. *I miss the smell of flowers.*

There is nothing to stop you breathing, Lilith. You just have to learn not to kill anyone. And that was the problem, wasn't it? Of course I could still breathe—my lungs hadn't dropped out of my body when I'd died—but if humans were around, then I sucked in their life force along with the scent of summer roses. There'd been enough killing already this year—I could live without being responsible for any more deaths, however accidental.

If anyone can do it, said the city, **you can.**

Just a little bit now and then, I thought. *I can handle it.* With a hollow laugh, I kept walking.

Despite the risk of witnesses, I decided to take the quickest route. Scrambling up the side of the Liver Building like Catwoman herself, I dropped into Eadric's rooms through a side window and bounced off the armchair positioned beneath the sill. Unfortunately for both of us, Nik was sitting reading in the chair at the time. I picked him up and rescued the paperback that had been knocked under a nearby bookcase, before straightening up ready to argue with the grownups. Elizabeth was sitting on the elegant velvet sofa opposite me, with Jude next to her. They were both looking at me with uncomprehending expressions on their faces. Eadric, however, clearly comprehended only too well and was already pacing the carpet in a fury.

"What the hell are you playing at?" he demanded.

The only way out is through. Never forget that.

"Ivo turned up to rescue Mab," I said, forcing myself to speak loudly and clearly. "She escaped, but Jude helped me capture Ivo. And then I let him go."

Eadric's expression was incredulous. "Why?"

"Because," I said, "Ivo isn't our problem. There's something else brewing—something only he knows about. The city—I mean, I—think it's vampires."

"So why let Ivo go?" Eadric asked. "Why not keep him and force him to tell us what's going on?" It was a reasonable question.

"Because Mab had already escaped," I said. "And if she gets back up north before he does, I suspect he's going to have a battle for his own territory."

"Why do you think the vampires are suddenly a threat?" asked Elizabeth.

I turned to look at her. "You know about the vampires," I said. "We talked about it in Highgate."

"We all have vampires," said Elizabeth, "even in London. The difference is what we each choose to do about them."

It had been a very long day, and my patience was wearing thin. "Why don't you tell me, then?" I asked sharply. "As you're clearly the expert?" I heard a thump from behind me and thought it might have been Nik's book hitting the floor again.

"How dare you speak to Elizabeth like that," said Eadric. "She came here to *help* you, Lilith. You will apologise." He stepped forward and caught hold of my arm.

"TAKE YOUR HANDS OFF ME, EADRIC SILVERTON." My voice sounded as though it had come from the very fabric of the world around us. Eadric's eyes widened in shock, but he didn't let go. I glared at him. "I WILL NOT TELL YOU AGAIN."

Elizabeth was still sitting on the sofa, and Jude bent to speak into her ear again. "No," said Elizabeth, loud enough for us to hear. "You're thinking of the character from the fantasy books. Lilith here isn't a walking, talking anthropomorphic personification, she's just being Lilith." She turned to Eadric. "I would suggest you let go, my dear. If Lilith believes that Ivo is better with his freedom, then that's her decision to make."

"We expect certain standards of behaviour," said Eadric, doggedly. He dropped my arm, though.

"You might," said Elizabeth with a delicate shrug, "but I've never needed it. People always insist on making an effort around me, of course, but I've never really understood why. I think perhaps the world is still rather too easily unnerved by a powerful woman. Wouldn't you agree, Lilith?"

"I'm not interested in your ridiculous undead bickering," I snapped. "I'm more worried about figuring out what the fuck is *really* going on." Eadric looked horrified, but Elizabeth just smiled. Jude's expression was utterly impassive. Nik had his book up in front of his face, but by the way his shoulders were shaking, I suspected that he, too, was struggling to take Eadric's etiquette worries seriously. "Anyway," I went on, "like I said, there'd have been no point holding Ivo prisoner. If we—you—kept him here, that would leave the north-east unprotected. I'd bet good money Mab would take immediate advantage of that. And Mab isn't ever going to back us up, however much we need it."

"And you think Ivo will?" asked Elizabeth.

"Yes," I said. "He needs us as much as we need him."

"What's to stop him joining forces with Mab?" asked Eadric. "She's presumably got some of her mother's powers, and he'd be in control of her."

"Ah," I said, "there's a very good reason why I don't think that's going to happen."

***

"His *daughter?*" Elizabeth was staring at me in astonishment. "But how?"

"Exactly what I asked him," I shrugged. "But ol' Casanova himself informs me he has no problems in that department."

"I can understand the physical ability," said Elizabeth, who looked distinctly as though she was trying not to snigger, "but I had no idea it might be possible for a revenant to impregnate a human female." If Eadric had been capable of vomiting, I'd have been passing over the sick bucket by now. He was currently sitting at his desk with his head in his hands. "And you say this Mab is human?" asked Elizabeth.

"I have no idea what Mab is," I said, honestly. "She's not any one thing, I don't think. Her father's a revenant and her mother was at least half witch. She has certain...powers."

"Such as?" asked Elizabeth. Jude was sitting next to Elizabeth on the sofa, watching me intently. There was no animosity in their gaze, but I was pretty sure it would take a while for me to earn back any trust Jude may have had in me.

"She brought my brother to me," I said flatly, "despite the fact that he died twenty-two years ago. Mab couldn't have known he even existed, yet she made him appear in front of me looking as real as you all do now."

"How?" asked Elizabeth. "An enforced vision of some kind? Perhaps a form of hypnotism?"

"It seemed absolutely real to me," I said, remembering Cally's odd socks. "And she can't have known the details. I think she somehow pulled it from my actual memories."

"Her mother could do the same," said Eadric suddenly. We all turned to look at him. He slowly raised his head to face me. "She liked to torment me with it," he said. "When she thought I was being particularly difficult."

"And you didn't punish her for this?" asked Elizabeth softly. "Why didn't you simply cast her out the first time she did it?"

Eadric was silent for a moment. "Because her favoured weapon was visions of my first wife," he said finally. "Golda. The only woman I truly loved, and who I lost through my own stupid actions. Maria knew how it made me feel, and she used it against me." This was the first I'd heard of Eadric having any wife other than Maria. By the looks on the other faces in the room, it was news to them as well.

"But you stayed with her," I said, stupidly. "For decades. You could have got rid of her, like Elizabeth says. Or just cut her bloody head off and saved me a job!"

"If it meant seeing Golda again," said Eadric, "I could tolerate anything. I did love Maria, at least some of the time. But she couldn't bear to be thwarted in anything and took revenge when she was. Maria liked to make Golda appear in front of me as though she were real. She would allow me just enough time to sink into a fantasy of what might have been, before ripping her away again. It tore out my heart anew every time she did it. But what she never realised was that each time she brought Golda to me, my heart filled up once more. When Maria...died," he glanced at me, "my grief was for Golda. Because my chances of ever seeing her again also died that day."

"I never knew," said Nik. "All this time we've been friends, and you'd never thought to mention your first wife to me?"

Eadric turned to look at Nik with a shadow of a smile on his face. "Have you ever told me the details of your true love?" he asked. "The real one?" Nik looked shifty. "No," said Eadric, "I thought not. I've long had my suspicions, of course. But I'm not crass enough to question a friend about their personal troubles."

"John Fitzgibbon," I blurted. Suddenly I knew who Nik really was, and why Mum had been so flustered when she met him in the Birds Nest café. Dead poets society, indeed. Everyone turned to look at me. "I, er…" I stumbled, "Things are coming back to me. Sorry. Some of it's a bit…unexpected."

"What does this person have to do with the current conversation?" Eadric asked. But it was Nik I was looking at. He'd turned even paler than usual and his eyes were fixed on me.

"How do you know that?" he finally asked, his voice quiet.

"I don't know," I said. "I must have read it at some point. Maybe when I was doing my degree?" Nik's expression was unreadable. "I'm sorry," I said to him, "I didn't mean to upset you."

"You haven't," said Nik, getting up from his chair and heading towards the door that led into the Silverton's personal quarters. I'd never even been close to seeing inside Eadric's rooms, but I'd once spent an afternoon with Nik in his. I'd discovered he had a penchant for large squishy sofas with horribly real fur throws. 'They're all so ridiculously vintage that they barely count as animals these days,' he'd said. But he didn't argue when I bought him several faux fur replacements from the big TK Maxx up on Church Street. "Anyway," said Nik, "I'll leave you to it." The door closed behind him. We all gazed silently at it for a long moment.

"Well," said Elizabeth, breaking the tension, "what do we do now? Or rather," she looked from Eadric to me, and back again, "what will *you* do?"

"Same thing we do every night," I said. "Try to take over the world. Ignore me," I went on hurriedly, "that's from something else. I swear I don't know what's going on in my head right now." Elizabeth smiled, not unkindly.

"Anyway," I said to her, "what are you doing up here? In Liverpool, I mean. I thought you didn't leave London if you could help it?"

"If I can help it," she said. "But I thought it worth the effort on this occasion. Just after you and Nikolaus left us, we had warning that Mab was perhaps going to try something. No one could be exactly sure what that something might be, so I—we," she put a hand on Jude's shoulder, "—decided to follow you. We flew, of course." Of course. I tried to imagine either of the Highgate revenants sitting on a Ryanair plane filled with stag parties and failed miserably. "Even Jude and I can't run that fast. And anyway, people tend to stare if a runner overtakes their car. So we came up to Liverpool for a little family reunion." The ghost of a wink. "It was agreed that I would stay here with Eadric and discuss future tactics, while Jude would head over to Anfield in case you needed help." She tilted her head at me. "But it appears you are perfectly capable of making your own decisions."

"What might the future tactics involve?" I asked.

"You're assuming anyone wants to discuss it with you, Lilith," said Eadric. I raised an eyebrow, but before I could open my mouth and drop both feet in it yet again, Elizabeth intervened.

"I would suggest," she said to Eadric, "that you consider dropping the habit of a very long lifetime, and allow someone else to share the burden of power."

"Oh no you don't," I said, before Eadric could reply, "I don't *want* any power. Eadric can keep it. It's all his, absolutely nothing to do with me."

"The problem," Eadric sighed, "is that it's not your decision to make. Nor mine, for that matter. How are you getting on with that extra baggage in your head?"

You were never going to be able to keep us secret.

"What are you talking about?" I asked, but I knew it was futile.

"The city's never tried to speak to me," Eadric said. "And I know from talking to Elizabeth here," she nodded, "that she hasn't experienced anything like it in London, either."

"Which is a good thing," said Elizabeth firmly. "No one needs a city in their head."

"Except me, apparently." I said. "Whether or not I agree to it."

We'd apologise, but it would make no difference, said the city. *The fate of the whole is more important than the needs of the individual. And we need you.*

I wish I could pretend to be flattered, but I'd rather not feel entirely insane, if it's all the same to you.

Sorry.

No, you're not. There was silence inside my head. Which was a pleasant novelty after the night I'd had. "It's a steep learning curve," I said to Eadric eventually. "But I'm slowly getting used to it."

See, there was definitely a pleased tone to the voice in my head, *you love us really.*

"Anyway," I said, "we'll have to sort the details out another time. I've got a vampire to re-home."

Super Furry Vampire

I'd tried to argue my case for using the Alfa, but Eadric had certain absolute lines he would never cross. Allowing a filthy vampire to be transported in his beloved car was, apparently, one of them. "No animals in the car," was his exact response. I countered it with a brief lecture about the perils of bigotry against other races, while Elizabeth and Jude looked on—Elizabeth smiling, Jude absolutely impassive. Which is why I was currently driving through Liverpool city centre with a terrified vampire in the back of my Beetle. Basil might be old, but he's well looked after—especially since the incident with Maria and the tunnels and his subsequent stay at the VW rehab centre. Much to everyone's disgust, I'd crowned his aesthetic renaissance by fitting a set of black, furry seat covers. Nik suggested I finish things off properly with a pair of fluffy dice hanging in the middle of the front windscreen and I'd spent quite some time searching for them online, despite Nik's protestations that he'd been joking, actually, for god's sake Lilith have you got *no* taste, etc. Anyway I eventually discovered they'd been all but banned in the UK because they had an unfortunate tendency to block a driver's view of the road. So I made do with a black tree-shaped air freshener dangling from the mirror, like every other car owner in Britain. Looking in said mirror as I negotiated the roundabout in front of the World Museum, I saw that Rachel was still curled up into a tight ball on the back seat, with a duvet draped over her back and her face wedged into the fluffy upholstery. *I hope she doesn't drool*, I thought to myself, teeth clenching as I pulled onto Dale Street and narrowly avoided being rear-ended by someone in a black BMW who hadn't bothered to check for other traffic as they pulled out of the Queensway tunnel. Making the universal hand signal for 'try using your eyeballs next time, dickhead,' I slowed down and resigned myself to sitting in traffic for the next fifteen minutes. Luckily, it was still early enough that I'd be able to park Basil up at Harrington Street before the barriers went up for the day. I gazed down the road towards the Town Hall, watching pedestrians dodging puddles and jumping out of the way of cars that were still managing to send up water spray, despite traffic being at a crawl.

"Would have been quicker to walk," I said idly. There was no response from the back seat. "You'll like Flora's," I went on, determined to make conversation, even if it was one-sided. I'm the same in taxis, insisting on chatting to drivers whether they like it or not. The ridiculous thing is that I rarely even *want* to speak. And the drivers always give the distinct impression they'd be happy to continue listening to the non-stop rotation of cheesy hits that always seem to be playing on *Liverpool Live.* And I genuinely like that radio station, because there is nothing better than dancing round the kitchen to a bit of Lionel Richie and this is a hill I would absolutely die on, if I wasn't dead already. But nope—something in the primal section of my brain insists I fill all silences with *something* in order to make contact with strangers. We were at a standstill less than a single Basil's length from where I needed to turn onto Castle Street. I looked down towards the Liver Building to see if Bertie was behaving, and noticed movement on the roof. It was Nik—I'd recognised that flouncy outline anywhere. I watched as he settled himself down at Bertie's feet. No doubt the poor bird was going to have a morning of dramatic poetry, whilst Nik got the angst out of his system. I felt a bit mean, as it was almost certainly my fault for accidentally mentioning Nik's lost love up in Eadric's office. I'd have to apologise at some point. And then probably apologise to Bertie as well. "Comfy back there?" Still nothing.

Are you sure this is a good idea? asked the city. I sighed. Just when I'd begun to think I was once again the sole occupant of my own head.

Ach, I replied silently, *it's just one little vampire living in the flat below me. She'll stay out of everyone's way and at least I'll know she's safe. What could possibly go wrong?*

Quite a lot.

Oh ye of little faith. I finally managed to turn left onto Castle Street. Both the city and the vampire stayed quiet until I was pulling onto the southern section of Harrington Street and waiting for a woman pushing a pram to untangle her pug, who'd got its lead wrapped around one of the pram's wheels just as she was crossing in front of me.

"Stay-with-you," came the voice from the back street. I looked in the rear-view mirror and could just see Rachel's blue eyes peeking out from underneath the pile of bedding I'd borrowed for her from Missy. I say 'borrowed'—it was more a case of me stomping around and glaring at Missy until Alan had nudged her and said maybe it would be easier to just let me take the contents of the airing cupboard. The clincher had been me suggesting Rachel could maybe just stay with them until I'd got the flat kitted out with basics, at which point Missy had thumped up the stairs and banged around dramatically, before throwing a random pile of laundry down and telling me to help myself.

"Yeah," I said, "you're coming home with me." I waved to the woman with the pram who'd finally untangled the dog and was mouthing apologies at me, then pulled into the narrow road. The part of Harrington Street that Flora's sits on is quiet and pedestrianised, but the first section—between Castle Street and North John Street—is open to traffic. It's also a handy spot to park for many local workers *and* it was bin day, so I drove slowly, careful not to scratch Basil's paintwork on the endless wheelie bins that were jutting out into the street. I finally made it across onto 'my' section and pulled Basil into his parking space next to Flora's, just as Izzy appeared from the Button Street end. She must have stayed at her flat last night, rather than with Damon. The rain was easing off now, but Izzy still carried an umbrella. It was bright red with black spines and had a pagoda-style design that would have her accusing me of cultural appropriation, had I dared carry it myself. It suited Izzy perfectly, because of course it did. She was dressed in a fifties-style flowered number that was more rockabilly than tea dress and had black ballet pumps on her feet. By the way she was tiptoeing around puddles, I guessed the pumps weren't waterproof. "Wait here," I said to Rachel, as I got out of the car. "I need to go explain things to Izzy." Rachel closed her eyes tightly and hunched down again, pulling the duvet over herself so that from outside the car, it looked as though I was just home from the laundromat.

"Hey, dead girl," called Izzy, grinning at me as she negotiated a last puddle just outside the door to Flora's. "You haven't forgotten you're working with me today?" My face must have given me away. "Aah," she said, rolling her eyes.

"It's fine," I lied. "I haven't got anything on." I paused. "Thing is," Izzy turned to look at me, her key already in the lock and one neat eyebrow sharply raised, "I'm moving a tenant in today. Into the flat below mine."

"What sort of tenant?" she asked, rightly suspicious. I pulled a face. "Oh," she said flatly. "*That* sort of tenant. Well," she unlocked the door and stepped inside, "you're the boss. Apparently."

"I know I'm not here enough at the moment," I said. "It's just really difficult fitting everything in."

"Zombie life busier than you expected, is it?"

I stepped into the doorway after her and slumped back against the wall. "Everything is *entirely* stupid," I sighed. Izzy gave me a sympathetic look before heading behind the counter to fill the coffee machine.

"Sean was asking after you," she said, noisily tipping coffee beans into the hopper.

"Huh," I grumped, "did he have the lovely Sophie with him?"

"Who's Sophie?" asked Izzy, scrunching up the empty coffee bean bag and dropping it into the bin. She reached up to unhook her apron from its hook next to the door into the staff room. "Oh," she looked up as she tied the apron strings behind her back, "that blonde woman?" I nodded. "You missed the drama," Izzy grinned. "Can't believe I forgot to tell you!"

"What happened?" I kind of hated myself for being so obvious, but it wasn't going to stop me catching up on the gossip. "They looked properly loved-up last time I saw them."

Izzy snorted. "Yeah," she said, "that's what I thought, an' all. Mind yourself,"

I stepped back as the bakery delivery man appeared in the doorway.

"Had to pull in at the end," he said as he slid past me with two large boxes in his arms, "bloody barriers have gone up early. Anyway," he placed the boxes onto the counter in front of Izzy, "how are you lovely ladies today?"

"We're very well, Frank," said Izzy, "thank you for asking. How about you?"

"Ah, y'know," said Frank, "no rest for the wicked." We both smiled and nodded as expected. Frank gave Izzy the invoice and she tucked it down the side of the till. "Got some extras in there today," he said, nodding at the boxes. "Laura's started a new line of Danish pastries, she thought you might like them. Apparently," he turned to me with a wink, "they're your favourite."

"Always here for a Danish, Frank," I agreed, cursing the fact I could never actually try them out. I'd have to get Izzy to let me know how they tasted, just in case I ever bumped into Laura and she asked. Not for the first time, I sighed inwardly at the irony of the owner of a cafe renowned for its cakes being unable to actually eat anything off the menu.

"Nice and warm, they are," said Frank, "just like my heart." I stepped backwards into the disused inner hallway that led up to the empty flats. *Shit*, I thought, *I've left Rachel in the car.* As if the Fates were listening, that was the moment the screaming started. I barged past Frank, nearly sending him flying across a table, and got round to where Basil was parked just in time to see Grimm throwing the grandaddy of all hissy fits on the bonnet. He was up on all four tiptoes, his back arched more impressively than the Chinatown gateway and his copious fur sticking out in all directions. It took me a confused few seconds to realise that the target of his ire was the shrieking vampire inside the car. Rachel was flapping her hands at the inside of the windscreen, presumably in an attempt to scare Grimm off, whilst simultaneously emitting a noise not unlike a freight train hitting its emergency brakes. Basil was rocking on his tyres and Grimm had his claws extended in order to grip himself onto the rubber seal that ran round the base of the windshield.

"Pack it the fuck in!" I yelled as I strode across to the car. Grimm sank down slightly and turned to look at me, his huge owlish eyes unblinking as I approached. He then slowly turned his gaze back to Rachel, who had indeed packed it in. She was frozen in position, leaning across from the back seat with one hand on the steering wheel. As I opened my mouth to speak, her hand slipped and landed heavily on Basil's old-fashioned, loud-enough-to-make-your-teeth-clench, added-by-me-at-Eadric's-expense-without-him-even-knowing, airhorn. Grimm leapt off the car in an explosion of fur, using my shoulders as a stepping stone to the safety of the fire escape. I actually heard my skin rip under his claws. Rachel was now screaming as loudly as I've ever heard anyone scream in my entire life—which was impressive, because she'd slid down into the rear footwell and was hunched back into a tight little ball. "ENOUGH!" It was my full 'Tales from the Crypt' voice, and it had the required effect. The noise from inside the car stopped as if the audio had been cut at the mains. I turned slowly round to see Frank staring at me from outside the door to Flora's, a look of abject fear across his face. To balance things slightly, Izzy stood behind Frank with her hands on her hips and an expression on her face that implied I'd probably be better off out of it, for an hour or so at least.

"Got some voice on you these days, lass." I hadn't even noticed Billy taking up position in his doorway while I was inside Flora's. "It's a fair pair of lungs you have, and no mistake."

"Things just get a bit much sometimes, is all," I said, turning my back on his amused grin. I opened the driver's door of the car and leaned in, pretending not to see Frank making a run for it while my back was turned. "Come on," I said to Rachel, "let's get you inside." I'd had the car windows open while driving through town, but had closed them when I parked up. The stench rising from the vampire filled the car with an odour strong enough to singe the hairs from my nostrils, and that was without me even breathing. "I'll run you a bath," I said. "Won't that be nice?"

***

Rachel had taken some persuading to leave the security of the car. She

214

hunched down into the footwell and pulled the duvet over her head like a small child, making quietly pained squeaking noises as I tried to physically pull her out. In the end, I went with threats of pure violence. "If you don't get out of this car right now," I said, "I'm going to send in the cat." After a few seconds of tense silence, Rachel's head slowly appeared from under the duvet, her eyes tight with fear. "Come on," I said sternly, "inside the cafe and up the stairs, before he spots you." The vampire literally scuttled across the car park to the door to Flora's, despite me knowing damn fine she could walk upright. Perhaps she thought keeping a low profile would help her hide from Grimm. Billy watched the entire thing play out in amused silence, sitting in his blanket nest like a kid waiting for the Saturday morning cartoons to start on tv. As I'd given Rachel a shove through the doorway to the inner stairwell that I never used, I caught a glimpse of Izzy inside Flora's. She was refilling the little bowls we use for salt and sugar sachets and looked up as we went past. She rolled her eyes dramatically and I heard a heavily weary sigh through the closed door, before she turned her back and disappeared behind the counter.

I got Rachel upstairs to the flat immediately below mine, only to realise just as I opened its front door that I'd forgotten it had no furnishings. Laid out exactly the same as my own flat on the floor above, Rachel's new home was bare of anything except a bedroom filled with storage boxes. If my memory was correct—and I suspected it was, judging by my recent upsurge in forensically accurate recollections—the boxes contained nothing more useful than chairs, tablecloths and an endless array of framed paintings of the style favoured by old-fashioned cafes in the 1980s. It had all been taken out of Flora's by me and Izzy, just after I'd signed the lease a couple of years earlier. Time certainly flies when you're having...well. Not *fun*, exactly. But no one could deny the fact that I was certainly living in Interesting Times. The rain had given way to sun, and it was already warm enough for me to suspect the heatwave was going to attempt a comeback. In the bright light coming through the uncovered windows, Rachel looked absolutely pitiful. I wrapped the duvet back round her and sat her down in a corner of what was, in theory, the living room. "I'm going to fetch you some things," I said, as she gazed blankly up at me with those huge blue eyes of hers. There was something different about Rachel, and it wasn't just that she had blue eyes, rather than the brown-black that was standard vampire issue. She'd told me she didn't drink blood, but surely she couldn't have meant it literally? If she was telling the truth, then I didn't think she'd been a vampire for very long—and she wasn't likely to survive. Vampires aren't like revenants—they have no option but to feed. If they don't, they lose both their strength and cognitive abilities really fast. I'd have to go talk to Joe at some point—maybe he'd have some ideas for potential meal replacements for her. There was nothing I could do right now—I'd just have to get her as settled as best as I could and worry about the rest later. "Stay here," I said to her. "I won't be long."

I left the vampire curled up on the floor and raced up the short flight of stairs to my flat on the floor above. As I put my hand on the door to open it, I remembered it was bolted from the inside. I'd never got round to fixing the lock broken by the vampires who'd prompted my accidental death in the spring, relying on the inside bolt and my own supernatural powers for protection from potential intruders. "Kitty?" I called, loudly, "are you in?" I heard noises from inside the flat, then steps coming towards the door. Heggie must have stayed overnight. *Oh god,* I thought, *I forgot to tell Heggie that Mapp was safe. Well, safe-ish.* At least I'd be able to give him some reasonably good news. But to my absolute astonishment, when the door opened, it was Kitty standing there in the tiny hallway corner I barely used. She had a grin on her face to rival that of the Cheshire Cat. "Crikey," I said, "you're really improving!"

Kitty laughed and pointed downwards. "It wasn't me," she said. I looked down to where Grimm was sitting at her feet and casually cleaning himself.

"You're not seriously trying to tell me Grimm's learned to open bolts?" And it was a heavy bolt—the sort you more usually find on garden gates that need an extra bit of security.

"I told you he was clever," said Kitty smugly. "Anyway, why are you coming in this way? I've never known you to use the staircase."

"I'm putting a new tenant in the downstairs flat," I said. "It's a long story.

Anyway, there's nothing in the place and I need to at least give her some basics."

Kitty's face lit up. "Oh," she squeaked, "I'm so pleased you're finally making friends!"

"What on earth are you talking about?" I stepped through into my flat and saw Heggie asleep on the sofa.

"He's so tired, bless him," said Kitty, appearing beside me. "Stayed up all night hoping for news on Mapp, but couldn't help nodding off this morning. I haven't had the heart to disturb him."

"Leave him be," I said. "Mapp's safe." Kitty looked relieved, but didn't ask questions. I thought Heggie's need to sleep probably answered my wonderings about whether or not he was a revenant. Although if Mab was anything to go by, there was nothing to say Heggie wasn't a happy little mix of all kinds of things. Clearly, the supernatural world was as varied as the human one. With hindsight, I wondered why it hadn't occurred to me before now that even undead races might not be entirely isolated. That would give David-the-pharmacist something to get his research teeth into. If he was still alive, of course, which I doubted very much. I headed into my bedroom and knelt down to look under the bed. Bingo. I pulled out the storage box filled with spare bedding. Then I rooted through my clothes drawers and found a complete set of clean clothes. Rachel was a good bit thinner than me, but the brown pyjama bottoms with drawings of cookies all over them had a drawstring waist, so hopefully she could pull them in enough to make sure they stayed up. And they were made of fabric that was heavy enough to do for outdoor wear if needs be, as were the vest top and t-shirt I added to the pile. A couple of pairs each of pants and socks, and I figured it would do for now. I went into the bathroom and pulled a bottle of foam bath liquid and a Lush bubble bar out of the little storage tower that held my few toiletries. I still loved my baths, but these days the smell of most bath foams is too much for my ridiculously oversensitive sense of smell, so I'd thrown most of it away since I'd died. Hopefully Rachel would appreciate a bit of luxury. "I'm off back downstairs," I said to Kitty, as I walked back into the living room. Heggie hadn't moved, and Kitty was sitting in the armchair with Grimm happily curled up on her lap. He opened his eyes slowly and gazed at me with an expression of complete disinterest. "Need to sort out the other flat."

"So, who's your new pal?" asked Kitty. "Will we like them?" By 'we', I assumed she meant herself and the cat.

"Depends whether or not you like vampires, I guess." I pulled the door open and shoved my foot against it to stop it from closing again. "Can you lock this after me?" I said. "I'll come back the normal way once I'm done."

"You're not seriously moving a vampire in downstairs?" asked Kitty, as she walked across to hold the door. Actually *hold* the door, I noticed. Grimm padded over to stand by her feet.

"This isn't your standard vampire," I said. "She saved my life, apart from anything else." Kitty looked unconvinced. "I treat people the way they treat me, Kitty," I said. "Rachel—the vampire downstairs—put herself at risk to help me, so I'm going to help her in return. Because if I don't, the rest of the bloodsuckers will probably kill her."

"Is she nice?" asked Kitty, unexpectedly.

I squinted my eyes at her, trying to decide whether she was taking the piss. "I don't know yet," I said, stepping out into the stairwell. "But I don't think she's dangerous, if that's what you mean. Not to any of us, anyway. And like I said—she saved my life."

"Okay," said Kitty, "then we help her." Without another word, she stepped backwards and let go of the door. As it closed, I watched her and Grimm walk back to the window together, like the world's weirdest double act.

I went back downstairs to the no longer empty flat and let myself in. Rachel was also staring out onto the street. She turned to look when I walked in and gave a silent smile of acknowledgment before turning back to the window. I left her to it and went through to the stash of storage boxes in the bedroom. I found what I was looking for in the third box—a pile of cushions from a set of outside garden chairs that had long been handed over to the scrap-iron man. We'd only kept the cushions because he'd refused to take them, saying they were probably mouldy and that he was only going to sell the frames for their scrap value, anyway. I'd been all for dropping them into the first open skip we found, but Izzy had some idea about re-covering them in a brighter fabric. They'd stayed in the box ever since, and I was fairly sure Izzy would have forgotten they even existed. There was also a set of ragged but serviceable curtains in a splodgy shade of dark grey. Although Rachel didn't have to hide from sunlight like most mythical vampires, I figured the curtains would give the flat an appearance of normality. I carried my trophies into the living room to find Rachel still staring out onto the street. "Anything interesting going on?" I asked, as I tipped the cushions onto the floor. My plan was to bodge together something like a sofa bed with the cushions and duvets. "Why don't I run you a bath?" I asked. Silence. She was still staring out of the window, so I went to stand by her and looked out to see what was so interesting. Harrington Street was quiet, which was a rarity in itself these days. Billy was curled up in his customary 'pretending to be sleep' position and all was quiet. A couple who, from the view I had of the tops of their grey heads, were probably in their seventies or more, sat at one of the outside tables in front of Flora's, sharing a pot of tea. They each had a plate in front of them—one classic scone and a piece of the carrot and walnut cake I used to love so much. It had sultanas in it—a blasphemy according to cake classicists, but to me it was food of the gods.

And now I would never taste it again. Or if I did, I'd have to spit it out, which kind of defeated the object. I was going to have to think up some replacement indulgences, before the afterlife became nothing but murder and boredom—two things you wouldn't normally put together, but which between them currently seemed to fill my life. I looked up and down the street, still unsure what Rachel was finding so fascinating. Other than a security guard leaning against the wall outside the hotel at the end of the street, there was no one else to be seen. "I was human," said Rachel, suddenly. Her voice still wasn't exactly clear, but it was definitely more coherent than it had been. "Wasn't I?"

"I'd imagine so," I said, shocked into truthfulness. "At some point."

"Not from here," she said. "From another place." She still had a raspy tone to her voice that made it difficult to make out an accent, but I thought I could detect a hint of Bristolian.

"How old are you?" I asked her. There was a long silence as we both stared out of the window and pondered our own thoughts.

"Dunno," she said eventually. "Not long dead."

I turned slightly and leaned back against the window frame to look at her. "You'll be properly dead soon," I said, "if you don't start eating."

"Not bad," she said, her face crumpling as though she might cry. "Good. Always good. I..." she trailed off for a second, before apparently getting a second wind. "I like people."

"Well, that's a start," I said. "Let's get you in the bath. You'll feel better for being clean." And I'd be able to stop worrying about potential complaints about the entire building smelling of decomposing corpses. It couldn't have seeped down as far as the cafe yet or Izzy would have been upstairs to yell at me, but it was only a matter of time. Rachel was staring out of the window again, so I left her to it and went to run the bath. The taps clearly hadn't been used in a very long time, and it took a fair bit of strength to wrench them to the 'on' position. The pipes clanked ominously for a few seconds, before there was a loud glugging sound and suddenly the hot tap began spewing brown water. I pulled the plug back out hurriedly and let the water go straight down the drain until both taps were running clear. Once I was reasonably sure any lurking legionnaires disease had been washed out, I put the plug back in. While I was waiting for the bath to fill, I went back into the living room to where Rachel was still standing at the window. "Do you want bubbles?" I asked. Nothing. Oh well, she could have them anyway—maybe they'd help dislodge some of the grime. It wasn't all that long since I'd had to wash Daisy in my own bath upstairs and I didn't fancy repeating the experience. Rachel absolutely stank, but didn't appear to be as physically dirty as Daisy had been when I first met her. Maybe vampires just naturally reeked. I went back into the bathroom and poured half a bottle of the bubbles into the tub, then chucked in the entire bubble bar for good measure. Heading back into the living room, I saw Rachel perching on the windowsill, her head resting back against the frame. She looked wistful, and much younger. "Bath's running," I said, with forced jollity. She still didn't respond, so I set to arranging things as best I could. The cushions were big enough to make a narrow approximation of a bed on the living room floor, and by the time I'd wedged the last two against the wall beside them and covered the lot with duvets, it looked—well, if not welcoming, then at least marginally more comfortable than it had before. I even got the curtains up, threading them onto the old pole that was fixed lopsidedly above the window. Rachel ducked out of my way when I needed to climb up onto either end of the windowsill, but otherwise stayed absolutely put. Finally, the bath was full of bubbles and the bathroom was filled with steam. The scent was way too strong for me to last long in there, but I was pretty sure it was the sort of bath I'd have happily floundered in for hours, back when I was human.

It took some persuading to get Rachel undressed and into the bath. In the end, I threatened to bring Grimm downstairs if she didn't shift her bony backside. It worked—she ducked behind the bathroom door, threw all her clothes out from behind it and was sliding under the bubbles in less than two minutes. "In!" she called through the door and, other than throwing a flannel in after her and pushing the clean clothes through the slightly open door with my foot, I left her to it. She'd currently been in it for almost an hour. I'd kept myself busy by running up and down between the two flats, digging out any spare items from upstairs that might make Rachel's new digs more homely.

On my third visit upstairs, I found Heggie sitting up on the sofa. He looked bleary-eyed, but his face brightened when he saw me come in through the door. "Kitty says you saved Mapp," he said, sounding genuinely choked with emotion. I stepped over to give him a hug, but he flinched back quickly enough that I turned it into an inelegant attempt at fluffing up the sofa cushions.

"Ah, he'd have saved himself," I said, "eventually. He's up at Missy's, I told him to get some rest."

"Oh, oh," said Heggie, "I must go to him!" He got up off the sofa and literally hopped from one foot to the other in his excitement. "Thank you," he said. "Thank you, thank you!" With that, he headed for the back door.

"No need to thank me," I said, as he scrabbled the door open. "It's all part of the service." The last few words hit nothing but fresh air, as Heggie disappeared down the fire escape.

"Awww," said Kitty, coming into the living room, "young love."

"Young?" I gave her my patented 'wtf are you talking about,' look. "Mapp's about nine hundred years old, by my estimate."

"What about Heggie?" asked Kitty. "How old do you think he is?"

"I have absolutely no idea," I said. "In fact, I'm not sure Heggie's even entirely human. Anyway," I stepped past her into the kitchen, "I'm just picking up some more things for Rachel. I thought I'd give her a couple of plates and glasses, for…" I trailed off, unsure why I was actually sorting out crockery for someone who didn't eat.

"The glasses are for blood, I assume?" Kitty arched an eyebrow. "I hope you know what you're doing, Lil. It's one thing letting her stay here, but it's quite another putting Izzy and the customers at risk." My own blood would have run cold, if it ran anywhere at all.

"It'll be fine," I said, trying to convince myself as much as anyone else. "Maybe we've got the key for her fire escape door. She could use that instead of the stairwell."

"That would be a good idea, I think," said Kitty evenly. "Anyway, shouldn't you be getting back to her?" Just then, my phone rang out with *The Final Countdown*. Sighing, I fished it out of my jeans and opened my text messages to see what Eadric wanted now.

"I should," I agreed, sliding the phone back into my pocket. "And then, apparently, I need to go do a stint as a chauffeur for the bloody Silvertons."

"Who's so important they need a personal driver?" asked Kitty. She was wearing a cornflower blue sundress today. It had little daisies embroidered across it and was short enough that her bare knees were showing. If I could figure out a way of making Kitty's clothes actually real, I could make a fortune on a vintage market stall. As it was, her outfits all seemed to just disappear into the ether when she wasn't wearing them.

"The queen and her consort are going home," I said. I started digging around in the junk drawer next to the sink. "Aha!" I held a bunch of keys up triumphantly. "One of these should be the key to Rachel's fire door. Now all I have to do is teach a vampire how locks work." I dropped the keys into one of the glasses and gathered everything up.

"You're driving all the way down to London again?" Kitty said, clearly fretting. "How long will you be away?"

"It won't take too long," I reassured her. "Now I know the car and the route, I'm happy to go alone. So I'll just run Elizabeth and Jude down to Highgate, then turn round and head straight back." I was actually looking forward to having the Alfa to myself for a while. If nothing else, the 'recommended for you' suggestions on Eadric's Spotify account were certainly going to look a bit different by the time I'd finished hollering to myself up the motorway.

"What about the vampire?"

"I'll go get her out of the bath," I said

"And if she refuses?"

I gave Kitty an evil grin. "I'll send in the cat."

Smile At Your Enemies—It Makes Them Nervous

W ho even knew vampires love bubble baths? Although to be fair, maybe even vampires don't know—I can't imagine they get much chance to try it. After all that griping about getting into it in the first place, Rachel was now, as Kitty had predicted, refusing to get back out. More worryingly, she'd figured out how to turn on the taps. The water level was now ominously close to the top of the ancient bath. "Five more minutes," I said sternly, "or it's the cat for you." She flashed a brief, yellow smile that made me wonder if Eadric knew of any vampire-friendly dentists, then slid straight back underneath the water. *Wonder if she'll soak it up like an undead sponge*, I thought randomly.

Why would that happen? You lie in the bath for what seems like an age, yet you never appear to be waterlogged.

Have you been watching me in the bath? I asked, indignantly.

We don't see you in the way you think we see you. You're just an extension of us. We're not interested in what you look like, Lilith.

Aah, so you want me for my brain rather than my body?

Yes. Funnily enough, I didn't find that remotely reassuring. I went into the kitchen and turned Rachel's water supply off at the mains, just in case I came home to find the entire building under water. Then I called Eadric and took instructions as politely as I could manage, after which I threatened Rachel with a visit from Grimm until she finally dragged herself out of the bath. It took her an age to get dry and put on the clean clothes, but she figured it out eventually. Which was a relief, because that time I'd had to bathe a newly rescued Daisy-the-Mersey-mermaid had reinforced my long-held belief that I'm definitely not the maternal type. I'm a caring person in general and happy to look after anyone who needs it, but only on special occasions. I showed her how the key worked and, to my surprise, she figured it out straight away. After unlocking the kitchen door, she peeked out and then immediately backed into the flat and locked it again, clutching the key tightly against her chest.

For reasons known only to the previous tenants—a group of students with doubtful housekeeping abilities—there was an old pair of army surplus boots discarded in the space where a kitchen bin would normally be. In a fit of inspiration, I unfastened a long stringy lace from one of the boots and held out my hand to Rachel. "Give me the key," I said. "I'll make sure you don't lose it." After a short and mostly silent argument, she handed it over. Careful to make sure she could see what I was doing in order to avoid any panic, I slid the key onto the string and knotted it tightly. "Stand still," I said. She stood, but probably through fear rather than obedience. "I won't hurt you, I promise," I said, reaching up and dropping the knotted string over her head. Her eyes widened as she clutched at the key now hanging around her neck. "There you go," I smiled, "all safe now." Rachel immediately tucked the key underneath the ancient Ramones t-shirt she was now wearing and shot out of the kitchen and back into the living room. Poking my head around the door, I saw she was already wrapped back up in the duvet. I stepped across and closed the curtains, thinking she'd prefer the darkness. She made a low grumbling noise and shook her head vehemently at me. "You want them left open?" I asked. She nodded, so I did as requested and was rewarded with what I took to be a happy sigh. "I've got to go out," I said, "but you'll be safe here." Worried eyes peeked up at me from inside the duvet nest. "You've locked the back door," I pointed out, "and I'll go out through the stairwell and lock that one behind me." *And then I'll go hide the key somewhere inside Flora's*, I thought. Better that than risking a surprise visit from a vampire when the place was full of potential snacks. I was confident that, whatever the vampires might be like in other towns, the local variety definitely didn't usually favour humans. But I couldn't be entirely sure if that was by choice, or whether it was just because scousers were a feistier target. Probably best to not let Rachel get too close to any tasty tourists, just in case. I gave her one last reassuring wave, then let myself out onto the stairwell. Gloomy and damp-smelling, it hadn't been used since the last intake of students did a moonlight flit after not paying the rent for weeks. Probably in rebellion at living in such grim conditions, I thought. My own flat hadn't been much better when I'd first moved in, but there's more incentive to redecorate when it's your own business taking up the ground floor and you're less likely to be evicted. Of course, these days I was as secure as it was possible to be. Eadric wasn't ever going to turf me out, although I knew he was still hoping I'd take him up on his offer of the apartment down in the Collonades. *As if I'd ever leave Harrington Street*, I thought to myself as I skipped down the stairs. *As if I'd leave my home.*

It is, said the city. **You belong here.** Cheered by the fact that even the city itself agreed with me, I pondered giving the stairwell a bit of a makeover. It would hardly ever be used, but it felt as though the entire building was slowly coming back to life. And it would be nice to make it all seem a bit more cared for. I bounced out onto the street and back into Flora's via the front door. Izzy was serving customers and Todd was behind her, busily stacking the dishwasher.

"Thought I'd cut my losses and get Todd in," said Izzy when she saw me. "Hope that's okay?"

"Of course it's okay," I said. "It's my fault for being unreliable." I was expecting her to snip back at me that I was, indeed, the least reliable revenant on the block, but she surprised me by smiling.

"It must be difficult," she said, passing a large cappuccino over to the woman standing at the counter and nodding thanks. She waited until the woman was out of earshot before speaking again. "Trying to be normal. I mean," she grinned, "not that you've ever been entirely *normal*, but compared to the rest of us."

"Yeah," I admitted, "it's difficult. Most of the time, actually. And it's also bloody complicated." I leaned against the serving hatch. "Who even knew there were so many oddballs hiding away in Liverpool?"

"You're doing really well, Lil," said Izzy. "And I mean that." To my surprise, she leaned over and gave me a quick, tight hug. "I know I keep asking you to stay safe—and if I'm honest, I've given up actually believing you when you say you will—but I'd really struggle if anything happened to you, y'know?" For a second, I thought she might actually cry. Then she gave herself a visible shake and smiled again. "Anyway," she said brightly, "you know what you're doing. Mostly."

"Mostly," I agreed. "As for the rest of it, I guess I'll just have to keep muddling through."

***

Eadric had, unsurprisingly, decided the Alfa was a better option this time. "Oh," I griped, "so Basil's good enough when I'm driving the locals round, but the queen deserves the fancy wheels?"

"Exactly," he agreed. It was probably for the best, anyway. Aesthetics aside, Basil was going to have to sit behind Flora's with his windows open for a couple of days, in order to air out the revolting scent of eau d'vampire.

"Why do I have to do all the work round here?" I grumbled, taking the keys from him.

"Because you're clearly the revenant on the go," said Elizabeth, coming through the pedestrian door into the car park with Jude following close behind her. "Down with the people, I think they say?" I didn't bother explaining to her that no, no one ever said that and settled for smiling blandly as I bounced the car keys in my hand. I'd been almost disappointed when I'd called Eadric to make arrangements, only to discover I wasn't driving down to London after all. Elizabeth and Jude's speedy arrival up in the not-so grim north had, it turned out, been down to them chartering a helicopter. Flash bastards. They were travelling via Speke airport rather than dropping directly into town, apparently because it was 'less ostentatious.' I'd pointed out to Eadric that anyone who thought hiring a helicopter was a normal thing to do was pretty ostentatious by default, but he'd ignored me.

The Middlesex contingent were immaculately dressed, as usual. And they didn't appear to have any luggage, so either they'd sent out for a change of clothes or they kept spares up in the Silverton's rooms. Elizabeth was wearing gold Roman sandals underneath yet another long and ridiculously feminine dress. This one was constructed from layers of green chiffon, with puffed sleeves and gold embroidery. Jude had opted for a wide-legged black pant suit over shiny black loafers. I narrowed my eyes at the lack of socks, but said nothing. Jude gazed blandly at me, their face utterly devoid of expression. Elizabeth looked reasonably pleased to see me, at least. "Such a shame we couldn't stay longer," she said with a smile, although I didn't believe her for a second.

"Thank you for helping," I said. "I mean it." Jude raised an eyebrow fractionally and got into the back of the car without saying a word. I was fairly sure Jude *could* speak if they chose to. They'd certainly communicated with Elizabeth easily enough when they wanted to tell tales on me. Maybe they really did think I just wasn't worth the effort.

"I've enjoyed it," said Elizabeth. "I wouldn't like to do it very often, but it's fun to remind myself that there's an entire world outside the walls of Highgate." She slid into the car next to Jude and I walked round to where Eadric stood waiting by the driver's door.

"I am not a bloody chauffeur," I hissed at him, "so don't be making a habit of this."

"Enjoy the car," he said with a grin, and turned to walk away.

"Eadric," I called after him. He turned and gave me a questioning look. "You're okay," I grinned. "I suppose."

He looked confused for a brief second, then his mouth twisted into the tiniest of smiles. "So are you," he said. "I suppose." I'd have liked to have honked the horn at him as we left, but by the time I'd remembered how to switch on the electronic ignition, he'd disappeared back up into his tower.

***

Speke Airport was renamed 'Liverpool John Lennon' in 2001, making it the first British airport to be named after an individual person. The airport operators really leaned into this new identity, installing an enormous bronze statue of the man himself in the passenger terminal, replacing the company logo with Lennon's famously scribbled self-portrait and adopting the slogan 'above us only sky', which proves even corporate management occasionally has a sense of humour. Despite the amount of effort put into the change, most people still call it Speke, because clearly there is no romance left in the world. I'd assumed I was dropping off at the passenger terminal, but as I started indicating left at the roundabout, Elizabeth leaned forward from the back seat and touched her hand to my shoulder. "No," she said, "we're along to the right." I turned as directed and Elizabeth pointed out what looked like an industrial unit further down the road. "Down there."

'Down there' turned out to be the airside offices of an executive jet company. A smartly dressed representative came scampering out to greet us as soon as I'd turned the Alfa into the car park and opened the door for Elizabeth and Jude to get out. "I'll say this for the modern world," said Elizabeth, leaning down to my open window and putting a delicate hand on my shoulder, "the transport options are rather marvellous." With one last swish of golden hair, she turned away from and was gone.

It was yet another beautiful day, so I decided to make the most of it. I pulled the Alfa out of the airport, but instead of turning off to head back down towards the city centre and the riverfront, stayed on Speke Hall Avenue. I'd call in on Martha and tell her Eadric had agreed to find her somewhere to live. I hadn't had chance to discuss it at length with him, but he'd agreed it was a small price to pay for being able to keep an eye on her. Not that we'd let her know we were doing any such thing, obviously. Silverton Properties didn't currently have anything vacant in Anfield, but there was a semi-detached house a bit further out in Walton that would be empty soon. Eadric's 'people' just needed to evict the current tenants first. When I'd asked why they were being evicted, Eadric muttered something about only letting to tenants who were at least sentient, and wouldn't be drawn on it any further. As Hillfoot Road turned into Menlove Avenue, I kept an eye out for Aunt Mimi's house on the right. It was so ordinary-looking that I wouldn't have spotted it if it hadn't been for the blue plaque on the front wall. Funny how a little boy who grew up in a thoroughly average house on an ordinary street could end up having the entire airport named after him. The houses on my left gave way to the greenery of Calderstones Park, then I took a right onto Queen's Drive, which carried me right up into Anfield. My knowledge of this part of town was embarrassingly scant and I was only navigating it so easily because of the Alfa's onboard satnav, so it was a relief when I got far enough back down into town to recognise places again.

It was only when I was turning off onto Priory Road yet again that it occurred to me to wonder whether Martha could actually be trusted to behave herself once she was installed in Walton. Okay, so she was getting a pretty good deal out of a shitty situation. A situation that she almost entirely brought on herself. And she very nearly killed Mapp in the process, which was something I'd never forgive her for. But I knew only too well how clever and welcoming the late Maria Silverton could be, and how easy it might have been to believe her pretty tales about immortality. I had to wonder, though, what Maria had been getting out of the bargain. Martha must have been able to offer her something in return, even if she didn't have a clue she was doing it. Not wanting to risk leaving the Alfa wedged on the verge, I pulled into the petrol station near the cemetery gates and parked up. Luckily, there was a cash machine. I withdrew a small wedge of cash and snuck it to the cashier behind the counter in return for a fervent promise the car would be looked after, before hopping the back fence and heading into the cemetery. It wasn't as dark this time and I was reasonably confident the vampires wouldn't be in a hurry to attack me again. At least, not until they'd found themselves a creepy new leader to replace the one I'd destroyed. I comforted myself with the knowledge there was also a growing list of people who would back me up if it ever came to an all-out fight. Probably. Some of those—Izzy, Billy and Kitty, for starters—were absolute definites, although they were also the three who would struggle to actually do anything very useful. Grimm would almost certainly have a go at scratching out the eyes of anything that threatened to interfere with his feeding schedule, so that was something. I thought Eadric and Nik would support me if it came to the crunch, although I wasn't quite as convinced about it as I'd like. Elizabeth was definitely in my corner, but her support might wane if my actions ever directly threatened her own safety. Jude, I was fairly sure, wouldn't give a fuck whether I lived or died and would only help me out if Elizabeth commanded it. Not that I could blame them, given recent events. Interestingly, I thought Ivo Laithlind might take my side in certain situations, but—like Elizabeth—it would depend entirely on whether he was likely to benefit from it personally. I didn't even consider Gaultier Mapp or the rest of the Renshaw Street Knitting Club. I knew they'd all come to my aid if I needed it, but equally, I didn't want to ever put them in that position. It had been scary enough seeing Mapp chained up in the crypt; I couldn't bear it if something similar happened to Heggie or Alan. Missy, on the other hand, could definitely look after herself, but I still wasn't entirely sure she'd come to my aid in an emergency.

I was walking slowly, enjoying the peace and quiet as I headed to Missy's house. The back fence opened as I neared it, and Alan stepped out into the cemetery. Today's outfit comprised a very flouncy gold shirt, tucked into the tightest pair of drainpipe trousers I'd ever seen. "Hey," he called cheerily as I approached, "come to spend some quality time with your favourite man?"

"Alan," I said, "between that quiff," I nodded at the enormous blond wave crashing down over his forehead, "and your ego, I doubt you could fit me into your life even if I wanted you to." Alan opened his mouth. "Is Martha home?" I added, before he had a chance to speak.

"She's gone out, girl," he said, recovering himself admirably quickly. "Said she was going to sort some things out from her place up there." He nodded towards the back of the cemetery. "Spend some time, say her goodbyes, sort of thing." Then, in a hopeful tone, "You can wait here for her, if you like?" He ran his fingers self-consciously through his hair. "I'd appreciate the company, sure enough."

"Maybe another time," I said.

"I'll hold you to that," Alan gave me a wide, bright grin that made him look years younger. "Anyway, Missy took Mapp home earlier, so I was thinking of popping in to see how he's getting on. Maybe have a wander through town. Catch up with the scene, sort of thing."

"With the scene," I said. "Uh huh."

"Tell Martha I've left the door unlocked for her," he said, already stepping backwards away from me down the path. "And that Missy says she'll drown her like the witch she is, if anything's touched when she gets back." With that, he turned and loped off into the gloom. I jogged up the main path that led to the catacombs, relieved to have made it so far without seeing so much as a human, let alone any undead threat. As I got closer to Martha's crypt, I wondered what furnishings she might need for her new accommodation. Rachel had been easy—vampires, by default, generally don't care much about their surroundings. But Martha was still human—sort of—and would probably expect to at least have the basics. Maybe I could take her to the Emmaus place up in Seaforth. Me and Izzy had driven up there in Basil not long after I'd moved into Flora's and spent a happy afternoon hunting for random bits of mismatched furniture, most of which still sat in my flat to this day. Eadric would probably fork out for new stuff if I asked nicely, but I suspected Martha's tastes were a bit more eclectic than that. And if she helped me choose, she'd have more emotional investment in the new house. Once I'd got her properly settled in, she could help me work out a timetable for knitting classes in Flora's and start paying back her debt to society. Feeling pretty good about things for the first time in ages, I swung myself over the railings outside the catacomb and into the ruins of the main surface-level room. The hatch in the floor that led down to the crypt was open. I froze where I stood and listened carefully, hoping to hear Martha bustling around below my feet. Surely she'd still be putting the kettle on, however much younger she was? I still like the occasional cup of tea and I'm in my thirties. Although I favour Earl Grey with both milk *and* sugar, which Izzy says makes me a heathen by default. Careful to make as little noise as possible, I crept slowly forwards. Crouched near the edge of the hole to avoid being spotted by anyone below, I peered in. The evening sky was still bright despite the sun dropping over the horizon, and it took my eyes a while to adjust to the darkness below. The only noise came from birds settling in to roost in the trees around me and the occasional distant car engine. A train suddenly passed through on the line to the north of the cemetery and the noise made me jerk back slightly—into something heavy, up against my back. Where there absolutely shouldn't have been. But before I could do anything, whatever it was slammed hard between my shoulder blades and I dropped into the darkness.

This wasn't the first time I'd been pushed from a height, and being immortal was definitely an advantage. But undead or not, landing on the rubble-strewn floor of the crypt was still enough to knock the wind out of me and I floundered for a few wasteful seconds before pulling myself upright. There was no sign of Martha. Getting to my feet, I backed up against the wall before looking round the room. Early evening light was coming through the open hatch and it was the first time I'd been able to see properly down here. It was actually better equipped than I'd realised. There was a large, double-height cupboard in one corner, of the sort often used as pantry storage in old-fashioned kitchens. One of the doors on its lower section was slightly ajar, and I was pretty sure I could see bags of sugar inside it, which would confirm my theory. If childhood memories of Granny Ivy's house were anything to go by, the upper cupboard would hold measuring cups, wooden spoons and a rolling pin. And maybe a small bottle of Harvey's Bristol Cream, just for special occasions. Martha's chair was exactly how it looked when I first came down here, its shape almost entirely disguised by the blankets draped haphazardly all over it. An open packet of digestive biscuits sat next to a half-finished cup of tea on the upturned crate next to me. To the right of it, the kettle sat on the camping stove. Touching my hand gingerly to the kettle, I realised it was still hot. If no one was at home, why had the kettle been on? Stepping nervously backwards with the kettle still in my hand, I looked around the room again. The only thing out of place was a pile of old clothes that I'd been standing on without realising. Bending down to pick up the clothes, sticky dust fell out of them and all over me. *"Oh fucking hell,"* I screeched, frantically wiping it from my hands. *"Shit shiiiit—"* Looking down, I could see a clear footprint where I'd stood right in the centre of what remained of Martha's crumbled face.

"Hello, Lilith," came a horribly familiar voice, "I see you've found Martha."

Mab was standing on the other side of the room and gazing coolly at me. She was feigning casualness, but nothing could hide the glint of murderousness that lurked in those eyes. "Such a shame she didn't get chance to make the most of her second youth."

"You are fucking *insane*," I yelled. "What did Martha do to deserve—" I gestured at the floor, *"that?"*

"She stole what was rightfully mine," said Mab, stepping forward. "I simply took it back."

"What for?" I planted my feet more steadily on the floor, in case she made a sudden lunge. "Your mother is *gone*, Mab! There's no getting her back. Not ever."

"That's what you'd like to think," said Mab. She was slowly getting closer. "But you still don't know what I'm truly capable of, Lilith." I was expecting it this time, but it was still a struggle not to scream when the world around me suddenly turned white. It was brighter this time, and however far I twisted my head, I couldn't find the edges. "Look, Lilith," said Mab, so close to my face that I banged my head against the wall in an attempt to pull away from her. "Look who's here." Taking an automatic breath in order to prepare myself, I was struck by a sudden and overwhelming sense of loss. Loss and guilt and a deep-rooted fear of ever looking back.

Don't be scared.

That's easy for you to say, I hissed silently at the city. *It's not your dead brother about to make an appearance.*

It isn't Cally she's showing you, said the city. **It's her interpretation of your thoughts. Never forget that.**

I gritted my teeth and breathed in again. The same feelings were there, but this time they were overlaid with something else—something even darker and way more powerful. "Look, Lilith," said Mab, right up against my ear. "Look what you did to your brother."

I looked. Cally was standing no more than six feet in front of me, his little eyes wide with fear. "Whatcha doin', Lil?" he asked. "You need to come get me. Don't let me drown again, Lil. It's cold and there's things in the water—"

"*Stop it!*" I yelled. Cally stared at me, a shocked expression on his babyish face. "You're not real," I said, more calmly. "You died, Cal. You *died*. Years ago."

"Why didn't you save me, Lil?" his voice was quieter now.

"Because I was ten years old! If I'd gone in after you, we'd both be dead now. Can't you see that?"

"But I'd have you with me," he said sadly. "I'm lonely, Lil." A taller shadow materialised behind him, growing bigger as it stepped forward to put a hand on his shoulder. Details materialised as if coming out of a mist, the soft edges turning into a face surrounded by dark hair. Dark chestnut hair that flowed down to the newcomer's shoulders and set off her perfect little doll face.

"Hello Lilith," said Maria Silverton.

A Tiny Knife

If I'd still been human, I'm pretty sure I'd have passed out from sheer horror. Maria Silverton—Maria *fucking* Silverton—stood in front of me. Bold as brass and with her hand on my brother's shoulder.

"Told you," whispered Mab in my ear. I shot out an elbow, hitting her as hard as I could. She made a satisfyingly pained yelping noise. I was rewarded by a heavy slap across the face. "You will behave yourself," she hissed, "in my mother's presence."

"How's tricks, Maria?" I asked the shadow ghost. She was almost completely solid now, dressed in the neat dark skirt suit and stiletto heels that were pretty much her uniform when she still lived in the Liver Building. Grinning, she pulled Cally up hard against her. He tried to wriggle away, but her grip tightened.

"Owww," he whined, "you're hurting me! Lil, tell her! Tell her to stop hurting me!"

It's all just a product of your thoughts and memories.

"You're not real, Cally," I said. Then, more firmly, "You're not real because you died a long time ago. I'm sorry. I did what I could, but it wasn't enough. You're dead, Cal. You should probably go now."

"No," he said, "I'm here. I'm here in front of you, Lil." His voice was deepening now, and getting harsher.

She creates him from your own fears.

"I can't keep carrying guilt for an accident that wasn't my fault," I said. "You are *dead*, Cally. Dead, gone, passed on. You've run down the curtain and joined the choir invisible. You are no more, you have ceased to be…" I trailed off, wondering where on earth that had all come from. My brother's eyes were darker now, hardening with the realisation I wasn't going to play the game any longer.

"You have to save me," he said, but he was already fading out around the edges. "You're a bad sister, Lil."

No more avoiding my parents because I couldn't bear to look them in the eyes, no more dreading the turnoff to Shrewsbury... "I'm done," I said firmly. "No more guilt. You need to go, Cally."

"What if I refuse to let him go?" said Maria. But when she tried to grab him, her hand slipped straight through. Cally's mouth moved as though he was speaking, but no sound came out. In contrast to his dramatic departure the last time Mab had forced him to appear, he just quietly disappeared into nothing.

"What if you accepted that you're dead and gone?" I said to Maria. "But if you're going to insist on hanging around, then your daughter here could maybe do with some lessons in manners." My peripheral vision was darkening now and reality was starting to seep back in. Thank fuck for that. "And you should probably have a chat with her father," I added. "Turns out he was leading you both a merry dance."

"Who cares what her father did," asked Maria, "so long as we get what we want?"

"I think Mab cares," I said. "I think Mab cares very much about the fact she was abandoned. By both of you."

"*Shut up, you stupid bitch!*" Mab moved to slap me again, but this time I grabbed her arm.

"I've still got your knife," I said, conversationally. "Had it sharpened and everything." I was pretty sure she didn't believe me, but there was enough of a flicker in her eyes to make me think she wasn't entirely sure. '*You only have to hit them once,*' Dad had once told me, when I was being bullied at school and didn't want to tell the teachers, '*just make sure you do it properly.*' Taking advantage of her distraction, I swung round and smacked the hot kettle across her face with all my strength, the crunching noise making me fairly confident I'd smashed her cheekbone, at least. Mab went flying across the room and crashed into Martha's pile of plastic recycling bags. She lay there screaming as I turned back to Maria. "Your daughter needs you." Maria's eyes hardened as she stepped towards me.

She's not real.

Wanna bet? Faint light was still trickling in through the hatch to the outside world. I could see the gold highlights in Maria's hair and the glint in her—*what colour were Maria's eyes?*

How would we know that? Anyway, someone's coming.

Fucking brilliant, I thought. *Knowing my luck, it's probably the local vamp squad, here to join in the fun.*

"I have been waiting a very long time," said Maria. She was almost within grabbing distance.

"So why are you hanging about now?" I asked. "Get on with it Maria, we haven't got all night." Another step forward and I might be able to hit her. I'd lost the kettle to Mab, but I hadn't been lying about the knife. I put my hands on my hips in a show of defiance, using the movement to slide the iron blade out of my pocket.

"I thought you'd never ask," said Maria, launching herself at me. I feinted then ducked, leaving her to spin round on her spiky heels.

"Not as easy as you'd expected?" I taunted. I could hear Mab moaning from the corner and although human me would have been worried about what damage I might have inflicted with the kettle, undead me was just relieved I had one less person to think about. "Aren't you going to help your daughter, Maria? She's clearly in pain over there." Maria's eyes flicked over to Mab, but her expression of one of scorn rather than concern. "I thought losing Mab was the cause of all your problems? Isn't that what turned you into a vengeful little bitch? Not that I could blame you for that," I moved fractionally sideways in order to get a better angle, "anyone would lose their mind after what you went through. But she's here now, Maria." The tiny knife felt disproportionately heavy in my hand. "Surely you should be looking after her?"

Hold your nerve, said the city. **Let her get close before doing anything.**

Cheers, Tyson fucking Fury. You're not the one facing up to a bloody psycho right now.

Oh, but we are. We're with you. We see what you see.

Yeah, but you won't get killed if I lose, will you?

Ah, well that's where it gets complica—

The city was cut off mid-sentence by a loud scream from the corner. "Why aren't you helping me?" howled Mab. It took me a second to realise she was talking to Maria, not me. "Get me out of here and we'll come back for her," she nodded her head towards me, "another time. I'm *hurting*, mama!" Maria hadn't taken her eyes off me throughout Mab's pleading. She tilted her head slightly, as if judging how best to attack.

"Are you really so awful," I said, "that you'd rather fight me than help your own child?" Not a flicker. "You really don't care, do you? You don't care about the child you've been yearning for this last century or more. Not very motherly behaviour, is it?" Maria's only reaction was to take a small step forward. I gripped the knife hard, readying myself. Her eyes glittered like jewels in the dim light, her gaze never leaving me.

"Mab," I said, trying to keep my voice casual, "I don't suppose you remember what colour your mother's eyes were?"

"They're brown," Mab said from the corner. "Like melted chocolate. I can still remember her looking down at me, before..." she trailed off.

Maria narrowed her green eyes at me and I knew my window of opportunity was going to be very narrow indeed. "How exactly did you bring her back, Mab?"

"What the fuck does that have to do with you?" Even as she spoke, Maria began to circle me. I moved in the opposite direction, careful to keep the distance between us.

"HOW DID YOU DO IT?" The voice came out at full force, and even Maria took an involuntary step back. She watched me carefully, and I knew she was only biding her time.

"I...prayed," said Mab. "I thought she might be secretly buried somewhere here in the cemetery. Or hidden in one of the crypts. So I came back here and sat with Martha. Told her she had to help me get my mama back. And I prayed."

"Who—what—did you pray to?"

"Anything that would listen," Mab said, her voice getting quieter. "I just wanted my mama back."

"I know you did," I said. "But I don't think this is your—" Maria flew at me before I could finish my sentence. I swung round and hit her with the little iron blade with all my strength—and found myself sprawling on the floor of the crypt. Twisting and jumping quickly back to my feet, I looked round, but Maria had disappeared. I turned slowly on the spot, waiting for her to make a move. Mab was still sitting on the floor, one side of her face looking red and horribly raw where the kettle had hit her. The pile of rags that were all that was left of Martha were still on the floor where I'd been standing. There was no sign of Maria anywhere in the room. Then she hit me, and it was like a tidal wave. There was nothing solid about the roiling grey cloud that spun around me, but I could just make out the shape of a face in the centre. It wasn't Maria's face. This one was older and stronger. With bright green eyes that were now glowing pinpricks, focused sharply on me. Fuck.

Indeed, said the city. **She's been waiting a long time.**

You know who this is? Why the fuck didn't you warn me?

We saw her as you saw her, it said. **We saw Maria Silverton—and now we see the wraith.** Whoever—whatever—it was hit me again. A writhing mass of darkness spun over and against me, as though trying to find a way in. I felt fury and vengeance, betrayal and pure, keening insanity, all fighting to find a chink in my mental armour.

Do not let her in.

Wasn't planning to. I was just wondering whether the phantom whatever-it-was would follow me if I managed to get out of the hatch into the open air, in the hope it would buy me some time, when something else hit me. It was Mab, screaming and thrashing at the darkness, trying futilely to grab hold of it.

"I thought you were my mama!" she howled. The spinning cloud knocked her off her feet and she fell to the floor, still kicking out. "You told me you'd help me! You told me…" Mab was sobbing now—big, choking gulps of agony, "…you told me you loved me." The wraith rose upwards and, as it did so, the face within it became more defined. It had a narrower face and higher cheekbones than Maria, and a viciously determined expression even she'd have been proud of.

"Thank you for resurrecting me," it said in a syrupy voice. "You did well, child. But now your work is over." The wraith spun around and scooped Mab up, carrying her towards the ceiling of the crypt. Before I could do anything, it threw her hard against the opposite wall. The blow stunned her, and she slumped heavily down onto the floor. The wraith rolled forwards and picked her up again, twisting to gain impetus. Okay, so Mab had been trying to make my life as uncomfortable as possible, but I *had* killed her mother and could understand her motives. And okay, so she'd also inadvertently freed some kind of evil spirit that was definitely not the sort of person we'd want popping into Flora's on the reg, but in her defence, she'd believed she was resurrecting her mother. Again, understandable. I was going to have to at least *try* to save her—I just had absolutely no fucking idea how.

Before I could waste any more time worrying about it, something dropped through the hatch. The new arrival went right through the centre of the wraith and knocked Mab out of its grasp. She hit the ground hard, but groaned loudly and began dragging herself upright.

It's clearly the week for superhero cosplay, I thought, as the figure stepped through into the room. Mab scrabbled backwards as it became fully visible in the gloom.

"Hey Red," said Ivo Laithlind.

It's A Gas

"What the *fu*—" I began, but Mab beat me to it. Injured or not, she leaped to her feet and started pummelling Ivo, screaming and crying as she clawed at him. He grabbed her wrists and pushed so she was forced to step backwards and look at him.

"You need to get out," he said to her. "Now." He shoved Mab towards the hatch. I knew she could get out of it because I'd seen her do it only the day before. Jesus, was that really only twenty-four hours ago? I was going to need some time off after this shitshow had sorted itself out. Maybe Eadric had contacts in the Med who'd put me up for a few nights.

"I'm not going anywhere without my mama," Mab howled, fetching Ivo a ringing slap around the face.

He turned on her in fury. "Your mama isn't—"

"*Ivo*," I yelled, "*look behind*—" The dark cloud hit him hard enough to send him crashing into Martha's little kitchen corner. Crockery smashed across the floor and the camping stove hit the wall. The gas canister broke away from the stove unit and went rolling across the floor. Ivo was already picking himself up when the wraith went in for a second go, smacking into the side of his head and sending him reeling. Mab looked as though she was about to join in, so I took advantage of the mayhem to grab her from behind and drag her away from the fight. "Stay right there," I hissed in her ear as I dumped her on the floor, "or I swear to fucking god I will rip your stupid bloody head right off." I turned round just in time to see the wraith surround Ivo. But instead of attacking him, it wrapped around him like a shroud. I thought it was absorbing itself into him. Being possessed by a malevolent spirit didn't seem like much fun to me. Ivo began to rise up into the air. As I watched, I saw there was a gap between the wraith's darkness and Ivo's limp body. He began glowing faintly, like in those old television adverts for instant porridge.

It's draining him.

Draining him of what? We're not human, for fucksake!

In the same way Martha used Mapp to regain strength, said the city. **It's taking his life force in order to strengthen itself.**

Well, fuck that *shit.* I launched myself forward and grabbed hold of the grey mass, which was just as weird as it sounds. Despite being ephemeral, there was something in it solid enough to allow me to cling on. I began pulling frantically, using my feet against it for leverage. "YOU WILL LEAVE HIM," I yelled, Van Helsing mode fully engaged. Digging my fingers deep into the cloud, I pulled hard and managed to wrench it away from Ivo's head. His face looked grey and drawn, and suddenly much, much older. "GET AWAY," I howled, "YOU DO NOT BELONG HERE." My hands were suddenly holding fabric, rather than grey air. Shock made my grip falter and I fell backwards as the wraith pulled itself up, dropping Ivo heavily to the floor.

"You dare to tell *me* where I *belong*?" The wraith twisted and turned in on itself, writhing upwards until it was at least a foot taller than me. It had a head and limbs that vaguely resembled arms and legs, but everything looked weirdly out of proportion, as though the creature was struggling to work out what it was supposed to look like. "I have been trapped here for longer than you could ever imagine, Lilith O'Reilly." What was *with* all these creepy-ass paranormal weirdos knowing my name without us even being introduced? "Trapped in darkness, with nothing but my thoughts for company. Do you know how that makes people feel, Lilith O'Reilly?"

"Absolutely fucking psychotic, by the looks of it," I said.

The wraith chuckled, and it was not a comforting sound. "You think you can take over this territory and not have to face us? What a stupid little child you must be." It was solid enough now that I could no longer see through it, but the grey smoke still swirled irritably. I thought I could see the outline of clothes beginning to emerge. Foot-like shapes pushed themselves out at the end of its strangely elongated legs and the bottom hem of what I thought might be a skirt started widening out above its ankles. It was floating towards me, slowly but surely. As it moved, it became increasingly human. Arms stretched out towards me and long, thin fingers groped the air like tendrils, looking for something to cling to.

"For the last bloody time," I said, "I am not taking over *anywhere*. The sooner you weirdos accept that, the better." I ducked, swung hard around behind the wraith and, by some minor miracle, hit my target on the first try. Which was lucky, because I'm pretty sure I wouldn't have managed a second attempt. The small iron blade on Mab's pocket knife slammed into what felt horribly like human flesh. Hanging my entire weight from the blade, I felt it crunching against bone as I dragged downwards. The wraith screamed—such an unbelievably awful noise I thought it might burst my eardrums. With an almighty howl, it managed to pull away from me and floundered across the room, before falling to what passed for its knees. To my relief, I saw Mab scrabble to her feet behind it and, with one last desperate glance back at me and her father, propel herself up and out of the hatch. I reached for Ivo while I still had the chance and dragged him across the floor, so he was next to me. Worryingly, there was no noise or movement from him, even when his face bounced off a rock. The wraith began to crawl slowly and painfully towards me. As I watched, it reached one of its arms up and behind its back in an unnatural movement which dislocated the shoulder. The joint popped out at a sickening angle, but the wraith didn't stop. Slowly, as I stood frozen in panic, it pulled the blade out of its own back and threw it across the floor in triumph. In a freakish stroke of luck, the knife bounced off the nearest wall and I managed to catch it as it came spinning towards me. As I lunged forward to grab it, I breathed without thinking and the smell made me gag. The gas had leaked from the disconnected camping stove and was filling the room. The hatch was still open, but it was small and there wasn't much breeze. Also, I'd remembered my grandad once telling me—during a discussion about how no, I couldn't use the portable gas stove as a heater in the makeshift tent me and Cally had built in his garden—that propane gas was heavier than air. Which means it sinks to the ground in the event of a leak. Grandad even did a little drawing of someone lying on the ground and how the gas would just suffocate them in their sleep. Okay so technically, neither me nor Ivo needed to breathe. But I was pretty sure that, even when it wasn't terminal, gas inhalation could lead to brain damage. It was bad enough having to face the prospect of living forever, but it would be a damn sight worse if I had to do it without all my faculties.

Carry him.

How the fuck am I going to get him out, though?

We don't know. Well, at least it was honest. **But you have to try.** The wraith was already pushing itself upwards. As I watched, it lifted its head and glared straight at me, its eyes burning with gleaming hatred. The entire scenario was like something out of a Japanese horror movie. Time to get moving.

I might have superhuman strength, but Ivo Laithlind hadn't survived twelve violent centuries by being weedy. I wedged Mab's knife back into my pocket, before dragging Ivo up from the floor and flinging him over my shoulder like one of the sacks of rice we used to have delivered when I worked at the Bluecoat. Ivo's weight forced me to tilt sideways to counterbalance, and I was pretty sure bouncing out of the crypt would be all but impossible this time. He groaned as I adjusted the weight, which at least reassured me he wasn't entirely drained of whatever it is that keeps us going. But the smell of gas was getting stronger, and the wraith was determinedly clambering to its feet. Neither option seemed like a fun end to the evening. I tried taking a couple of running strides and bouncing up towards the hatch, but Ivo's weight made it impossible to get closer than just scraping my fingernails against the ceiling. I peered up into the twilight and wondered if it would be worth throwing him as hard as I could and just hoping he didn't land on any of the twisted iron bars that made up the fence around the catacomb. A noise made me turn round. "Leaving so soon?" An elegant, middle-aged woman stood in the middle of the crypt. She wore a floor-length dress made of heavy, dark green fabric, with leg o'mutton sleeves. Her steel-grey hair twisted into a knot on top of her head and an ornately jewelled necklace hung around her high, tight collar. "Aah," she said, in a strong voice that was devoid of any accent I could detect, "I'm feeling much more myself now. Why don't you stay for a cup of tea, dear?" The words sounded normal—at least, as normal as a morphing wraith inviting you for tea in a gas-filled crypt ever could—but her eyes were absolutely wild. She appeared to be struggling to focus on me. In fact, I strongly suspected she was struggling to literally keep herself together. There was something majorly odd about the dress and the jewellery all appearing out of nowhere, and that's me speaking as someone who's had to develop a very high tolerance for odd. Of course, Kitty can change her outfits to suit, and clearly Billy's also picking up the talent. But they looked as though it all fitted together. Like they really would have dressed like that when they were still alive. Whatever was standing in front of me right now, it had never, I thought, been fully human.

She is the embodiment of those who cannot rest.

Oh, I sniped, shifting Ivo's weight so I wouldn't get a permanent crick in my neck, *now you come up with a theory. Couldn't you have figured it out a bit earlier? Maybe in time for me to just exorcise the entire fucking cemetery, rather than waiting for me to be trapped underground with a murderous...something...and an unconscious idiot?*

As we keep explaining, came a hurt-sounding voice inside my head, **we don't always see things any better than you do. We're just an avatar of the city's spirit, Lilith. We're not mind-readers.**

Your theories are all a bit too bodged together for my liking. It's almost as though you're making this shit up as you go along.

Aren't we all? To some extent?

For fuck's *actual* sake, now even the voices in my head were trying to get metaphysical. And I still had a fully-grown adult man hanging over my shoulder, like a baby that needed a good burp. "That's it," I said out loud, "I'm done. We'll be off now." With that, I made a really good attempt at leaping up against the side wall in order to propel myself up towards the ceiling and what was currently looking like a very small and unlikely escape hatch. Somehow, I managed to grasp the edge of the hatch with one hand, but it wasn't enough to pull us both through to the outside. I hung from the opening with my feet dangling in mid-air as Madame Creep slowly walked towards me with the most unsettling smile I'd ever seen in my life on her face. I'd discovered fairly quickly after the first day I woke up dead that being immortal and pretty much impervious to injury doesn't stop things hurting. Which is a bit of a let-down on the part of the whole 'eternal life' thing, if you ask me. My shoulder was making its displeasure at having to carry the weight of both me and Ivo very clear and I wasn't sure how long I'd be able to hang on. Maybe I could build up some impulsion. I remembered teaching Cally how to get going on a swing when he was really small. He was desperate for me to keep pushing him but I wanted a go on a swing myself, so I told him to do it himself. After a lot of yelling of the 'waaah it's not fair' variety, he'd eventually got the hang of pushing with his feet until his own bodyweight began to propel him higher. Eventually he got good enough at it that we'd compete to see who could get highest and would talk excitedly about how it surely must be possible to one day swing a full loop, if only we tried hard enough.

I swung my legs forward then back, gritting my teeth to stop myself screaming as the weight pulled down on the wrist that was attempting to cling to the ledge. I thought it was impossible and was about to drop back down in the hope I could fight the wraith-woman off, when I felt Ivo move. "Hold tight, Red," he said and, before I could do or say a single thing, he'd used his own weight to swing us both off my arm and up high enough for him to grab the edge of the hatch opening himself.

"*Fuuuuuuuuuuuuuuuck!*" I howled, as my shoulder twisted. Just as I was losing my grip, Ivo somehow pushed me up out of the hatch and got his elbows up onto it to drag himself out after me. I dropped to my knees and caught hold of his arms, pulling him with as much strength as I could manage, given that one of my arms was completely numb. "Come *on*," I yelled at him, "get out!"

Ivo looked up at me with what looked horribly like a defeated expression on his face. "She's got my legs, Red," he said. "I can't keep holding on. You need to save yourself."

"No!" To my absolute mortification, I started to cry. Except revenants can't actually cry, so I made do with angry gulps of agonised frustration. "Don't you *dare* give up on me, Ivo Laithlind!" The feeling was coming back in my arm now and terrified fury was adding to my strength. The wraith howled as it hung from Ivo's legs and I could see its green eyes staring up at me from the darkness. Ivo groaned as we pulled him like a horribly sentient Christmas cracker and suddenly I knew what to do. "Ivo," I said, *"duck!"* He slammed his head down against the stone floor of the outer catacomb just in time for Mab's knife to skim past his ear as it flew down into the crypt. The explosion as it hit stone and sparked the buildup of gas was enough to send me flying backwards, dragging Ivo with me. I ended up flat on my back with him lying face down on top of me. "Well hello there, Red," he croaked into my ear, "I thought this might never happen."

"Go fuck yourself," I growled, shoving him hard. He rolled off and lay on his back next to me.

"I'd rather—" his far-too-obvious response was cut off by the sound of tortured screaming coming from the crypt. Flames were licking up and out of the hatch. They carried a strange green tinge that made me very grateful I didn't have to breathe the air around us. We lay there recovering a while, listening to the wraith's tortured screams. Just as it occurred to me to ask the obvious, smart-arse question about how on earth a phantom could feel pain, there was a loud whooshing noise and it shot out of the hatch and up into the night sky, spinning until it finally disappeared from sight. Sirens started up in the distance.

"Shit," I said, clambering to my feet, "someone's called the bloody fire brigade. We need to run."

"Umm," said Ivo quietly, from down by my feet, "I don't think I can manage that just now, Red." I looked down at him. His face was still tinged with grey and he looked hollow-eyed and weirdly shrunken.

"Then I'll just have to carry you," I said. "Up we come." I bent down and hoisted him up and over my shoulder like a sack of potatoes.

"Oh god," he groaned, "I think I'm going to be sick."

"You're not capable of being sick." I started walking and Ivo kept groaning. I hadn't even got as far as the main path down to the gates before I'd had enough. "That's it," I said, dumping him onto the grass, "there's nothing else for it." I picked him up again, but this time cradled in my arms like a baby. "For fuck's sake," I hissed as he floundered, "even Mapp wasn't this dramatic! Stop flopping your head around, you bloody idiot. Put your arms round my neck." Ivo did as he was told, and I finally got a proper hold of him. "You'd better hold on tight, spider monkey," I said, snorting at my own humour as I sped off.

You know all those 80s movies you find when you're trawling Netflix and are getting to the bottom of the list where they shove all the retro stuff? The ones where a gallant man—usually in military uniform—swoops in at the last minute and literally sweeps the heroine off her feet and into his arms? Anyway, me and Ivo did not look like anything out of one of those movies. I jogged down through Anfield cemetery with him hanging around my neck like an enormous toddler who was well overdue a nap. He'd lost one of his expensive shoes—presumably when the wraith was hanging off his leg—and his jacket was torn. "Who the hell wears a suit when they're about to stage a rescue, anyway?" I muttered, taking a left in order to avoid passing Missy's house. Things were complicated enough without having to explain to her why I was carrying Ivo Laithlind around like a baby. I was forced to take another left as I realised two fire engines had pulled in by crematorium buildings.

"Hey!" Someone in full protective fire kit had spotted me and was waving. "What are you doing in there?"

Shit. "Hang on," I warned Ivo, and ran as fast as I could away from the humans. Normally I'd have just scaled a discreet fence, but carrying a fully grown man was cramping my athletic style. And I had to stick to the paths, for fear of accidentally stamping on graves or tripping over tombstones. As I reached the southern end of the cemetery, I veered right towards the boundary fence that ran behind the garage where I'd stashed the Alfa. "You're going to have to help me here," I said and, without stopping, flung Ivo upwards at the fence. He hung over the top like a literal dead weight as I vaulted it and grabbed his arms to pull him down on the other side. He fell awkwardly, and we tumbled together into a heap on the ground.

"You trying to take advantage of me again, Red?"

"You wish," I said. As retaliation, I threw him back over my shoulder and determinedly ignored the moaning coming from behind my head. A souped-up Honda Civic was pulling away from the fuel pumps as I stomped across the forecourt, its occupants leaning out of the window as it passed us.

"Ooh," called a young man in the passenger seat, "fancy kidnapping me after you're done with him, girl?" Raucous laughter came from inside the car as they drove off.

"It's weird," I said as I wriggled the car key out of my pocket and unlocked the doors, "that because I'm a woman and you're a bloke, people think this," I gave him a shake, "is funny. How do they know I haven't murdered you and am just off to hide the body?" Ivo let out a small groan, which I decided to take as agreement with my observation on human behaviour. "Do not leave so much as a fingerprint in this car," I warned him. "I'm not sure how Eadric's going to react to me saving your stupid ass as it is. Giving you a seat in his beloved car might be the final nail in both our coffins."

"He won't argue with you," Ivo mumbled. "The city won't let him."

"I wish I could share your confidence," I said, pulling out onto the main road. "Right now, I just want to go home. I'll worry about the rest of it tomorrow."

***

It's only a ten-minute drive from Anfield down into the centre of town, so I was already heading towards the traffic island by the World Museum before I remembered the barriers would be up on Harrington Street. And I couldn't park the Alfa back at the Liver Building, on account of how my passenger was currently top of Eadric Silverton's shit-list. "Might as well make the most of it being in Eadric's name," I said, "if I get done for this."

"Done for what?" mumbled Ivo from the passenger seat, as I drove straight across onto Haymarket and down to Whitechapel. He really didn't look good. I was beginning to wonder just what level of trouble I'd got myself into. If Ivo died—*permanently* died—on my watch, would that be a good or bad thing for my undead reputation?

"Doesn't matter," I said, pulling the Alfa onto the pedestrianised area that goes right down into the centre of town. It would usually have been an impossible manoeuvre, because if there's one thing Liverpool council enjoys spending money on, it's traffic bollards. But I knew one of them had stopped working a few days earlier, because all the construction companies working on the re-stabilising of Mathew Street had been using it as a short cut. I wriggled the car through the narrow gap and drove slowly down to the turnoff for Button Street. It seemed far narrower in a car than it had ever done on foot, and there was a distinctly squeaky moment as I navigated the angled turn into the top of Harrington Street. Luckily for me, there was no one around to see me performing a fifty-seven point turn in order to get the Alfa backed into my car park, next to Basil. "I'm going to take you to my flat," I said to Ivo, as I unclipped my seatbelt, "until I figure out what to do next." No answer. *Christ,* I thought, *I hope he hasn't just run out of power completely.* I'd assumed that so long as there was some 'life force' left, Ivo would be okay until I had chance to prop him up somewhere busy. My plan had been to sit him in the staff room at Flora's and hope human energy was strong enough to waft through, although I hadn't yet decided how to explain it to Izzy. Were revenants like batteries? Could energy levels get so low that they couldn't be revived?

He'll be fine, said the city. *So long as he's with you.*

Why does it have to be me? I said. *All he ever does is drag me into trouble.*

If not you, then who? Silverton cannot be trusted with him.

Why are you worried about Ivo? Surely you'd be better off without him fighting for dominance all the time.

There was a brief silence in my head, which was actually a pleasant novelty. Then, *Someone has to lead the North. If not him, then who?*

Whoever bloody wants it, I said, getting out of the car and going round to the passenger side. Opening the door, I gave Ivo's slumped body a tentative prod.

"Nnnghhhhh," he mumbled. "So tired." I thanked all the gods of the undead universe for at least keeping him alive until I could get him out of the car. I had a sneaking suspicion Eadric wouldn't have appreciated gunky revenant remains getting stuck in his nice upholstery.

"Come on," I said, hoisting him out of the seat and back over my shoulder, "it's sleepy-nap time for you." I kicked the door shut—carefully—with my foot, and managed to press the lock button through the fabric of my jeans. The Alfa shut itself down with a solid-sounding *thunk* as I carried my undead parcel over to the fire escape.

The person who truly wants it, the city went on, **wants everything. Never forget that, Lilith.**

Okay, so I'm going to need to know who— I was cut off by a movement in the shadows.

"Whatcha got there, Red?" said Billy from the darkness. Shit. "Been out hunting for a mate?"

"Don't you bloody start," I said, one foot already on the stairs. "It's Laithlind, if you must know." Billy sat up at that. "I saved him from an evil...something or other. And don't bother asking me what, because it has been a *very* long day."

"What are you going to do with him?"

I started plodding up the steps. "Dunno," I called back over my shoulder, "I haven't decided yet. Might keep him as a slave."

"That is morally corrupt," said Ivo, from behind my head. "I like it."

"He can't stay here!" Aunt Kitty was pacing the living room in an exceedingly agitated manner for a ghost who didn't even pay rent. "What will people think?"

"Kitty," I said from the armchair, where I was once again attempting to unravel my tangled knitting, "you lived through the 60s. Well, some of it, anyway." She scowled at me. "Oh, come on," I said, "who gives a shit what anyone thinks?" Grimm was sitting on the back of the sofa, washing his paws. He turned towards me and blinked, very slowly. "Is it just me," I said, "or is that cat becoming creepily sentient?"

"Grimm has always been sentient," Kitty said indignantly, leaning over to stroke him lovingly. She was solid enough to do it properly now, I noticed, her hand visibly pressing down into the cat's fur as he pushed up against her in delight. He looked at me again with what I was fairly sure was a deeply smug expression. "You just haven't bothered to take any notice."

"Cheers," I said, "I'll remember that next time I'm spending a fortune on his ridiculous cat food."

"Only the best for our boy," said Kitty, unrepentantly. "Anyway, he deserves it. He's been helping the vampire downstairs. Haven't you, you clever boy?" She squished the cat again. If I'd done that, he'd have taken my hand off.

"Devious, is what that cat is," I said. "Which isn't the same as being clever. Hang on," I belatedly registered what she'd said. "What do you mean by 'helping the vampire downstairs'?"

Kitty flopped into the sofa and Grimm immediately slunk down to hang around her neck like an animated fur stole. She grinned at me. "So our Rachel's a vegetarian, right?" One hand went up to scratch Grimm's ears as she spoke, and a rumbling purr started up. "But she can't survive on thin air for long. And we all know there's a rat problem out back. So Grimmy here convinced her she'd be doing us all a favour if she got over her aversion and helped him sort out the rodent issue."

There was so much going on in that one single sentence that I didn't know where to start. "Firstly," I said, putting the knitting down, "isn't she going to turn, well—*ratty*? Cos that's what happened with the others living down in Joe's tunnels."

"So what if she does?" asked Kitty. "Are you judging people on their attractiveness now?"

"Of course I'm not," I said, possibly a bit too quickly. "But how am I going to explain having Rat Girl living in the flat below me?"

"You think that's any worse than trying to explain away a vampire?" Kitty looked at me pityingly. "Honestly Lil, I thought you'd be getting the hang of all this by now."

"Well I'm sorry for taking a while to get to grips with immortality," I said. "Never mind the endless fighting and general angsty drama."

"You're doing better than you think," said my aunt in a kinder voice. "Don't forget that."

"Humph. Anyway," I remembered what I'd been about to say, "what did you mean by Grimm having convinced Rachel to eat the rats? She was terrified of him when she came here! Why is my cat talking to vampires, anyway? And, more importantly," I glared at Grimm, who turned his head away, "since when could he *talk?*"

"I told you," said Kitty, "he's a clever boy. You just choose to ignore it."

"Fucking *hell*," I said, getting to my feet. "Everything and everyone in my life is completely and utterly *insane*."

"Where are you off to?" Kitty asked.

I looked down at where she was still sitting with Grimm. He'd now slid down into her lap and was rolling around on his back. Kitty was scritching his belly, and he appeared to be genuinely enjoying it. "That," I said, pointing to the cat, "is absolute proof that nothing is normal round here anymore. I'm going to go chat to Billy for a bit."

"Oh yes," came a voice from the bedroom, "because sitting out in the street talking to a ghost is completely normal behaviour."

"You," I said to Ivo, "need to shut up. Or I'll turn you over to the zombie narcs. I'm going out," I said, turning back to Kitty. "Don't let that cat do anything he shouldn't." As I walked out of the living room, I swear I heard a feline-sounding snigger.

You'll Never Walk Alone

"How's it hangin', Red?" Billy grinned up at me as I bounced down the fire escape. When I got to the first floor, I jumped the railings and swung off them like a monkey, before dropping lightly onto the car park. "Come to hang out with the proles?"

"Shove up," I said, sitting down next to him, "and give me some blanket." I pulled a scraggy old duvet over me and hunched up over my knees. Billy sat silently next to me, waiting for me to speak.

"I need to check in on Mapp," I said, eventually. "There's been so much going on that I'd actually forgotten about him." I sighed heavily. "I'm a pretty shit friend when it comes down to it."

"Ach," said Billy, "won't you listen to yourself, being all waily there. Mapp's just grand, I saw him myself earlier on."

"You're kidding? He looked like he wasn't long for this world, last time I saw him."

Billy grinned. "He was sitting out on Bold Street just this afternoon," he said. "Bold as brass and twice as shiny, with Heggie fussing around him like an Italian mama. Taking in the healthy human air, you might say." He nodded up towards my flat. "You'll be needing to do the same for your man up there, I'd be thinking. How are you going to manage that without people knowing what you're up to?"

"I honestly don't know," I said. "It's all just an absolute bloody mess. Eadric's going to lose his shit when he finds out that not only have I saved Ivo yet again, I'm now harbouring him in my house. The house Eadric technically owns."

"Ah, I don't think the Silvertons are going to argue with you too much, Red," said Billy. "They haven't survived this long by not knowing when to keep their beaks out of things."

"Something's coming," I blurted. "The city warned me. Well, sort of," I shifted around on the pavement. It doesn't matter whether you're dead or alive, nerve-endings still complain if you sit too hard on your tailbone.

"The city?"

"Yup," I said, leaning back against the wall and turning to look at him. "Got an entire city chatting away in my head." A city that had been noticeable by its absence since I'd brought Ivo back to the flat. Perhaps I wasn't the only one who needed a rest. "Which was a bit of a surprise, I can tell you."

"The stories were true, then," said Billy.

"What stories?"

"Oh," he said, "just the old wives' tales. You know the sort. They say this city is alive."

"I reckon they're probably right," I said.

"And it's there in your head," he said thoughtfully. "Fancy that."

"Why do you bother with the blankets, Billy?" I asked abruptly. "You don't need them."

"Neither do you," he said reasonably, "but you're still tucking yourself up there, sure enough."

We sat in silence for a while, lost in our own thoughts. Or at least, I was. For all I knew, Billy might just switch into standby mode, same as Kitty sometimes does. "Humans are ridiculous," I said finally.

Billy sighed companionably. "They are, that."

"We're so institutionalised into the basic pattern of what it means to be human," I went on, "that we don't even know why we do half of it. For god's sake, Billy," I sat up, "I still go to bed most nights, but I haven't actually slept since the day I died! So fuck knows why I still bother."

"When was that, again?" He leaned back against the wall and I could sense his eyes on me. "When you died, I mean."

"April," I said. "Just over four months. I haven't slept in sixteen weeks, yet I still go to bed at night. Because that is what humans do."

"Four months isn't long," Billy said. "Not in the scheme of things. You'll drop some of the human habits eventually,"

"Yeah?" I turned to face him. "How's that working out for you, then?" I nodded at the pile of blankets and sleeping bags that made up his nest. "Been a good century and a half now, hasn't it?"

"Aah," he grinned, "but you're forgetting I'm an actor, Red. These," he grabbed the blankets and shook them, "are my costume. With these, I'm invisible. With the blankets and rags and whatnot around me, I can sit here for hours, just watching the world go by. And in return, the world mostly ignores me."

"That doesn't sound very nice," I said.

Billy looked at me. "You get used to it," he said, "when you're on the streets. It's worse for those still living, believe me."

"I guess my life is easy compared to many," I said. "I should probably stop moaning."

"Oh, I don't know about that, Red," said Billy. "You've got a Norseman in your bed and a vampire living downstairs. Your housemate is a hippy ghost, and your cat...well." He looked up to where Grimm sat at the top of the fire escape, watching us intently. I hadn't even noticed him up there. Me and that cat were going to have to have words. One day. If I dared. "Well," Billy went on, "it's probably best not to talk about the cat. At least, not in his hearing, anyway. Seriously, Red," he tilted his head to look at me, "how do you keep up with it all?"

"I honestly don't know, Billy," I said with a laugh." It's certainly been a busy week." I gave him a friendly shove with my shoulder. To my surprise, he put out an arm and pulled me close up against him. Instead of feeling weird, it was strangely comfortable. Having Billy there next to me made the world feel solid and safe, even if it was only temporary. I took a breath and smelled honeysuckle and jasmine, wild garlic and meadowsweet.

"Anyway," my ghostly companion said, and I could hear the smile in his voice, "what are we going to do next?"

"Same thing we do every night, Billy," I grinned. "Try to take over the world."

THE END

Turn the page for a taste of what's to come in
LARK RISING:
Netherweird Chronicles, Book Three

LARK RISING

Wake up.

"No." I wasn't asleep anyway, and the voice knew that.

Wake up wake up wake up wake up WAKE UP!

"Fucking hell!" I shrieked, sitting bolt upright in the bed, "can't a woman get any peace and quiet round here?"

The city never sleeps. And neither do you. A pause. *And neither does the vampire downstairs, clearly.* The flat was in darkness, but steady banging came from the floor below, as if someone was slowly and methodically hitting their head against the wall in frustration. The flat underneath mine is occupied by the most tormented vampire in history, and sometimes I regret letting her move in. Seriously, Louis de Pointe du Lac has nothing on Rachel and her wailing. But she once helped saved my (after)life and one good turn deserves another. I had a brief daydream about taking Eadric Silverton up on his offer of the apartment down in the Albert Dock. I'd actually got as far as going to look at it, purely to humour Aunt Kitty. Kitty might have been dead this last sixty years, but she still appreciates a good view. And there was no getting away from the fact that the apartment was incredible. But I wasn't going to leave Harrington Street and everyone knew it. I don't have much hands-on input in the coffee shop downstairs anymore, but that's because my best friend Izzy has proved herself more than capable of looking after it without my help. Also Izzy's a living, breathing human, and apparently customers prefer that to being served by someone who occasionally forgets it isn't normal to pass someone their coffee before they've even finished asking for it.

Albert Dock would certainly be more suited to someone with your power and status, said the city in my head. It's not actually the city itself, you

259

understand—more the spirit of those who've made Liverpool what it is today. And what Liverpool mostly is today is a fucking weird mash-up of both human and supernatural inhabitants, the human side of which is, for the most part, happily oblivious of the others' existence. Either way, there's a voice in my head and sometimes that voice is really fucking annoying.

"I didn't have you down as a snob," I said, but the city didn't answer. Giving in to the inevitable, I climbed out from under the duvet, toppling Grimm onto the floor as I did so. The banging had stopped, which was a relief. I don't really get headaches these days, but the noise had been going on for long enough that my teeth were clenched and I could feel tightness behind my eyes. "Your reactions are sometimes very slow, for a cat," I said to Grimm. He arched one furry eyebrow and stalked out of the room, presumably to get himself a midnight snack. Grimm mostly sorts his own meals out these days, which suits me just fine. But when I walked into the living room, he was sitting on the windowsill and Kitty was next to him. They were both looking down onto the street and had serious expressions on their faces. "What are you two looking at?"

"Billy's talking to someone," said Kitty, without turning round. "And he doesn't look happy about it." Anyone walking past the pile of old blankets and sleeping bags that's permanently installed in the empty doorway opposite Flora's would suppose Billy was just another of the endless rough sleepers that call the city centre their home. It's certainly what I'd assumed for the first couple of years I'd owned Flora's. But then I'd died and everything got extremely strange and the upshot is that I'm still here, but now I know Billy is actually a ghost. Like I said—Liverpool is *weird*. I walked over to the window and peered out into the darkness. Billy was standing in front of his blanket nest, gesturing at someone in the middle of the street. The second person had his hands in his pockets and a casual posture, his pomaded quiff glinting under the streetlights.

"It's Alan," I said. At that moment, both men looked up towards the building. I ducked quickly.

"What are you doing?" asked Kitty. Banging started up again from the floor below.

"Hiding from Alan," I said, "obviously. He'll be hoping to see Rachel, but she's clearly not in a good mood and I can't deal with any more madness right now." I crawled away from the window before getting back onto my feet. "I'm going to see Eadric, won't be long. If Rachel kicks off again, bang the floor."

"What do you need to see Eadric about at this time of night?"

"Stuff," I said, then relented. "Just boring stuff." Kitty looked unconvinced. "Honestly. Bella needs some maintenance and I've promised to sit with her whilst the work's done." I shrugged. "She gets nervous when people start welding around her feet." Bella's the Liver Bird that faces onto the river and, although she's generally better tempered than her brother Bertie, she sometimes needs a bit of support. I figured it was much like taking a kid to the dentist and holding their hand whilst they had a filling done. "I just want to know when it's scheduled, cos I'm working in Flora's a bit this week. And it's not as though Eadric will be in bed."

"Izzy's allowing you back behind the counter?" asked Kitty. "I thought she said never again, after that incident with the bread knife and the delivery man?"

"He shouldn't have snuck up on me like that," I said. "Anyway, I only nicked his ear. And I said sorry."

"Didn't Izzy have to find a new supplier of coffee beans?"

"It was time for a change, anyway," I said archly. "Anyway, I'm off out. Mind you behave yourselves." My deceased aunt and my very-much-alive cat watched me go out through the kitchen door, before turning back to the window. I bounced my way down the fire escape at speed, and was past the pair of bickering ghosts before either of them could drag me into their ridiculous argument. And it *was* ridiculous—I knew that without even having to get involved. Alan had a crush on Rachel, and Billy didn't approve. There wasn't any jealousy on Billy's part, he just didn't think Rachel should be getting into relationships with ghosts until she'd got used to being a vampire. I'd tried telling him that Rachel seemed quite keen on Alan in return and maybe Billy should drop the dad act a bit, but it hadn't made any difference.

We're basically just one big happy, argumentative family—it's just that most of us are dead.

***

As I approached the Liver Building, I could see from Bertie's clock that it had just gone two in the morning. I gave him a wave and he creaked a small nod in response, before going back to staring out over the city. Because it was dark and quiet, I didn't bother with the official entrance and instead just went the direct route, scaling the side of the building like a red-headed bug. When I reached the windows of the Silverton's rooms, I tapped the window.

"Have you forgotten how doors work?" asked Nikolaus Silverton, as I dropped in over the stone windowsill. Nik was wearing an embroidered silk dressing gown and his bare feet poked out from under what appeared to be satin pyjamas.

"All you need is marabou slippers," I said, ignoring him, "and that outfit would be perfect."

"Who says I don't have any?" he replied. I was about to snark back at him when the door from Eadric's office opened and the man himself stalked into the room. Now, Nik Silverton is undeniably handsome, if you like your men on the foppish side. But Eadric is something else entirely. Tall, with distinctively sharp features and wavy chestnut hair, he looks like he plays guitar in an indie band in-between writing poetry and painting masterpieces. What Eadric actually is, is a notoriously powerful leader of the undead realms who celebrates his one thousandth birthday sometime this century. I suggested a party, but apparently he can't remember the actual date on account of how that sort of thing becomes less important once you've been around a few hundred years. Right now, he had a look on his face that suggested he wasn't in the mood for jokes.

"I've just had Laithlind on the phone," he said. Tension was visible on his face.

"I thought you were never going to speak to Ivo again?" asked Nik. Ivo

Laithlind is even older than Eadric, and they were friends for centuries—until we discovered Ivo had been shagging Eadric's wife. Anyway, I'd chopped her head off (long story) by the time the secret came out and Ivo had wisely done a bunk. But then I'd saved his undead life and Eadric clearly thought I shouldn't have bothered, so we'd all agreed to just not talk about him. I certainly didn't mention the not so pure thoughts I occasionally had about Ivo. Things like that are best kept between a girl and her closed bedroom door.

"He had information he felt we needed," Eadric said. "And he was correct to warn us. We will have no alternative but to work with Laithlind in the very near future, I fear. I must warn Middlesex." He was already pulling his phone out of the pocket of his immaculately tailored trousers.

"Whoah," said Nik, putting a hand up, "want to tell us what's going on before you speak to Elizabeth?"

Eadric looked at each of us in turn—me in my scruffy nightclothes with a definite case of bed-head, and Nik looking worried yet immaculate next to me—and appeared to be wondering just how he'd ended up with such a ragtag pair of sidekicks. "It's happening," he said, "after all these centuries. After everything we've done to secure our place in the human world. Ivo has had suspicions for a long time, of course. We had discussed it before…well. Before." He shook his head. "But now it's confirmed."

"What's confirmed?" I asked. I was feeling nervous myself now. Eadric looked me in the eye and seemed to consider his words for a long time before he eventually spoke.

"The Bastard's back."

COMING AUGUST 2023

Sign up to my mailing list to be the first to hear about upcoming releases and other interesting stuff - and get a FREE short story from

Netherweird!

tinyurl.com/netherweirdstory

Author's Note

Once again, I've taken liberties with some of the real-world history, geography and architecture of the people and places that make Netherweird what it is. But as always, most of it is based on at least some elements of truth.

The unmarked grave that Elizabeth talks about lies in Highgate Cemetery West (the 'old' side). In it are the remains of ten women who died in Highgate Penitentiary—aka 'the House of Mercy'—between 1862 and 1909.

Anfield Cemetery does indeed have a pair of very old catacombs, which are usually locked away from public view. I've been lucky enough to have been allowed inside them in the past and they're incredible buildings.

Shrewsbury Market Hall truly is one of the best in the country (and has awards to prove it). The Birds Nest cafe is real, and well worth a visit.

Many of my characters are based on real people from various points in history, although some details have been changed. Some are probably easier to identify than others, but if you figure them out, let me know!

***

As is the same for most authors, it's not just about thinking up a story and throwing it out into the wild—a lot of other people help out along the way. Hugest thanks to:

Toni Hibberd and Jayne Hadfield, without whom this book would probably make very little sense; Sal Geere, who is the Queen Of All Pedants and a brilliant editor because of it; Emma Kalson-Leadley; Emily Davies; Tilly Melia; Lisa Webster and James Webster for awesome photos of randomly interesting Liverpool buildings; Li Zakovics, for endless tea and gossip; Winston Gomez, for generally making life nicer. And my boys, Jaime and Oscar. Love you.